Hester Pengelly

A Memoir of William Pengelly, of Torquay, F. R. S.

Geologist, with a selection from his correspondence

Hester Pengelly

A Memoir of William Pengelly, of Torquay, F. R. S.
Geologist, with a selection from his correspondence

ISBN/EAN: 9783337093402

Printed in Europe, USA, Canada, Australia, Japan

Cover: Foto ©Raphael Reischuk / pixelio.de

More available books at **www.hansebooks.com**

A MEMOIR

OF

WILLIAM PENGELLY, F.R.S.

a

A MEMOIR OF
WILLIAM PENGELLY,

OF TORQUAY, F.R.S.,

GEOLOGIST,

WITH A SELECTION FROM HIS CORRESPONDENCE.

EDITED BY HIS DAUGHTER,

HESTER PENGELLY.

WITH A SUMMARY OF HIS SCIENTIFIC WORK
By the Rev. Professor BONNEY, F.R.S., F.G.S.,
HON. CANON OF MANCHESTER.

LONDON:
JOHN MURRAY, ALBEMARLE STREET.
1897.

LONDON:
PRINTED BY WILLIAM CLOWES AND SONS, LIMITED,
STAMFORD STREET AND CHARING CROSS

LONDON:
PRINTED BY WILLIAM CLOWES AND SONS, LIMITED,
STAMFORD STREET AND CHARING CROSS

TO MY MOTHER,

WHOSE LOVING AND UNFAILING SYMPATHY

MADE LIGHT AND PLEASANT TO MY FATHER

MUCH WORK WHICH MIGHT OTHERWISE HAVE PROVED

LABORIOUS AND IRKSOME,

I DEDICATE

THIS BOOK.

PREFACE.

IT is to be regretted that circumstances have made it needful for the author to put into other hands than her own the work of setting a short preface to the grateful task which she has so assiduously and lovingly laboured at, and so ably carried through.

The regret experienced is, however, somewhat softened by the consideration, that one unconnected with the subject of the memoir, except by the tie of friendship, is under less restraint than his daughter has shown herself to feel, in estimating his many sterling qualities, and remarkable capacity.

The biography has been written under no inconsiderable disadvantage, from the fact that Pengelly was as little anxious and careful for posthumous fame as he was for celebrity and notoriety while living. Not only had he neglected to keep any diary from which many valuable particulars of his life might have been gleaned, which are now irrecoverably lost, but he had moreover, in his latter years, destroyed a vast quantity of memoranda and correspondence, which would have been of the greatest service to his biographer. Happily, enough remains to show what manner of man he was.

How excellent and entertaining a book would have been given to the world, had Pengelly employed himself on an autobiography or recorded his reminiscences, may be fairly judged from the passages penned by himself concerning his early life, with which the volume so happily opens. In their transparent truthful simplicity they recall the inimitable verisimilitude of Defoe.

But when one becomes awake to the high pressure under

which the most vigorous years of his life were passed, it will be readily understood that Pengelly could have kept a diary only at the sacrifice of some of the important work which he continually had in hand. In truth, not a minute of his time, for very many years, could be said to be unemployed, or employed otherwise than usefully.

In his last days, the present writer, charmed by the interest of his reminiscent conversation, asked to be allowed to bring with him some one skilled in shorthand who should, for an hour or so at a time, take down at least some occasional recollections of his active years; but he only shook his head, and murmured, "Too late! too late!"

It can scarcely fail to force itself on the reader of the ensuing pages, that the special note of William Pengelly's character, apart from the energy, perseverance, clear-sightedness, wit, and abundant good humour which distinguished him, was his extraordinary unselfishness. This quality may sometimes be esteemed to be engendered in people by a love of approbation; but this cannot be said to have been the case with Pengelly. He "stood four-square to all the winds that blew." No man was ever more ready to oppose what he deemed to be wrong or erroneous, or more willing to espouse the cause of truth and justice, as he saw it, at any cost or inconvenience to himself.

From the days when, as a cabin-boy, he was accustomed to read aloud to entertain his messmates, to the time when, as a popular lecturer, he had the power of holding large audiences spell-bound by his eloquence, his first thought was the benefit he was able to afford to others, his last consideration the personal profit he might derive from his labours.

This it was that caused one who might have stood in the first rank among men of science, in an age prolific of great men, to confine his residence to the place of his adoption, though on several occasions he was strongly urged, by those fully capable of judging of his ability and capacity, to accept one of the positions offered to him in London, at Oxford, or some other great centre.

It was indeed fortunate, for the cause of one branch of science, that Pengelly was not possessed with the ambition to engage in what might have been considered a higher or wider sphere. In that case the important cave explorations at Brixham and Torquay, to which he devoted himself heart and soul with untiring energy for sixteen years, might have been indefinitely delayed. The result of such delay must have been the postponement of the evidence of the antiquity of man, which, by the aid of the discoveries made in the course of his explorations, Pengelly was able to set forth so fearlessly, and establish so clearly, as to put it beyond all danger of refutation, and out of the pale of reasonable controversy.

On this important point in the history of the world Pengelly was one of the first to speak with no uncertain voice, when many other men of science still held back from full expression of opinion on the subject.

It will be well understood that a man so unselfish as Pengelly, and so devoted not only to the increase of the sum of human knowledge, but also to its diffusion among his fellowmen, took little heed of the accumulation of worldly wealth, or even of providing very amply for the day when his power for work should fail him. It may, therefore, be told far more in his honour than in his derogation, that his means, as old age approached, were such as to cause him no little anxiety. This induced some of his scientific friends to make appeal to the Government of the day to place his name on the civil list. Strange to say, although the memorial was signed by all the names most eminent in the scientific world, its prayer was refused by the Gladstonian Government. The only recognition that was offered was a grant of a sum of money, which was courteously declined.

Happily, by a circumstance so remarkable that if it were introduced into a work of fiction it would be derided as a weak way of making the story end happily, Pengelly was, during the last decade of his life, placed in the ease and affluence he so richly merited, without being beholden to any government aid.

Those persons living, and they are many, who had the good fortune to hear Pengelly lecture, will bear ready witness to the complete mastery he always had of his subject, and of the faculty of imparting his knowledge. Even when speaking upon abstruse subjects to a mixed audience, he would make his matter perfectly clear without in any degree appearing to talk down to the capacity of those he was addressing. In this respect he would compare favourably with such masters of elocution and exposition as Faraday, Tyndall, Huxley, and Ruskin.

His manner was no less pleasing and attractive than the language in which he clothed his ideas was grateful to the ear. His voice, though not strong, was resonant and impressive. Perhaps no man has ever passed through the fire of adulation, flattery, and patronage, more completely unscathed than Pengelly, or was rendered less vain by the success he met with, and the society to which he was introduced.

Throughout the most prosperous part of his career he was ever cordial to the humblest genuine inquirer after knowledge, and as accessible as he had been when he himself was a struggling and unknown student, ardently seeking his way towards the light, destitute of patronage, and unacquainted with people of wealth and influence.

In person Pengelly was tall, erect of carriage, spare of habit, fresh coloured, without marked features, but with a countenance indued with extraordinary mobility of expression, and lit up by intelligent eyes that, incessantly twinkling with humour and kindliness, seemed to speak the feelings by which he was animated. It is not too much to say that, for nearly half a century, the place which he had made his home, acquired a special lustre and interest from being the residence of William Pengelly.

The author desires to express her sincere thanks to all those of her father's correspondents who have kindly permitted the use of letters which add so greatly to the value and interest of the work.   F. S. ELLIS.

LIST OF ILLUSTRATIONS.

A MEMOIR OF
WILLIAM PENGELLY.

CHAPTER I.

EARLY YEARS AT SCHOOL AND AT SEA.

JANUARY, 1812-1830.

WILLIAM PENGELLY was born at East Looe, in Cornwall, on January 12, 1812, and christened shortly afterwards at the Parish Church of St. Martin. His father, Richard Pengelly, was captain of a small coasting vessel, while his mother, whose maiden name was Prout, belonged to the same family as Samuel Prout, the famous water-colour artist. She came from Millbrook Creek, in the parish of Maker, Cornwall. The name Pengelly is, as the sound implies, Cornish. It is interpreted in Bannister's "Glossary of Cornish Names" as signifying "head of the hazel grove." Though an uncommon surname in other parts of England, it is not unfrequently met with in Cornwall, and occasionally in Devonshire.

Passing his early years in the picturesque fishing village of Looe, it is not surprising that Pengelly acquired a strong attachment to the sea, which was rendered doubtless the more intense through hereditary influences, for on his father's side he was descended from a long line of sailors.

It is, however, needless to attempt to trace back the ancestry of the subject of this memoir, for no one ever took less heed of the matter than himself. In later years he was constantly written to about it, as people persisted in supposing that he belonged to the same family as Sir Thomas Pengelly, who rose to be Chief Baron of the Exchequer in 1726, and left certain sums for the discharge of debtors from the gaols of Bodmin and Launceston. In answer to one of the many letters addressed to him

on this subject, Pengelly sent the following characteristic reply :—
" With regard to Sir Thomas Pengelly, I had some years ago a
correspondence respecting him with Mr. Peter Taylor, M.P., whom
I put on the trail of a picture-dealer in London, named Bryant,
who had a portrait of Sir T. Pengelly, and was wont to write me
about it very frequently. I have an impression that Mr. Taylor
bought it. I declined to do so, as I don't care to claim any
connection with him." Later on, he writes, " The Parish of
Whitchurch, near Tavistock, appears to have been a great home
of the Pengellys, and the church, I am told, is rich in their
monuments, but I have never seen it."

When little more than an infant, he was sent to the Dame's
school in his native village, where his progress in learning was so
rapid that, before he was five years old, his mother betook herself
to Mr. Rundle, the master of a school for bigger boys, to arrange
for her son being taught there, with the result that he declined to
take so young a pupil. Not long afterwards, when walking down
the street the schoolmaster happened to pass the Pengellys'
house at the open door of which the child was sitting, engaged
in his favourite occupation of reading the Bible aloud, and the
wonderful fluency and accuracy of the reading so greatly impressed the pedagogue, that he entered with the announcement,
" Mrs. Pengelly, you may send your son to me at once, I was
not in the least aware that he was so advanced."

The life destined to endure for upwards of fourscore years,
and to be productive of so much valuable work, ran the risk of
being cut short by an accident at a very early period.

The particulars of the occurrence have been preserved by
a friend who heard them from Pengelly's own lips, when he was
one day descanting on the fact that circumstances which appear
in themselves trivial may materially affect the whole course of
a man's life. The trivial circumstance referred to in his own
case was the arrival of an aunt, on a visit to his parents, one day
sooner than she had been expected. Early the following morning,
when sitting at her bedroom window, wrapped in a thick woollen
shawl, she was horrified to see her little nephew Wiliam rushing
out of the house enveloped in flames. She hurried after him,
and managed to stifle the fire with her woollen garment, and
thus saved the child's life, though she was so badly burnt herself, that she carried the scars till her dying day. The little boy
had got up early, as was his wont, and had set about to kindle a

LOOE, CORNWALL.　　　　　　[*To face p.* 2.

fire, that he might go on with his lessons before any one else in
the house was astir, with the result that he set light to his
clothes, and except for the premature arrival of his aunt, must
certainly have been burnt to death.

At Mr. Rundle's school he remained until twelve years old,
when he accompanied his father to sea. Though study was
always a great pleasure to him, his school life could not have
been particularly happy, as the unusual abilities he possessed were
quickly discovered by the elder boys, who used very forcible
means to keep him hard at work during play-hours, preparing
their lessons, in addition to his own ; thus exemplifying how
unenviable is the position of a very small boy as the head of a
school. He never received any external instruction or intellectual training after the age of twelve. When it is remembered
how imperfect his education must have been, it is indeed remarkable that, by his unaided abilities and industry, he should have
succeeded in ultimately winning for himself a distinguished place
amongst the scientific men of his day.

Some account of his seafaring experiences, with descriptions
of his shipmates, can fortunately be given in his own words.
He writes :—

"Our voyages were short. I do not remember an instance of being
at sea more than three consecutive days ; so that, except when 'wind-
bound,' we were almost always taking in or taking out cargo. The
work was hard, but the food was abundant, and on the whole the life,
though rough, was not unpleasant.

"To me—thinking nothing of the pecuniary aspect of the question—
the most enjoyable occasions were those which fierce contrary winds
brought us, when we had to seek some harbour of refuge. These were
by no means necessarily holidays, for, if the weather were dry, advantage
was taken of the enforced leisure, to give our craft a thorough cleaning,
or to repair her rigging, or to make up the books. Moreover the crew
employed me to write letters to their wives from their dictation. These
epistles were generally of a remarkable character, and some of them
remain firmly fixed in my memory. The opening clause, was that
which—so far as my experience went—was invariably employed by the
labouring classes of the period ; 'this comes with my dear love to you,
hoping it may find you in good health, as it leaves me at present ;
thank God for it.' The foregoing labours disposed of, and foul winds
still prevailing, we had a washing-day ; or, better than all, a bout of
tailoring, which did not generally get beyond repairing, though occasionally the ambitious flight of making a pair of trousers was attempted.
On tailoring days it was understood that my clothes should be repaired
for me, in order that I might read aloud for the general benefit. We
assembled in our little cabin, where the stitching and smoking went on

simultaneously, and with great vigour. My poor library consisted of a
Bible, the eighth volume of the *Spectator*, Johnson's ' English Dictionary,'
a volume of the *Weekly Miscellany*, which I have some idea was
published at Sherborne, the history of 'John Gilpin,' 'Baron Mun-
chausen's Travels,' Walkinghame's 'Arithmetic,' and a book of songs.
My hearers were not very fastidious, but allowed me to read pretty
much what I pleased, though, truth to tell, the *Spectator* was not a
favourite ; some portions of it were held to be nonsensical, and others
were considered to be so lacking in truthfulness, that it was generally
termed the ' Lying Book.' This ill repute was largely due to the story
of Fadallah (No. 578). Walkinghame was by no means unpopular.
I occasionally read some of the questions, and my shipmates endeavoured
to solve them mentally ; and as the answers were all given by the
author, I had to declare who had made the nearest guess, for it was
very often but little more. Of all the questions, none excited so much
interest as that which asks, What will be the cost of shoeing a horse,
at a farthing for the first nail, two for the second, and so on in
geometrical progression for thirty-two nails, and which gives for the
answer a sum but little short of four and a half million pounds sterling.
This was so utterly unexpected, that it went far to confer on Walkinghame the same name that Fadallah had given to the *Spectator*."

Pengelly relates some of the experiences which he had heard
from different members of the crew, beginning with those of his
father the captain, who, as a boy, had been brought up on
his uncle's farm, but wearying of the life there, was turning
his thoughts towards seafaring, and while still in doubt was
determined by what he deemed divine direction. As is common
among men of Keltic origin, Richard Pengelly had a firm belief
in supernatural appearances, and his son describes how this
belief influenced his way of life.

"Our skipper had no doubt whatever that ghosts sometimes
appeared, and he held that they were sometimes sent in answer to
prayer. Indeed, his firm belief that he had seen his father's spirit,
altered the whole course of his life. After completing his fifteenth
year he was thinking of going to sea. When he was sixteen, his father,
who was a sailor, was drowned almost within sight of his home. The
effect on the boy was to make him pause, and on his friends, to urge
him to give up the idea. For some months these influences kept him
quiet, but at length his restlessness returned so strongly, that he would
have gone to sea at once, had he felt satisfied that his father would
have approved the step. To ascertain this point he prayed frequently
and earnestly that his father's spirit might be allowed to appear to him,
with a pleasing or frowning aspect, according as he might approve or
disapprove. At length, he believed his prayer to have been answered,
and that when in the field ploughing, he saw his father, who passed by
looking intently and smilingly at him. This decided him. He became
a sailor at seventeen, and as such died at a good old age."

It will have been seen that young Pengelly's labours as an amanuensis were much appreciated at sea, but his great conversational powers were not equally valued, and his comrades used sometimes to say, " Here, Bill, put up a mop and talk to that, for we have not time to listen to you." The mate of the vessel, John Pengelly, was an elder brother of the boy's father, and the only member of the family who had ever been engaged in smuggling, then so common in England. His early life had on this account been full of stirring and hair-breadth escapes, certain of which are thus described by his nephew.

" The mate's life had been one of considerable adventure. Almost from his infancy he had been a smuggler, and to the excitement of that career, he had occasionally added those of a privateer. He had an unconquerable aversion to the Royal Navy, as was manifested by the following incident. The smuggling cutter to which he belonged was chased by a frigate, and just before sunset was overtaken near the Scilly Isles. Though a part of her contraband cargo had been disposed of, sufficient remained on board to condemn her. She was accordingly made a prize of; her crew were transferred to the frigate, from which a prize-crew was sent with orders to take the cutter to Plymouth. During the great French war, it was usual for trading and smuggling vessels to have concealed ' berths,' in which to secrete such members of the crew as were liable to be taken in the event of a visit from the press-gang. When he saw that the cutter must be captured and condemned, our mate retired to one of these concealed berths, but in his hurry left part of his dress projecting, so that the sliding panel was not completely closed.

" After parting with the frigate, some members of the prize crew proceeded to investigate the cutter, in the hope of meeting with articles of dress or other waifs which they might appropriate. One of them catching sight of the projecting portion of dress just mentioned, took hold of it, and by tugging, opened the panel, exclaiming as he did so : ' Here's a pair of blue trousers.' ' Yes,' said their proprietor, ' and here's a man to wear them.'

" He was at once taken to the prize-master, or lieutenant in charge, who received him kindly, expressed his regret that he was unwilling to serve the king, but added that, since he was not willing, he could not be blamed for concealing himself in the hope of escaping. He then said : ' You know the cutter better than I do. Come below, and help me to get a glass of grog.' Whilst in the cabin together, a message was sent to the effect that there was a light ahead which they were nearing rapidly. He replied, ' It is the frigate, probably. Keep under her lee.' Very soon after, a second messenger came down, who said : ' It doesn't look like a ship's light, sir. We are getting very near it. I wish you'd come on deck.' ' What nonsense !' said he, ' it must be the ship.' Then, turning to the smuggler, he said, ' Come on deck, my man ; I must put you on board the frigate now.' When arrived on deck, he was satisfied it was not a ship's light, but did not know what light it was. The captured man at once said, 'It is the Longships lighthouse. We shall be on the rocks in five minutes, unless you put about at once.' 'For God's sake, take the helm, if you know the coast,' said the officer. 'We are none of us well acquainted with it.'

"'I know every rock and creek between this and Plymouth,' was the reply, 'and I will take charge, if you will promise, on your honour, to set me ashore perfectly free before you report the prize at Plymouth; but if you will not, we will all go to the bottom together.' 'On my honour, I'll do so.' 'Then, stand by. About ship; hard lee!' shouted the smuggler; and the cutter, almost within the breakers, answered her helm in a moment, as he knew she would. For a time all was breathless suspense, which was not relieved until the pilot, as he may now be called, relinquished the helm to him from whom he had taken it, remarking as he did so, 'You may keep her full, as we are all safe for the present.' Then, taking the prize-master to the cabin, he pointed out on the chart, the Rundle Stone, the Wolf Rock, and other dangers near the Land's End, as well as the Stags off the Lizard Point, and stated that he would undertake to pilot the craft to Penlee Point at the entrance to Plymouth Sound, on the understanding that he was set ashore there. This was at once agreed to, and was duly carried into effect early the next morning. This was by no means his only narrow escape of becoming a man-of-war's man. During the last seven years of the great war, he seven times fell into the clutches of the press-gang. On each of these occasions, he was taken on board a sea-going ship, and his name was entered on her books; but in no more than one instance, when he was taken to the West Indies, did his enforced service extend beyond a few days, as in every other case he succeeded in 'running' very soon after being captured, as he ultimately did from his West Indian ship also.

"On returning from this foreign cruise, his ship was ordered to the Cove of Cork, near Queenstown; and a day or two after arriving there, a boat's crew, of which he was one, were sent under charge of a midshipman to Haulbowling Island to make spun-yarn. Whilst engaged in their work, they all agreed 'to run,' and not to return to the ship. The following was their programme. On finishing their work and getting into their boat, the coxswain was to ask the midshipman to allow them to go to Cork to get 'something to drink.' If he consented, well; but if not, they were nevertheless to go. In any case, they were 'to run' the moment they reached the shore, and, if possible, all in different directions. They were so fortunate as to get a reluctant consent from the officer to go to Cove, and on touching the Strand, they simultaneously leaped ashore and fled. Our mate and another man took the same direction, the former having a good start ahead, and to them the midshipman gave chase. Just as our fugitive turned a sharp corner of the street, he passed a young woman who had seen and at once comprehended the affair. Her house happened to be the first round the corner, and as he was passing the open doorway she pushed him in, followed him, and immediately secured the door. Thinking it possible that she had been observed, and that her house would be searched in consequence, she hurried her involuntary guest to a bed-room, took the bed and bedclothes off the bedstead, bade him lie on his face on the sacking, with his nose and mouth in an aperture between the lacing, and then replaced the bed and bedclothes; in short, she 'made up' the bed on him. In the course of the day her suspicions were realized. The house was thoroughly searched by a party of marines from the ship, who not only looked under the bed where the fugitive lay, but crept under it, examining the floor for trap-doors. On the following day they came again and made a similar search, but never thought of examining the bed itself, and hence failed to find the man. Whilst lying there secreted, his generous hostess fed him through the aperture his nose and mouth occupied. He remained a prisoner in her house for ten days, when, the ship having sailed, she secured him an opportunity of working his passage to England in a vessel proceeding thither. Before leaving, he had to inform her that it was utterly out of his power to make her any remuneration, as the clothes he wore were his only property; and he asked her what had induced her to show such great kindness to an entire stranger. She replied that her only brother, a sailor, had been impressed, was serving against his will on board a ship-of-war, and would certainly take the first opportunity of running. Hence her sympathy with him. She expected no recompense, but hoped that some one would be ready, if necessary, to do for her brother what she had done for him."

Another of Pengelly's favourite stories related to a shipmate named George, in whom he had always taken a lively interest, and of whom he writes—

"George was a man having an experience utterly unlike that of either the captain or the mate. He was the son of a well-educated father, who, having failed to make proper use of the opportunities put in his way, had remained a poor but by no means respectable relation. To add to his sins of commission and of omission, he taught his only child to love strong drink, and to hate his wealthy relatives; and he allowed the streets and quays to complete his education. To the end of his life his son was ignorant of the alphabet.

"George's early seafaring career was in merchant-vessels, in none of which does he appear to have remained long. The last of the series was a large brig belonging to merchants in the north of England, and bound to some foreign port. Not long after they had got clear of the Channel, one of the crew sickened and died. He was followed by another and another, until the captain, George, and a boy, alone remained. Before reaching this very alarming condition, the ship's head had, of course, been turned towards England, and some progress had been made thitherward. One evening, the weather being moderate, the captain said, 'George, I will lie down on the locker for an hour or two. Call me at ten o'clock, and then you can have a spell below.'

"At the appointed hour George went to call him, leaving the boy at the helm; but seeing, by the light he carried, a too-well-known expression on his face, he felt convinced that the disease had seized him, and stood a short time watching him. As he did so, he heard him say, 'My dear Peggy,' and with his wife's name on his lips he died, leaving the brig in the hands of a young man and a boy, both ignorant not only of navigation but of the mere art of reading.

"At this part of his tale I have seen my old shipmate, who had subsequently faced death in many forms, so overcome with emotion as to be utterly unable to proceed for some time. For a few days the weather continued moderate, and they kept on the course which they had been steering at the captain's decease. At length it began to blow heavily about sunset, and they attempted to reef the fore-and-aft mainsail; but whilst thus engaged, the main-boom struck George so heavily as to prostrate him. He lay for some time on the deck in an unconscious state, from which he awoke to find the brig driving before the wind, and the boy standing by him crying bitterly. He brought her back to her course, but she had too much canvas spread; before morning, however, some of the sails were blown from their ropes.

"Where they were they had no idea, nor had they any hope of being seen by a passing ship; for the gale, having blown itself out, was succeeded by a dense fog. The only thing they could do was to steer in the direction in which they supposed England lay.

"At length the fog cleared off, and they were delighted to find themselves not far from land—land, too, with which George was well acquainted. He found they had come up channel, and were abreast of the Start Point. A few hours enabled him to sail into Dartmouth harbour, with which he was familiar, where without delay he handed the vessel and boy over to the care of the authorities, and made a statement before the magistrates of all that happened. This done, he started for Plymouth, and feeling sick of the merchant service, entered on board a ship-of-war, which in a few days sailed for a foreign station. For many years he remained a true man-of-war's man, and was at length invalided on a pension, the amount of which brings out his character prominently.

"When the admirals, before whom he had to appear in order to obtain his discharge, told him that he was to receive twenty pounds a year in consideration of his long services, and of the wounds he had received, they asked where and how it should be made payable.

"He replied that he should wish to receive it at his native place, which he named, and in quarterly payments, and added: 'Your honours will see that I must drink the king's health when I receive my money, and as I should not wish to change the five-pound note, perhaps you will let me have an extra shilling each quarter.' This suggestion, at once loyal and prudent, met the cordial approval of the court, and the additional shilling a quarter was secured to him. His wife, however, has often told me, that it was the shilling, which in many cases he did not change, but carefully brought to her, after the five pounds had been expended in drinking his majesty's health. During his long service in the Royal Navy he visited many foreign stations, the Mediterranean, the Cape of Good Hope, both the Indies, and Madagascar and the neighbouring islands. He appeared to have availed himself of every opportunity of visiting noteworthy and famous localities and objects, and he often gave minute descriptions of

Gibraltar, Malta, Bombay, the Cave of Elephanta, the Isle of France and Madagascar, as well as of the strange animals he had seen. One of the latter secured for him a nickname, by which he was better known than by that given him at the font. The animal which he chiefly delighted to describe was one of the flying squirrels, which he, however, always called a 'flying fox.' The idea of a fox having the power of flight was so much too large for his customary auditors, that they utterly rejected it, and to mark their estimation of the tale, called George 'Old Flying Fox.' With a literary shipmate, who had read him the story several times, he had made a study of all the localities in the Isle of France connected with St. Pierre's tale of 'Paul and Virginia.' The same crony had often read him the 'Paradise Lost'; and George, whilst tailoring, would sketch the outline of the poem, concluding with the invariable remark that it was 'a very deep book.' Indeed, he regarded it as the exclusive privilege of the most talented and learned men fully to comprehend it. My first acquaintance with the character of the works just named was made through the oral descriptions of my shipmate, and when I subsequently read them, I was greatly surprised to find how faithful his sketches were. His pension was clogged with no other condition than that he should not ship on board vessels trading to foreign ports, thus leaving him at full liberty to form part of a coasting crew.

"His favourite beverage was beer, of which he could carry off enormous quantities without, as he phrased it, 'losing his reckoning.' Indeed, I only once knew him utterly incapable of taking care of himself. He was very garrulous, but never quarrelsome, when tipsy. At one well-known stage in his inebriation, he became religious, would talk much and with great admiration of the labours of the well-known 'Boatswain Smith,' and quote Scripture largely. Propped against the bulwarks, he would hold forth at great length, and certainly not cease without repeating the text, 'He brought me up also out of an horrible pit, out of the miry clay, and set my feet upon a rock, and established my goings.' On pronouncing the last words, he would commence an illustrative march, and usually gave evidence that his goings were not very firmly established. I once witnessed an amusing conflict between the poor fellow's respect for his 'promise' and his love of drink. One of our crew * had been rescued from drowning by an innkeeper, at whose house our skipper, by way of showing his gratitude, gave a supper to the crew, the landlord, and a few friends. George, on being invited stated that he would gladly be of the party, but that, on account of a quarrel with the innkeeper, he had made a 'promise' never to drink again in his house. This was met by the remark that the promise did not extend to *eating*, and that he should be left at perfect liberty to drink or not, as he pleased. On this understanding he came. As may be supposed he was a good deal chaffed, but this he managed to bear with great firmness and good temper. At length, however, it was unluckily suggested by some one, that there was nothing in his 'promise' to prevent his taking a glass of beer outside the house and drinking it there. At this compromise he caught eagerly, and marched

* William Pengelly himself.

gravely to the door every few minutes, drank his beer, and then resumed his seat.   At length the captain argued that if he had put his head out of the window of the room and took his draught, his 'promise' would be by no means broken, as he certainly would not be 'drinking in the house.'

"George, aided by the potations he had already taken, was convinced by this logic, and at once acted on the suggestion.   At length the innkeeper, desirous of reconciliation, thus addressed him: 'George, my boy, I am very sorry that there was ever any misunderstanding between us.   There's my hand, and here's my heart, and I love you like a brother, don't take the trouble to put your head out of the window any longer.   If you must do something of the kind, here's a large corner cupboard with nothing in it; put your head into that and drink.'   The speech and suggestion were cheered by the party, and the landlord was declared to have behaved like a man.   George seized the proffered hand, informed the innkeeper that he bore a strong resemblance to 'Boatswain Smith,' and then proceeded to go seriously through the farce of keeping his 'promise' in the manner just prescribed."

The account of Pengelly's shipmates has been given at some length, so as to enable the reader to form an estimate of the companions amongst whom he was thrown during his most susceptible years, and thereby understand something of the conditions of life at sea, early in the present century.   His escape from drowning (which has been mentioned, in connection with the supper at which "George" had such a struggle with his conscience) was not the only preservation from great peril for which he had to be thankful whilst engaged in a seafaring life.   Together with the rest of the crew, he suffered shipwreck during a violent gale, and on two subsequent occasions he was rescued from drowning, once after so long an immersion, that animation could only be restored with extreme difficulty.

Space forbids our dwelling on many other incidents of his boyhood, but the following account of a remarkable danger from which he was delivered is worth recording.

One bitterly cold night at sea, he and some of the other sailors having closed the cabin door and lit a charcoal fire, had all fallen asleep, when fortunately one of the crew entered the cabin.   He found the greatest difficulty in awakening his comrades to sufficient consciousness to enable them to stumble up on deck and get a breath of fresh air, for their sleep had wellnigh become that of death.   The strong and hardy seamen soon recovered, but the boy was so seriously affected that, long after he had been carried upon deck, he could not be roused, and was only restored to consciousness by means of prolonged exertions on the part of his shipmates.

When in his sixteenth year he lost his younger brother, Richard Pengelly, who had been seriously hurt during some school games. It was soon found that the child's illness would terminate fatally, but his kindly nature prevented him from revealing the name of the boy who had injured him, though he was frequently urged to do so. After his sad death, their mother was too anxious about her only surviving son, to be happy whilst he remained at sea. By her urgent wish, her son William returned home, and thus his seafaring life came to an end. The courage and self-reliance which he had gained as a young sailor were, no doubt, most useful to him all through his career, and though the life must have been one of some temptation, he seems to have been singularly unharmed by it. He was always moderate in speech, at a time when oaths were not uncommon, and consistently abstemious, when hard drinking was almost universal. In later years he became a total abstainer, and never took any alcoholic beverage, even when urged to do so by medical advice. Those who consider for a moment the many allurements to evil that beset a youthful sailor's life, will appreciate the strength of mind and nobility of character which enabled the young mariner to escape them unscathed.

The keen sense of humour, high spirits, and love of fun, which made Pengelly so much liked at sea, rendered him afterwards equally popular with his pupils and scientific colleagues.

No doubt his unfailing cheerfulness greatly assisted him to overcome the difficulties and anxieties that are always incidental to a long and active life ; but joined to this sanguine disposition, he possessed in large measure the extreme sensitiveness and highly-organized nature which is so often a characteristic of men of Keltic origin.

It was a perfect passion with him ever to side with the victims of injury or oppression, and though in later life he bore misrepresentations of his own scientific work most cheerfully, he was instantly roused to indignation by any injustice shown to his friends, or even to entire strangers. The knowledge of unfairness of any kind, or even the receipt of a distressing letter, would be sure to give him a weary and sleepless night. It was his nature to be perfectly honest and truthful, and his sympathies remained undimmed to the end of his life.

CHAPTER II.

FOR a few years after giving up the sea, Pengelly lived at Looe, but of this time little record remains. It is, however, certain that, notwithstanding the severe labours he was engaged in during the day for a bare maintenance, he nevertheless devoted many hours of every night to study, with the determination to make himself a master of the science of mathematics. This difficult task he carried on, not only without tuition, but also under the great disadvantage of not possessing any really good books on the subject. In spite of these drawbacks he succeeded in attaining such proficiency in his favourite pursuit, that in a comparatively short time he became a mathematical tutor of no mean order.

This period of home life is uneventful, but there was one day that lived happily in his recollection, when he made a pedestrian journey of more than thirty miles, to Devonport and back, that being the nearest town where he could procure some of the books he so earnestly longed for. For this purpose he had saved up his money for a long time, and, needless to say, it was all quickly expended. He returned home with empty pockets, but feeling rich indeed in having become the possessor of the works of some standard authors; for while he was specially devoted to mathematical studies, he was at the same time an omnivorous reader.

It will be easily understood that the books thus obtained opened a new world to him, and assisted materially in promoting his intellectual progress.

He records some years later the history of his self-education.

"'I could a tale unfold' of struggles, long-continued and severe, during my early pursuit of knowledge. I could speak of the intellectual isolation of my early years, when panting after information ; no one at hand to direct me in my inquiries, to solve my numerous questions, or to cheer me onward in the path I had resolved to pursue. No book-seller's shop within sixteen miles, and but little money to spend in it, if there had been. My only chance of obtaining a book was through an old pedlar, who occasionally visited our village, and of whom I bought my first ' Euclid.' Well do I remember the delight with which, on one occasion, I purchased twenty volumes of books at a secondhand book-shop at Devonport—ay, and the pride, too, with which I carried my treasure in a bundle on my shoulder, to my village home, sixteen miles across the Cornish hills. I could tell, too, of the derision of some of my acquaintances, the dissuasive advice of others, and the firm, though kind and well-meant, opposition of my parents. In short, I stood all but alone ; few, very few, sympathized or cheered, but many scoffed."

It is not difficult to see that, though this mental isolation must have been extremely irksome, the determined struggle, and the self-reliance gained in consequence, tended in a remarkable manner to assist his self-development.

In a fragmentary sketch, hastily written and unfortunately never completed, my father describes a well-known character in his native place, whose sayings and doings had made a deep impression on his youthful mind.

"Dick Harper," he writes, "before my time had been a farm-labourer, but, when I knew him, he had grown old though still hale, was a sort of 'odd man,' could assist in loading or unloading a coasting vessel, could act as a scavenger, supply the place of a river bargeman for a day or two, work in a garden, and, in short, turn his hand to several things, none of which, however, needed much skill. He had mastered the alphabet, and could spell out a word if time were given him, but beyond this his scholastic attainments did not extend. He had a huge fund of good temper and dry humour, and a tolerable stock of stories. According to the villagers, Dick had an answer for every-body ; in other words, if any one began to chaff him, he usually proved to be fully their equal in that line. He must have been a pretty good actor, for during the great French War a press-gang which visited our village carried him off to a ship-of-war, where he played the fool so continually and consistently that he was set on shore, whilst other landsmen, no more efficient than he, were retained and converted into sailors.

"Dick was sincerely religious, and very fond of hearing religious books read. He once came to me with the following statement :—

"' I was working yesterday in Mr. R——'s gardens, and 'e was there most part of the day reading. When 'e went away 'e left his book on the seat, and I took en up and look at en. 'Twas called " Milton's Paradise Lost." Did 'e ever 'ear tell o'n ? '

"Now it so happened that I had heard much of the work, and had once caught a glimpse of it, about two years before, for a quarter of an hour only. I knew that the word 'Paradise' had caught the old man, and that he expected it to be a sort of religious tract. Still I knew him well enough to believe he would enjoy it when read to him. I accordingly replied—

"'Oh yes, I've heard a good deal about it, and indeed saw it once for a very short time. I should be delighted to get an opportunity of reading it. Do you think you could borrow it?'

"'I dunnow, but I'll try if so be you'll promise to read en out loud to me.'

"'Oh, by all means; that's a bargain! Get the book, and you shall hear it from end to end if you wish.'

"At the close of his next day of gardening at Mr. R——'s, my old friend came to me, and with a look of triumph said, 'I've got en,' and we at once arranged that, as the days were near their greatest length, we would, the weather being fine, meet for the purpose of reading at seven o'clock on Tuesday and Friday evenings, at the head of his orchard. And there the old man of seventy and the boy of sixteen duly seated themselves under an apple tree, on a mossy bank which commanded a view of the harbour and the sea, and steadily read the 'Paradise Lost' through from end to end, and very thoroughly they enjoyed it. I must make two confessions, however. First, the mythological allusions puzzled us a good deal, but with the aid of a small edition of 'Johnson's Dictionary' containing a chapter of the heathen gods and goddesses, our principal loss was that of time. Secondly, we both chuckled a good deal over the puns put into the mouths of Satan and Belial in the sixth book in the matter of the devilish inquiry. Indeed, I had to read that section a second time.

"When we reached the end, the last five lines so impressed us that we committed them to memory, and when we occasionally met afterwards and had time to do so, each repeated to the other—

> "'Some natural tears they dropt, but wiped them soon;
> The world was all before them, where to choose
> Their place of rest, and Providence their guide:
> They, hand in hand, with wandering steps and slow,
> Through Eden took their solitary way.'"

It does not appear that whilst acquiring other branches of knowledge Pengelly paid any special attention to that science with which his name afterwards became associated.

His earliest geological experience was not particularly encouraging; it occurred when he was a sailor-boy weather-bound on the Dorsetshire coast, and he used thus to relate it:—

"I received my first lesson in geology at Lyme Regis, very soon after I had entered my teens. A labourer, whom I was observing, accidentally broke a large stone of blue lias, and thus disclosed a fine ammonite—the first fossil of any kind that I had ever seen or heard of.

"In reply to my exclamation—

"'What's that?'

"The workman said with a sneer—

"'If you had read the Bible, you'd know what 'tis.'

"'I *have* read the Bible. But what has that to do with it?'

"'In the Bible we're told there was once a flood that covered all the world. At that time, all the rocks were mud, and the different things that were drowned were buried in it, that there's a snake that was buried that way. There are lots of 'em, and other things besides, in the rocks and stones hereabouts.'

"'A snake! but where's his head?'

"'You must read the Bible, I tell 'ee, and then you'll find out why 'tis that some of these snakes in the rocks ain't got no heads. We're told there, that the seed of the woman shall bruise the serpent's head. That's how 'tis.'"

Some years later he was brought a second time into contact with geology, and writes thus of the occurrence :—

"A few of my brother villagers started a reading club, and I became a member. We met in a dame's schoolroom, at eight o'clock on every Thursday evening during the winter; paying no rent, but finding our own candles and fuel. Our practice was for one member to read aloud, whilst the others listened. One of our laws secured to any member the privilege of stopping the reader for the purpose of asking a question, stating an objection, criticizing, commenting, or amplifying, and the law was by no means a dead letter. Amongst other books we read Rowland Hill's 'Village Dialogues,' Chalmers' 'Astronomical Discourses,' and Dick's 'Christian Philosopher.' The 'Philosopher' contained a geological section. On reaching this the reader paused, announced what was immediately before us, and remarked that, as geology was very likely to be extremely dry, and as many good men thought it dangerous if not decidedly infidel in its teachings, he would propose that the section should not be read. This was passed by acclamation, and the reader passed on to astronomy."

While still quite young he was induced by a relative of his mother to settle at Torquay, which, though at that time a small place, was more interesting to his ardent and enthusiastic nature than his native village. From the following description it may be judged that life at Looe must have been somewhat monotonous.

"In the village in which I was born and bred," he writes, "I knew every individual, from the worshipful the Mayor down to the scavenger, and was not uninformed respecting the amount of their incomes, their rates of expenditure, the letters they received, where they bought their new garments, what they cost, and who made them; whether they lived on the fat of the land, or on the barest gleanings; in short, their general domestic arrangements and concerns."

Shortly after arriving in Torquay, he opened a small day-school on the Pestalozzian system, and was one of the first to introduce the use of the chalk and black-board, in giving instruction. The school rapidly increased, from six scholars to thirty, and afterwards to about seventy, and amongst his assistants he had the advantage of reckoning the Rev. Ebenezer Jenkins, subsequently well known through his writings, and as President of the Wesleyan Conference.

Soon after beginning his career as a schoolmaster the subject of geology was for a third time brought before his notice, and in such a manner on this occasion as at once to arouse him fully. Looking over some books that appeared likely to be useful to his scholars, he came unexpectedly upon one volume (published by the Brothers Chambers, with both of whom he afterwards became well acquainted), which devoted a single chapter only to Geology. On reading it carefully through, he was at once struck by the extent of knowledge that had been already gained in this department of science, and with the opportunities of further research which it afforded.

Scientific studies now began to occupy Pengelly's attention, and he devoted himself with great earnestness to geological pursuits, although it was many years before he undertook those investigations in the caves of Devonshire, which were brought to such a successful conclusion, as to gain for him a foremost place in the ranks of British geologists. It is remarkable that his efforts were so successful, for it will have been seen that his early years had passed without any of those opportunities of special training which might have proved of such great assistance to him. But he was a keen observer, very fond of work, and a capital walker (no mean requisite in field-geology), and having once taken his hammer in hand, he pursued his investigations with eager delight.

In 1837 Pengelly married Mary Ann Mudge, who was related to his mother, and this early marriage put an end to his cherished scheme of matriculating at the University of Cambridge. His wife's health was always delicate, and he suffered much anxiety on this account. He also felt acutely the loss of his eldest boy, who died when only a year old, and often afterwards he spoke of the terrible grief which he endured at the funeral of his first-born child. It took place on a beautifully bright sunny day, and the happy stir of life and movement

around, with all the freshness of the blossoming spring, were in sharp contrast to his own sorrow and distress. He was always extremely fond of children, and a most kind and thoughtful father, but it was some time before his home was again gladdened by the presence of a little child.

To the present generation, accustomed to railway journeys, it may be interesting to have an account of Pengelly's sensations on first travelling by train. He had to go as far as Taunton by coach, the railway not being extended further westward at that time. After arriving in London, he writes thus to an intimate friend :—

"Nothing of importance having occurred on the road, I have the less to write; nevertheless I would, were it in my power, describe my sensations in passing along the rail-road ; this, however, is beyond me. I was delighted with such an astonishing application of science, and also with the precision and regularity of the arrangements and movements at the various stations. I cannot say I was perfectly at ease during the first hour. There was one idea that presented itself to my mind throughout the entire journey, namely, that I was attached, with many other things, to the tail of some huge animal in the manner that boys sometimes treat cats or dogs, and that I was drawn along by its efforts, made in the extremest agony, to free itself from the articles attached to it."

In 1837 he was instrumental in the re-organization of the Torquay Mechanics' Institute, for which he laboured with his wonted energy. He continued for more than twenty years to feel a warm interest in the success of the undertaking, and contributed greatly to it by the delivery of lectures and affording other valuable services.

To one whose love and appreciation of natural science was so far in advance of what had hitherto been his means of study, the first opportunity of inspecting the treasures of the British Museum, and other great institutions in London, was naturally a period of intense enjoyment.

At the same time, the delight recorded in the following letters addressed to his friend, Mr. William Wilson, reads curiously in the consideration of what the collections were, that came under the student's view in 1843, as compared with what they have grown to be, in another half-century.

The letters bear the following dates :—

"*London, June* 20, 1843.—Yesterday I paid my first visit to the British Museum, and now find that I know little or nothing about it; the multiplicity of objects confused me. I paid most attention to the

Ornithological and Zoophytic rooms, in each of which the variety of forms, under which Nature presents itself really astonished me; still I do not think a strait waistcoat will be necessary. I need not tell you that I shall go again."

"*London, June* 30.—Yesterday morning I called on a medical student in the London University, who very kindly conducted me through those parts of the university most interesting to a stranger; that which struck me most, was the museum of anatomical and physiological preparations. Unfortunately, my friend's time was very short, so that I left the room very reluctantly, and with an earnest desire to revisit it."

"*London, July* 1.—I went this morning to visit the museum of the College of Surgeons, and was very much delighted indeed. It is impossible to say what I saw, I saw nearly everything in the museum; and I should think that it contains all that the anatomist and physiologist can desire. I was probably equally pleased with each department. Sometimes I think that of comparative anatomy the best, sometimes that of morbid anatomy, and sometimes that illustrative of fœtal development and existence; the fact is, they are all best. Some of the fossils are magnificent. I scarcely know which to admire most, the museum, or the kindness of my guide.

"After leaving this I went to King's College, and accidentally became acquainted with Mr. Edwards, one of the Professors, and known to me as an author; he very kindly showed me all he could then, which was a museum of models and apparatus. There I saw Babbage's calculating machine—at least, so much of it as has been perfected; I saw it cube several numbers, but do not by any means understand the principle on which it acts, or the movements of the complicated machinery. I also had the pleasure of seeing Mr. Wheatstone, inventor of the electric telegraph, electric clocks, etc. I saw the telegraph at work on a small scale; but this, too, is beyond me. Let the self-sufficient in knowledge visit the London institutions, and he will be cured if curable.*

"I again returned to the Museum and spent some time in the insect-room, and was very much pleased with the gay attire in which Nature has decked herself in this department. I found that a considerable quantity of fossil bones had been set up since my last visit."

"*London, July* 4.—I have called on Mr. Webster, Professor of Geology at the London University, and found him a kind-hearted simple old gentleman, having no desire to keep his knowledge a secret. I spent some time with him, and had one of the most agreeable chats since leaving home. He is much afraid that all the movements made for the improvement of society will be abortive, he is rather inclined to take a gloomy view of things. I fear he has been disappointed; his whole life has been spent in scientific research, and it does not appear to have enriched him. The privileges of the London University are not appreciated by the public to the extent that was expected.

---

* This letter contains Pengelly's first mention of Babbage and Wheatstone, with both of whom he afterwards became well acquainted.

Mr. Webster tells me it has almost become a medical school only. I promised him some of the fossil treasures of South Devon; the effect of this communication was something like that of an electric shock, the good old man appeared quite delighted."

"*London, July* 5.—Yesterday morning I went in search of the Museum of 'Economic Geology' of which I have read much, and which I had been informed, at the British Museum, was at, or near, Charing Cross; therefore, to Charing Cross I went, and inquired of the first well-dressed person I met; but he knew nothing about it, could make nothing of the phrase 'Economic Geology.' I applied with similar success to at least twenty different persons; by some I was directed to the Adelaide Gallery, by others to the British Museum, to the Polytechnic, to some Phrenological shops, but most persons declined to direct, declaring they knew nothing about it, having never heard the phrase 'Economic Geology' before. At length, a philosophical instrument maker directed me to Craig's Court, into which I went, and met a gentleman, who again directed me out of it into Scotland Yard, on reaching which I found the museum of the United Service; this not being what I wanted, I recommenced my search, and was directed by a shoemaker to Craig's Court again, and, on getting there, I found it; and a very interesting place it is. Here are immense numbers of polished cubes of marble, sandstones, elvan, granite, and serpentine, all with tickets containing their names, localities, by whom presented, and the chief buildings in which they had been employed. The Babbacombe, Ipplepen, and Ogwell marbles were amongst the choicest specimens; another large room contained the metallic minerals, or ores of metal, with which I was very much interested. On leaving this, I called on Mr. Edwards, of King's College, who took me to a class of boys, who were being instructed in singing by the famous Hullah; I was much pleased to find that Mr. Edwards could descend from the pedestal of the teacher, for he sat down among his pupils, and sang away as heartily as any of them; he afterwards told me he was going regularly through the course. Mr. Hullah found great difficulty in keeping up the attention of his pupils generally. They were taking their first lesson in the minor key, and I suppose found it somewhat difficult; nevertheless, several boys answered the questions he put them very expertly and correctly, and on the whole I conclude the boys did very well. On the breaking up of the class, Mr. Edwards informed me that Mr. Hullah would be at the College again the next day, and have a larger and more advanced class, and invited me to call again.* He then took me to Christ Church School, of which he has been an examiner for the past ten years. This appears to be an immense place, and I should think the boys were very comfortable there."

"*London, July* 11.—On looking over the time I have spent in London, I find nothing to cause me to repent of coming; it will be an important period in my life, many things have occurred since being

* Pengelly had studied the theory of music, was extremely fond of it, and sang well himself, so that this visit must have interested him greatly.

here, for each of which I would have come up from Devonshire. I have had an intellectual feast, the viands have been various, but I hope wholesome. I am inclined to think I must be removed from the order Bimana to Ruminata, as I shall certainly reproduce my food and chew it over and over again. There are a few things I could have wished to have seen, but I must have stopped somewhere. I could spend a fortune here in purchasing philosophical apparatus and models, maps, diagrams, and books, but I have not a fortune to spend, and as I must stop somewhere I have stopped short of purchasing anything; indeed, I know not what choice to make."

"*Southampton, July* 14.—I find this to be an interesting place; it possesses a scientific institution, termed the Polytechnic, possessed of a museum and reading-room, the society has a good many members, lectures are regularly given during the winter, there is no difficulty in getting an ample supply of lecturers. I visited the museum and found many good things in it, but miserably arranged—or rather, not arranged at all.

"About two miles from the town, on a common, an artesian well is being sunk; this I visited, but could not get access to the works; this was a disappointment, nevertheless I very much enjoyed the walk. In the afternoon I rambled to Netley Abbey, a ruin not far from the shores of Southampton Water, about three miles from the town. To reach it I had to cross the Itchen, on which a steam bridge plies; I found the walk to the ruin very beautiful, a considerable part of it is by the water, commanding a view of the country, the harbour, and the Isle of Wight. I found the ruin to be very splendid; though time has done much injury, the modern barbarians have done much more, both in destroying and rebuilding; the latter being perhaps more destructive of the beauty of the old pile than the former. I should like to spend some time in the Isle of Wight, but it will be altogether useless to think of visiting it during my brief tarriance here."

During his holidays, Pengelly began to make longer journeys, and greatly enjoyed his first expedition to Scotland, a country which he often revisited. He was delighted with the beautiful scenery of the North and Western Highlands, and the picturesque islands of the coast. Edinburgh, with its grand situation and deeply interesting old town, particularly attracted him. Whilst in the Northern capital he had the advantage of making the acquaintance of the late Professor Jameson, who gave him much valuable information concerning the geology of the Isle of Arran, which he was about to visit. The Professor concluded his remarks with the following hint: "On your return I hope you will call on me again, when the first question I shall ask will probably be, 'Did you write your notes on the spot, or at the Inn at the close of the day?' If you reply, 'On the spot,' I shall be glad to hear them; but, if not, I am afraid I shall not think them of much value."

From that time Pengelly acted on this suggestion, and there is little doubt that the advice so opportunely given him, when a young man, greatly helped to form those habits of extreme accuracy which characterized all his scientific work.

Mr. Edward Vivian was one of his earliest friends in Torquay, and the similarity of their tastes, both in scientific and local matters, tended to foster the friendship thus begun. In 1844, with the assistance of Mr. Vivian, Dr. Battersby, and other friends, Pengelly founded the Torquay Natural History Society, and was untiring in his efforts to contribute to its permament usefulness, by assisting with gratuitously-given lectures, papers, and gifts of fossils. His power of organization was great, and certainly did not mean, as is sometimes the case, doing little work and taking all the credit.

A writer in "*Natural Science*" for May, 1894, thus alludes to the subject :—

"It was indeed mainly due to Mr. Pengelly's energy that the autumn of 1844 witnessed the foundation of the Torquay Natural History Society. Over its early fortunes he exercised the most watchful care, and in 1851 he was induced to accept the office of honorary secretary, an office which he continued uninterruptedly to hold, to the unspeakable advantage of the Society, for no less than nine-and-thirty years. Under his guidance it became a scientific power in the county. Year after year he lectured there, tincturing the locality with his own enthusiasm; and from the Society there ultimately sprang the Museum in Babbacombe Road, with its admirable local collections. In the reading-room attached to the Museum there fitly hangs an oil-painting of the man whose individuality is unmistakably marked upon the entire institution—William Pengelly."

The following notes from a paper written in 1894 by his old friend and pupil, Mr. A. R. Hunt, M.A., F.G.S., F.L.S., give some reminiscences of Pengelly's work at the Museum and show the pleasant feeling that existed between him and his pupils.

"Without entering into needless detail, it may be confidently asserted that the Torquay Natural History Society was founded by a few enthusiastic naturalists, associated for the sole purpose of mutual assistance in original research. The founders were able men; but men, however able, cannot work without books; so these gentlemen devised a plan by which their individual subscriptions should be augmented for the purchase of the needful scientific literature. Having much to say, and being able to say it well, they organized lectures, open to the public, simply and solely for the purpose of turning in the wished-for cash. These lectures, delivered in the winter season, have continued to the present day. . . .

"Owing to the fact that the Society was founded by men of mark, notable visitors and neighbours have often been seen at the lecture-desk, such as Scoresby, Tylor, W. Froude, Goldwin-Smith, and Sir Samuel Baker, together with many others of high eminence in their respective walks of science and culture. . . .

"In course of time the Society took up its quarters in the Freemasons' Hall, where Mr. Pengelly's wonderful lectures attracted crowds of hearers of the most miscellaneous character, and abstruse questions of astronomy and geology proved attractive to men with no scientific training whatever. Given a little common sense, and the lecturer seemed to require nothing more. We have all seen the celebrated Kodak advertisement, 'You touch the button; we do the rest.' Mr. Pengelly might have said with equal truth, 'You come and listen; I will do the rest. The lecturer's style was quite *sui generis*. He seemed to force his hearers to form their own conclusions, rather than to accept the speaker's opinions. Indeed, these as mere opinions were very seldom allowed a prominent place. Astronomy was a favourite subject. I well remember, as a boy, hearing Mr. Pengelly explain and illustrate the retrograde paths of the planets in the heavens in so perspicuous a manner that it was impossible not to understand the phenomena. Of course, in astronomy Mr. Pengelly was not an original worker; but, as the facts on which he lectured were acknowledged facts, and not questions of opinion, he was always on safe ground. As a geologist it was, of course, otherwise; here he was not only an advanced worker, but in the special branch of cavern deposits he was an authority. When expounding this, his favourite science, his power was quite extraordinary, and his courses of elementary lectures were more instructive than any text-book could be. He used to say that he never wrote his lectures, or delivered identically the same lecture more than once. A few skeleton notes seemed to suffice for a text, on which there was always more to say than time would allow, though the mistake was never made of attempting to crowd into an hour more than it could contain.

"At the time the Society occupied the Freemasons' Hall, the Darwinian theory was comparatively young, and was even more often than at present the subject of eager controversy. The majority of naturalists had been brought up in the orthodox belief that plants and animals had been created perfect at definite times, in the common acceptation of the meaning of the word creation. Besides this, the six days of creation was a doctrine very commonly taught and accepted. Perhaps the two most distinguished naturalists who have made Torquay their home were Mr. P. H. Gosse, F.R.S., and Mr. Pengelly, F.R.S., the former a staunch exponent of the literal Mosaic doctrine of creation, the latter an early convert to the theory of creation by evolution. . . .

"Mr. Pengelly, as I have elsewhere stated, remarked at a public meeting that he wanted to hear what Mr. X. *knew*, not what he *thought* —a sentiment which is the very key to all true progress, and which involves building on the firm foundation of what is known, and doubting every scientific assertion based on conjecture and opinion. The Apostle's precept, 'Prove all things, hold fast that which is good,' is the very soul of sound research; but such sentiments can naturally find no place in the nursery or class-room, where docility is more valued than scepticism, unless, indeed, in those exceptional cases where the teachers are fellow-students with the taught.

"This calls to mind another remarkable trait in Mr. Pengelly's character. As soon as his pupils were men, all idea of teacher and taught was swept away, and the master did not even seem to appreciate the incense of his pupils' gratitude. He would far prefer their attacking him, and so giving him the pleasure of returning the compliment. This again reminds me of a personal incident. Mr. Pengelly having publicly attacked one of my papers, I replied in the most rebellious spirit, fighting every point, conceding nothing, and even gibbeting my critic in parallel columns to try and convict him of inaccuracy in his own work. A fearful retribution might have been expected! This is what happened. Mr. Pengelly quietly said one day, 'I have read your reply. It is, of course, open to me to write a rejoinder; but these controversies must stop somewhere, and, so far as I am concerned, I intend to let the subject drop.' Mark the generosity! Though he left me with the last word in the *Transactions of the Devonshire Association*, he went out of his way to set me at my ease in private as to his future intentions—a very important matter to a student when his opponent is a man of the calibre of Mr. Pengelly. But, on looking back to years of fencing with my old master, I note especially the absolute trust which he always inspired. It was impossible for him to take a mean advantage of an opponent, or to try and make the worse appear the better part. To play a science game with him was like playing any game of skill, such as golf, racquets, or lawn-tennis, with gentlemen who can be trusted to attempt no sharp practice, and to give the benefit of the doubt to their opponents rather than take it themselves. Thus, if any one scored a point off Mr. Pengelly, he would be the first to proclaim it."

He worked so unceasingly, as frequently to call forth the remonstrances of his friends, one of whom writes, in April, 1846—

"I am fearful for you, on hearing of such continual exertions, far beyond the health of the strongest; continual mental exertion from five o'clock to midnight is more than any one can bear with impunity, especially as you can allow no time for meals. On this account I was pleased to hear you were contemplating giving up your school at midsummer, and trusting to private tuition alone, which will save you a vast amount of wear and tear, and not materially diminish your resources, I hope, from the increased time it will afford, for other pursuits. Torquay is becoming such a large place, and you are such a public character, that there can be little doubt of your finding full employment and time for geologizing again, and making fresh discoveries in the fossil treasures of Torquay."

In 1846, his private pupils had grown to be so numerous that he was able to give up his school altogether, and become a tutor of mathematics and the natural sciences.

His success from this time was extremely rapid, and is most striking, when it is remembered that he enjoyed so few advantages of education, was without access to a single good library, had no influential friends, except those whom his own ability and worth attracted, and suffered constant anxiety from having no private means to fall back upon in case of illness. His pupils were representative of all classes, from the scions of more than one royal house, and the children of people of distinction, to those in the humbler walks in life. Many of them afterwards achieved celebrity. He was deeply interested in the welfare of all, but most particularly in that of the working-men and lads, whom he taught gratuitously at an evening class that he had established in 1839, and at which he worked very hard, after his long day's professional toil. He was always anxious to encourage a love of knowledge, and to assist in any educational work among the people, wishing that others might have those advantages which he himself had never had the good fortune to enjoy. Among his papers, the following note, written about this time, was found : " I spent a considerable part of to-day in turning over a host of manuscripts, chiefly mathematical exercises, including arithmetic, algebra, plane and spherical trigonometry, and navigation. They are the results of severe study, under terrible privations; now they are altogether valueless, and I believe I shall burn them, though it really pains me to do it."

One of the earliest of the numerous testimonials presented to him was from his pupils. It took the form of a valuable microscope, which he greatly prized, not only for its intrinsic worth, but also as a proof of the kindness of those who had cheerfully undertaken the task of getting up the testimonial as a mark of their appreciation of his work.

After giving up his school, he was able to find a little more time for general society. One of his most valued friends at this period was the Duchess of Manchester, who showed him great kindness, and took the keenest interest in all his scientific pursuits. Her death, in the autumn of 1848, was a great sorrow to him.

He also became intimate with Sir Culling and Lady Eardley,

who were very desirous that he should accompany their son to Palestine; but, interesting as the expedition would have been, he had regretfully to give it up, as it would have involved too great a sacrifice of his time and work at Torquay. It will have been seen how highly he valued mathematical studies, but that his zeal was surpassed by one of his friends the following extract from his narrative of a holiday ramble will show.

"I one day learned that my road lay within a couple of miles of the rectory of my old mathematical friend D——. We had been great friends when he was a curate in a distant part of the country, but had not met for several years, during which he had been advanced from a curacy of about £80 to a rectory of £200 per year, and a residence, in a very secluded district. My time was very short; but, for *auld lang syne*, I decided to sacrifice a few hours. On reaching the house, Mr. and Mrs. D—— were fortunately at home, and received me with their wonted kindness.

"The salutations were barely over, when I said—

"'It is now six o'clock; I must reach W—— to-night, and as it is said to be fully eight miles off, and I am utterly unacquainted with the road, and with the town when I reach it, I cannot remain with you one minute after eight o'clock.'

"'Oh, very well,' said D——, 'then we must improve the shining hours. Jane, my dear, be so good as to order tea.'

"Having so said, he left the room. In a few minutes he returned with a book under his arm, and his hands filled with writing materials, which he placed upon the table. Opening the book, he said—

"'This is Hind's "Trigonometry," and here's a lot of examples for practice. Let us see which can do the greatest number of them by eight o'clock. I did most of them many years ago, but I have not looked at them since. Suppose we begin at this one'—which he pointed out—'and take them as they come. We can drink our tea as we work, so as to lose no time.'

"'All right,' said I; though it was certainly not the object for which I had come out of my road.

"Accordingly we set to work. No words passed between us; the servant brought in the tray, Mrs. D—— handed us our tea, which we drank now and then, and the time flew on rapidly. At length, finding it to be a quarter to eight—

"'We must stop,' said I, 'for in a quarter of an hour I must be on the road.'

"'Very well. Let us see how our answers agree with those of the author.'

"It proved that he had correctly solved one more than I had. This point settled, I said, 'Good-bye.'

"'Good-bye. Do come again as soon as you can. The farmers know nothing whatever about trigonometry.'

"We parted at the rectory door, and have never met since; nor shall we ever do so more, as his decease occurred several years ago.

During my late long walk to W——, my mind was chiefly occupied with the mental isolation of a rural clergyman."

Pengelly's name being so well known in connection with Kent's Cavern which had already partially been explored by the Rev. J. MacEnery, a Roman Catholic priest (to whose labours he always referred in the warmest terms of appreciation), and again in 1840 by Mr. Godwin Austen, it is worthy of note that in 1846 he received, in conjunction with Mr. Vivian and Dr. Battersby, a grant of a small sum from the Torquay Natural History Society, to enable them to make some further examination in the cavern. The results obtained were very valuable to science, but public opinion was not then prepared to receive some of the most striking conclusions. It was not until the year 1864 that "at the Bath meeting of the British Association, mainly by the influence of Sir Charles Lyell, who was then president, a powerful committee was appointed for the systematic exploration of the cavern."

Allusion has been already made to Pengelly's temperate habits, but his kindness of heart extended even to inebriates, and occasionally led him into curious adventures. It was well that he did not expect any gratitude for his assistance, as his help was often received in quite another spirit. He has recorded one of these occasions, when he was endeavouring to enact the good Samaritan, so the incident can be given in his own words.

"One cloudy, moonless night, when walking, about ten o'clock, from a considerable town to my lodging in one of the suburbs, I saw something lying in the road, and supposed it to be a dog. Having no fondness for any of the *caninæ*, I gave it a wide berth, but steadily watched it. At length, feeling sceptical about the dog hypothesis, I approached, and found it a man, fearfully intoxicated. On being raised to his feet, he fell immediately he was left to himself, and when propped against the wall his efforts to walk very soon brought him again prostrate in the middle of the road. To leave him there was to render it very probable that he would be seriously injured—perhaps killed—before the morning by some one running over him. Happily, his tongue was not quite so drunk as his legs, and, after many efforts, he succeeded in giving me his name and address.

"Being familiar with the district—another suburb—I decided on taking him home. The labour was by no means trifling, as the distance was fully two miles, the night was dark, and he was a heavy man. We reached his house at about one in the morning. My knock was answered by his wife, with whom I had the pleasure of the following chat—

"' Is this your husband?'

"'Yes, unfortunately.   I wish he was in heaven.'

"' I found him lying in the road, and could do no less than take him home.'

"'A pretty story to tell me!   No doubt you've been drinking with him.'

"'Good night, ma'am.'

"And in this way I disposed of my charge and of hers."

CHAPTER III.

HIS GROWING FAME AS A GEOLOGIST.

1848-1850.

SOME letters written by Pengelly to a favourite pupil, with whose family he was intimate, may be inserted here, inasmuch as, though they contain no striking incidents, they throw some light on his opinions, and the great amount of work that he undertook successfully at this time.

"*Torquay, October* 5, 1848.—. . . Inclosed are the remaining propositions of the third book of Euclid. I should wish you to read the first book a second time, and very thoroughly, before proceeding further. I hope my scrawls will be of use to you sooner or later. I received a copy of the paper of which Hugh Miller is editor (the *Witness*) last week, and which I have sent you by this post, and find that he has commenced a new series of papers on his geological rambles. Are you aware that the Queen has been pleased to confer knighthood on Lyell the geologist?"

This is Pengelly's first reference to Sir Charles Lyell, afterwards one of his warmest friends, and with whom he was most intimately connected during his investigations into the antiquity of man in Britain. About a hundred letters from Sir Charles Lyell are preserved amongst Pengelly's papers.

"*Torquay, October* 12, 1848.—. . . Our winter visitors are flocking in, and I hope to be very fully occupied; my pupils are on the increase, and by this time next month I shall probably have much less leisure than now. I got two additional members for the Palæontographical last night; we are now a goodly number in this place. I have just been exhibiting my fossils to a gentleman of Cheltenham, who has a splendid *general* collection; he sadly broke the tenth commandment over my Devonians and Silurians (I was not without fears that he would break an earlier one)! He thinks he can add with great advantage to my Cretaceous and Oolite specimens, and has kindly promised to do so. . . ."

"*Torquay*, 1848.—. . . You say that you are concerned at having taken up so much of my valuable time; if my time is really valuable, it is because I can employ it serviceably for others. I do not think that Nichol does Adams justice.* He attempts to excuse, if not to justify, the neglect of both Airy and Challis. The passage in which Nichol compares Leverrier to Columbus is very fine, certainly, but not original; the idea was contained in a speech made by Sir J. Herschel at the meeting of the British Association at Southampton, 1846. I think the passage still finer than that of Nichol; judge for yourself. The planet had not been discovered, yet Herschel expressed his belief in its existence thus: 'We see it as Columbus saw America from the shores of Spain. Its movements have been felt along the far-reaching line of our analysis with a certainty hardly inferior to ocular demonstration.'"

"*Torquay, October* 26, 1848.—. . . Be dull as you please about your geometry. I will try to enlighten you as often as you think fit to apply to me. . . . Hyperion, the eighth satellite of Saturn, seems to have been a double discovery, see *Athenæum*, October 14th. Pray how do *you* know that my geological collection is 'already beautiful?' Come and see it, then give an opinion. . . . My lessons and lectures leave me but little leisure at present, moreover the committee meetings of the Mechanics' Institute and Natural History Society must be attended, so that, on the whole, I am tolerably occupied. . . . I have just been reading Scott's 'Lady of the Lake' and had some trouble to close the book for the purpose of writing you. What a beautiful poem! It bears reading again and again. I know the scene perfectly, which greatly increases my pleasure in the reading. . . ."

"*Torquay, November* 6, 1848.—. . . I think you are mistaken in your notion that the inhabitants of the coast do not enjoy the sea so much as their inland friends; the former doubtless say least about it, because it has no *novelty* for them, the latter most, because it is *novel* and not because it is the sea. You and I have both seen the sea, and have both admired it, yet I do not think you would or do pine after it so much as I should, and have, after a very few weeks' absence. I really think this point conclusive. The story of the retreating Greeks, under Xenophon, is quite in point, I fancy. . . ."

"*Torquay, November* 20, 1848.—. . . Early last week we learned that the gentleman who was to have lectured for us this evening could not do so. As is usual in these cases, I was asked to supply his place, and consented to do so. I had consequently a good deal to do in preparing diagrams. . . . I am happy to be able to inform you that my wife is much better, and came downstairs yesterday for the first time. . . . I heartily wish I could manage a holiday at Christmas, but it cannot be. I must 'make hay while the sun shines.' . . . Most sincerely do I wish that I could spend every evening in a cheerful intellectual circle of about a dozen, it would do me all the good in the world. I am sincerely attached to the vocation of the teacher, and

---

* Prof. John Couch Adams of Cambridge, discoverer of the planet Neptune, an astronomer, and, better still, a *Cornishman*, for whom Pengelly entertained a strong admiration.

earnestly do I wish that I could afford always to do it without pay-ment. I do not like to be paid for thinking, and to think on stated subjects, at stated hours. Would that I could throw off the harness, and live independently, no matter how humbly; but I have children to settle in the world, and if I can do it, they shall never pass through the fearful struggle that I did. I have at this moment a very vivid recollection of myself at a late, lonely, and humble supper; the little table at which I wrought theoretical and practical mathematics; the very small pile of books (but oh, how valued! and then how really valuable!); the wretched light, the fireless grate, the damp cold stone floor, the aching head, the swollen feet, the shivering frame, and that which enabled me to bear the whole, the determination to know something of the beautiful and astonishing universe. I thank God that I was enabled to persevere, that He has crowned my efforts with success, and that I have a reasonable prospect of competency for myself and family. . . . I am very sorry to hear of poor ——'s great affliction, it seems almost too long for a merely temporary attack. I hope, however, almost against hope, that it is not; I cannot but think that there is something wrong in your philosophy or your theology, when you say, 'How wonderful it seems such an affliction should befal such a thoroughly amiable and intelligent young man.' I am far, very far, from denying the doctrine of a particular Providence, but I certainly think it undesirable to call in extraordinary means to explain an ordinary phenomenon. I believe —— to have been very amiable; but he, or some of his progenitors, may have (and in my opinion certainly have) broken a law of which his present calamity is the unavoidable penalty, irrespective of his *moral* excellence. . . . It is, as you suppose, a great pleasure to spend the evening cosily with some favourite author, but this I can only occasionally do. There is also a pleasure, a great one with me, namely, a game of romps with my children; it would do your heart good to see us roll over each other on the floor."

" *Torquay, November* 25, 1848.—. . . I am very happy to be able to inform you that my wife is sufficiently well to be able to send away her nurse this evening. . . . Once more I request you to send me your mathematical difficulties as soon as they occur. You say, 'I am not to correct them until it is convenient;' I promise I will not, but you will allow me to add that it will always be convenient? . . . Before this reaches you, you will probably have heard that the Duchess of Manchester is dead. She was an excellent woman, eminent for her piety and good works; as come-at-able and unassuming as she could possibly be. I never felt more at home with any one in my life, it really was a treat to have a chat with her, as I had three times a week at her tea-table during the winters of 1846–47."

" *Torquay, February* 1, 1849.—I have no doubt that you could understand Herschel, but it would require all your mathematics and much study. I would rather that you deferred it for some time, more especially as Sir John is known to be engaged on a more elementary work. . . . I went to Exmouth on the 10th ult. The day was very bright, but there was a heavy gale off the coast, which, acting on the sea breaking on the shore, blew the spray seaward very beautifully. In the railway carriage with me there was an elderly lady and her son; the latter I judged to be a midshipman of the Royal Navy, just returned from a foreign station, with evidently very shattered health. His mother was very attentive and kind to him, and directed his attention to the spray, which I have mentioned above. He looked at it for a moment, and whilst she exclaimed, 'How very beautiful!' he turned from it with a sigh, and said, in the most heart-breaking tones, 'Oh, mother, I have seen quite enough of that lately—quite, quite enough! I care much less about the sea than I once did.' There was nothing in the words, but much in his manner of uttering them, which instantly recalled his kind mother, and spoke to me of ruined health and disappointed ambition, and which made me somewhat gloomy till I found myself on the platform. . . .

"My lecture [at Exmouth] was well attended, and very well received. Speaking of lectures, I delivered one yesterday at the Natural History Society (Torquay) on 'Organic Remains,' and have eleven more to come on geology. . . . And now for geometry; but, would you believe it? I thought to put my hand at once upon your paper, but I cannot find it anywhere. Though I cannot remember where I put the paper, I *do* remember that neither of your exercises were quite right. You really ought to be very angry with me; but still I hope you will not. . . .

"I agree with you in thinking of the punishment by death for any crime as unchristian, impolitic, and worse than useless."

"*Torquay, May* 12, 1849.— . . . On Friday I left for Exeter by the six o'clock train, delivered a lecture on the 'Moon' before the members of the Literary Society at the Athenæum, finished just in time for the last train, and reached home just after eleven. . . . Do not be surprised that you feel some discouragement respecting teaching; all honest teachers do that. Do the best you can, and leave the result to Him who will not allow honest endeavours and sincere motives to go unrewarded."

The correspondence is soon after broken off by the summer holidays, which Pengelly spent partly in a ramble amidst the beautiful scenery of the river Wye, and partly in a walking tour with a friend in South Wales. His letters to his pupil begin again in the autumn.

"*Torquay, September* 21, 1849.— . . . I am sorry to hear that the cholera is so bad with you; it has been rather alarming here, but I am happy to say that it is better at present. I am far from denying the doctrine of judgments in the abstract, or that we have not again and again deserved them as a nation, as well as individually; but I hold it unwise to call in supernatural causes when natural ones will account for phenomena, and in the present case I quite think they will do so. I fully believe that the cholera has a mission, that it will accomplish much moral and physical good, and that the laws of which it is the penal sanction are the laws of God. . . ."

"*Torquay, October* 20, 1849.— . . . On account of my Cornish journey I was unable to get my letter to you off before. On my journeys on Thursday and Friday I never saw so much to admire in the autumn tints. The orchards of Devon were looking truly lovely; rosy-cheeked and golden apples were hanging on the boughs in most inviting luxuriance; the wild clematis was climbing every tree and covering every hedge; the leaves were all in the warmest colours; here and there a grey limestone rock showed itself with beautiful effect. . . . The walk to Looe from Liskeard is at all times lovely; it is through a magnificent valley, charmingly wooded. Ever since I can remember it has been a great favourite; but now I was approaching the home of my boyhood and of my parents. . . . My reception in the lecture-room at Looe was very flattering. The audience was very large, every face well known to me—old schoolmates and playmates, and one or two with whom I had once thought of mating in a more serious sort of way. And then there was such shaking hands and 'How d'ye does!' that there was some fear about the lecture beginning at all. But being begun, it was listened to with an attention that did my heart good. They did not give vocal demonstrations of approval or disapproval from beginning to end; but I could read their eyes, and was more than satisfied. But didn't they cheer at the close! The president got up and thanked me, as is usual; sceptics got up and thanked me for having cured them; ladies and gentlemen came up and shook hands with me again, and thanked me individually. Then came the invitations to supper. I could not accept them all, so allowed myself to be carried off by a dear old lady with whom my mother came to Looe, and who has always felt an interest in me.

"I left next morning at nine; but before doing so, a deputation waited on me to ascertain whether I considered myself a West Looe man or an East Looe man, as both parties claimed me, and I was called on to decide, which I did by informing them that I was born in East Looe.

"'I know that,' said one; 'but you were reared in West Looe, and West Looe is your parish. So if you want parish relief, you will be sent there!'

"This reasoning would have been deemed sufficient, had I not hinted that I had gained a parish in Tormohun [the old name for Torquay]."

"*Torquay, October* 25, 1849.— . . . I have received a letter from Colenso. He acknowledges the error in his answer. If you care to have the letter as an autograph, I will send it you. As I expected, his reply is written in a kind, friendly spirit. . . . I spend the greater part of my evenings in covering the boards on which I put my 'geologicals' with blue paper. You would be amused to see me at work. My dear children call themselves my servants, fetch and carry the boards, and hand me papers, and honestly believe they are helping me, and are extremely happy in the delusion. . . . I forgot to tell you in previous notes to cause your pupils in algebra to get all Colenso's *text* carefully up. I don't mean by memory, but so as to be able to answer any question you may put them respecting it, more especially the *demonstrative* parts. These are of more importance than all the mere rules in the world. Excuse me, but if you only teach them to work algebraic exercises by the rules, without their being fully acquainted with the *rationale* of these rules, you will have done nothing for them ; nay, worse than that, their time will have been lost. To work algebraic exercises will not be of use to one lady out of a million—they will never go far enough into the science to turn it to account in any branch of natural philosophy ; but the habit of close investigation and severe analytical reasoning acquired by following an author through his illustration of principle is beyond all value. . . ."

" *Torquay*, 1849.— . . . 'Herschel' would not do at all for the purpose you propose [reading to pupils], but you cannot do better than study it yourself should you ever get time. Unfortunately, I have Darley's intolerably stupid book ; by all means discontinue the reading of such trash, and never allow any book in *any* department of science, when arranged in the *form of dialogue*, to be seen by your pupils ; they are quite as likely to remember the blunders of the learners in the chat, as the corrections of the teacher, perhaps *more* likely. . . . I think you had better read A's book fairly through, than merely select fine passages. I need not tell you that I do not dislike poetry, but I do dislike it out of its place, and I certainly think that the flights in which he indulges, especially at the end of his chapters, are not only misplaced, but quite absurd generally. I wish all science could be thrown into the form of Euclid or reduced to the form of an equation. . . ."

" *Torquay, January* 3, 1850.— . . . At my lecture last week I made the acquaintance of Lady Shelley, and her son and daughter. They attend the lectures at the Royal Institution when in town, which they usually are. They have been at my house to-day to see my fossils, with which they profess to be quite delighted. I am to spend next Wednesday evening with them. I lectured this evening and met a Dr. Alliott, with whom I was greatly pleased. . . ."

" *Torquay, January* 21, 1850.— . . . Since I last wrote I have been very much occupied in the preparation of lectures, and in reading mathematics with a young student at the East India Company's College at Addiscombe. . . . My lectures at the Natural History Society Museum have been well attended. I lectured to-day on 'The Physical Constitution of the Sun and Planets.' I expect to lecture at Exeter, on Comets, on February 1st, and at Exmouth on the Wednesday following. . . . As on former occasions, my lectures at the museum are all gratis. . . ."

" *Bethesda, North Wales, July* 8, 1850.— . . . We left Beaumaris at eight a.m. by omnibus for the Menai Suspension Bridge, and were set down on the Anglesey side. Our first labour was to descend nearly to the level of the stream for the purpose of seeing the fastenings of the bridge, which we accomplished by entering a tunnel one hundred yards long. This done we crossed the bridge, which is a very beautiful object ; everything about it seems not only useful but also ornamental, and indeed *appears* to partake more of the latter than the former quality. We next ascended the Carnarvonshire side, about one mile, to the tubular bridge, and availed ourselves of the permission given to walk on it. In this way we again entered Anglesey, and returned by the same route. What a stupendous monument of human genius and daring, and what a surpassingly fine view it commands! Almost the entire range of Carnarvon's giant hills is visible, and the entire Menai Strait is spread out before one, looking like a very beautiful river, its shores covered with sweet villas, hamlets, and rich woods; here and there small islets add to the beauty of the scene, which is still further increased by the steamers, ships, and boats on it and Beaumaris Bay. The ebb tide was running westwards at the rate of fully five miles an hour. From the bridge we walked to Bangor, and thence to this place. The distance is about five miles, and a more beautiful road can scarcely be travelled, it runs by the river nearly the entire way. This stream commands attention by noisily falling over its rocky bed, its banks are luxuriantly clothed with beech, larch, oak, and other trees.

"We reached this place about half-past two. Our sitting-room commands a glorious view of the famous Penrhyn slate quarries, the distant hills, and the Ogwen. The inhabitants seem to live entirely on slate; they, by some chemical magic, extract all they need from the mountain side."

"*Carnarvon, July,* 13, 1850.—I leave it to my companion to describe our triumph in ascending Snowdon yesterday. Whilst breaking a few stones for fossils, on the summit of the mountain, a gentleman, whom I shall call *Stranger* at present, stood watching me, and at length the following conversation passed between us :—

"*Stranger.* 'Your hammer is rather light for these rocks, sir.'

"*Pengelly.* 'It is; it was made for the Cornish slates, and has done me good service among them, it has helped to disinter many a fossil fish.'

"*Stranger.* 'Indeed! my old friend, Mr. Peach, has worked a good deal among the Cornish ichthyolites.'

"*Pengelly.* 'Yes he has, sir; I know him well. When Peach dropped the investigation at Talland sand-bay I took it up, and have continued it with success to the Rame Head. This year I have been working on Looe Island and have found good specimens; on the whole I have a capital collection of these ancient fishes.'

"*Stranger.* 'I am really glad to find some one is still at work there. Has Sir Philip Egerton seen your specimens?'

"*Pengelly.* 'He has not.'

"*Stranger.* 'I hope the Permian fishes will be shortly given to the world in splendid style.'

"*Pengelly.* 'By whom?'

"*Stranger.* 'By Professor King of Newcastle, for the Palæontographical Society.'

"*Pengelly.* 'Indeed, I am glad to hear that. I am one of the local secretaries of the Palæontographical.'

"*Stranger.* 'And I am the general secretary.'

"*Pengelly.* 'What! are you Bowerbank?'

"*Stranger.* 'Yes, I am.'

"*Pengelly* (*presenting his card*). 'I think you will remember my name, sir?'

"*Stranger.* 'I should think I ought. We are greatly obliged to you for the trouble you have taken for the Palæontographical. I hope you were pleased with Milne Edwards?'

"*Pengelly.* 'Indeed I was,' etc.

"It is useless to pursue this further; you will suppose that an interesting conversation followed, and, amongst other topics, we talked of the strange manner and place in which we, who had so frequently corresponded, met for the first time."

Dr. Bowerbank had written in the spring to introduce Milne Edwards, who was greatly pleased with Pengelly's corals and fossil fish, and showed him much kindness when, later on, he visited Paris.

Pengelly's lectures at the Torquay Natural History Society became extremely popular, and were attended by large audiences. Though still poor, he took no payment for these courses of lectures, which he said were a pleasure to him, and a labour of love. A thoughtful and attentive audience always gave him intense encouragement. His friends remonstrated at this disregard of his pecuniary interests, one laughingly telling him "that money was not dirt." But he was quite satisfied to look on the work itself as the best payment. There is no doubt that the diffusion of scientific knowledge was much needed in Torquay, and indeed in other parts of Devonshire, which, though so large a county in extent and population, and very rich in distinguished names of artists, authors, prelates, soldiers, and sailors, had not yet produced any great number of scientific men.

About this time he made the following note :—

"I accidentally met the Earl of Wicklow and Lord Hatherton to-day, who asked me whether I delivered the lectures, on which I am at present engaged, on my own account, or if I am engaged by the Natural History Society. On being informed that I delivered them gratuitously, they thought me wrong in doing so. Lord Hatherton advised me to pack up and settle in some larger town, where I should doubtless do greatly better than I am doing here as a lecturer, adding, that no man in Torquay is so underpaid as I am, and though it might be all very well to preach down money in the pulpit, it nevertheless is a good thing and a necessary one in this world. I said I quite thought it a valuable thing, that I was very well satisfied with Torquay, that the public had been very liberal to me, and that it became me to be liberal in return."

Every one associates the name of William Pengelly with

geological research, but it will have been seen that astronomy also greatly interested him, and that many of his earlier lectures were on that subject.

At a soirée in December, 1850, held in his honour, Pengelly was presented with a very valuable telescope subscribed for by several of his friends. The document accompanying the presentation set forth that the signatories of it were desirous of marking their appreciation of his high scientific attainments and of the value of the lectures which he had delivered during a long course of years at the rooms of the Natural History Society and Mechanics' Institute at Torquay, and at the same time of expressing the great esteem in which they held him personally. Among the signatures affixed to this address were those of the Earl of Beverley, Viscount Newark, Lord Hatherton, Lady Sinclair, Sir John Morrenden, Sir Culling E. Eardley, Lady Eardley, Lady Shelley, Dr. Sutherland, etc., etc.

He was deeply touched by this presentation, and thanked his friends in these words :—

"Never have I been so desirous of correctly and appropriately expressing my thoughts and feelings. At no time have I so decidedly regretted my lack of eloquence as at this moment, when accepting this highly interesting and valuable proof of your munificence. I am intensely anxious to convey to you a correct idea of my sincere gratitude, not only for your having judged me worthy of a testimonial from you, but also for the kind and delicate way in which the funds have been raised, as well as for the *form* which you decided your testimonial should take. Nothing could have been so gratifying and valuable to me as a telescope. Never shall I forget my intense delight when I first followed the astronomical mathematician, step by step, through the processes by which he determines the distances, bulks, masses, and densities of the bodies composing the solar system. And not a whit inferior to this has been the enjoyment with which I have occasionally read a page of that marvellous record, inscribed by the finger of Nature on rocky tablets, respecting the mighty changes, organic and inorganic, which have passed over this world during periods incalculably remote. You must give me no credit for disinterestedness with respect to my public lectures; for next to the pleasure of acquiring and possessing knowledge stands the pleasure of communicating it. I have been addicted to, and fond of, teaching from my earliest years. The fact that the same persons have again and again, year after year, attended these lectures, has more than repaid any pains that may have been taken in their preparation. It was my happiness to take a prominent part in the formation of the Natural History Society, and also in the reorganization of the Mechanics' Institute. Could others have been easily found, the lecturer's rostrum would never have been so frequently occupied by me; but, rather than see it empty, I slipped into it, little thinking that the act would elicit expressions of approval from an assembly like the present.

"This telescope is a really magnificent instrument. I prize it highly; it is to me most valuable. But I prize this paper much more, and attach a still higher value to it. It contains the expression of your esteem . . . The list speaks, too, as with a voice from the tomb. The death of Lord Newark, one of the subscribers, is not without its significance; it reminds me that the most prosperous earthly career must terminate, and that there are subjects, infinitely more sublime than science, which should pre-eminently occupy the attention of every human being.

"Once more, allow me to thank you most sincerely for so kindly enabling me to 'consider the heavens.' I hope and believe that the effect will be to impress me more deeply with the greatness of God, and His infinite condescension and benevolence in visiting man, and being mindful of him."

CHAPTER IV.

HIS FRIENDSHIPS WITH MEN OF SCIENCE.

1850 TO MARCH, 1853.

THE year 1850 had been a busy one for Pengelly. He had
given more than two thousand lessons to private pupils, delivered
a large number of lectures, and taken part in many public meetings.   He had also been elected a Fellow of the Geological
Society of London ; and in the success both of that and of the
Palæontographical Society he took great interest.   In addition
to his other pursuits, he now devoted himself with increasing
zeal to geological researches.

It has been naturally supposed that he must have been of
very strong constitution to get through his multifarious undertakings unaided ; but this was not the opinion of the medical
men, whom he had occasion to consult at different times.   He
suffered frequently from quinsy, and had always a delicate throat,
though he managed to speak frequently and with great clearness in public.   Another difficulty under which he laboured
was his liability to serious attacks of fainting ; yet such was his
power of will, and love of science, that he succeeded incarrying
through his varied and severe labours, without hindrance from
this or any other constitutional disadvantages.   Like the late
Sir Andrew Clark, he firmly believed that hard work was
injurious to no one.

He had already formed a warm friendship with Charles W.
Peach, a special bond of union being the interest they both took
in certain fossil fish, which Peach was the first to note the
existence of, in Cornwall.   The importance of the discovery was
at once acknowledged, but it was supposed by Prof. McCoy
that the "fishes" were merely fossil sponges.   Peach and Pengelly both held to their opinion in spite of this adverse criticism,

and had the satisfaction of proving their surmises to be correct before the controversy closed.

Dr. Henry Woodward, F.R.S., in a biographical notice of Pengelly, in the Presidential address delivered at the Anniversary Meeting of the Geological Society of London, on February 15, 1895, thus alludes to this subject :—

"One of Pengelly's first recorded papers was 'On the Ichthyolites of East Cornwall' (1849–50).* These interesting remains were first identified as FISHES by C. W. Peach in 1843; after eight years they were referred to SPONGES, under the name of *Steganodictyum Cornubicum*, in 1851, by McCoy †; then to the Cephalopoda by Ferd. Roemer (as *Archæoteuthis Dunensis*) in 1855; and back again to the Fishes as *Scaphaspis Cornubicus* ‡ by Huxley in 1868. Pengelly mentions in one of his papers, that he had no fewer than 300 fragments of these fossil fishes from the Devonian of Cornwall and Devon in his own cabinet." §

Early in the Spring of 1849 Pengelly had received the following kind letter from Hugh Miller.

" Edinburgh, February 24, 1849.

"I ought long ere now to have acknowledged receipt of your kind note, and its interesting accompaniments, but my health is not strong and my engagements are engrossing, and so I have very frequently to throw myself on the good nature of my correspondents. Neither from its mineral character nor organic contents could I identify the Old Red Sandstone of your part of the Island with that of the North of Scotland. But the Old Red of Russia serves, it would seem, to demonstrate their identity, by exhibiting in the same beds the organisms of both. It is a curious circumstance that Great Britain should be as it were tipped at both its ends by fossiliferous rock-systems.

"The waves of the English Channel, and of the Pentland Firth, are laying bare along their respective shores fish and shells that were contemporary. I send you in the accompanying box a little fish, that was disinterred from out a bed of rock which overhangs at a height of rather more than a hundred feet the western extremity of the bay of Thurso, nearly the most distant point in Britain from the rocks in which the Ichthyolitic remains you have so kindly sent me were found. It is of an undescribed species of *Asterolepis*, and exhibits the curved form so common among the Old Red ichthyolites, and which is regarded by Agassiz as indicative of violent death. The smaller kind of fishes when suddenly deprived of life do certainly at first stiffen into

---

* *Trans. Roy. Geol. Soc. Cornwall*, vol. vii. pp. 106–108 and 115–120.
† *Ann. and Mag. Nat. Hist.*, ser. 2. vol. viii. (1851), p. 482.
‡ Huxley, *Geol. Mag.*, 1868, p. 248 ; H. Woodward and E. R. Lankester, p. 247, and p. 437, and *Quart. Journ. Geol. Soc.*, vol. xxiv. (1868), p 546.
§ *Trans. Devon. Assoc.*, vol. ii. (1868), p. 440, and *Geol. Mag.*, 1869, p. 77.

such a curve, though they again straighten as they become flaccid. People in the neighbourhood of fishing towns in the North of Scotland regard the herrings which they purchase as fresh, in the most perfect degree, when they find them still retaining the bend.

"Should business or amusement ever lead you into this neighbourhood, I trust you will afford me an opportunity of introducing you to its various objects of geological interest.

"My own collection you would, I am sure, find worth examining. It is not very large, but it is rich in fossils, in which many large collections are poor; and exhibits pretty fully those portions of the fauna of your own Devonian which Devonshire has not yet presented.

"P.S.—The ichthyolites of the Caithness schists are usually of a substance less destructible than the rock which incloses them, and in consequence the stone frequently weathers from around them, leaving them so little attached that upon a small blow dealt by the hammer, they leap out entire. The fossil inclosed is in this state, and is retained in its original bed by a little glue.—H. M."

Pengelly, as already mentioned, had communicated to the Roy. Geol. Society of Cornwall (of which he was a Corresponding Member) an article "On the Ichthyolites of East Cornwall" in the autumn of 1849, and contributed a second paper on the same subject in the following year. His letters on this question are, unfortunately, nearly all missing, but some from his friend Peach with regard to it have been preserved.

C. IV. *Peach to Pengelly.*

"*Peterhead, August* 28, 1850.—. . . I was greatly obliged and delighted by your kind remembrance of me. I got your letter on the eve of my departure for Edinburgh. I laid it aside in the hope of answering it on my return ; at present I have not met with it again— it is put safely away with a lot more which I want. However, I well remember that you had found lots of fish remains on Looe Island ; this *I always suspected*, but, somehow or other, never set foot on it. I passed the island once at low water, or nearly *inside*, and I could see the colour of the rocks agreed with the fossil beds. . . . Mr. Hugh Miller and I had a snug chat after the meeting of the British Association (which, by-the-bye, was a splendid meeting), and I showed him a *lot* of my best fossil fish specimens from Cornwall, and he could *only see one bit like* the Old-red *fishes*, and it was the piece I named *Asterolepis*. This, he said, 'if he had found it in the Old-red of Scotland he should call an *Asterolepis*,' and so I am quite satisfied it is. Professor Sedgwick saw the fish fossils and they are *all new to him ;* it is odd *no one knows them*, they are puzzlers, so work away, dear friend. I am no more (at least for the present) personally in Cornwall—my heart is there, and I shall feel great interest in all connected with her, especially the geology. But, dear Pengelly, the *strangest of all* is to be told ; I have

LOOE ISLAND, CORNWALL.

[To face p. 40

found veritable *Graptolites* in our rocks—there for you, what do you think of that? I have always hoarded these fossils with miserly care. I have asked many what they were, and, until I got hold of that kind Palæontologist, Professor E. Forbes, no one either could or would tell me, he pronounced them Graptolites. I got them very near the Gribbon, and have asked a friend there to get a lot of fossils from the spot. Of course I want all I have told you to come out at the meeting.* I shall look with some anxiety for the report of your paper, for I am more anxious than ever, and Cornish news is so dear to me now I am so far removed from the dear old spot, as well as because I quite expect some of the *Lions* of Geology will be visiting Cornwall, and we then shall get them regularly christened. . . ."

From Pengelly to C. W. Peach.

"*Torquay, May* 12, 1851.—. . . My dear friend,—On Good Friday last I had the good fortune to meet Mr. Landsborough, the Scotch Algologist, etc. In the course of conversation he told me that he had just engaged to write a work on British Zoophytes, and that he was very anxious to find some one who would kindly furnish him with information on Cornish Zoophytology, when I took the liberty of speaking of your labours in that department, and ventured to add that I believed you would readily render him any assistance in your power. At Mr. Landsborough's request I engaged to write you on the subject, and allowed him to use my name if he found it desirable to write you. Mr. L. is a dear old fellow, as simple-minded as a child, and almost as enthusiastic as C. W. Peach, Esq.! . . . I shall be glad to hear from you, when you have a moment which you have no better use for."

C. W. Peach to Pengelly.

"*Peterhead, May* 14, 1851.—. . . I have been very closely attending to the Zoophytes on this coast, and have *doubled* the list of those known in the County of Aberdeen, in fact have got several new to Scotland and two new to the *British list*, and I believe I have an Actinia now living which will prove also an addition to the *British list*. I am almost getting a *little conceited* about these things, from having very many times brought forward new things before these great men and authors, who would not listen to their being so at the time, but have been compelled to submit after all—to wit, I exhibited a most beautiful collection of Echini at Southampton (Brit. Assoc.), and described one as differing from all the other British; I was opposed by Forbes and Agassiz, still they said there was *room for suspicion.* At the meeting at Edinboro' last year, Forbes laid it before the British Association and confessed I was right, and it proves to be the *Echinus Melo* of the Mediterranean, and is the largest of the British species. I say this not as boasting, but just to justify my 'lectle conceit' (Sam Slick). . . .

"Like yourself, I believe that, although my friend Miller does not think our *fish* fish, *I do;* and they *must be fish*, and *shall be fish.* He

* *Royal Geological Society of Cornwall.*

judges from a *few specimens.* When you go to Looe again, be sure and
examine the slates on the beach, from the harbour all along eastward,
and trace them into the cliff beyond the Chough Rock, Mellendreth,
etc.; you will get some very curious and strange forms. I should like
to be with you; you will find, I fancy, amongst the fish remains some
will prove to belong to the *Sepidæ.* Still, there are plenty of fishes."

Writing of Pengelly's work in connection with the Cornish
fossil fish, and the Geology of the West of England, Mr. Howard
Fox, F.G.S., President of the Royal Cornish Geological Society,
remarks in the Annual Address, November, 1894—

"William Pengelly, F.R.S., was connected with this Society as
Corresponding or Honorary Member since 1856. His career is a
striking example of the brilliant success that may attend the study of
Geology in the intervals of a busy professional life.

"The seventh volume of your *Transactions* contains nine of his
papers; three 'On the Ichthyolites and Geology of South-east Cornwall,' commencing at Talland Sands Bay (the point at which Mr.
Peach's labours eastward terminated), and comprising the coast of
Cornwall, thence to the Tamar. . . . His attention in later years was
naturally turned to the geology of his adopted, rather than to that of
his native county; but further papers on Cornwall appeared in other
publications. . . . He has been described by Prof. Boyd Dawkins[*]
as 'one of the last survivors of the heroes who laid the foundation of
Geological Science,' who 'died full of years, and with his services
honourably recognized by his private friends and by the scientific
world. He has left behind an example of what one man can do in
advancing knowledge by energy and perseverance.'"

Pengelly was not in 1851 acquainted with Sir Roderick
Murchison, and in a letter to a friend, he mentions his disappointment at failing to meet and have a geological chat with that
eminent scientist.

"*Torquay, January* 5, 1851.— . . . On Friday last I was bidden
by Lady Shelley to meet Sir Roderick Murchison, and was requested
to prepare myself to discourse very learnedly on 'Beekites.' Accordingly, I charged myself to the very muzzle with scientific jargon,
respecting decomposing limestone nodules, conglomerates, and water
holding chalcedony in solution. Mr. Vivian, who was also bidden,
went fully primed about Kent's Cavern; he could scarcely open his
mouth but stalagmite, stalactites, flint knives, and elephants' teeth,
came tumbling out. . . .

"I found Lord Glenelg and Mr. Hippisley, and one or two others
whom I knew, and a couple of gentlemen and ladies whom I did not
know. One of these I expected was the great Sir Roderick; but alas!

* *Nature,* April 5, 1894.

alas! for human expectations! Sir John Shelley soon sent all my glowing anticipations flying. He had received a letter from Sir Roderick, by which he had learned that Lady Murchison could not leave her room, and consequently was still in London, and not in Torquay. . . ."

He had afterwards the pleasure of entertaining Sir Roderick at his own house, and of taking him to see many geological points of interest in the neighbourhood of Torquay. He thenceforward enjoyed the intimate friendship of the great geologist.

During February, 1851, Mrs. Pengelly's health, always delicate, completely broke down, and her death took place towards the end of that month. After this bereavement he wrote at once to his parents asking them to come and live with him. This they were able to do for a considerable period, much to his comfort. His son Alfred, and his daughter Mary Ann, survived their mother for some years, but both died before their father.

Of the period immediately succeeding his wife's death little of his correspondence remains, but some months later he writes to an intimate friend :—

"I owe you very many thanks for having induced me to read Arnold's 'Life.' I would apologize to you for not having acted on your advice earlier, but that I am rather glad that I have seen Fox How, to which he was so very sincerely attached, and the many other lovely nooks which he must so thoroughly have enjoyed. So far as I have read, I like him best as a husband and father, then as a friend, next as a teacher, next as a scholar, then as a reformer; and last, and therefore least, as a divine. I find myself differing from him rather frequently as a theologian, but very, very seldom as a Christian. He carried his Christianity into every character I have mentioned, and never seems to have paraded it. Would I could be a sort of miniature Arnold!"

Some idea of Pengelly's kindness of heart will be seen in the following extract from his letters to the same correspondent.

"W——* gave me a very bad account of his wife's health. He has not been able to settle with me. I could not press him, poor fellow. . . . During my perambulations last night, I found a little boy in the hands of the police for having stolen nuts from an itinerant confectioner. I paid the complainant one shilling for the nuts, and had the boy set at liberty. I took possession of his cap, and the nuts which he had stolen in it, telling him to call at my house for his cap this morning. He has

* An improvident friend, to whom he had been extremely kind.

been, and I have given him a little lecture, and then accompanied him to his home. I find that his mother is dead ; his father is a sailor, and is married again. Both his present parents are in London ; he is with relatives of his stepmother. It seems a sad case of neglect. I quite feel that I must occasionally look after the child. . . . I have finished Arnold's 'Life,' and have been delighted with it. I hope to begin Paley's 'Natural Theology' next week. . . .

"I am glad you are reading the 'Vestiges,'* and have no doubt you are pleased with the work. . . . I think you are aware that I read Geology with Miss Bird. When at their house last evening, Mrs. Bird brought a little girl into the room, and told me that she was anxious to be present during the lesson. Mrs. Bird, at the same time, told me that the child is a daughter of Kingsley, the author of 'Alton Locke,' and other similar works, and that Kingsley had married her sister. Of course, I was greatly interested. Rose Kingsley is one of the most intelligent children I ever met with. . . ."

Being now a widower, with both his children at school, Pengelly was able to give more of his scanty leisure to geological excursions, and he jotted down in his note-books some of the incidents which amused him most, from which the following extracts are taken.

"Once, soon after midday, I found myself at a lone wayside inn, and encountered a forlorn-looking hostess, with a black eye, of whom I asked—

"'A crust of bread and cheese, and a glass of beer.'

"'Can't 'ave it, zur.'

"'Why not?'

"'Cause me and my old man 'th valled out.'

"'I'm sorry for that. But what has it to do with my having refreshment?'

"'I tell 'ee, we've valled out, and he'th carried away the kay; so you can't 'ave it. You may 'ave some of they there 'orts—whortle-berries—if you like ; but there's nort else.'

"I declined the ''orts,' and proceeded on my journey, which after a walk of twenty miles brought me to an inn where the host and hostess lived amicably. Finding that a bed was obtainable, I ordered tea with ham and eggs.

"Slipping off my collecting basket, but leaving my hammer in the belt in which it was carried, I took a seat on the 'kitchen settle,' and thereby joined three men, apparently masons, who had just 'left work,' who were enjoying a glass and pipe before going home. They all eyed me intently ; but for a time no one spoke. At length one of them took the pipe from his lips, and emitted the accumulated smoke in that long thin thread which seems to betoken a desire to make the most of a good thing. When his lips were at liberty, he said—

* "Vestiges of the Natural History of Creation."

" ' Ax your pardon, sir, for making so bould ; but what trade be you ? '

" ' I can't say I have a trade.'

" ' Cause of your hammer, sir, I took the liberty.'

" ' Oh, my hammer !   I can only say I break stones on the road.'

" The trio exclaimed in chorus—

" ' We won't believe that.'

" ' If you'll open my basket, you'll see the stones I've broken.'

" I had spent the day before in a richly fossiliferous Greensand district, and had collected many very fine specimens ; whilst the rocks of the locality in which the inn stood were, so far as was known, utterly destitute of fossils.

" Taking me at my word, one of the masons opened the basket, and took out the first stone that came to hand.   It proved to be a piece of Greensand with an unmistakable shell firmly embedded in it, yet standing out in bold relief.   Instantly their pipes were snatched from their lips, their mouths fell open, and they all stared at the specimen as if they would at once penetrate the mystery connected with it.   Never had I seen looks in which ignorance, wonder, and admiration were so obviously blended and so strongly pronounced.   At length one of them exclaimed—

" ' Why, how did thekky'—a provincialism for that—'shell get there ? '

" Obviously fossils, with their wondrous teachings, were new to them.   My attempt to reply to their question eventuated in a sort of conversational lecture ; and so far as my experience goes, no audience was ever more attentive or more interested.   The discourse was at length cut short by the landlady's announcement, ' Your tea's ready, sir.'   And she intimated that I was to adjourn to the adjoining parlour, which, however, was within earshot of my audience.   As I took my place at the table, the following flattering remark reached me—

" ' Lord ! what a scholard he ez !   I reckon he writ'th a booteful hand, ef we cud zee it.'

" Before my meal was over, they had left the house ; and I have never seen them since.   This, however, seems to have been no fault of theirs—as the following incident shows.

" On finishing my breakfast the next morning, I told the hostess I wished to pay my ' reckoning,' to which she replied—

" ' My maister wishes to spaik to 'ee 'bout that, sir, plaize.   May he come in ? '

" ' Oh, certainly ; I shall be very glad to see him ! '

" But what it all meant I had no conception.   The landlady at once withdrew ; and the master of the house very shortly entered, apparently very ill at ease.   He shuffled into the room, constantly shifted himself from leg to leg without advancing, giving himself the appearance of a ship rolling in a heavy sea which struck her on the beam ; then he bit his nails, and finally scratched his head.   In short, his appearance when translated into words, was to the effect, ' Dang me if I know how to begin.'   To help him, I told him it was a fine morning.   He seemed grateful for the information, assented to its truth, and then said—

"'Where be gwain?'

"'I am about to walk to M——.'

"'Be in a hurry for a day or two or a week?'

"'I can scarcely say that I am in a hurry; but I wish to get there to-night.'

"'The men was very much pleased with what you told 'em last evening.'

"'I thought they were interested.'

"'Oh, ees—uncommon, I 'sure 'ee. I hope no offence, sir; but ef you'd stop 'ere for a foo days, or a week, and talk to the men in the evenin's, you shud be welcome to meat, drink, washing, and lodging free gratis. I'm sure lots o' men wud come an' hear 'ee, and I should zell an uncommon zight o' beer.'

"'Your offer is extremely handsome, and most tempting; and I am much obliged to you for it. But my plan was to reach M—— to-night, and I don't like to make any alteration. Thank you very much; but I must get on.'

"I was accordingly allowed to pay my 'reckoning,' and to proceed.

"I was one morning overtaken by an active, hale old fellow, who had been a soldier and seen a great deal of service, but was at the time a river bargeman.

"In our journey we passed a directing post, with arms in good condition, and containing full information.

"'Do'ee know what that is?' said my companion.

"'A directing post, of course.'

"'I call 't a passon.'

"'A parson! Why?'

"'Cause 'ee tell'th the way, but doth'n't go.'

"Before we separated, we passed a second post, which was very dilapidated, and had lost its arm.

"'If the post we saw just now were a parson,' said I, 'what's this one?'

"'Oh, he's a bishop.'

"'Explain.'

"'He neither tell'th nor go'th.'"

This happened many years before the establishment of the Bishopric of Truro, and the increased activity of the clergy in the West of England.

Pengelly was always extremely interested in the religious history of Cornwall. The fine old church which occupies the site of the ancient Cathedral of St. Germans appealed to his antiquarian taste, and he experienced great pleasure in visiting the Cathedral now being erected at Truro. But beyond all he recognized, as a hopeful sign for the future, the quickened zeal and generous devoted lives of many of the clergy, who have during recent years shed the light of religion alike upon the busy, crowded town, and the lonely country parish.

The journey from the north of England to Torquay, at present so rapidly accomplished, was in former days a tedious affair, as will be seen from the following letter which Pengelly wrote at the end of 1852. He had started early in the morning, hoping to reach Torquay the same night, and says—

". . . . By clever dawdling at some pigmy stations, we managed to be fully half an hour late at Bristol, and on our arrival found that the three o'clock train to Plymouth had just left. Having about an hour and a half to spare, I rambled towards Redcliff church, and then studied various print-shops. In due time I returned to the station, and had the pleasure of waiting some twenty minutes for the train which should have left at 5.6 p.m. At length we were off for Exeter; all hope of my being able to reach Torquay before to-morrow having vanished. Things went on tolerably until ascending the inclined plane preparatory to entering the tunnel between Wellington and Tiverton Road. Our train was of enormous length, the rails very wet and slippery, and the engine by no means potent, so that at last we came to a stand, when near the steepest part of the plane, and then we began a retrograde movement, which was checked by the breaks. The gradient on this plane is 1 in 100 only, whilst that of the Bromsgrove Lickey is 1 in 37. At length it was decided to divide the train into two parts, and to take the first up to a siding, of the down line, about two miles on, and then to send the engine back for the second part. I being in the remaining or second part, got out to walk a bit, as did one or two other persons. After waiting a considerable time I heard an engine coming up, and supposed it was ours returning, but remembering that possibly it might be an up train, I thought it no longer prudent to walk on the up line, so I got into my carriage again. I had scarcely shut the door when an up goods train swept over the ground with a velocity that almost made one shudder. . . . We had now been waiting more than an hour, and began to feel desirous of the return of our engine as a *down* train would be due in a quarter of an hour.

"At length the engine came to us, but though it tugged and snorted, and snorted and tugged, it could not move us, and a feeling of alarm, respecting the expected down train became more or less general. By this time, however, the engine of a goods train had been obtained, and, this applied to our rear, whilst our engine did its best in front, we were set in motion and in no long time were brought up to the portion of our train which had been taken on. . . . There certainly ought to be an engine kept at the bottom of the incline. At length, however, we got fairly on the down line, and then ran down the incline to Tiverton Road at more than express speed, in the hope, I suppose, of recovering the almost two hours that had been lost. We had the happiness of reaching Exeter between 10 and 11 instead of at 8.45. . . ."

There he had to spend the night, and go on to Torquay by

the earliest train the next morning to fulfil his numerous engagements.

Pengelly's circle of friends was now becoming very large. In March, 1853, he writes, in answer to a correspondent—

"I feel much obliged by *your* acquaintance wishing to make *my* acquaintance, and hope they may some day have that '*distinguished pleasure*,' but as H. B. Stowe said in reply to the good Scotch ladies, who had invited her to visit them, 'I was never anything to look at;' and I will add that 'study and its physical results have by no means improved me.'"

He then goes on to write of his great grief at the loss of his friend, Mrs. Edward Vivian, whose unfailing kindness through a number of years he warmly appreciated.

"I have deferred the worst part of my letter to the last. Torquay has sustained a loss to-day not easily repaired; poor dear Mrs. Vivian is taken to her eternal home. I was there this morning and learned from her almost distracted husband that she had had a wretched night, that at that moment she was unconscious, but that she seemed to rally a little at rare intervals. I endeavoured to express my deep and sincere sympathy with him. Poor, poor fellow, what a terrible blow. I learned just before returning home, that she departed about six o'clock. The poor of Torquay have lost a warm-hearted yet most judicious friend, and Torquay one of its greatest ornaments. May her bereaved husband be supported under his terrible loss. May it be sanctified to him and bring him more closely to God, who only afflicts to draw His loved ones to His own bosom. . . ."

CHAPTER V.

THE statement which has more than once appeared in print to the effect that Pengelly came "of a Quaker stock," is altogether erroneous. Neither on his father's side, nor on that of his mother, had he any connection with the Society of Friends. The account that has been given of the struggles of his early life would be a sufficient contradiction of the statement to any one acquainted with the constitution of the Society.

Such a connection would indeed have been of inestimable benefit to Pengelly, for beyond any other body of people bound together by special tenets, the Society of Friends has been careful that every birthright Member should have a sound and adequate education, as witnessed by the foundation and endowment of the well-known school at Ackworth (where the late John Bright and other leading men among the Friends received their education), and other establishments of a like nature. If Pengelly had been eligible for such instruction as he certainly would have enjoyed, had his parents belonged to the Society in question, how much of the trouble and hardships he underwent in his determination to acquire knowledge, might have been spared to him !

It was not until early middle life that he became acquainted with some of the Members of the Quaker body. Among those with whom he was intimate may be mentioned Joseph Sturge, Robert Were Fox, F.R.S., and his daughters Anna Maria and Caroline Fox, H. Bowman Brady, F.R.S., and the Hanbury, Lister, and Burlingham families. Deeply impressed with the devotion, spirituality, and unworldliness of the Friends, and the warm solicitude which they displayed in promoting the welfare

E

of their fellow-creatures, he soon joined their Body. Later on he became attached to Lydia, the youngest daughter of William Spriggs, a Member of the Society, descended on his mother's side (who belonged to the Savory family) through several generations of Quaker ancestry. One of the family, Hester Savory (who died shortly after becoming the wife of Charles Dudley), was greatly admired by Charles Lamb. On her death, he wrote the well-known lines beginning—

> "When maidens such as Hester die,
> Their place ye may not well supply,
> Though ye among a thousand try,
> With vain endeavour."

Mr. Spriggs and his wife always gave hearty support to those benevolent and charitable undertakings, which the Members of the Society of Friends, have supported so largely and honourably. Mrs. Spriggs, when a girl living with her widowed mother, had enjoyed the friendship of the great philanthropist Thomas Clarkson, who was often an honoured guest at their house. In later life, she had the privilege of going with Elizabeth Fry to visit the prisoners in gaol, a sight so touching that it once made Sydney Smith weep bitterly, and say, "to see her in the midst of the wretched prisoners, to see them all calling earnestly upon God, soothed by her look, animated by her voice, clinging to the hem of her garment, worshipping her as the only being who had ever loved them, or taught them, or noticed them, or spoken to them of God, was a sight which broke down the pageants of the world."

Pengelly's second marriage took place on June 28, 1853, and he thus gained a most devoted wife, but of the extreme happiness of this union it is out of place to speak here. Mrs. Pengelly entered with ready zest into all her husband's scientific pursuits. Though in politics she remained, like her parents, a Conservative, while he was always a consistent Liberal, this difference of opinion, never occasioned the slightest cloud in the brightness of their exceptionally happy and united married life. Her artistic powers were of the greatest assistance to him, as she was indefatigable in drawing and colouring diagrams for his lectures. This she continued to do till the end of his lecturing career.

The following letter, to his wife's sister Hester, was written by Pengelly on his wedding journey:—

"*Bettws-y-Coed, July 9th.*—You must take great care not to thank me for this letter, as I am really writing just to kill time. The rain has been most pitiless all day. I did just manage to get to the post-office, where I found a letter and two papers; but since that I have been a close prisoner. I have read Shakespeare's 'Lear,' and I have also done my best to criticize Lydia's sketch, now in progress, of the splendid hill in front of our window. The newspapers have been duly gone through, and the guide-books consulted, and, as a last resource, I take my pen to say I have nothing to write about. Had the day suited, we were to have seen the falls of the Conway. . . . *July 10th.*—We have ascended the beautiful hill over the way this afternoon. But what would you have given to have had a glimpse of the glorious mountain range westward—including Snowdon—all in one view? In the course of our ramble we suddenly came upon a mountain lake of which we had not heard. Oh, how tranquilly it lay, reposing on the heart of the mountain! How it seemed to invite one not to return to the bustling money-getting world. . . ."

We get some glimpses of Pengelly's life, after their return from this journey, in his wife's letters to her mother.

Mrs. Pengelly to her Mother.

"*November*, 1853.—. . . Joseph Wolff's lecture here created quite a sensation; it was very crowded, some were delighted, others thought it only rigmarole. . . . We have just had a very pleasant visit from Bishop Carr; he came to see the fossils again, and was extremely interested in them, particularly the 'Beekites.' He stayed to take tea with us, and told us such interesting facts about the Syrian Christians, the Malabar Jews, the Indian population in the Deccan, Ceylon, etc. He says he was at Torquay forty years ago, when there were only a very few houses here. William has been several geological rambles with him, and likes him very much. The bishop was with the Princess Esterhazy * when she died, poor thing. He said her throat was in such a dreadful state that she could take nothing but Devonshire cream for the last two or three weeks. In fact, it was nothing but that which had kept her alive. . . . The bishop mentioned several amusing things about his correspondence in India; occasionally he received letters addressed 'T. Bombay, Esq.' His account of the suffering caused by the terrible floods in his diocese was most sad. . . ."

Pengelly to a Botanical Friend.

"*Torquay, November* 21, 1853 — . . . Please to inform your brother Thomas that I made careful inquiries after the *gentleman* whose acquaintance he desires, namely, *M. Asplenium lanceolatum ;* but he has left this district about three years ago, and has wisely gone into Cornwall. So says my friend, C. Parker,† a man who calls on, and therefore knows

---

* Lady Sarah Villiers, daughter of the Earl of Jersey, who died at Torquay.
† An excellent local botanist.

the exact whereabouts of, every member of the botanical family living in this district. . . ."

Mrs. Pengelly spent the Christmas of 1853 with her family, but her husband was not able to leave Torquay on account of the lectures he had undertaken to deliver. He writes to his wife during her absence.

"*Friday.*— . . . Now I'll just tell you what I've done this afternoon. Feeling the gardening fit strong upon me, I began operations. First I removed the stunted fir-tree, and the first larch that came to hand, next a *laurustinus*, a *phyllorea* (if that is not the correct orthography it ought to be). The destructive tendency is in the ascendant just now, which, were it spring, the trees would soon find to their decided loss. . . . I have gone roughly through my lecture for Monday, and called on the Birds. Last night I took up 'Hypatia,' and got more than half through the first volume before going to bed. Really, it is first-rate. Miss Bird told me that Kingsley and his family are coming here for the winter, and have taken Livermead House for three months.

"*Saturday.*—I finished the first volume of 'Hypatia,' and got so absorbed in the second that the midnight hour found me still reading. . . . There was a splendid sea yesterday, and I think I never saw so fine a sky; I wished you here. How can any one leave the ocean, a fine climate, and a lovely district, for a land of fogs, and a place where the ocean is not ! ! ! I am promising myself a long letter to-morrow, and hope it will bring a good report of my better *nine-tenths*—it would be an insult to call you better *half*, any woman comes up to that standard. I think in one of my cross moments I said I would not tell you how I was. In order to please you, and also to keep my word, let me tell you how I am *not*. I am *not* at all unwell. I am *not* satisfied by a week's experience that a wife is by any means a useless thing! I am *not* at all unlikely to give you a hearty welcome again, though I am *not* sorry that you have gone, nor do I wish you to curtail your visit in any way. . . ."

Pengelly to his Wife.

"*Torquay, December* 16, 1853.— . . . I have been promising myself the pleasure of commencing another letter to you this evening; and now the day's work being over, and the evening come, I gladly set about it. Mr. H—— inquired kindly after you to-day, and told me he thought me most kind 'to *allow* my wife to leave me so soon.' I cautioned him not to use such words as 'ALLOW,' with reference to wives, in the hearing of any lady if he ever hoped to get married. He laughed, but was quite ready to do battle for his proposition, so I left the besotted creature in the belief that he will have power to 'allow' or disallow after being 'noosed.' I met Toogood recently, who played off on me the following—'Of what rascality was Power guilty when he produced the Greek slave? D'ye give it up?' 'Yes.' 'Why, he chiselled a young woman out of her clothes.' . . . Miss H. Bird told me she had just received a letter from Lady Verney, who is at Malta with her family. They were all to have gone to Constantinople; but Sir Harry was informed by the admiral at Malta that it was no place for ladies now, so he went alone. Lady Verney has sent some particulars respecting the geology of Malta, all of which she says I can expound. The young Boyles asked me this evening if I had seen the Haytian prince, so that it seems we are beginning to wake up to the honour thrust upon us."

It was during the early part of 1854 that Charles Kingsley and his wife passed some time at Livermead, near Torquay, for the benefit of Mrs. Kingsley's health. Pengelly had long admired Kingsley's works, and a sincere friendship sprang up between the two men, in whose characters there was much in common. Both were enthusiastic students of nature, and both were endued with noble frankness and breadth of view on the subjects of the day, especially a ready and unflagging interest in the labour question, then hardly so prominently before the public as at present. Pengelly's sympathies with, and desire to promote, the true happiness of working men, remained active and keen throughout his long life, and in times of trouble and distress no one appealed to him in vain for counsel or assistance ; he has been aptly described as "an ardent and thoughtful Liberal, a friend of the people, and a lover of truth, in the widest sense of the terms."

Mrs. Pengelly to her Mother.

"*March*, 1854.— . . . Lady Louisa Percy and two other ladies came to see the moon through the telescope last night ; but William was gone out, so I had to entertain them till his return—not a difficult task, as they were extremely bright. The moon would not be viewed, however, so they are coming again, when I hope they may be more fortunate Sir Paul Hunter, who also came with the hope of seeing the moon, is loud in his praises of John Bright's last speech (on the Crimean War), which he says is the best on the subject. Sir Paul Hunter is rather Russian in his tendencies, as his wife's mother is a Russian lady—Mrs. Bosanquet, whose husband has written a pamphlet on the war, called the 'Cross and the Crescent.' Sir Paul seems to think the English are by no means alive to the nature of a war with Russia. . . ."

In the autumn Mrs. Pengelly writes to her mother—

"How dreadful are the accounts of the dynamite explosion at Newcastle ; and yet that seems to fade by comparison with the accounts of this terrible engagement (in the Crimea).

"One of William's pupils, Lieutenant Montague, grandson of his friend the late Duchess of Manchester, was killed on the spot. His poor sister living here, who is an orphan, feels it exceedingly, and refuses to see any one but Mrs. Bird.

"Major Lysons,* a fine man, also a pupil of William's, and who attended all his lectures last winter, saved Sir G. Brown's life by shooting a Cossack who was taking aim at him. Another of his pupils, who is invalided home, Captain Fearon, came to see us a day or two ago, and looks very ill; he was aide-de-camp on Omar Pasha's staff. We hear much of the war just now, as many of William's old pupils and friends are engaged in it."

Whilst staying with friends in London during the spring of 1855, he was for the first time present at an evening meeting of the Geological Society, and thus describes it in a letter to his wife written from Upton, the charming residence of Mr. J. J. Lister, the distinguished discoverer of the principle upon which the Achromatic Microscope is constructed, and whose scientific tastes were shared by his son Sir Joseph † Lister.

" . . . You will see that I am now in Essex, a thing I could never say before. I wish you could see this place; such glorious cedars of Lebanon, and such a wistäria! I must now give you my promised account of my visit to the Geol. Soc. There were probably about forty persons present, which I believe is considered a good attendance. We were rather late, and found on our arrival that a paper was being read descriptive of Manna Loa, the volcano in Owhyee. At its close, Austen,‡ a well-known geologist, and who once lived at East Ogwell, read a paper on the 'Probability of Coal existing at workable depths near London.' . . . A discussion followed the paper, in which the author was by no means spared, as the various speakers expressed themselves freely. This part was extremely interesting, not only on account of the remarks made, but also because it gave me an opportunity of seeing and hearing many eminent men, as Lyell, Murchison, Col. Portlock, Sharpe, Smyth, Prestwich, Morris, etc. Daubeny and Percy were also there, but did not speak. Lyell is a merry-looking fellow, very bald, and, according to C. Hanbury, junior, like me in a 'general way.' C. Hanbury introduced me to a few persons. I seemed to get on best with Morris, the author of the great Catalogue. After the meeting we got into a tea-room, and did ample justice to the good things there spread. In leaving the Geological, the author of the paper on Manna Loa came out with me, and appeared very sociable; he told me he was seven days in reaching the top of the mountain, which is about two and a half miles, and that the cold was so intense that he could not sleep a wink. . . ."

A letter written by Pengelly this summer shows the interest he continued to take in his native county.

"*Torquay. July* 24, 1855.—. . . You are aware that we visited

---

* Now General Sir Daniel Lysons, Constable of the Tower.
† Now Lord.   ‡ Mr. R. Godwin-Austen.

Looe, and probably dear Lydia has given all the information of a serious character, but possibly there are a few facts that have not been mentioned and that may interest you. We journeyed from Plymouth to Looe by a Cornish van, having a boy driver, and a middle-aged man, as a sort of guard, and who is at the same time proprietor, and father of the driver. I happened to have in my pocket an interesting book entitled 'Cornwall, its Mines and Miners,' which commences with a description of a van by which the author performed the same journey, viz. from Plymouth to Looe, and he dwells minutely on the great number of things stowed in, on, and under the van by the boy driver. In order to amuse our fellow-travellers I read my book aloud, and with one accord it was agreed that Bob (our driver) must have sat for the portrait (quite an error), but Bob himself thought there was nothing of the kind in the book, but gave me credit for the manufacture of the text there and then, and that I was only pretending to read. On being allowed to take the book he saw his mistake, and thenceforth on being drawn into conversation would suddenly stop short with, ' I must take care what I say, else it will get put into a book, I s'pose,' for he would have it that I was author of the book in question. Whilst at Looe, I got a donkey for Lydia, who rode some miles in the country by the side of the river, I acting as guide. Being a hot day I stopped at the Well to drink, my wife scolded me for not having taken her from the saddle in order that she might drink *first ;* of course I was intensely sorry to be so wanting in politeness, especially as it turned out to be the Well of St. Keyne.* Another day my father took us by boat to Polperro, we called on Jonathan Couch, the Naturalist, and had a most interesting hour spent in geological chat with him. Lydia was delighted with Polperro, but had not time for more than one sketch. She bargains for a week there on some future occasion. We fully reckoned on going to the meeting at Liskeard, but dear L. managed to get toothache and declined it. I attended, and I greatly enjoyed the day. I had the pleasure of sitting between Miss Tregelles and her sister at dinner ; indeed, I was just in clover, next beyond sat Mrs. William's, an astonishing woman truly, upwards of eighty years of age, and possessing all the activity and vivacity of most women not half that age. She had to walk about a mile from the meeting to dinner, but made nothing of it. At dinner she gave us some of her theatrical reminiscences in her early years, especially of Mrs. Siddons in the character of Lady Macbeth ; and almost electrified a mild guest opposite, by an imitation of the great actress, in the passage, ' Out ! out damned spot ! ' in the sleep-walking scene. We greatly enjoyed our visit to Looe. The week after our return home I took the first train on Monday for Plymouth, and on arriving there took boat, by which I got landed on the east side of the Sound ; my object being to ascertain whether or

* Southey's amusing poem, explains the desirability of drinking *first* at the renowned well, of which Fuller gives the following account :—

" I know not whether it is worth reporting that there is in Cornwall, near the parish of St. Neot, a well arched over with the robes of four kinds of trees, withy, oak, elm, and ash dedicated to St. Keyne. The reported virtue of this water is this, that whether husband or wife come first to drink thereof, they get the mastery thereby."

not the rocks contained the peculiar organic remains which have been denominated 'Cornish fossil fish.' I did succeed in finding one very inferior patch, but nothing further. The coast is a fine one, and I greatly enjoyed the ramble, especially the superb view from the mouth of the river Yealm, the river itself being finely wooded to the water's edge; then came the ever-glorious sea with upwards of fifty craft of all rigs, and then the coast of Cornwall from the Rame Head to the Lizard entire; rarely have I seen anything so fine of its kind. About nine p.m. I found myself at the mouth of the river Erme (Ivy Bridge river), and took up my abode for the night at the Jolly Sailor, at the small out-of-the-world village of Mothecombe. I had inquired of a lad for the best inn before I entered the place, and was by him directed to the Jolly. On presenting myself at the door I found a butcher engaged in dressing the carcase of a pig, which he had just killed, and said piggie was hanging in the doorway (the front door). There seemed no help for it, so I demanded a bed of the old woman whom I supposed to be mistress of the house, but was answered by the butcher, who proved to be mine host, in the following words, 'Yes, sir, you can have a bed, so please to walk in, and take a seat in the kitchen; I would ax you to go into the parlour, but my missus is there cleaning part of the pig, and perhaps you mightn't like the smell o't.' Being of his opinion I acted on his advice, and soon got a capital ham rasher and (for me) a passable cup of tea; the old lady whom I first encountered (mother of the landlady) sitting by to cheer me on to the attack. Having disposed of the ham I commenced an onslaught on the butter, of which a very small piece was placed before me, but the dear old creature requested me not to be 'afraid of the butter, cos there's plenty more in the 'ouze, but 'tis allays best to finish up the bits and scraps.' On Tuesday I started to ascend the Erme, and had a splendid day. At the mouth the river is very tame and insignificant and uninteresting, but soon became very lovely, and only lost this character to become grand. Like the Yealm it rises on Dartmoor; it falls into Bigbury bay (the Yealm does not). I stopped to bait at Ermington, famous only for its leaning spire, and the wretched orthography and poetry on the headstones in the graveyard, of which I copied several examples. A couple of miles more brought me to Ivy bridge. I continued to follow the stream three or four miles above the bridge—in fact, got quite on Dartmoor—but as I had to get home that night I could not reach the source of the river; it certainly is a very delightful ramble, and artists might find many a delightful 'bit' in the district.

"Last week we went down and up the Dart; it is a charming cruise. The helmsman on board the steamer informed me that he had been told by many travellers that 'if the old rocks and old castles be a leaved out, the Rhine is not finer than the Dart.' Something like playing *Hamlet* with the character of the prince omitted. Yesterday Mr. Battersby and I were out all day dredging, and got many good things, the ground we selected is that between Berry Head and Brixham. Well, now I must close, I fear my scrawl will not repay the trouble of reading, but it will serve as a proof that I have not quite forgotten you. . . ."

Pengelly to his Wife.

"*London, May* 29, 1856.— . . . I proceeded to Sheppard's, and started with him in a cab to take up Stella, and her aunt,* on our way to the Regent's Park Flower Show. Many azaleas formed complete cones four feet high, and rich and tasteful was the grouping. Veitch, as usual, carried off many prizes. . . . I strolled on from the park, having declined to return with the Sheppards, and then to Somerset House to attend the meeting of the Geological Society. Two papers were read, one by a Mr. Moore on the rocks of Wigtonshire, etc., which was discussed by Col. Portlock, Murchison, and Salter; the other was by the famous Babbage, on the formation of sedimentary outliers, etc., which called up Portlock, Lyell, Salter, Stephenson the engineer, Prof. Tyndall, Huxley, etc. It was a magnificent meeting, and made me wish for a town residence. Whilst we were 'coffeeizing' I renewed my acquaintance with many old friends."

The following extract from his geological journal describes a ramble during which he visited Burr Island, situated on a wild and almost unknown part of the Devonshire coast.

"*July* 15*th*, 1856.—Left Bantham about eight in the morning, crossed the Avon at the ferry, and walked along the sands to Borough or Burr Island. The ceaseless hum of the sea, the wild scream of the sea-gulls, the magnificent expanse of water, the fine slate cliffs, and the glorious morning, made me feel unusually free and buoyant. Commenced my tour round the island on the eastern side. Drab and chocolate slates. Fine natural arch, through which the waves have cut a passage at east end. Several thin continuous layers of quartz parallel to the plane of stratification. Rocks at the back, *i.e.* sea side of the island, accessible by boat only. Island not so large as Looe Island, parts of it extremely wild and even approaching to grandeur. Rabbits very numerous, difficult to avoid slipping into their burrows, rabbits flitting in every direction, gulls abundant, frequently perched most picturesquely on romantic crags. The coast gives striking evidence of the long-continued erosive action of the sea, several almost completely detached parts of the island, and traces of landslips in places."

At this time Pengelly was giving special attention to "Beekites," which are found in considerable numbers in the Torquay district, although not often met with elsewhere in England.

The following letter on the subject, from the late Mr. Robert Hunt, Keeper of Mining Records at the Museum of Practical Geology, is worth quoting, as it shows how little was then known concerning these specimens.

"*Museum of Practical Geology, Jermyn Street, London, July* 1, 1856.— . . . I can obtain very little information respecting the Beekites.

* Some Torquay friends.

It appears that very little has been said or written respecting them since Dr. Beek, of Bristol, drew attention to them. They are found on the Greensand fossils of Black Down. We have no specimens here—a few would be a very acceptable present. Professor Morris tells me that he is engaged in a full examination of siliceous concretions, amongst which he classes those Beekites—but, as yet, he has not arrived at any conclusions. At any time I shall have much pleasure in obtaining, if possible, information for you. . . ."

In the summer of 1856 the British Association met at Cheltenham. It was the first meeting attended by Pengelly, who gives his impressions of it, in a series of letters to his wife.

"*Cheltenham, August* 7, 1856, 7.30 a.m.— . . . You are, of course, like a true woman, dying of curiosity to know about *our* proceedings at the British Association. And mark the word *our ;* it reminds me of the story of the wasp, which had sat on the horn of the ox all day, saying, '*We* have ploughed an acre of ground to-day.' About 7.30 p.m. I found my way to the college—the meetings are to be chiefly held there. I found the company rapidly assembling. . . . As I had come to the meeting to hear Dr. Daubeny's address, and knew something of the talking powers of the ——s, I retreated to my original seat. At length the platform filled ; in the chair sat the Duke of Argyll, the retiring president. He made a few introductory remarks, and resigned the chair to Dr. Daubeny. He read his address, but his voice is not strong enough for the room, so that I did not hear half his address, though I am inclined to think it a good one, and have no doubt it will read well. On his right sat Lord Wrottesley, and next to him sat the famous Mr. Close, of Cheltenham. He moved a vote of thanks to the president in a very good speech. On the left of the president sat Lord Stanley, who seconded the vote in a not telling but good speech, good, because decidedly in keeping with the tendency now gaining ground, of introducing science into our educational institutions ; next him sat Professor Phillips, the General Secretary, a man about my height, just as bald, a year or two older. He was the last speaker, and in a very facetious speech told the meeting what is to be done during the Association week. He kept lords and commons in a roar. Next Phillips sat Sir Roderick, and next him sat his great antagonist Sedgwick. Daubeny in his address used the expression 'the Silurian and Cambrian rocks,' which no doubt grated on Murchison's ear, and agreeably tickled Sedgwick's. The meeting over, we withdrew to an adjoining room, where a chatteration took place."

"*Cheltenham, August* 9*th.*— . . . At the reception-room yesterday morning I met Grindrod, who introduced me to Symonds,* of whom we read so much in connection with the Malvern Naturalists Club. . . . At the Geological Section, Symonds began by reading a paper on some part of Malvern, condemnatory of a view held by Ramsay ; of course

* The late Rev. W. S. Symonds, of Pendock.

the latter replied.   Phillips and Harkness both spoke approving of the paper.   Then came a paper by Buckman,[*] on the Cotswold Hills ; it was followed by two papers from Owen, on different fossil mammalia. Old Sedgwick grew enthusiastic and eloquent in commenting on them ; he was followed by Professor Macdonald, of St. Andrew's. . . . Then came a series of papers, the first by Hull, on the Cotswold Hills—this paper, or rather the author, was introduced by Murchison ; the second was by Dr. Wright, of this place, and was an attempt to show that what is usually called lower Oolite is the upper Lias.   The third of this series was by Moore, of Bath, his object being to disprove what Wright had attempted to prove.   He really startled the whole section by professing to be able to tell what nodules contained fossils, and of what species they were, and proceeded to verify these by breaking nodules before us, and, lo and behold, he was right in every instance !   ' The first instance,' said Professor Ramsay, ' of Geological clairvoyance that I have ever met with.'   A discussion should have followed, but our time was too nearly gone for that, so it is deferred until to-day ; still there remained a little time in which Mr. Edward Lee made two communications, both on fossils which had been given him by persons, who professed to have found them where they ought not to be found.   I had encouraged him to introduce them, but told him he would be told he had been cheated, and the result verified my words.   This ended the sitting.   I was extremely sorry for many of the authors ; there is at times such a racket of seats by persons leaving or entering the room, that they can scarcely hear themselves speak. . . ."

" *Monday, August* 11*th*.— . . . I do not recollect having informed you in my last, how Friday evening was spent, so that I had better begin this by informing you that Sir H. Rawlinson gave a lecture on his Assyrian researches ; the great room at the college was closely packed, some said there were two thousand people there, but that I greatly doubt, and am only willing to believe half I hear.   Sir Henry has a good voice, and tells his tale pleasantly.   On Saturday we commenced with a debate arising out of papers read the day before, the point in dispute being the exact boundary of the Liassic and Oolitic rocks ; then came a paper by Brodie,[†] on some new species of Lias corals, and one also by him on a new species of *Pollicipes* in the inferior Oolite.   The author is well known as a collector of fossil insects.   This was followed by Professor Hennessy reading a paper ' On the Relative Distribution of Land and Water affecting Climate.'   Poor fellow, he looked extremely ill.   Then came a paper from the famous Salter ' On the great Pterygottis.'   This drew Sedgwick, Murchison, and others into a discussion as to the exact line separating the Silurian and Devonian Systems ; then came a paper by Etheridge, of Bristol, as to whether the Bone Bed of Aust passage should be considered Liassic or Triassic ; thus have we had, in one day, three attempts to draw well-defined divisions in Geological Chronology.   The attempt is in my judgment absurd, such lines have no existence in Nature.   Had the world been at various times

* The late Professor J. Buckman, of Cirencester.
† The Rev. B. P. Brodie.

entirely depopulated, or had the earth's crust again and again been completely broken up by physical disturbances, then such lines or divisions would exist, and perhaps might be ascertained. Then we had a paper 'On the Time required for the formation of Rolled Stones,' by Moggridge; the author was not present, it was read by the secretary. Then came Sorby with a working model to illustrate the formation of Drift Bedding, which Murchison characterized as giving the greatest possible amount of information in the least possible time. Then came Vivian, with Kent's Cavern, and introduced his own views as to the formation of the cavern, which gave me an opportunity of replying, and this I did at some length. Robert Chambers took up the theme, so did Professor Rogers, of America. Beete Jukes, the chairman, pronounced in my favour, and Vivian acknowledged very handsomely that he thought me right. There were one or two other papers, and the sitting ended."

The following extract is also taken from a letter written at Cheltenham, the date of which is missing.

"Owen has a most gentle expression, he is extremely courteous to every one desiring information from him. Phillips spoke at some length on Owen's paper, and was followed by Sedgwick, who has unmistakable lines of decision of character in his face; he strongly condemned the frequent use of negative evidence, stating in reply to Owen, that it is quite unlikely, and must be considered exceptional, that the remains of a land animal should find their way to the sea, and be found in a marine deposit; and that hence we ought not to infer that terrestrial mammals did not exist in early geological times, from the negative fact that their remains are not met with in early strata. Owen replied that negative evidence was worth much more than Sedgwick admitted; he felt satisfied that mammals did not exist in early times, for we do not find the remains of marine, *i.e.*, cetaceous, mammals in the rocks in question. Again, he did not believe that marine reptiles lived in the earliest times; their remains are not found, and such creatures were not needed, as the saurian fish, that then abounded, performed the same functions; that is, kept down superabundant marine life. On which I remarked that Owen's conclusions respecting the non-existence of early marine reptiles had not been drawn from the negative fact of their remains not being found, but from the positive fact that fish remains were found capable of doing the same work, and I concluded by asking, 'Is Professor Owen acquainted with any early animals which discharged the functions now performed by the cetacea?' He replied that 'early fish did the work both of the later reptiles and the present cetacea.' I have much to say on this point, but not now."

"*Cheltenham, August* 12*th.*—Last night we had a lecture from Grove,* on 'The Correlation of Physical Forces,' a subject of which he is a thorough master, and on which he published many years ago. The

* The Rt. Hon. Sir W. R. Grove, D.C.L., F.R.S.

room was densely packed.   The lecturer is a thoughtful, studious-looking man, has a good voice, and a perfectly felicitous simplicity of illustration. It is certainly a wise plan to hold these evening lectures, in which men are selected who have the power of making profound subjects popular ; it helps to diffuse knowledge, whilst it may be hoped that the sectional meetings help to extend its boundaries. . . . five o'clock.   My paper has been read.   (On Beekites.)   Tennant considered Beekites as one form of silicious concretions, and thought the fossil character of the nucleus purely accidental.   I am coming home to-morrow, if all be well.   My home is very, very dear to me. . . ."

CHAPTER VI.

FIRST VISIT TO IRELAND.

1857 TO END OF YEAR.

AT the opening of the Abbey Road Public Schools at Torquay, in January, 1857, Pengelly briefly addressed the meeting. In his speech, he expressed his belief that the present age was not one " of *education*, it was an age of *instruction ;* the difference was momentous. If true education prevailed, would Mormonism have existed ? Would the belief in clairvoyance, spirit-rapping, table-turning, and such-like fallacies, as had recently disgraced this and other countries, have existed ? The fact was that the majority of scholars of the present day were taught to be rather passive recipients of knowledge, than active inquirers. What was required was to teach comparatively few things, but to teach them thoroughly. Parents should be less concerned about the rapid passing over of a great number of rules in Arithmetic than that what their children learnt should be thoroughly learnt, so that when they left school they should be in a position to acquire knowledge for themselves. It was true that vast improvements were constantly being made in the various departments of science ; but he did not think that public enlightenment had kept pace with the progress of science. People were surrounded on all hands by wonders, and what was wanted was to get them to think. Once successful in that respect, the love of acquiring knowledge naturally followed."

Pengelly was at this time President of the Torquay Mechanics' Institute, the members of which presented to him a copy of the " Encyclopædia Britannica " as a testimonial.

The volumes of the " Encyclopædia," bore the following inscription :—

" Presented
to
W. Pengelly, Esq., F.G.S.
By the Members and Friends of the
Torquay Mechanics' Institute,
as a tribute of esteem,
and in recognition of his untiring services
during a period of more than twenty years.
March 25, 1857."

Mrs. Pengelly to her Mother.

" *March* 28, 1857.—. . . William's old friend, Dr. Scoresby, the Arctic traveller, is to be buried this morning at Upton Church ; he has been ill a long time with heart complaint. It is a great loss to Torquay, as he has several times given us lectures here, and those with regard to the search for Sir John Franklin have been especially interesting. . . .

" William's Testimonial from the Mechanics' Institute, in acknowledgment of his more than twenty years' work, was presented to him last week at the close of Mr. Vivian's lecture there. . . ."

Of the *twentieth* lecture of a course on " Physical Geography," which Pengelly delivered at the Museum at Torquay, on March 30, 1857, his wife writes to her mother early in the following month.

" *April*, 1857.—. . . Most gratifying votes of thanks were moved to William at the conclusion of his course of lectures, in which it was said that none such could be heard in England, out of London, or a University town. Miss Burdett Coutts came up afterwards, very warmly expressing her extreme interest in them, and introduced me to several of her party, who were all equally pleased ; they praised my diagrams much more than they deserved. . . ."

Notwithstanding his engagements at this time with the work of the Mechanics' Institute and his lectures at the Torquay Natural History Society, Pengelly found time to lend a helping hand to many other matters, both in his own locality and elsewhere.

Pengelly to his Wife.

" *Stoke Newington*, 1857.—. . . On my arrival in the evening, I found an invitation to join my friends next door at a party at Alfred Tylor's, where I found Babbage, Sorby, Morris, and Rupert Jones. Was it not a little, or indeed, a good deal vexing, to find that Ruskin had just left ? Babbage and I got on well ; indeed, with Sorby, we made a little group and went into Slaty Cleavage, Transportation of Mud, Plurality of Worlds, etc. I was delighted to hear Babbage begin to hold forth that, for anything that appeared to the contrary, there might possibly be a world of intellectual whales; the very thing I have frequently said in reply to Whewell's book. Only keep Babbage in a good temper, and he really is quite charming. He told us a good story of Brewster. You are aware that Brewster was a leading man in the Scotch Free Church Movement, and also that he has recently married a young Miss *Kirk* Palmer; some wag has said, since the marriage, that Brewster has at last embraced the true *kirk*. . . ."

Pengelly to his Wife.

" *Stoke Newington, May 26, 1857.—.* . . Having fixed to meet Mrs. Yorke at Jermyn St. Museum, at 11 o'clock on Monday morning, I took omnibus here yester morn for Charing Cross, and getting there early, I started to see G. Wilson before I was due at the Museum. I pushed on, and had to pass close to a large number of soldiers with bands in full pipe preparing for a review, great crowds of people were moving towards them from all quarters. It really is a brilliant spectacle, and military music is truly fascinating, every nerve seems excited, and appears to suggest motion to all one's muscles. I found my Peace principles rapidly oozing out of me, but happily, before I had come to the resolution to enlist, the band having struck up 'The girl I left behind me,' I recollected there are two sides to the picture, and I was no longer in danger. On reaching the Museum I found Mrs. Yorke had not arrived, so hunted up some old geological acquaintances, officers of the Museum, amongst others Robert Hunt, Bailey, Ramsay, and Salter. Hunt introduced me to Bristow. I introduced Mrs. Yorke to Ramsay, and we went into the question of well-defined lines of demarcation in Geological Chronology, the existence of which, you will remember, I strongly deny. Ramsay admitted that their existence could not be proved, that the progress of discovery was daily rendering their existence less likely, but contended that we were not yet in a position to assert their non-existence. He then kindly showed us the specimens, on which he founds his belief that Glaciers existed during the Permian age, and certainly the evidence is striking. You will remember that I frequently had to allude to this during my lectures on the Temperature of the Earth."

Pengelly to his Wife.

" *Stoke Newington, 1857.—.* . . The Hanburys would not hear of my sleeping out, so I decided on taking a cab home, on leaving Miss Coutts'. But Alfred Tylor, being engaged to go to Burlington House, to hear the great Surgeon, Paget, read a paper on the rhythmic action of the heart, before the Royal Society, wished me to accompany him; but as that was quite out of the question, and as Burlington House is little more than a stone's-throw from Miss Coutts', he agreed to call for me. . . . On entering the drawing-room, I found Mr. Barlow

(Secretary of the Royal Institution) there. I was directly introduced to him, he was most cordial; desired me to come as frequently as possible to the Royal Institution, and especially wished me to come on Saturday to hear Scott (Principal of Owen's College) lecture on Moral Philosophy. Barlow had been invited to dine, but had a prior engagement, so left very soon. . . ."

"At length the guests began to arrive. First came a clergyman named Stokes, I had met his sisters at Miss Coutts' at Torquay; then Charles Dickens, beard, white waistcoat, fancy shirt and all—he is splendid company certainly, but strikes one as being altogether an actor; then came my friend Captain Gordon, and then Wheatstone; Sorby was to have been there, but did not turn up through some mistake. At dinner we talked of Education, Extension of the Electoral Franchise, etc. Dickens talked with good sense on all topics. Dinner over, puns and riddles flew thick and fast; unfortunately, Mrs. Browne had a lot without the answers. To one of them, 'When is most beef tea made?' I replied, 'When John Bull is dissolved in tears;' the answer was accepted. . . ."

In the summer of 1857, Pengelly visited York.

Pengelly to his Wife.

" *York, August* 6, 1857.—. . . The city seems quite an old-world place, but not so strikingly so as Chester, and not so un-English or un-nineteenth-century as Dartmouth. There are numbers of new names on the signboards,* but not many whimsical ones. The only ones I have thought worth noting down are, 'Toes,' 'Nutbrown,' 'Boast,' and 'Winspear.' I am told there is a 'Longbones,' but I have not had the pleasure of catching him. The streets are not generally named 'streets' but have some distinctive name, no doubt historical, such as 'Bootham,' 'Holgate,' 'Micklegate,' 'Skeldergate,' 'Lendal,' etc. . . . I took a peep into the Cathedral, or rather Minster, which is certainly magnificent, but I was not able to see all of the interior. I went also to see the Museum, which is really splendid, situated in extensive and beautiful gardens, which contain on one side the ruins of St. Mary's Abbey, and a Roman Multangular tower on the other. The antiquarian collection is an extremely fine one. . . ."

Later in the month he had the pleasure of visiting his old and greatly valued friend Mr. William Wilson at Mansfield, and the following letter to his wife shows how much he delighted in the traditions of the neighbourhood.

" *Sherwood Hall, August* 13, 1857.—. . . Yesterday after dinner we drove through a circuit of about twenty miles perhaps, through Sherwood forest, and extremely enjoyable it was, such a number of splendid old oaks, and such charming drooping birches, with abundance

---

* A subject in which he took much interest.

of heather just bursting into flower. Among the objects of interest we had first the 'Parliament Oak' under which King John, in a great emergency, once summoned a Parliament; next the 'Butcher,' or 'Shambles Oak,' a huge hollow trunk, nearly thirty feet in circumference, with a still vigorous top. Within the trunk tradition says that Robin Hood, Esq., used to hang his uncooked venison; it is said that the hooks on which the joints hung were *in situ* very lately. I don't know when I enjoyed a drive more; emphatically the land of legend and ballad, with an abundance of living vegetable witnesses of the scenes of other times, and the usages of a bygone phase of civilization. We got home a little before nine p.m., and after supper Mr. Wilson drew his dear old mother out to repeat portions of the ' Night Thoughts;' it was really beautiful to listen to her reciting, with good taste and fine emphasis, Young's tersely epigrammatic lines. . . ."

After spending a few days at Manchester with his wife, and seeing the magnificent Exhibition of Pictures just then assembled there, he proceeded to visit Ireland in company with his brother-in-law, and records, in a series of letters to his wife, his first impressions of the country with which he afterwards became more familiar.

" *Bush Mills, North of Ireland, August* 18, 1857.—. . . I am extremely concerned that I could not conveniently write you this morning, more especially as I am sure you will be curious to know my first impressions of Ireland. We reached Fleetwood a little after time, but as the steamer always waits the arrival of the train, that did not matter; we were taken by the train quite to the steamer's side, and in a very few minutes found ourselves on board. W. and not a few other landsmen looked gravely at the sky, and feared a rough passage, and when they found the boat pitching more freely than they had expected, they believed their fears fully realized. Some of the old salts, on the other hand, talked of a 'nice breeze,' of a 'splendid passage,' and in reply to the remark that 'it was rough,' said that, ' were it always smooth, all the old women in the country would be sailors.' I confess that I do not remember having ever enjoyed a voyage more. We made acquaintance with an artistic gentleman. Of course W. came in for the lion's share of the talk, which suited my desire to talk as little as possible.* About ten we went below for the purpose of 'turning in,' as we sailors say. The scene which met our eyes was whimsical enough; all the seats were transformed into beds, and above them were placed other beds, looking as much like coffins as anything; other beds were arranged on the floor, and every bed found an occupant—I am not sure that it would be safe to say sleeper. W. and I occupied one each. Beneath us, on the lockers or seats, lay others, inside us on the same level, and in close contact, lay others on the floor. I could not sleep much, so that I was able to sit up in the night at times, just to study the strange group.

* He had been suffering from one of his throat attacks.

I got up finally at half-past four, and went on deck, hoping to catch a glimpse of the Isle of Man, which I had failed to do last night, but I was again disappointed. I found Ireland ahead, and Scotland on the weather bow, and it seemed to carry me back to my seaboy life, to watch the gradual coming on of day, the steady development of the land we were approaching, the various craft we passed, and the sea-birds that floated and wheeled around and by us. Soon after six we entered Belfast Lough, and one by one the passengers came on deck all looking more or less seedy. About half-past seven we landed at Belfast, which we found having all the appearance of prosperity, activity, wealth, and taste ; it did not come up, or come down, whichever you like, to my idea of an Irish town, and it was not possible to believe it Ireland, until we reached the railway station, whither we at once drove to deposit our luggage, and there we found that, at any rate, it was not England, seeing that a railway porter appeared 'taking a shock of his duden,' alias, 'smoking his pipe,' which quite put my pipe out. Next we breakfasted, and then strolled through the town, and soon after ten set off by rail for Portrush, the nearest railway approach to the Causeway. The first half of the journey was performed pretty well, but the latter half was slow indeed. About two, in due time, we reached Portrush, about seven miles (Irish) from the Causeway. Between the point reached and that to be reached the coast is superb so that we decided to walk, and started for that purpose soon after three.

The first object that attracted us was a series of very fine chalk cliffs, famous on account of being altered by the basalt of the Causeway. This chalk is in horizontal beds, is harder than chalk usually, in consequence of the heat of the basalt, and contains great numbers of flint nodules, sometimes, but not always, in parallel layers, and many fossils of unquestionable chalk types. I only saw Belemnites, but I obtained *Terebratulæ* and an *Echinus* from a quarryman. The chalk is much fissured and caverned by the sea, in most cases it is overlaid by the basalt which has clearly overflowed. Some of the sections are of great beauty, and made me frequently wish for you to make sketches. Up to this point we had seen no columnar basalt, but found it spheroidal with occasional bands of volcanic ash. Leaving the chalk we next reached (also on the coast) the ruins of Dunluce Castle, which has undoubtedly been lauded beyond its deserts ; still there are points from which the remains form an interesting and picturesque group, and the situation is certainly very fine. Beyond this we had traces of the columnar form, but nothing more than faint predictions of what we hope to see to-morrow. Soon after seven we reached the Causeway hotel, and found it full, so had to turn back to this village, and here the chief hotel was also full, so we took the second, which is not quite up to the mark, but we have frequently done worse. I have very much enjoyed the day ; it is a district of new geological features to me, and would afford me much interest for a longer time ; indeed, I feel that we shall not half do the North of Ireland, but it cannot be helped, and I less regret it, as I have decided to devote myself to the geology of Devonshire. The district through which we have passed, *i.e.* the district from Belfast, seems entirely volcanic. We do not suppose we have seen genuine Paddy yet. . . ."

"*Portrush, August* 20, 1857.—. . . Yesterday we started pretty early from Bush Mills, and walked a second time to the Causeway. Arrived there, we courageously declined the services of the guides who prowl about. We were quite prepared from reports, etc., to be disappointed, and so indeed we were, but then it was a most agreeable disappointment. To attempt description would be to display my weakness. Whether regarded as a geological phenomenon, as a subject for a picture, or rather a series of pictures, or as a great cyclopean terminus, the Causeway is a singularly splendid object. Having penetrated as far as possible under the cliff we retraced our steps, and then I rambled on the margin of the precipice to a much greater distance, and as point after point opened, I became sensible that we were leaving much too much unexplored, so that we agreed to alter our plans, to remain in the North until Saturday, and to reach Moyallen that evening, to give up Killarney and the West, and consequently to hope for a second Irish trip. After breakfast we started by boat for Bally Castle, a distance of nearly twenty miles. I was much pleased to find Lias with Ammonites, in contact with Trap, by which it is much hardened, yesterday on the beach here. This is a most charming spot, there is a splendid sea walk, with a glorious open sea having no land nearer than America. Whilst strolling on this walk yesterday, I met my old friend and pupil Urquhart, and had a pleasant stroll with him and his wife. . . ."

"*Bally Castle, August* 20, 1857.— . . . We are now journeying southwards, and have had a splendid day, though it did not commence very auspiciously. I think I mentioned in my last that we were intending to reach this place from Portrush by boat. The voyage would certainly have been a very splendid one in suitable weather; but though the sea was as smooth as could be wished, and there was very little wind, and that little fair, yet a dense fog, which increased with the morning, rendered the attempt at best an unwise one, so we abandoned it, and made our journey by car. Between eleven and twelve o'clock the fog all but left us. Our road was by the sea, which was perfect in colour; the cliffs and islets, and the distant island of Rathlin, looked their very, very best, and we intensely enjoyed the drive. On the way we stopped at a spot famous in these parts, under the name of Carrick-a-Rede, an island separated from the mainland by a chasm sixty feet wide. This chasm is spanned by a bridge mainly of ropes, on which rest some not over-safe or strong planks. The bare idea of crossing made me sick; of course, we neither thought for one moment of attempting it. I would not try it for a thousand guineas, a false step would precipitate one down ninety feet to the sea; and yet it is said that during the salmon-fishing season (to facilitate which the bridge was put up) children cross it in perfect unconcern.

"We reached this soon after three o'clock, and at once started on a walk to see a famous headland known as Fairhead, about three miles off. We did not quite reach it, our object being rather to see it than to see from it. It is truly a magnificent headland, upwards of six hundred feet high, the upper two hundred columnar basalt quite vertical; the lower part slopes with a steep talus to the sea, and consists of beds of the carboniferous formation. I saw a great many fossils, shells, crinoids, stigmaria, lepidodendrons, etc.; but none worth taking. All being well, we travel by mail-car along the coast to Belfast, or near it, to-morrow; and I shall feel I am by so much nearer to you and my home. I have very much enjoyed my trip. . . . But why should I bother myself about the geology of this or any other distant district, when there are so many unsolved problems connected with the pre-Adamic history of lovely Devon? . . ."

" *Moyallen, August* 25, 1857.— . . . Though I have little or nothing to communicate, I do not like breaking through my practice of a daily letter. We took a drive of several miles yesterday. The district is essentially a manufacturing one; and though there is no large town, there is a large population, apparently in comfortable condition. It seems that spinning and bleaching are the principal employments. Our kind hosts wish to detain us till to-morrow, and as we can reach Dublin to-morrow quite in time for the first meeting of the Association, we have concluded to remain. I have quite decided to return by way of Holyhead; it will cost me little more in time or money, and will afford me the pleasure of once again seeing beautiful Conway. I forgot to tell you in the right place that on our way from Cushendall we met a respectably dressed man, so very drunk that the road seemed hardly wide enough for him. I have already described the road as one of great beauty, winding along the coast, and about from ten to twenty feet above the sea. This road is bounded by a low parapet on the sea side. Just after we passed him, the poor fellow staggered against the parapet and went head over heels completely over it. Of course we concluded that he must have killed himself, and two of us ran back, regardless of the assurance of the driver that, his being the mail-car, he could not wait one moment. Before we had run back ten steps, he was recrossing the wall, apparently unhurt, on perceiving which we returned to our seats, when the driver sagely remarked to me, 'Shure, the fall will waken him a bit.' . . ."

" *Dublin, August* 27.— . . . Last night we had our opening address, and it was indeed a great treat. Dr. Lloyd, the President, is a capital reader, and his address was at once profound and simple. The following point in it especially struck me, namely, the date cannot ripen her fruit at a lower temperature than 70°, and the pine cannot endure a higher than 70°, hence the climate in which these grow together cannot vary more than 1° on either side of 71°. The Bible assures us that they did grow together in early times in Palestine, and we know they grow together there now, hence we are sure that the climate of Palestine has undergone no change. This thought was much applauded. On the platform I observed General Sabine, Professor Phillips, Robinson, Hincks (the Orientalist), Nasmyth, Portlock, Lord Wrottesley, Jukes, Macdonald, Daubeny, Harkness, Lord Carlisle (Lord Lieutenant), Hennessy, and Sir W. Hamilton. Lord Carlisle moved the vote of thanks in a capital speech, and Lord Wrottesley seconded it. In addition to the sectional meetings, we are to have a soirée to-night, a lecture from Professor W. Thomson * on the Atlantic Cable to-morrow night, and a lecture from Dr. Livingstone on Monday night. On Thursday next there are to be excursions, one to Killiney and Wicklow, one to Galway, Isles of Arran, and one to Parsonstown, to see Lord Rosse's telescope. All of which are forbidden fruit to me, seeing that I must reach home on that day. Well, now comes the calling with the introductions Dr. Evanson so kindly sent me. I would sooner walk through the county of Wicklow than do it; but, of course, it must be done. . . ."

"*Dublin, August* 28 — . . . After breakfast I called on W——, and then repaired to the Section-rooms, where I met sundry old friends. I took my specimen from Cornwall, which, in spite of M'Coy, I have always pronounced to be a portion of a fish, and showed it privately to sundry bigwigs. They all individually, and without knowing the opinion of either of the others, pronounced me right, and without hesitation too; moreover, they all regarded it as a triumph, and a great fact in geology. You will not wonder at my being overjoyed about it. I showed it to Phillips, Bowerbank, Bailey, Jukes, and Lord Enniskillen (to whom R. Were Fox introduced me). Next to Sir P. Egerton, who is not here, Lord Enniskillen is the highest authority we have on fishes. The papers yesterday were not without interest, but were not likely to be popular. After dinner I went with my kind hostess, Mrs. Edmondson, and her children, to see St. Patrick's Cathedral. . . . The curator is himself a character, and tells some good things, much as Addison tells us the custodian of Westminster Abbey did to good old Sir Roger de Coverly. In the evening came a soirée in the museum-rooms of the Royal Irish Society, and a brilliant scene it was. Science, fashion, beauty, ugliness, were met in one room. There I saw Sedgwick and Rogers, who had not appeared before. I met, amongst others, Mr. Pim, his wife (J. J. Lister's daughter), and her brother, my old friend Lister. They wish me to dine with them to-morrow. It involves a short journey by rail; still, I think I may go. I was promoted at the Association, being placed on the General Committee, and also on that of the Geological Section. Well, now I must conclude. Tell baby I will write her a letter soon; thank her for her letter to me, and tell her I must bring it back for her to read. . . ."

"*Dublin, August* 31, 1857.—All things come to an end, and this month among them, it seems. Ends are serious things, dear, always serious, though sometimes pleasant, sometimes painful. I hope the end of this month, however, will be pleasant to both of us. But to my task of recording. On Saturday morning I proceeded to call on Sir Henry Marsh, M.D., to whom Dr. Evanson had sent me an introduction. I had a brief but very pleasant interview with Sir Henry and Lady Marsh, both very pleasant. They gave me an invitation to dine with them that evening, but most kindly allowed me to leave it an open question. Next I proceeded to the Geological Committee-room, and energetically assisted in the business there by reading the programme for the day, that is to say, I did nothing but talk, etc., because

* Now Lord Kelvin.

there was nothing else to do. At eleven the sections assembled as usual, and as usual I took my place in the Geological, which promised and proved to be of very high interest to the geologist, but probably not to the *vulgar*. Professor W. B. Rogers, of Boston, U.S., read a paper on the discovery of *Paradoxides* in New England, in rocks heretofore considered Azoic; another splendid hint from the stony volume of the insufficiency of negative evidence. Then came a highly interesting report on Earthquakes, on which I had a little to say. Then came the great subject of Slaty Cleavage in a series of papers from different authors, and a capital discussion on them, which ended in a confession that, though mechanical agency has probably produced the main phenomena observed, there are still residuary phenomena which cannot be explained, but which are probably the effect of molecular, perhaps polar forces, a conclusion amounting almost to a compromise, but which seems not unfairly to express the present state of our knowledge on the question, and which gratified R. W. Fox, who sat very near me all the day. On leaving the section, R. W. Fox introduced me to Mrs. Lloyd, the wife of the President of the Association. I informed her that Dr. Evanson had kindly sent me an introduction to Dr. Lloyd, and it was arranged that I was not to wait for ceremony, but accost the doctor wherever I might find him. Then came a promenade in the Botanical Gardens, which, as old Pepys would say, was 'mighty pleasant.' The grounds are very beautifully laid out, and are well kept. . . . In the gardens I met Dr. Lloyd and his wife, and talked with them awhile, then I met a Torquay friend, then a series of geological acquaintances, and amongst others Professor W. B. Rogers; we quite fraternized. Then in the evening came a soirée, at the rooms of the Royal Irish Academy, which contain a capital Library, and a Museum of Antiquities, rich to overflowing with early Irish remains. The tables almost groaned beneath microscopes, and photographic and other pictures of round towers, etc. A large garden connects the rooms with the Mansion House. All the public rooms in the latter were open to us, the connecting garden being covered with canvas, so as literally to convert the garden into a room. One of the rooms at the Mansion House is called from its form the round room; it was built in order to give a dinner to George the Fourth, and the Queen has dined in it. It is a very fine apartment. Here refreshments were provided, and every one partook at his pleasure. A band was stationed in the orchestra, and on its playing a lively air, some of the lighter spirits, male and female, got up a wee dance. I turned away, remarking that 'it was painful to see the understandings of philosophers shaken.' Then came the Lord Lieutenant, making himself very agreeable. I frequently came in contact with Professor W. B. Rogers, who remarked that he felt we must be drawn together by sympathy or polar force, or something of the sort, perhaps mesmerism. Well, now I must close, leaving the report of yesterday to another opportunity, if I can find one. . . ."

During the next month Pengelly received the following letter on the subject of fossil fishes from Peach—

" *Wick, September* 14, 1857.—Many thanks for yours of the 9th inst. I had been thinking to write to you about your paper on the Beekites. I was always much pleased and interested with them when living in Devon, and have frequently thought about them, and of late much more than ever, for when in Sutherland last month I obtained a great many fossils (Silurian) in a locality said to have 'been devoid of fossils' until I got a few in '55. I find them abundant, for in my last trip I got them in new localities, and had I time to have visited several other places I might have probably done more. You will probably hear about them one day from Sir R. Murchison. My motive for mentioning them at all is to ask you whether the enclosed piece of a fossil is *covered with Beekites?* It is evidently cherty or flinty matter, and is formed like the Beekite. This came from Durness metamorphic limestone. I should be glad to hear your opinion.

"Although Professor M'Coy pooh-poohed the fossil fishes of Cornwall, my opinion has never been changed, and although I have every respect for him I never felt that he was right altogether—his broom swept too clean. I am confident that two or three specimens which I obtained in the cliffs between Fowey and Polperro, are spines of fishes, and as well, there are other portions which belonged to fishes. One large specimen now in the Penzance Museum is much like the spine of the *Hybodus* of the Lias, but not serrated. One of them is very large. *None* of these spines were seen by McCoy. I wrote him and told him he was wrong in saying that *no* fish remains had been found in Cornwall. He said he might be. I have not yet seen his paper on the Cornish rocks and fossils. I did expect this; Professor Sedgwick would have sent it to me. But no—have you a copy? If so could you *lend it to me?* I would return it after reading it—if you would or could it would be a favour indeed. I live so completely out of the world of science, I see no scientific publications of any kind. When you were enjoying yourself at Dublin I was working away in the Highlands of Sutherland. I spent a month there and much enjoyed myself, and got a splendid collection of fossils from Durness.

"P.S.—I intended to congratulate you on being able to use such names as those you mention as having pronounced your fossil *Fish.* Long life to you and them. Of course I mean the *men* not the *fossil fish.*"

Mrs. Pengelly's letters to her mother give a glimpse of their life at this period.

Mrs. Pengelly to her Mother.

" *October 7th.*— . . . We paid a very pleasant visit last evening to our friend Thos. Christy Wakefield (William's kind host in Ireland). I was interested to find from him, that General Nicholson, now before Delhi, is his nephew. T. C. Wakefield spoke in the highest terms of him, says he was always so steady and thoughtful. He was taken prisoner by the Afghans in the Kyber Pass when sixteen years of age, at which place he lost two brothers; he was kept prisoner for many months by Dost Mohammed, who tried very much to persuade him to change his religion and become a Mohammedan. . . ."

Mrs. Pengelly to her Mother.

"*October* 17, 1857.— . . . Last night we attended Mr. Vivian's soirée at the Bath Saloon; it was quite a bright affair, every one seemed determined to enjoy it, and to be sociable; we had much chat with various interesting people; amongst others a lady came up and introduced herself to William, and she proved to be Mrs. Brockedon, the widow of the famous Mr. Brockedon (originally a watchmaker at Totnes), who made the remarkable discovery of hardening black lead powder by means of a violent blow, so as to make it perfectly solid to be used as pencils, etc. He made a large fortune by it. We were much pleased to have made her acquaintance. . . ."

"*November* 11*th*.— . . . William went a very pleasant excursion down the Dart yesterday with Mr. Gosse, the Naturalist. We see a good deal of him, he is an exquisite artist in his own line. . . ."

During the winter of 1857, Pengelly, whose ability as an instructor and former of character gave him a strong hold on the affections of most of the pupils for whose welfare he laboured during so many years of his life, had a very quick pupil in Frederick Myers. Writing many years afterwards to obtain some information, Mr. Myers thus refers to his tutor's lessons—

"*December* 30, 1883.—You have doubtless forgotten two little boys to whom you taught 'Heights and Distances,' and other trigono-metrical puzzles at Bronshill, Torquay, in December, 1857, and January, 1858. One of them, however, remembers those months as the only time in his life when he was vividly interested in mathematics—and consequently retains a clear image of his instructor. Mr. A. R. Wallace has just sent me a most interesting pamphlet of yours, called 'Is it a fact?' . . ."

CHAPTER VII.

BRIXHAM CAVERN AND THE DEVONSHIRE CAVES.

1858 AND 1859.

IN 1858 the discovery of a new Bone Cavern at Brixham greatly interested Pengelly, and he at once visited the spot, and entered into negotiations with the proprietor, on behalf of the Torquay Natural History Society, for a thorough exploration. While arrangements for this matter were pending, Dr. Hugh Falconer, having heard of the discovery, came to Torquay to make inquiries respecting it. The result of his deliberations with Pengelly led to the following arrangement—that, as the Torquay Natural History Society had not sufficient funds at its disposal for a systematic investigation of the cavern, Dr Falconer should obtain a grant from the Royal and Geological Societies for the purpose, Pengelly undertaking the superintendence of the work.

The remarkable discoveries which were made, formed the subject of Pengelly's paper, read that same year before the Leeds Meeting of the British Association, on "A recently discovered Ossiferous Cavern, at Brixham, near Torquay." A quarter of a century later, in his Address to the Department of Anthropology at the Southport Meeting of the British Association in 1883, he described the apathy and scepticism with which all geological evidence as to the Antiquity of Man had previously been received, even by British geologists of the first rank. He goes on to give a short summary of the history of the Cave, and the results that the explorations have had in stimulating scientific investigation.

The following extract from this Address is worth quoting:—

"Early in 1858, the workmen engaged in a limestone quarry on Windmill Hill, overhanging the fishing town of Brixham, in South Devon, broke unexpectedly a hole through what proved to be the roof of an unknown and unsuspected cavern. I visited it very soon after the discovery, and secured to myself the refusal of a lease to include the right of exploration. As the story of this Cavern has been told at some length elsewhere (see *Phil. Trans.*, voL clxiii. pp. 471–572 ; or *Trans. Devon. Assoc.*, vol. vi. pp. 775–856), it will here suffice to say that at the instance of the late Dr. H. Falconer, the eminent palæontologist, the subject was taken up very cordially by the Royal and Geological Societies of London ; a Committee was appointed by the latter body ; the exploration was placed under the superintendence of Mr. (now Professor) Prestwich and myself ; and, being the only resident member of the Committee, the actual superintendence fell of necessity to me.

" The following facts connected with this Cavern were no doubt influential in leading to the decision to have it explored.

" 1. It was a virgin cave which had been hermetically sealed during an incalculably long period, the last previous event in its history being the introduction of a reindeer antler, found attached to an upper surface of the stalagmitic floor. It was, therefore, free from the objection urged sometimes against Kent's Cavern, that, having been known from time immemorial, and, up to 1825, always open to all comers, it had, perhaps, been ransacked again and again.

" 2. It was believed, and it proved, to be a comparatively very small cavern, so that its complete exploration was not likely to require a large expenditure of time or of money.

" It will be seen that the exploration was placed under circumstances much more likely to command attention than any of those which had preceded it. It was to be carried on under the auspices of the Royal and Geological Societies, by a Committee consisting of Mr. S. H. Beckles, Mr. G. Busk, Rev. R. Everest, Dr. H. Falconer, Mr. Godwin-Austen, Sir C. Lyell, Professor Owen, Dr. J. Percy, Mr. J. Prestwich, Professor (now Sir A. C.) Ramsay, and myself—all Fellows of the Geological Society, and almost all of them of the Royal Society also.

" It was impossible not to feel, however, that the mode of exploration must be such as would not merely satisfy those actually engaged in the work, but such as would command, for the results which might be obtained, the acceptance of the scientific world generally. Hence I resolved to have nothing whatever to do with the " trial pits " here and there, or with shafts to be sunk in selected places ; but, first, to examine and remove the stalagmitic floor; then, the entire bed immediately below (if not of inconvenient depth) horizontally, throughout the entire length of the cavern, or so far as practicable ; this accomplished, to proceed in like manner with the next lower bed ; and so on until all the deposits had been removed.

" This method, uniformly followed, was preferable to any other, because it would reveal the general stratigraphical order of the deposits with the amount and direction of such 'dip ' as they might have, as well as any variations in the thickness of the beds ; it would afford the only chance of securing all the fossils, and of thus ascertaining, not only the different kinds of animals represented in the Cave, but also the ratios which the numbers of individuals of the various species bore to one another, as well as all peculiar or noteworthy collocations; it would disclose the extent, character, and general features of the Cavern itself; it was undoubtedly the least expensive mode of exploration ; and it would render it almost impossible to refer bones or indications of human existence to wrong beds, depths, or associations.

"The work was begun in July, 1858, and closed at the end of twelve months, when the Cavern had practically been completely emptied; an official report was printed in the *Philosophical Transactions* for 1873, and all the specimens have been handed over to the British Museum.

"The paper on the subject mentioned at the beginning of this Address* was read in September, 1858, during the meeting of the Association at Leeds, when I had the pleasure of stating that eight flint tools had already been found in various parts of the Cavern, all of them inosculating with bones of mammalia, at depths varying from nine to forty-two inches in the Cave-earth, on which lay a sheet of stalagmite from three to eight inches thick; and having *within* it and *on* it relics of lion, hyæna, bear, mammoth, rhinoceros, and reindeer.

"It soon became evident that the geological apathy previously spoken of had been rather apparent than real. In fact, geologists were found to have been not so much disinclined to entertain the question of human antiquity, as to doubt the trustworthiness of the evidence which had previously been offered to them on the subject. It was felt, moreover, that the Brixham evidence made it worth while, and indeed a duty, to re-examine that from Kent's Cavern, as well as that said to have been met with in river-deposits in the valley of the Somme and elsewhere.

"The first-fruits, I believe, of this awakening, was a paper, by Mr. Prestwich, read to the Royal Society, May 26, 1859, *On the occurrence of Flint Implements, associated with the Remains of Animals of Extinct Species in beds of a late Geological Period in France at Amiens and Abbeville and in England at Hoxne.*† This paper contains explicit evidence that the Brixham Cavern had had no small share in disposing its author to undertake the investigation, which added to his own great reputation, and rescued M. Boucher de Perthes from undeserved neglect. 'It was not,' says Mr. Prestwich, 'until I had myself witnessed the conditions under which these flint implements had been found at Brixham, that I became fully impressed with the validity of the doubts thrown upon the previously prevailing opinions with respect to such remains in caves.'‡

"Sir C. Lyell, too, in his Address to the Geological Section of the British Association, at Aberdeen, in September, 1859, said, 'The facts recently brought to light during the systematic investigation, as reported on by Dr. Falconer, of the Brixham Cave must, I think, have prepared you to admit that scepticism in regard to the cave-evidence in favour of the antiquity of man had previously been pushed to an extreme.'§

"It is probably unnecessary to quote further to show how very

* "A recently-discovered Ossiferous Cavern, at Brixham, near Torquay," by W. Pengelly.
† *Phil. Trans.* for 1860, pp. 277–317.
‡ *Op. cit.,* p. 280.
§ *Report Brit. Assoc.,* 1895; *Trans. Sects.,* p. 93.

large a share the Exploration at Brixham had in impressing the scientific world generally with the value and importance of the geological evidence of man's antiquity.   That impression, begun, as we have seen, in 1859, has not only lasted to the present day, but has probably not yet culminated.   It has produced numerous volumes, crowds of papers, countless articles in Reviews and Magazines, in various countries ; and perhaps, in order to show how very popular the subject became almost immediately, it is only necessary to state that Sir C. Lyell's great work on the 'Antiquity of Man' was published in February, 1863, the second edition appeared in the following April, and the third followed in the succeeding November—three editions of a bulky scientific work in less than ten months ! A fourth edition was published in May, 1873.

" Few, it may be presumed, can now doubt that those who before 1858 believed that our fathers had under-estimated human antiquity, and fought for their belief, have at length obtained a victory."

Scientific writers have borne generous and appreciative testimony to the value of Pengelly's work at Brixham.

In the *Geological Magazine* (No. 359, p. 238, May, 1894) he is spoken of as "one of that small band of Geologists, who assisted Falconer, Busk, Lyell, Prestwich, Lartet, Christy, Rupert-Jones, Boyd-Dawkins, and a few others to place upon a scientific basis, that inquiry into the evidence of Pre-historic Man which was systematically commenced, in this country, by the exploration of Brixham Cave in 1858.   This work, which was carried out, under the auspices of the Royal and Geological Societies, by Mr. William Pengelly, of Torquay, yielded most important results."

Professor Boyd-Dawkins thus alludes to the Cave work :— " The result of the exploration, established beyond all doubt the existence of palæolithic man in the Pleistocene age, and caused the whole of the scientific world, to awake to the fact of the vast antiquity of the human race.   From this time Pengelly's energies were mainly directed towards cave exploration." [*]

In *Natural Science* for May, 1894, the following reference to the same subject occurs.   "On the shoulders of Mr. Pengelly fell practically all the work of supervision ; but he had his reward, in finding ample corroboration of his previous conclusions ; for beneath the unbroken stalagmitic floor were brought to light relics of human handiwork in such intimate association with the remains of extinct mammalia, as to place their contemporaneity beyond all cavil."

It has been already mentioned that many scientific men were

------

[*] *Nature*, April 5, 1894.

unprepared for the results obtained by the Brixham exploration ; and the conclusions arrived at were received with some apprehension by the general public.

Probably the outcry raised against Pengelly's geological discoveries by the orthodox party of that day will appear extraordinary to this generation, which has long ceased to be disquieted by facts that are now so generally received. But many, even of his own friends, were filled with misgivings by the discoveries of science. Some of them endeavoured to reconcile the old and new views, as he himself at first hoped to do ; but he soon found that all such attempts were unadvisable. He saw that many of the facts brought to light by geology could not, in the present state of knowledge, agree with the long-accepted interpretation of the account of Creation ; and that the various well-meaning endeavours to harmonize the two had frequently only ended by making the discrepancies still more evident. Indeed, he felt that some writers who attempted a reconciliation did positive harm, either by their forced attempts to adapt the language of the Old Testament to scientific facts, even at the cost of rendering the Biblical language doubtful and almost unmeaning ; or, oftener still, by giving, from a complete ignorance of science, explanations which were utterly unphilosophical and unsound.

His own feeling on the subject is expressed in the following extract from a letter, written in answer to one of the many correspondents (chiefly total strangers) who wrote to him regarding the views of geologists—". . . Geologists see no mode of reconciling the commonly-received interpretation of the Mosaic account of Creation with geological science. . . . For myself, I am satisfied that Science can do nothing for the salvation of the soul, and that the Bible is able, through God's blessing, to make us wise unto salvation. . . ."

No doubts or difficulties were ever able to undermine his faith as a Christian. But, although his religious convictions were strong and intense, he was in many ways an advanced thinker, and always tolerant of the views of opponents. His position might be justly described by the following striking words of Erasmus—" The sum of religion is peace, which can only be when definitions are as few as possible, and opinion is left free on many subjects. . . . Wait till the veil is removed and we see God face to face."

The wider field of geological research which now opened before Pengelly did not hinder him from pursuing his work, as Honorary Secretary to the Torquay Natural History Society, with his accustomed activity.   After a course of twenty-three Lectures, which he delivered before that Society during the session of 1857-8, many of the members and his other friends expressed their sense of the value of his scientific labours, by presenting him, early in May 1858, through his friend Mr. Sheppard, with a purse of 80 guineas.   In response to this substantial proof of regard, he expressed himself in the following terms :—

"Whilst I have supposed myself simply geologizing during the winter now terminated, a note received during the last week, from my valued friend and neighbour, Mr. Sheppard, informs me that I have really been at the 'diggings,' and that I have been so very fortunate as to extract an extremely valuable 'nugget'—set in kindliest feeling and appreciation, more beautiful, and I trust more durable, than the most brilliant 'quartz.'   I cannot afford to value the *nugget* itself lightly ; but, believe me, I set a far higher price on the *setting ;* the first will, as I presume it is intended, take to itself wings and fly away, but the latter will long live in my recollection and my gratitude."

Shortly afterwards he paid a hasty visit to London to see Dr. Falconer, and writes home—

"*May*, 1858.— . . . I believe nothing occurred on my journey up worthy of record.   We reached Paddington at the time appointed, namely, 11.5, and on the suggestion of two respectable fellow-travellers, I got myself set down by the 'bus, at the Gloucester Hotel, Piccadilly, but, alas! they had turned away forty applicants for beds before my arrival, so I started on my travels loaded with my luggage ; one hotel after another was tried, but with a like result.   At length, heartily tired, I applied to the Police, who, though civil, could not help me, and when I proposed that they should lock me up for the night, they only laughed!   Good fortune smiled on me at length, and something before one I got a bed, and on the whole a pretty comfortable one. This morning I went to Falconer's, had a pleasant breakfast, but found that the Committee is to be held on Tuesday.   Thence I went to Jermyn Street Museum, where I found all the authorities agree in thinking my Cornish specimen an ichthyodorulite, as I think also, as you are well aware. . . . I forgot to say that I am to dine with Miss Coutts next Thursday, and after dinner to accompany her and party to hear Dickens read his 'Chimes.'   I am promising myself a decided treat on the occasion. . . ."

Whilst in London, Pengelly made the acquaintance of Dr. Percy, of the School of Mines.

Mrs. Pengelly to her Mother.

"*August* 28, 1858.— . . . William is very much interested in having made the acquaintance of Dr. Percy (of the School of Mines), who is spending the autumn here; he is going out with him in his yacht to-morrow. Charles Landseer is Dr. Percy's particular friend, and he is expecting him and Dr. Hooker both down on a visit shortly. W. had a letter yesterday from Dr. Falconer, who said he had just heard from Sir Charles Lyell from Germany, saying he had been shown there a fossil human skeleton, found in one of the geological (supposed) prehuman periods; it is a puzzle. . . ."

Mrs. Pengelly to her Mother.

"*September 8th.*— . . . I had a very interesting call last week from Dr. Falconer, Professor Ramsay, Dr. Percy, and Charles Landseer. I extremely enjoyed it. They were all most interesting, and C. Landseer very entertaining. They are all delighted with Torquay, and think it is not half as well known as it deserves to be. . . ."

During the British Association Meeting that autumn, at which Pengelly read, amongst other papers, one upon the result of his exploration of the Brixham Cavern, he writes to his wife—

"*Leeds, September*, 1858.— . . . The sections opened to-day, and though the papers did not promise much, they have been on the whole decidedly interesting. I took part in a discussion on submerged forests. Last night I attended Owen's lecture; it was about three hours long, too long decidedly, but truly excellent. I have been to see the Museum to-day, which is admirable. . . ."

To his Wife.

"*Leeds, September*, 1858.— . . . Your faithless husband has allowed a post to pass without writing you, not, however, from choice. . . . My papers were both read, namely, on the Ichthyodorulite and on the Trilobite. My views were fully confirmed on the first by Sir Philip Egerton, who spoke on it, and on the second by Salter, who spoke on that. There was a horticultural *fête* at Kirkstall Abbey, about three miles from Leeds, which I attended; the old Abbey is a fine ruin. . . . I have greatly increased my circle of friends both scientific and otherwise. . . ."

To his Wife.

"*Leeds, September*, 1858.— . . . I have read my paper (on Brixham Cavern) to a crowded house, all the great geologists came in apparently. Owen followed in very eulogistic strains, characterizing exploration of the Cavern, as the only satisfactory and good attempt of the kind that ever had been made. I was very much complimented at the close by sundry persons. Robert Chambers introduced himself, and proposes having a chat with me on the question. . . ."

The Rev. Canon H. B. Tristram to Pengelly.

"*Castle Eden, Durham, October 2, 1858.*— . . . I did not at once thank you for your kind trouble and interest in collecting and forwarding to me the Devonian fossils, as I was not sure of your Leeds address. . . . Do you take any interest in Tertiary fossils from Malta, Spain, etc. ? I got a considerable number of fossil shells in those regions last winter, and should be very glad to send you any that might interest you.

"I had hoped to be at Leeds, at the meeting, and had almost made arrangements to do so, but was kept at home by work in my parish. I was meditating a paper on the Sahara, but it must keep, D.V., till next year. Perhaps Aberdeen may tempt you to explore a kindred geological period to your Devonian. I saw with great interest the notice of your paper before the Association."

Mrs. Pengelly to her Mother.

"*October* 18, 1858.— . . . Dr. Falconer is intensely interested about the flint knives, and thinks he has discovered a larger implement, by joining some of the pieces together—they are sent up to the British Museum for the Savans to see. . . . I enclose an autograph of Charles Landseer, which Mrs. Percy gave me. He has the care of the Royal Academy, and it is said never hangs his own pictures well, which I think is very nice of him. We spent a delightful evening with him at the Percys', and had a good view of the splendid Comet, with Arcturus in the middle of the tail. . . ."

In addition to the exploration at Brixham, Pengelly found time to visit other Devonshire caves, amongst them a small cavern south of Berry Head, but no fossils of particular interest were found there.

Mrs. Pengelly to her Mother.

"*March*, 1859.— . . . We had a very pleasant evening, though disappointed of one of our friends ; but Mr. Gosse and his son Edmund (a nice boy),* Joseph Lister † and Arthur Lister, Miss Tuke, and others came. The gentlemen had all been with William to the cavern. We heard many interesting anecdotes about natural history, one story seeming to call out half a dozen others. . . ."

Mrs. Pengelly to her Mother.

"*April*, 1859.— . . . To-day I had the pleasure at William's lecture of watching Sir Roderick Murchison, as he sat between Miss Coutts (whose guest he is) and Mrs. Brown. He is rather a heavy-looking man, and does not interest you so much as Falconer, Prestwich, or Ansted ; but he is very pleasant and friendly. He is going this

---

* Edmund Gosse, the critic and poet.
† Now Lord Lister, the eminent surgeon.

G

morning with William to Hope's Nose, and to-morrow to Brixham and Berry Head. . . ."

During the spring of this year Pengelly took a short geological ramble, and made careful investigations amongst the numerous Devonshire caves. Indeed, his labours in this direction occupied so much time that one wonders how he was able to carry on his teaching and lecturing simultaneously. His geological journal abounds with descriptions of the caves, and he gives a graphic picture of one which he visited on April 22, 1859—

". . . Left Plympton for Totnes by first train. Walked thence to Buckfastleigh, to see the caverns said to be numerous there. It does seem to be the very metropolis of caverns, at least, so far as Devonshire is concerned. That which enjoyed the highest reputation was in a quarry, termed 'Baker Pits,' on the hill on which the church stands; indeed, it is immediately adjacent to the churchyard. Understanding it to be very large and intricate, I judged it best to secure a guide, and, after a good deal of trouble, was so fortunate as to find the cousin of the very quarryman who discovered the cavern, or rather laid it open by quarrying, about twelve years ago. The discoverer is named William Wilcocks, and my guide is named George Wilcocks, a lime-burner. We found it a desolate affair; huge masses of rock, which had fallen from the roof, lay in the wildest confusion, and strangely grotesque stalactites hung from the roof and lined the sides. Desolation, adorned with the most fantastic trappings, stared me in the face. The farthest point we reached, and which seemed to be the end, measured four hundred and eleven feet from the mouth. The mouth is itself a sort of funnel, twenty feet wide, and at its inner end is so small that a large man would scarcely pass through. So far as I could judge, the cavern may be said to consist of a series of chambers connected by galleries, with many under vaultings and lateral recesses. In some places the surfaces are much corroded, and in others they are eroded. About half-way in from the entrance the musical voice of running water was heard; it proved to be a small stream, but probably, in rainy seasons, would be considerably larger. No fossils have been met with, but it does not appear that any search has been made for them."

Mrs. Pengelly to her Mother.

"*April* 29, 1859.— . . . We have seen a good deal of Sir Roderick Murchison this week, dining with him and a large party at Miss Coutts' one evening; Lady Brownlow, Lord Churston, and many others were there. The next day William took Sir Roderick to visit the cave, and then joined Miss Coutts and party to lunch at Lord Churston's. The day after, Miss Coutts and Sir Roderick and Lady Murchison came to see the fossils—the latter is a most bright and pleasant old lady—and they talked a great deal about Russia; they seem to have been much attached to the late Emperor.* Sir Roderick stayed to luncheon, and then went for a geological ramble with William, round Lincombe Hill to Babbacombe and Petit Tor. In the evening met all of them again at a large party at Mr. Farrer's. Lady Brownlow, Mrs. Spring Rice, etc., there. It was a most pleasant evening. . . . To-morrow the Murchisons leave. Sir Roderick was speaking to-day of poor Hugh Miller; he says he completely brought on his illness and sad death by anxiety and overwork, and was going to tell me more, but was called away. . . ."

These rambles were followed by a visit to London, where Pengelly saw a good deal of Charles Babbage, who was much interested in the caves.

Pengelly to his Wife.

" *London, May* 20, 1859.— . . . I attended the Royal Society Club dinner; met Barlow, Sabine, Percy, Sir James Ross, etc. Went then to the Chemical, then to the Royal Society, where I met Babbage, and engaged to call on him shortly. Then with Percy to his house, just to see Mrs. Percy; all extremely kind, with kind inquiries after you. . . ."

Pengelly to his Wife.

" *London, May* 24, 1859.— . . . Yesterday I called on Babbage before the meeting. He was most agreeable, breakfasting in his library, which is really the den of a true literary man. He is greatly interested in the revelations made, and questions suggested, by caverns. He is preparing a paper which he thinks will at least show that Falconer's Palermian Caves do not *compel* us to believe that man is of such very high antiquity; his hypothesis is ingenious. . . . The Geographical dinner was a brilliant affair; it was held in the Freemasons' Hall, which was extremely well filled. . . . I sat next Rupert-Jones, and next to him was Balmat, the famous Swiss guide. Sir Roderick was supported by the Duke of Wellington and Lord Salisbury. The speakers before I left (soon after ten) were Sir T. Pasley, Sir John Pakington, the Earl of Ripon, the Danish Minister, and Lord Carnarvon, who was on his feet when I left. . . ."

During his stay in London (on Friday, May 27, 1859), Pengelly gave an evening lecture at the "Royal Institution," entitled "The Ossiferous Caverns and Fissures of Devonshire," in which he briefly explained his views on the probable origin of caverns in general, and on the Windmill-hill Cave at Brixham in particular. He concluded with some remarks as to the remains of extinct animals, which were found there in conjunction with "flint knives" of human manufacture, and the important

* Nicholas I.

bearing which these facts had on the antiquity of the human race.

The following month there are several letters from Pengelly to his wife, who was away visiting.

"*Torquay, June* 4, 1859.— . . . Feeling that it is time to give you some account of myself and my doings, I put on my retrospective cap, and take up my pen to furnish you with a record. Yesterday, I started soon after two, with Mr. Robertson and Mr. Carrol, for the Brixham Cavern in the yacht *Edith ;* we had a pleasant sail there and back, but found nothing *fresh* at the cavern, and very much that was *stale* in the Brixham odours. . . . I spent the evening letter-writing, and received a letter from Mr. Bastard, granting me permission to see the cave at Yealmpton. I think I told you yesterday I had written Owen offering him the Oreston bones, and also that I had been informed of the exhumation of more bones at Oreston. I started for Plymouth to-day at 11.30, found Robert Were Fox and his daughters in the train at Newton ; they gave me a pressing invitation to visit them at Falmouth. At the ferry I was joined by a Mr. Hodge, a good mineralogist, and a fair geologist, residing at Plymouth. He was aware of the recent ' find,' and was on his way to the quarry as well as myself. I purchased all the bones. . . ."

"*June* 5, 1859.— . . . This morning brought me a letter from Keep- ing (his head-workman at the cavern), announcing the discovery of gravel with a flint knife on the summit of the hill, sixty feet above the Cavern ; also a letter from Faraday. . . ."

"*June 6th.*— . . . Yesterday evening I took a stroll through the Abbey grounds and on to the new railroad,* just to keep up my geography. What a superb burst Torbay and Torquay will be to the stranger, who first beholds them from this station. I saw a thousand things in the sections of the line, that cry aloud to be fully worked out. . . ."

"*June 7th.*— . . . As I intended I went to Brixham yesterday, whence I have just returned. I have worked like a slave for a couple of hours, digging at the greatest depths we have yet reached, I was so fortunate as to exhume a large bone. We have now four labourers at work, so as to make a finish before midsummer. You never saw so filthy a wretch as I was on emerging. I attracted great attention ! . . ."

"*June* 8, 1859.— . . . Notwithstanding my visit to, and labour in the cavern yesterday, in order that no grass might grow under my feet, I took boat at 4.30 for Livermead Head, where I got some good Beekites, and was much interested in the caverns there, of which I had never seen so much before. This morning I took an early breakfast, and at 8.15 went to assist poor Miss Phillips, by giving her a lesson in the art and mystery of the ' Rule of Three,' which she is

* Then being made.

suddenly called upon to teach, but which she has never learned, poor thing ! I did my best for her, but it is sad to think of any one undertaking to teach a thing of which they really have no knowledge. On my way to her, I got your nice letter, for which many thanks. I saw the gravel at the top of the hill at Brixham yesterday, and the flint Keeping had found in it. It is perhaps no more than an accidental fracture, but I am by no means sure. There are no indications of bones, but the gravel is a great fact, and jumps quite in harmony with my conclusions respecting the origin of what I call the 'Berry Head Terrace.' . . . I began to put my library in order ; nothing having been done since we left, it is not by any means finished, but I have done a good stroke there. I then went to the Infirmary meeting, where and when a new house surgeon was appointed. Then home again at the library. Then did some gardening. . . ."

"*June 9th.*— . . . I have been at the library again all the afternoon ; no order visible yet. . . ."

Amongst Pengelly's pupils at this period were two nephews of the Czar, Alexander II.; the elder, Prince Nicholas, who was appointed by the Czar, in 1861, inspector of all the mines in his dominions, said, when leaving, "I shall often think of Mr. Pengelly."

"*June 10, 1859.*— . . . I called on Colonel Rehbinder, and engaged to read six hours weekly with the two Russian princes.* I have been to Barton this afternoon getting fossils for Oxford. At Barton a lime-burner took me to his cottage, to see 'such a specimen,' and indeed it is a good thing. 'Well,' said I, 'how much do you want for it ?' 'Why, sir, if you waz a downright regalar gentleman, and had a got your thousands upon thousands every year, hang me if you should ha'n for less nor half a crown, but since 'tes as 'tes, you may ha'n for a shilling ;' and for a shilling I obtained it. . . ."

"*June 12, 1859.*— . . . Though I have just sent off a budget, that does not seem any reason why I should not begin another. Last evening I had a short walk with J. Lister, always a treat. I have just read the first chapter in Bunsen's 'Signs of the Times,' and have been intensely interested. . . . The library is finished, and looks quite inviting. The Oxford fossils are not yet gone ; I am really working hard about them, going all the world over for them. They ought to be of prime quality, remembering who is the *donor* and who the *donee*. . . . I took boat at three for the Oreston, and never had a finer geological day. I came back richly laden with fine specimens. . . ."

"*June 14th.*— . . . Took 'bus to Brixham, went to the cavern, saw all right there, and then off to Mudstone to seek fossils for Oxford ; I have enjoyed the day. I have just written to R. W. Fox of Falmouth, respecting the Longitude of the Perihelion, and Ascending

* Nephews of the Czar Alexander II.

Nodes of the Planets, a subject on which we have frequently conversed. . . ."

"*June* 15, 1859.— . . . This morning brought me three letters, one from you, one from Prestwich, and one from Vincent of the Royal Institution. That from Prestwich, contained the information that Falconer is home. . . . I started off in proper time for the rush on the Russian princes. I saw them in the Apsley grounds shooting, with Mr. Stewart the surgeon. The boys soon came to me, and I began with the younger, a nice chatty little fellow, so very chatty, indeed, that had I felt inclined I might have known how many pairs of stockings he had, or anything else in his power to communicate, but of course I checked his loquacity. I only remember that his mother is expected here next month. The elder boy is equally agreeable, but less chatty. The engagement promises to be very pleasant, they are thoroughly simple. The *Athenæum* is very interesting this week; I have been much pleased with an abstract of a paper read before the Society of Antiquaries, 'On the occurrence of Flint Implements in undisturbed beds of Gravel, Sand, and Clay (such as are known to Geologists under the name of Drift) in several Localities, both on the Continent and in this Country.' . . ."

"*June* 18th.— . . . I was so extremely negligent yesterday, that I did not write you even one line. I was up early gardening, or rather cutting laurels; I have made such a slaughter amongst them, all round the garden. Whilst thus engaged, came there a note from Mrs. Yorke,* stating that she had returned, and inviting me to accompany her on the water in the afternoon. I wrote a note accepting the invitation, and fixing two o'clock as the starting hour, and stipulated to be on shore again at six, as I had previously engaged to go for a row with Mrs. Mallock and her party. At the right time, I went to the Russian princes; the younger is not very industrious, the elder, I think, is, and is desirous of distinction. I find that he is sixteen, and his brother twelve. We get on very nicely. Soon after two, I met Mrs. Yorke, on the quay, and we started across the bay. I landed at Brixham, in order to see how they were going on at the cavern; and then walking on to Mudstone to rejoin the yacht, Mrs. Yorke came in the punt for me, and we then examined that glorious coast, on the south of Berry Head, and went into the great cavern. I do not know when I have enjoyed a thing so very, very much; but, lo and behold, half-past five had come, and we were there still ! I was at once landed to go again to the cavern. Mrs. Yorke returned to the yacht, to pick me up once more at Brixham; the wind was against us, and consequently we reached Torquay at eight instead of six. So far from Keeping being glad that his time is almost up, I believe him truly sorry. I have copied my list of the Devonshire Cave Fossil Mammalia for J. Lister. . . ."

"*June* 21st.— . . . I went to Teignmouth by 10.10 train this morning, crossed the ferry, and walked under the cliff, almost to

* A geological pupil.

Maidencombe, and then returned to Teignmouth, carefully noting the prominent facts connected with the conglomerates; in fact it may with as much propriety be called *Breccia* as conglomerate. Many of the stones are astonishingly angular; and yet they have probably travelled far, as I know of no parent rock near, whence they could have been derived. Thereby hangs a puzzle, as I need not tell you. 'What was the agent of transportation?' . . ."

"*June* 22, 1859.— . . . I arranged some fossils, and reached Apsley House as appointed at three o'clock. On arriving there I found two carriages, into one of which the princes, Dr. Tillner (who speaks English, and is probably a German), and I got. In the other carriage were Colonel Rehbinder and Professor Bauer. We were about an hour in the cave, and saw it pretty thoroughly, and the whole party were pleased. We then proceeded in the same order to the cave at Ansty's Cove. Dr. Tillner and I became very chatty; he tells me that it is most likely they will remain here all the coming winter. From Ansty's Cove we took different routes. The colonel and professor returning directly home, whilst our carriage drove round to drop me at my own door. . . . The last *Athenæum* is worth looking at. The first article is 'Recollections,' by Rogers, and is charming; the second on 'Hallucinations,' almost fearful, and fascinating; then a somewhat interesting notice of books on America, but I am not going on *seriatim* (absurd affectation, speak English like a man or rather *write* it). There is an interesting letter, by Wright the antiquary, on the papers by Prestwich and Evans on their Flint Implements in the Drift. .n the list of meetings for the ensuing week there is an 'Extraordinary Meeting of the Geological Society at 8 p.m. on Wednesday (yesterday), to hear 'Further Observations on the occurrence of Human Art in the Bone Breccia in the Caves near Palermo,' by Dr. Falconer, and 'Reports on the Exploration of the Cave at Brixham,' by Dr. Falconer, also 'On Flint Implements recently obtained from the Gravel near Amiens,' by Mr. Flower. Flints are undoubtedly to the fore. . . ."

"*June* 26, 1859.— . . . There is an end to most things, I suppose; at any rate, the end of the Listers' tarriance here has come, so far as I am concerned at least. I shook hands with J. J. Lister this evening, and there is no prospect that I shall see him again, for some time at least. And the longest day, too, has been with us, and is gone, and shorter and still shortening ones will soon be here. I feel that I am the same person that some years ago wished Time would be less tardy in his movements; one might almost question one's own identity, for now I would rather that he would 'reserve his flight,' that is to say, as far as I am concerned, *not* society. I do not believe in 'Good Old Times,' taking 'Old' in the most limited signification, or any other. But enough of this. . . . I begin to see *land* ahead, but it may be mist merely; but I will confess to a hope that it is land, and that I may see you home this week. I hope you will remain until Saturday, if you desire to do so, or your mother wishes it; nevertheless, I will now say, and I think this is the first time I have allowed you to infer so much, that it is sadly dull here without you. I am pleased with Alfred's letter.* I think the journey is not likely to be thrown away on him; he clearly has a decided taste for Natural History, and will of necessity love the country. . . . This afternoon I wrote Salter and Prestwich. Did I tell you I had found a remarkable fossil at Mudstone? It is very much of the character of the Polperro sponges, *alias* fish; but much more definite in outline, than I have previously seen. I am most sceptical as to its being a sponge. Gosse called here and had a chat this afternoon. . . ."

In one of his letters at the conclusion of the Brixham Cavern exploration he writes :—

"*June* 27, 1859.— . . . We closed our labours at the cavern on Saturday evening last, Philp having allowed us to work a day and a half beyond the hour to which we were legally entitled. The workmen are all discharged, the key is returned to Philp, all the specimens not already in town, are at my house. . . . I felt a little sorry to give up the cavern. I have spent a good many hours there since last March, when I first visited it. . . ."

The Grand Duchess Marie, sister of Alexander II. of Russia, daughter of the Emperor Nicholas I., and widow of the Duke of Leuchtenberg, was at Torquay with her family in August of this year.

Mrs. Pengelly to her Mother.

"*August* 17, 1859.— . . . This morning we had a two hours' visit from the Russian Princess Eugénie, the Countess Tolstoi, and one of the tutors. We were extremely pleased with them all. The Princess is not pretty, rather small features, a very good forehead, and evidently very intelligent, and extremely interested in what William told her. They looked at the corals and fossils, etc., which she seemed to understand thoroughly, and asked leave to come again and bring the younger ones, who were much disappointed at not coming with them this morning. . . . I had a good deal of conversation with the Countess Tolstoi; she told me the eldest princess was on a visit to the Queen at Osborne with her mother the Grand Duchess, and that they were greatly pleased with the Isle of Wight. She said the young princes and princesses are so happy here. I said, 'I suppose on account of being so near the sea.' 'Oh no,' she said, 'they have a palace on the seashore, a very magnificent one; but they enjoy being here and living in a plain simple way.' The Grand Duchess telegraphed to the Emperor the other day after her arrival here, 'This is Paradise.' . . ."

Mrs. Pengelly to her Mother.

" . . . William went yesterday to Newton, with the Russian party, to a little picnic in the Bradley Woods valley; they seemed to enjoy

* His son by his first marriage.

it very much, and the little princess kept saying, 'Oh, it is so nice! I am so happy!' She had a hammer which the tutor had bought for her, and which soon broke. 'Oh!' she said, 'this is too fine, too pretty; I must have a large one like Mr. Pengelly's.' William says she is a witch, for he never found so many good fossils before. Like so many of his pupils, she enjoys her lessons greatly, and is much attached to him; Countess Tolstoi says she keeps running to the window to see if he is coming. One day he had a very pleasant interview with the Grand Duchess. The Princess Eugénie said the other day after leaving us, 'I would rather have Mr. Pengelly's fossils than all my diamonds. . . .'"

During September, the British Association met at Aberdeen. Pengelly was now beginning to take a prominent and useful part in the proceedings of Section "C"; and the meeting was especially noteworthy to him, as the question of the antiquity of man was warmly debated.

Mrs. Pengelly to her Mother.

"*September.* . . . William is very much occupied in preparing his paper for the British Association meeting at Aberdeen. I have drawn three large diagrams for it. I went on Friday to see the Grand Duchess, by invitation, and we were introduced to the Princess Mary, who has now arrived here, and is very nice. We paid a most pleasant visit, but I am sorry to say the Princess is not at all well, she is certainly a most interesting girl. The Countess gave a charming present to little Lydia, who went with me by particular invitation, and of whom they made a great pet. . . . The Channel Fleet are here now, fourteen of those splendid vessels including the 'Royal Albert.' . . ."

Pengelly to his Wife.

"*Aberdeen, September* 16, 1859.— . . . The meeting is a very large one. There are said to be two thousand seven hundred persons; if so, it surpasses Dublin, and ranks as one of the largest meetings. This, no doubt, is partly owing to the prince;* and truly he does seem to be very amiable and intellectual. . . . Many of my old friends are here, and all extremely cordial. Peach and I fraternize charmingly. Lyell's introductory address was a masterpiece of ability and frankness, mainly on the question of human chronology. The papers in our Section, *i.e.* Geology—the only one I attended—were good, and drew forth much valuable discussion. After the meeting Peach took me to call on Mrs. Hugh Miller. Sir W. Jardine, with his two daughters, and Symonds of Pendock, entered with us, so that she had a sort of *levée.* By some mistake at the soirée, the doors were not opened until 8.45 instead of 7.15 as was expected; the result was an assembly of about two thousand persons in the street waiting to enter, and about as

---

* Prince Albert was President that year.

many more to see them, with a strong body of police to keep
order. . . ."

To the Same.

"*Aberdeen, September* 17, 1859.— . . . Yesterday was a good day
here; I speak as a member of Section " C." The fourth paper was by
Rev. Dr. Anderson (author of a book in my library, under the title of
' The Course of Creation'), ' On Human Remains in Superficial Drift,'
in which he attacked all the evidence which has recently been produced
of ' Man amongst the Mammoths,' and a very great deal which no one
ever regarded as bearing on the question. After wading through a
great amount of rubbish, he boldly attempted to castigate Lyell for his
opening address; next he ridiculed Horner's argument of the pottery, etc.,
in the silt of the Nile. (Lady Lyell was within a couple of yards of him.
I did feel for her, more especially as she is so sweet and charming, to
be thus compelled to witness a bungler, mangling both her husband and
father.) Then he ran off to Germany to cudgel Bunsen, then back
again, pitched me into Brixham Cave, and did his best to bury the Cave
and myself in ridicule, and finally he gave us a yard or two of bad pulpit.
There was a considerable amount of orthodoxy in the room, and he got
a very undue share of applause. And now *per contra.* Lyell handled
him as a gentleman and a philosopher alone can do it. Next Phillips,
having rubbed his hands in oil, smoothed him down, but in such a way
as to scarify him; then Ramsay seized him by the button-hole, and
informed him of a fact or two connected with caverns, and finally
handed him over to me, upon which I seized him by the collar, dragged
him into Brixham Cave, and showed him its facts and their whereabouts.
Then came Symonds * and pulpited him. A few papers followed, and
then I read my paper, which was well received. . . . Last night Sir
Roderick delivered a lecture on the Geology of the North of Scotland—
a very able performance—after which a deputation from the Royal
Society of Edinburgh was introduced by the Chairman, and a gold
medal from the body they represent was presented by them to Sir
Roderick. . . ."

Pengelly to his Wife.

" *Aberdeen, September,* 1895.— . . . This evening I took a ramble to
Old Aberdeen, a distance of fully two miles; it seems a very decaying
old place, and a great and striking contrast to the New Town. Yesterday
I accompanied the ——s to tea with a person who has declined business,
having made a fortune. It was a very stiff affair. —— has realized a
good competency by trade, and hence must possess trade ability; but
that I contend is no proof of intellect, or it proves that trade sometimes
dries up our mentality. Be that as it may, I would rather be an inmate
of a Union Workhouse, with such powers as God has given me, than be
in the condition of Mr. —— (who boasted of having no interest in science
of any kind) for all the wealth that has ever been represented by all the
ledgers in existence. . . ."

* Rev. W. S. Symonds, Rector of Pendock.

Pengelly to his Wife.

"*Aberdeen, September* 19, 1859.— . . . You are anxious to know whom I have seen.   Well, then, I have seen, and been cordially received by, Murchison, Lyell, Owen, Phillips, General Portlock, Peach, Sorby, Ramsay, Hopkins, and all the stone-breaking fraternity.   Whether they have done wisely or not, I will not say, but they fully recognize me as a descendant of Thor, like themselves. . . ."

Pengelly to his Wife.

"*British Association, Aberdeen, September* 20, 1859.—Yesterday was a great day in Section "C."   In the Committee Room Lyell showed us a green stone instrument which had been given him in Aberdeen, during the present meeting, by a gentleman who five years ago saw a savage use it in Australia for the purpose of opening a tree.   Allowance being made for the difference of material, it was so precisely like the *flint* knives found in the *drift* at Abbeville, that the most sceptical must admit the latter to be of human origin.   Sir Charles also stated that in the recent drainage of the Haarlem lake no human bones had been found, though history assures us that positively thousands of bodies have fallen into it in the course of centuries.   In the Section, Moore of Bath read a valuable paper on Brachiopoda, which drew an eulogy from Owen.   A letter from Dr. Dawson to Sir Charles Lyell, stating that an air-breathing mollusk had been found in the carboniferous rocks of the South Joggings of Nova Scotia—a valuable fact, no such thing being previously known to occur below the Cainozoic rocks.   Then came a great discussion between Nicol and Murchison, supported by Ramsay, on the rocks of the North-west Highlands—a highly important, though local, subject.   Then a great series of papers on the Stagonolepis of Elgin, Huxley showing it to be a reptile of high order, and the other geologists showing that there is reason to believe the rock in which it was found is *Devonian.*   In the evening I dined with the 'Red Lions;' a most splendid time, Owen being Lion-in-chief.   After this I went to a lecture by Dr. Robinson of Armagh on Electricity."

Pengelly to his Wife.

"*Aberdeen, September* 21st.— . . . We had a capital day yesterday. Sedgwick opened in his own style, with a paper on the Lake district. Then came Rogers, on the Parallel Roads of Glen Roy, producing some new and important facts, and a monstrous hypothesis.   The other papers were of less interest, but excellent.   At the soirée, Anderson and I had a somewhat long and animated discussion on the flint knives. He informs me that Professor Macdonald is to lecture on 'Man' to-night (Wednesday), and is intending to 'pound me to dust.' . . ."

Pengelly was included among the members of the association, who, during the progress of the Aberdeen meeting, were honoured by an invitation to Balmoral.   Unfortunately the weather on the day of the visit turned out wet and stormy.   As several accounts of the expedition have already been recorded in other Memoirs, and as her Majesty has also mentioned it, in that part of her journal which has been given to the public, any further account of it is unnecessary.

Before leaving Scotland he received a kind and pressing invitation from Sir George Sinclair to stay at Thurso Castle, which time would not permit him to accept; this was the more disappointing as it prevented his making the acquaintance of Robert Dick of Thurso, who was already attracting the attention of geologists, as an active and successful worker.

Greatly as he enjoyed meeting scientific friends, Pengelly always looked forward eagerly to a return to his family and his quiet home at Torquay. His son Alfred was now old enough to accompany him on some geological expeditions, and was already distinguished by a love of Natural History, and great success in athletic sports and other open-air amusements. Mary Anne (the only remaining daughter of his first marriage) had died during the year, tenderly nursed to the last by her step-mother, to whom she was much attached.

Mrs. Pengelly had now a little daughter of her own, named Lydia, but generally called " Trottie " in her father's letters.

Late in the autumn of 1859, at a public dinner in Torquay, in response to an unanimous call for a speech, Pengelly pointed out that it was rather unwise to couple his name so frequently with the toast of " Prosperity to Torquay," lest it should become an established custom for him to respond to it. Speaking of the attractions of the place, he recommended as an addition " the establishment of a County Museum of Natural History in this town, which held out greater inducements than either Plymouth or Exeter. The district was rich in natural history. A large number of visitors came here in the winter for their health's sake ; and those visitors would be very thankful to the inhabitants, for providing the means of spending their time in a way not injurious, but beneficial to body and mind. The intellectual prosperity of the town must be looked to ; and geology, as an intellectual research, was very interesting." He concluded by strongly advocating the claims of the Natural History Society, the Mechanics' Institute, and the Working Men's Society.

CHAPTER VIII.

LECTURES AT THE ROYAL INSTITUTION, AND PAPERS READ BEFORE THE BRITISH ASSOCIATION.

1860 TO NOVEMBER, 1861.

IN 1860, Pengelly completed the formation of a fine collection of Devonian fossils, from the counties of Devon and Cornwall, which was presented in that year, by the Baroness Burdett Coutts, to the New Museum of the University of Oxford, in connection with the foundation of a geological scholarship. The fossils are known as "The Pengelly Collection," as indicated by the following regulation passed in a Congregation of the University of Oxford on February 16, 1860:—"The collection of Devonian fossils presented by A. Burdett Coutts shall be named 'The Pengelly Collection,' in honour of the gentleman whose scientific knowledge has enabled the foundress to make the collection."

Mrs. Pengelly to her Mother.

"*February* 17*th*.— . . . Much enjoyed the evening on Thursday at Miss Coutts' to meet Archdeacon Mackenzie, the new Bishop for Central Africa (sent out by the special fund raised at Oxford and Cambridge), and also the Bishop of Derry and his wife, and many others. Miss Coutts has lent us the printed regulations from Oxford, in relation to the Burdett-Coutts Scholarship, to read. William's collection of fossils, which he has made to be presented to the University, is by her wish to be called 'The Pengelly Collection.' Have you seen the very appreciative notices of it in the *Times*, and other papers? Dr. Falconer told me of them to-day, and seemed much pleased. William is reading Myers's Sermons to Miss Coutts, Mrs. Brown, and Rajah Brooke, and they are greatly interested, the latter says he shall get them. Lady Charles Wellesley is staying there now, and we like her very much. . . ."

Princess Mary of the Netherlands had now joined the ranks of Pengelly's pupils, and proved both agreeable and intelligent.

Mrs. Pengelly to her Mother.

"*March* 17, 1860.— . . . We spent an interesting evening with Sir John Bowring at Mr. Beasley's. Sir John looks much older than I expected—a keen, thin, and intellectual, worn face, with great animation. He is a capital talker and full of information. We talked of my old friends, the Ashworths; he says they were for some time at his house at Shanghai, but are now in London. Sir John Kennaway was there also, and we were invited to meet them the next evening at Mr. Vivian's, but had engaged to go to Miss Coutts'. . . . William has been, with the Prince and Princess of the Netherlands and the Russian Princes, to the Cavern; he is much pleased with the two latter, especially Nicholas the elder, who is reading Dr. Kane's Arctic Travels with him with great interest. They are coming to us one evening to look through the telescope. We had a long visit last week from Lord and Lady ——. He prides himself on having the best collection of marbles, I believe, in England; but some of the party appeared amusingly ignorant on some points, inquiring if our corals, etc., were Antediluvian! . . ."

At this time Pengelly also was actively engaged in a systematic examination of the deposits at Bovey. Sir Charles Lyell considered the work of great importance, and on its conclusion induced him to communicate a paper, entitled "The Lignites and Clays of Bovey Tracey," to the Royal Society.[*]

This work was supplemented by Dr. Oswald Heer's account of "The Fossil Flora of Bovey Tracey." The essays were reprinted, with a preface, as a separate volume, in 1863, with a dedication addressed to the Baroness Burdett Coutts, who had generously undertaken the expenses of the publication. Mr. Starkie Gardner's subsequent studies of the fossil flora of Bovey Tracey, have modified opinions respecting the origin and age of the deposits, and some doubt has been thrown on Heer's conclusions; but Pengelly's work is still considered to be of great scientific value.

Mrs. Pengelly to her Mother.

"*April 7th.*— . . . William is greatly interested in going about with Sir Charles Lyell, yesterday and to-day. It happened rather nicely, as he is taking a holiday just now, for a few days; so he was quite at liberty to go with him, and Sir Charles seemed intensely interested in the raised beach at Hope's Nose, etc.—had his note-book in his hand the whole time, and fully endorses William's views on the geology of this neighbourhood, which is entirely new to him. To-day they are going to Brixham, Berry Head, etc. Last night we had a nice long call from Robert Were Fox of Falmouth, who is taking his

---

[*] *Phil. Trans. Roy. Soc.*, vol. clii. (1862), p. 1019.

daughter Anna Maria away for a little tour to recruit.   He says his daughter Caroline is too ill to accompany them.   They are both nearly laid by with doing so much for the 'Navvies,' establishing Reading Rooms, etc., for them."

Sir Charles Lyell to Pengelly.

"*April* 8, 1860.— . . . Dr. Falconer leaves with me by the ten o'clock train to-morrow, for Newton, to go thence, and do what we can in the Bovey Coal-Field.

"He asked me to ask you for a note to Miss (Cooke?), the daughter of the late collector of fossil leaves of the Bovey Coal— also for any instructions you may have to give us, as to points to visit; but I think I understood you that we were to go to Bovey Tracey.

"The problem to be solved at Torquay is not only the relative age of three deposits—

" 1. The cave-deposits, including Kent's Hole with *Machairodus*, an oldish form? and *Hippopotamus?* which Owen, I believe, says came from Kent's Hole.

" 2. The raised beach.

" 3. The submerged forest, with *Elephas primigenius;* the tooth dredged up from it having, says Falconer, rather the form of the more modern varieties of the Siberian mammoth.

"Not only have we to correlate all these three, but to get them into comparison as to their age with four deposits near Brighton.

" 1. Elephant-bed, Brighton.   *Elephas primigenius.*

" 2. Raised beach, with recent shells and rolled granite pebbles.

" 3. Erratics of French granite, nine feet diameter—Pagham near Selsea.

" Marine mud, with *Elephas antiquus* and thirty species of marine shells.

" The granite pebbles of the raised beach, No. 2, were derived from the older bed of glacial period, No. 3, of Sussex Coast.

"No. 4, a præ-glacial deposit, with shells not like recent British fauna. . . .

"Has Mr. Battersby any of the fossils of the Hope's Nose beach? and has he identified the *Cardium*, the large *Cardium*, with the long one of your bay? or who has given a list?"

Mrs. Pengelly to her Mother.

"*April* 13, 1860.— . . . We have had such a pleasant visit from the Princess Mary of the Netherlands, who is a pupil of William's now, and a most agreeable one; she is about eighteen, an extremely simple open-hearted girl.   To-day we have had a visit of two hours from Miss Coutts and her party, and William is gone there to dine to-night. . . . The last time we went the Prince and Princess W. were there, Sir Charles and Lady Lyell, etc. . . . The Prince and Princess of the Netherlands are returning home.   Princess Mary and Mademoiselle von Doorn often walk down to town to meet William, when he is on his way to give his lesson there, though it is before eight in the morning. . . ."

Mrs. Pengelly to her Mother.

"*April 21st.*— . . . Had a delightful evening at Miss Coutts', meeting Baron and Baroness Hoenick, Rajah Brooke, Dr. Falconer, etc. Sir Charles Lyell and Dr. Falconer have set their minds on William's working somewhat in the Bovey coal-beds, which he himself has long been anxious to do—they contain so many plants new to science. One evening lately we spent at Mrs. St. John's (Sir Joshua Reynolds' great-niece), with a very pleasant party. She has a good painting by Sir Joshua. . . . Sir Charles Lyell has left; he has sent William a geological map by Murchison. We have Murchison's 'Siluria,' which he sent us himself last year, with a kind letter of appreciation respecting William's geological work. . . ."

Sir Charles Lyell to Pengelly.

"*May 7, 1860.*— . . . I am very glad of the prospect of our knowing something of the Bovey coal-plants. It is almost a reproach to English geology that they have been so little explored, as they are perhaps the only fossils of the Tertiary period to which they belong. I shall be glad to hear that Keeping's services are retained.

"All Barrandés' grand discoveries in Bohemia, and splendid collection of unique Silurian and pre-Silurian fossils, were made by opening quarries expressly for his geological researches.

"In this case the old pits are flooded, and whether they (the proprietors) will pump out the water again seemed doubtful.

"But I am not afraid that Miss Coutts will not be rewarded by bringing to light at least so much of the ancient flora as will enable Heer of Zurich to settle the age of the formation relatively to the other lignite and brown-coal deposits of the Continent.

"The only Miocene plants discovered in the British Isles we owe to the Duke of Argyll's exertions in Mull.

"I am going to beg you to send me any corrections you can suggest for my 'Manual,' fifth edition, confining yourself at present to the first part (say up to p. 235), or any of the earlier pages, as the last half may be attended to some time hence. Besides positive mistakes, I shall be glad of any hints and suggestions made freely, which your knowledge of the manner in which beginners are struck with certain passages may enable you to send us.

"Dr. Falconer may depend on a large audience in Burlington House when he reads his paper on the Welsh Caves. . . ."

Mrs. Pengelly to her Mother.

"*May 24, 1860.*— . . . William left for London yesterday; he is going to stay with Dr. Skey, a very nice old gentleman of eighty-six, who has been spending the winter here. The little trip to Cornwall with Miss Coutts, Sir J. K. Shuttleworth, and Sir James Brooke,* he enjoyed

* Rajah of Sarawak.

exceedingly. To-morrow night he lectures at the Royal Institution on Devonian fossils, in reference to the Oxford scholarship. On his return home he will be much occupied, using all his spare time in examining the coal deposit of Bovey Tracey, towards the exploration of which Miss Coutts has contributed £50, and which both Falconer and Lyell are most earnest for him to undertake, as they say it is quite a disgrace to English geology not to know where rightly to place these beds. They contain palm leaves two feet long. Bovey is twelve miles from this, so it will be rather far for him to go; but he has secured Keeping —his head man at Brixham—who is most careful and trustworthy, to work under him there. . . ."

During May and June of this year Pengelly gave a course of geological lectures at the Royal Institution, which passed off very successfully.

Pengelly to his Wife.

" *London, May 26, 1860.*— . . . I then went off to call on Falconer, found him very cordial, agreed to dine with him at the Geological Club next Wednesday. On leaving the house I met Mrs. M'Call, Miss Milne, and their uncle. Next I went to the Royal Institution, to hang my diagrams, etc.; found my specimens had travelled well. Faraday most agreeable. This done, I called at Tennant's, on my way to the meeting. Met Ansted there, and had a good chat with him; a very agreeable man. I then went to Barlow's. The only stranger at dinner was Archdeacon Sinclair, whom I had met at Miss Coutts' more than once. The lecture went off satisfactorily, I believe, yet I did not think I was so untrammelled as usual; I had paid too much attention to preparation. The subject was also too large; yet it seemed to give satisfaction, and I was frequently applauded. The specimens were greatly admired after the lecture. The audience contained a good number of truly great men—Babbage, Faraday, Murchison (in the chair), Tyndall, Grove, Bigsby, Daubeny, Wheatstone, and others. I made the acquaintance of Grove and Daubeny. . . ."

" *London, May 29, 1860.*— . . . Yestermorn Dr. Skey and I sallied forth, immediately after breakfast, to call on Lyell; he received us very cordially. He and I went through all my criticisms on his 'Manual,' most of which he thankfully accepted, and reserved the rest for consideration. I left him soon after eleven. I then called on Babbage, and could not get away until after one. He is a splendid talker. He seemed much pleased to see me, and complimented me very much on my lecture, in which he was evidently much interested. He is the most marvellous worker I ever met with. I never saw anything like the evidence of multifarious and vast labour which his 'workshop' presents; he sticks at nothing. One drawer full of riddles, another of epigrams, one of squared words, etc. . . . It is appalling! And then the downright fun of the fellow; it is almost intoxicating to be with him! He was so kind as to give me a copy of his 'Ninth Bridgewater Treatise.' I dined with the Listers; there was a large party. . . ."

H

Pengelly to his Wife.

"*London, May* 31, 1860.— . . . The days are rapidly flitting by, and drawing my tarriance in the Modern Babylon swiftly to a conclusion. I had received an invitation to dinner from Samuel Gurney, and accordingly found myself in Lombard Street at the appointed hour. Many old friends were present, and an Ojibbeway Indian woman, who has been sent over by her tribe to plead their cause before the Great Mother (the Queen). Hitherto she has not been able to obtain an interview. She is a Christian, speaks choice English fluently, is very self-possessed, and might pass muster easily for a rather coarse-featured Englishwoman. . . . Yesterday I took Salter to see my fossils at the Royal Institution. Then came the Geological Club dinner, which I attended as Lyell's guest. I was well received by all; many of them were old friends. Amongst them were Horner, Murchison, Lyell, Percy, Godwin-Austen, Smyth, Lubbock, Prestwich, and Falconer. It went off capitally. I sat by Lyell, who told me spontaneously he would gladly vote for me as F.R.S.! My lecture was much and well spoken of. Then to the Geological Society, where two papers were read by Falconer on the Gower Caves. There was nothing new on the question of human chronology. A good discussion followed, in which Lyell, Austen, Prestwich, and I took part. . . ."

At the end of June, Pengelly attended the meeting of the British Association at Oxford, and gives some account of the proceedings in the following letters—

Pengelly to his Wife.

"*Exeter College, Oxford, June* 28, 1860.— . . . I find, after all, I did not send you my hasty scrawl of yesterday. But what of yesterday? . . . I went to hear the opening Address of the President at four. You are aware, I think, that it is usual to have this address and the lectures at eight; instead of that, they are to be given at four here. I do not think the change is popular; but it is said the authorities are under oath not to allow lights in the building we should use on these occasions after a certain hour. Prince Albert attended, and in a short speech resigned the Presidency to Lord Wrottesley, who then delivered his Address. The customary vote of thanks was moved by Lord Derby, and seconded by Whewell. Neither of them succeeded in making a very effective speech. After this to dinner at the Star Hotel—a villainous substitute for a meal; so bad, indeed, in every respect that a large party of us went in a body, headed by Professor Macdonald, to the bar, and stated that we would never dine there again. Well, now you want to know who are here. Murchison, Lyell, Horner, Falconer, Harkness, Shuttleworth, Sedgwick, Moore, Chambers, etc. Phillips is very friendly. Oxford is truly a superb place; the new museum is, or rather will be, magnificent. It is far from finished.

" Well, now I must close. I want my breakfast, and do not yet know where I am to get it. It appears that the authorities only provide us with lodgings, meals we find where we can, or if we prefer it we can go without.   A grand-daughter of Lady Blakiston, an old pupil of mine, claimed me as an acquaintance yesterday ; she is here with her husband, Lionel Beale, Professor of Physiology, King's College, London.   She seemed much pleased to see me again. . . ."

Pengelly to his Wife.

"*Oxford, June 29th.*— . . . Now then for yesterday.   First I went to the Inquiry Room, where I stumbled on Faraday, then to the Committee Room, after which to Section 'C.' Sedgwick's opening Address most characteristic, full of clever fun.   Most imperative that papers should be as brief as possible—about ten minutes he thought— he himself amplifying marvellously.   The papers were not of a high order yesterday, excellent no doubt in themselves, but not of general interest.   There was one by my friend Mr. Tristram, of Durham (the clergyman to whom I sent fossils), on the Sahara.   Well, now, whom did I see ? Prestwich, Salter, Bigsby, and lots of 'em.   The evening soirée was very good ; it was held in the New Museum, from 1800 to 2000 people seemed lost in it.   There I met Sir Charles and Lady Lyell, Falconer, etc., etc.   I find that Prestwich is just over my head, *i.e.* he has rooms in the college, just over mine.   I suppose the great event of yesterday was a paper by Dr. Daubeny on the Sexual Organs of Plants, with special reference to Darwin's theory.   A most smart discussion rose on it between Huxley and Owen.   I tried to get in, but the room was most densely packed.   One consequence of Sedg- wick's law about time was that the section got through its business so as to adjourn at two instead of three. . . ."

Pengelly to his Wife.

"*Oxford, June* 29, 1860, 11.30 p.m.— . . . This has been a very busy day.   In the morning got journals, then off to hang my diagrams, then to committee, and then section, where Dr. Daubeny read a paper on the Elevation-Crater theory, which of course brought up Lyell to defend himself.   This took an hour.   Then came a paper on Dolomitization, which took half an hour.   Then came mine.   Dear old Sedgwick wished it compressed.   I replied that, ' I would do what I could to please him, but did not know which to follow, his precept or example.'   The roar of laughter was deafening.   Old Sedgwick took it capitally, and behaved much better in consequence.   My paper was splendidly received, and drew forth an hour's discussion, in which Phillips, Austen, Salter, Jukes, etc., took part ; they all spoke highly of it, and many expressed a hope that it would be printed at full length.   We went off at the close of the section to hear Professor Walker lecture on the Sun ; it was a capital lecture.   A vote of thanks to Professor Walker was moved in an eloquent, though, as I think, unsound speech, by the Bishop of Oxford.   The unsoundness consisted in his laying it down as a law, that all things were made for man, and are useful ; in fact, this idea seemed to run through the lecture too.

"I begin to feel that a short time will close proceedings, and put me into harness again. . . ."

Pengelly to his Wife.

"*July* 1, 1860.— . . . Yesterday was a great day. Called on Mrs. Yorke by appointment to meet Moore of Bath, who was to show us his fossils. They are really wonderful, upwards of forty thousand fish teeth, and many thousands of other fossils, many of them microscopic, dug or rather picked out of three cart-loads of rubbish. Next to committee, where I found Sedgwick very cordial, took my address, and talks of paying me a visit. A paper by Mrs. Yorke's Genevese friend, M. Favre, on the 'Structure of the Alps,' was given in French, but it excited much attention. Then Moore's paper, which truly and deservedly astonished the section; Lyell and Falconer spoke on it. The latter said ' Mr. Moore was made for the Bone Bed, and the Bone Bed was made for him.' Then left Section 'C' and went to 'D' (Zoology) to hear a discussion on a paper which has direct reference to Darwinism. The room was densely packed. The Bishop of Oxford, Huxley, Dr. Hooker, Professor Beale, Lubbock, and others spoke on it. The excitement was excessive, quite as great as at a political meeting. . . ."

" *Exeter College, Oxford, July* 2, 1860.— . . . Several good papers at the sections to-day, especially one by a clergyman named Lister of Wolverhampton, on some Reptilian Footprints from the New Red sandstone north of Wolverhampton, a new locality, and therefore an important fact. We shall get them in our New Reds by-and-by. The section adjourned at two, to attend a meeting in the theatre, where the degree of D.C.L. was conferred on Lord Wrottesley, Sedgwick, and some one else, whose name I have forgotten ; it was a pretty spectacle. At three, to General Committee, and settled the next meeting shall be at Manchester. Then to theatre, to hear Sherard Osborn deliver a Lecture on Arctic Enterprise. At six to dinner with Professor Walker, in Hall at Wadham College. We were about a dozen, amongst others Professors Rankine and Earnshaw, Sir Edward Pechell, and Gassiot. Lots of fun. . . ."

Pengelly had now completed the notes which Sir Charles Lyell had asked him to supply for the fifth edition of his manual which was being prepared.

Sir Charles Lyell to Pengelly.

"*July* 2, 1860.— . . . I have been reading over your useful criticisms, all of which I have adopted or attended to, except where a recast of the page or chapter had already superseded the necessity of adopting them. I have to thank you much ; and shall only say a few words on your reference to Mr. Hopkins' paper, vol. viii., *Quart. Jour. Geol. Soc.*, which I am glad to have been called upon to read over again, as I might have omitted to do so.

" I had already considered it before the publication of my last edition of the Manual, but found it would take me more time and space than I could then afford to discuss it. So far as the Manual is concerned, I am almost in the same state of feeling now, but should have liked to have had a talk with you on the subject ; for, if I mistake not, you threw out some critical remarks on Hopkins' hypothesis of the change of the course of the Gulf Stream, when I was at Torquay, and I should be very glad if you would repeat them in a letter.

" My first difficulty is this. The glacial phenomena of the North American continent imply, I think, a more southern extension of the severe cold than do those of Northern Europe.

" Hopkins' theory, instead of helping us to comprehend this, diverts the Gulf Stream, so as to warm up the American side of the North Atlantic and cool the European side.

" 2. The delta of the Mississippi is, according to my notion, a hundred thousand or two hundred thousand years old. And prior to that was the older delta implied by the upraised 'loess' of Natchez, d, Fig. 23, 'Principles,' 9th Ed. p. 265 ; and the older deposit was, I think, more modern than the period of erratic blocks.

" All this time it is out of the question to suppose that the valley of the Mississippi was a bay of the sea, connecting the Gulf of Mexico with the Arctic region.

" Therefore we should have to throw back the Glacial Period very far, in order to admit Hopkins' hypothesis, etc. Now, I have no objection to give it an antiquity of several hundred thousand years, but this would make us suppose it contemporaneous with the European Northern drift, in which case I should require rather to cool the Gulf of Mexico than to make the hot waters of that Gulf flow northwards for a thousand miles or more.

" Nevertheless I am willing, on the other hand, to suppose great local developments of cold, owing to elevation of mountain chains and other combinations, so as to produce great north and south or meridional lines of glaciation, for that would help us to introduce Darwin and Hooker's migrations of North Polar species of plants and animals into the equatorial mountains, and thence into South Temperate zones, without a universal chill, or a simultaneous freezing of both hemispheres, annihilating in Pleistocene times all the tropical forms of vegetation, etc., and requiring a new creation of the same in Post-pleiocene times.

" Please to let me hear from you, if you have any thoughts on the subject, for or against Hopkins' scheme.

" I suspect that Hopkins is in error in imagining that in an island like Great Britain (or British Isles) there could not be an upheaval of several thousand feet without contortion of strata. Take the steepest of railway gradients, and see to what a vast height you may rise in a few hundred miles.

" In a hundred miles with a slope of an angle of two degrees, which would be to the eye horizontal, you would more than reach a height above the sea-level of three miles or the height of Mont Blanc.

" But I must not run on. I wish you merely to tell me whether you think there is so much weight in Hopkins' Gulf Stream diversion hypothesis, that I ought to modify my southern curve of the lines of cold in the Glacial Period, on comparing North America and Europe.

" My letters will be forwarded to me abroad wherever I may be after Friday next, 6th inst., when I leave after post-hour. But in case you write after that, do not write on very thin paper, as some of my friends do. Any news of the meeting after I left would be acceptable. I have just seen Baron Anca, who has really found the *Elephas Africanus* in the Sicilian caves, accompanying one of the extinct Sicilian Hippopotami. . . .

"Your paper on the Devonian fossils made a very favourable impression; and under less chilly auspices I should like to have said something on the conclusion to which it pointed. Shall you send it to the Geological Society?"

During August, 1860, the British Medical Association met at Torquay, and Pengelly, in response to a request from several medical friends, delivered a lecture before the members.

The lecture is thus referred to in a letter from an enthusiastic pupil. "The day I left Torquay I was in a railway carriage full of doctors, all speaking of your lecture the night before, and seeming delighted. They spoke of it with rapture. . . . "

Sir Charles Lyell had been consulted by Pengelly with reference to his collection of plants, and he wrote :—

Sir Charles Lyell to Pengelly.

"*December* 12, 1860.— . . . I have been considering what I should do, if I had myself collected the plants you allude to, and had to get them figured, for I should require the same kind of help which you are desirous of getting.

"As Dr. Hooker, who is just returned from Syria, and is overwhelmed with arrears of work accumulated in his absence, is out of the question, the next person I thought of as the most competent is Sir Charles Bunbury. But he will not be staying in town till February. I might get him to do something then; but he could not be hurried, and would take perhaps longer time to it than you could spare. Still I think he might help greatly in February.

"The other person whom I should turn to is Professor Morris, High Street, Kensington. You might address a letter to him, and say I suggested his assistance, and try to get an appointment. Perhaps you might offer to him, for the University College Museum, which is under his charge, a set of duplicates. I gave him some good fossil fish from the United States Trias, for that Museum, as an acknowledgment of some help he gave me in the geological way a year ago.

"Morris has written an Appendix to a paper of Prestwich on fossil plants of Colebrook-Dale Coal, and has studied also Tertiary plants, and would, I think, be a safe adviser. I will call in and see your plants; but, even if I were not most fully engaged in trying to get out my new edition, I really could not undertake the task for want of knowledge on the subject.

"I am glad to hear of your having so many specimens of palms.

"I can see no objection to the course you are taking, or in that proposal by me on the score of its interfering with Dr. Falconer. It must be desirable to get drawings made before some of the specimens fall to pieces, which they may do, if like those I saw at Bovey. . . .

"I saw Miss Coutts lately, and talked to her of your discoveries."

Some letters written by Pengelly to his son Alfred during this and the following year, are valuable, not only for the evidence they afford of his own occupations at this period, but also as showing his ready sympathy with his son's pursuits.

Pengelly to his Son.

" *Torquay, June* 7, 1860.— . . . I was extremely pleased to find you had been so successful in Chemistry. The failure in Geometry was to be regretted, but it is not irreparable, we will hope. I do not believe anything can compensate for a low amount of Geometrical knowledge; so read up and read hard, my boy. I rather regret your giving up your Entomology. 'A rolling stone gathers no moss,' it is said, and truly. If you have an *enlightened* conscientious objection to fly-catching it is clearly your duty to give up the practice, and I desire to encourage you to do so (in this matter as well as in all others). I quite think no one should destroy life without a sufficient motive, and in my judgment merely doing what others do is *not* a sufficient motive, nor are we justified as I think to take life in order that we may make a collection of things more or less pretty, and which, when well grouped and arranged, will make an attractive show. But if the object is *clearly* to study the works of Creation, I hold it to be a sufficient motive, and I should have no scruple to kill any infra-human animal in order the better to accomplish such object. If this is your view your duty is first to ask yourself, 'What is my object in killing insects?' This answered satisfactorily, I think you may safely kill them with a clear conscience; still, if you think otherwise, desist, for if you cannot clearly answer the question, you ought not to kill. So far as it is a question of cruelty, I cannot but think that the Aquarium is the worst. The animals in it generally die more or less lingeringly, while in the hands of a good entomologist, insects die suddenly and on the whole with greatly less pain; but still it is a matter of individual feeling and judgment. I must leave it to yourself.

Since I last wrote you I have been in town, and very much I enjoyed myself. I should like to spend some weeks there yearly. I reached London a little before midnight on 22nd ult. On Friday I dined with the Secretary of the Royal Institution, and afterwards gave my lecture to a good, and eminently scientific, audience. The subject was the *Devonian* fossils of Devon and Cornwall. I had compiled large tables showing the statistics of the question, *i.e.* the number of species in the various classes and their distribution in Time and Space. I took up seven trays of specimens for illustration. It is considerably more than a joke to lecture to an audience composed, as mine was, of such men as Faraday, Tyndall, Babbage, Grove, Daubeny, Wheatstone, Murchison, etc., and also a crowd of non-scientific folk; the task then becomes difficult, as a lecture is required to be at once profound and popular—a not very frequent combination of qualities, and perhaps not a desirable one. On Monday morning I called on Sir C. Lyell and spent two hours with him criticising his 'Manual.' Then I called on Babbage, the author or constructor of the calculating machine, one of the most remarkable and talented men the world has ever produced. On Wednesday I dined with the Geological Club; we were about thirty, including some of the most eminent geologists. After dinner we went to the Geological Society, where a paper was read by Dr. Falconer descriptive of some ossiferous caverns near Swansea; he made the astounding statement that between ten and eleven hundred antlers *of the Reindeer* had been taken out of ONE cavern. There is no manner of doubt about its correctness. On Friday, the last day I spent in town, I heard Dr. Tyndall lecture at the Royal Institution on a 'Winter Visit which he made to the Swiss Glaciers.' It was extremely interesting, and he is a truly charming lecturer. During my visit I was the guest of an old gentleman who wintered at Torquay last season; his name is Dr. Skey, he is eighty-six years of age, and very bright indeed."

Pengelly to his Son.

" *Torquay, May* 11, 1861.— . . . My last visit to town was a very agreeable one. My lecture was warmly applauded. I left home on Tuesday, so as to have a day at Oxford on my way, in order that I might have an opportunity of arranging the 'Pengelly' collection of fossils. I got there just in time for Dr. Daubeny's dinner (I think I told you I was to be his guest). We went in the evening to Magdalen College, at the invitation of the President thereof. Next day I arranged the fossils, and left for town at four o'clock. This I was sorry to do, as Dr. Daubeny had invited a large dinner-party of all the eminent men resident in the University to meet me. There was no help for it, however, as I had made a previous engagement in town. Before leaving, Dr. Daubeny informed me that a wish had been expressed by the Vice-Chancellor of the University that I would deliver a lecture on the 'Pengelly' collection of fossils before the University some time before June 10th. I reached town just in time for dinner, after which we all went to a large party at the Bishop of London's. I met Murchison there, who told me that all the geologists connected with the flint instrument question are to be immortalized in 'Punch' next week. Your dad in the number."

Pengelly to his Son.

" *Torquay, September* 1, 1861— . . . I fancy I ought to have written you this day week, but truly I am almost worked to death (that is a strong expression). My correspondence is becoming a grave affair. I have four papers for Manchester. I do not suppose I shall be able to get them all in, but that will not trouble me. I hope to leave this on Tuesday, and go on, with Mamma, next day to Manchester. I hope you are doing as much as you can towards the examination. Let me advise you very, very strongly against taking up more than one thing at a time. The classical subject and nothing else until that is fairly conquered, ditto mathematics, ditto Milton, etc., etc. Speaking of Milton, I strongly advise your reading the 'Paradise Lost' quite through from end to end, so as to get a general idea of the poem, then return to the two books, and take them up critically.

"There is a splendid critique on the poem by Addison in the *Spectator*, which you should read by all means. If it is not in your school library, it ought to be. I have engaged to deliver a course of six lectures on Geology at Norwich in January next.

"Heer, the Swiss Fossil-botanist, has made out forty-one species of plants at Bovey, and has pronounced the formation to be decidedly Miocene. I am extremely busy professionally now, have no time for gardening or geologizing."

Pengelly to his Son.

"*Torquay, October* 21, 1861.—I was sorry not to be able to write you as usual this day fortnight. I went to London the day before to look over the Bovey specimens with Dr. Falconer and Sir C. Lyell; they were both delighted with them. I dined and slept at Miss Coutts' residence at Highgate, and returned home on Monday. You probably remember that the huge pit at Bovey had a considerable quantity of water in it when you were there. I am happy to say that by the, for us, well-timed continuous pumping, which has been lately undertaken, the water is so far gone that we reach the bottom of the pit at the western end and work there with comfort. You will probably remember that the lignite beds were divided into two series, an upper and lower, by a thick bed of sand. We have made a complete section from top to bottom of the lower series, thereby revealing the thickness, character, and fossils of the beds, and of the clays, etc., by which they are separated. We purpose doing the same by the upper series, and shall probably begin to-morrow. I purpose going to Looe on Tuesday next, to deliver a lecture on 'Fossil Organic Remains.' Next day I go on to Penzance, to read my paper on the Distribution in Time and Space of our Devonian fossils—the paper indeed which I read at Oxford somewhat amplified. I am glad to find you liked Mr. Greenbank's professional visit to you, and still more that you 'got on pretty well' at your Reading meeting. Good reading is a valuable, but almost equally rare, accomplishment."

In the summer of 1861 Pengelly delivered lectures, which were well attended, at the Royal Institution and at Oxford. While in London, General Wyndham asked him to go to India in order to make a geological survey for the native prince of the Cashmere region.

Pengelly to his Wife.

"*Royal Institution, May* 23, 1861.— . . . My lecture is just over, and I am again breathing freely. We reached town safely about a quarter after time yesterday. The dinner-party went off well. There were about forty, amongst them the American Ambassador, Lord and Lady Elgin, Sir Hope Grant, Sir Thomas Cochrane, General Wyndham, Lady Charles Wellesley, Tyndall, Wheatstone, Sir J. K. Shuttleworth, the President of Magdalen, etc. I had a good deal of talk with General Wyndham. Mr. and Mrs. President of Magdalen are also stopping in Stratton Street. . . . Please remember to send my diagrams in good time, and then I'll praise you to the skies. . . ."

Pengelly to his Wife.

"*London, May* 24, 1861.— . . . Well, breakfast over, yesterday, I went to hang my diagrams, and then returned here to meet General Wyndham, to take him to Jermyn Street to introduce him to Murchison, as the general is desirous of getting a geologist to proceed to India to survey for the native prince of the Cashmere region. He offered me the place, but it is out of the question altogether. We were not so fortunate as to find Sir Roderick, and shall make another attempt to-day. I then proceeded to Tennant's to take a Devonshire Madrepore table, which he had promised to lend me to illustrate my lecture to the Royal Institution. I went to Dr. Skey's, and then returned to my lecture, which you will remember was on the Corals and Sponges. It was quite as well attended as ever, and my audience was very attentive. The polished specimens excited very great attention, and the audience lingered long over them, and asked a multitude of questions; then called on Sir C. Lyell. The only remarkable person at dinner at Miss Coutts', so far as I know, was Babbage. I was so fortunate as to sit very near him. I forgot to say that Fechter, the great Shakesperian actor, was at dinner. After our meal we went off to an immense upper room on the first floor, which was soon filled to the brim with men and women of all degrees, from dukes and bishops to artisans, to hear Fechter read selections from *Hamlet*, which he did most charmingly. In the company were Mr. Horner and Lady Lyell, Dr. Daubeny, Crawford, and lots of others whom I more or less knew. I arranged with Lady Lyell to go to Harley Street to-day at 1.30, to see Sir Charles. I will report progress in my next."

Pengelly to his Wife.

"1, *Stratton Street, May* 25, 1861.— . . . Yesterday I went by appointment to meet H—— at the Royal Academy, and spent an hour in a mortal squeeze. This is a thing which I *did* enjoy (not the squeeze, but the paintings); but it is in your line, not mine. Thence to Jermyn Street, to meet and introduce General Wyndham to Murchison. We found Sir Roderick, who was very gracious, and named a Dr. Hector as the very man for the Indian geological business, and promised to set to work about the affair. Before I left Murchison invited me to dine with him on Monday, at the Geographical dinner. . . . Then off to Lyell's, where I had engaged to take luncheon. We talked over the Bovey affair, and thus it stands: I am to prepare a paper to be read at the Royal Society, at the first meeting in November. Heer is to be asked to describe the plants, and the drawings, and some of the more portable fossils are to be sent to him, unless he thinks it necessary to come to England, to examine the collection and locality. . . ."

So much has been already written on the subject of the celebrated "Essays and Reviews," that, though they greatly interested Pengelly, it will not be necessary to quote more than one letter of his on the question. After attending a meeting in London, where the Essays had been discussed with much warmth of feeling, he writes to his wife as follows :—

" 1, *Stratton Street, London, May* 27, 1861.— . . . On my arrival at the meeting I found ' Essays and Reviews ' were under condemnation. I was sorry I was not there in time to hear B——'s speech on the question, as from what I heard incidentally and allusively from other speakers, it must have been a good speech. I am told that C—— was most violent in his anathemas. After my arrival (don't suppose I mean because of it), the speeches were temperate, which I was glad of, as otherwise I should have felt it right to caution the meeting not to persecute what they regarded as heretical opinions into notoriety, and possibly to have said something like protesting against any opinion being given on the work by a large miscellaneous body, composed of persons of whom probably not three were capable, either from their knowledge, or mental power, or freedom from prejudice, of giving a verdict worth anything. The matter, however, was closed without any remark valiant or otherwise from me. I dined at the Listers', where I met amongst other old friends, R. W. Fox of Falmouth ; A. Tylor ; my friend Joseph Lister ; and most of the family. R. W. Fox and I contended that ' Essays and Reviews ' had met no refutation, and could not be scoffed down, nor easily replied to. A—— thought otherwise ; but, good man ! he will not be a philosopher for a day or two to come at least ! F—— was somewhat impatient, so soundly orthodox is he. I was not sorry that he left very early, as I am quite certain he is illiberal to a very remarkable degree. . . . I think I forgot to tell you, that I learned from Lady Lyell that the great Darwin has taken a house in Hesketh Crescent." *

Pengelly to his Wife.

" 1, *Stratton Street, May* 28, 1861.— . . . . I left the meeting soon after six, to attend the Geographical dinner. The company was a large one. Amongst those known to me were H. Rogers, R. Chambers, C. Landseer, E. W. Cooke (marine artist), H. Christy, S. Gurney, Murchison, King, and a few others. . . ."

" *London, May* 29, 1861.— . . . I dined with the Listers, where was a large party. I got back just in time to go to a conversazione at Dr. Lankester's. The scene is fairly drawn in one of the numbers of

------

* At Torquay.

the *Cornhill.* Such a squeeze! I had pleasant chats with R. Chambers, Dr. Gladstone, Dr. Daniel (a great scholar and traveller), and Mr. Yates. I got home soon after eleven, and found Lyell had called. . . ."

Pengelly to his Wife.

"*London, June* 7, 1861.—This is probably the last letter I shall write you from town for some time; and indeed, this will not be completed here, as I intend just to put in a line at Oxford, all being well, so as to say how my lecture there goes off. Before my lecture yesterday I called on Dr. Bigsby, and, I hope, prevailed on him not to take any steps in my individual case with the Council of the Royal Institution, leaving him to do as he likes with the general question. He told me my lectures had been considerably better attended than Owen's, which were concluded just before mine began. My last lecture was very well attended, and gave much satisfaction, I think. The cuttlefish were a decided hit, and were in no way offensive. After the lecture I called on Dr. and Mrs. Percy. At dinner our party was a small one of fifty; amongst them Lord Lansdowne, Lord Hanover, Fechter, Sir Roderick, Wheatstone, John Young, etc. I took in Lady (Philip) Egerton, so, of course, we talked of the lines in *Punch.* The whole affair went off capitally, and I to bed at half-past one. I shall not be able to get away from here before eleven to-day, which will make me later at Oxford than I could wish. . . ."

Pengelly to his Wife.

"*Botanic Gardens, Oxford, June* 8, 1861.— . . . I have not much to communicate, but must keep up the daily letter. Our dinner-party last night was a very agreeable one. Besides the Vice-Chancellor, his wife and two daughters, there were Daubeny, Professor Phillips and Miss Phillips, Dr. Thompson and wife, Professor Smith, Westwood, and two or three others, whose names have escaped me. This morning we had at breakfast a Mr. Jenyns, well known as a naturalist, related to Dr. Daubeny.

"Next I went to the Museum, saw Dr. Rolleston, the distinguished physiologist, and had a long gossip with him (he is shortly to marry a Miss Davy of Ambleside, daughter of Dr. Davy, and therefore niece of Sir Humphry). Then I had a chat with Westwood, who is one of the professors at the Museum, as is Rolleston also. Next I strolled by the river, and saw the students afloat, and all the fairy-like character of the river. I am writing this partly for the purpose of making known these important facts, and partly for the purpose of resting myself; for, truth to tell, I am indeed very tired. The Vice-Chancellor was very eulogistic about my lecture, and declared there was a family likeness between Phillips and myself as lecturers. We have a dinner-party to-night, so I must conclude. . . ."

The deposits at Bovey Tracey were now arousing considerable attention in the scientific world; the part which Professor Heer took in the examination has already been referred to.

Sir Charles Lyell to Pengelly.

"*June* 17, 1861.— . . . I received your letter returning Mr. Key's; but you did not acknowledge one I sent you, giving you an abstract of what I had written to Professor Heer. You will see by the enclosed that he has made himself a good English scholar, so that I need not have written in French. I am exceedingly glad that he can come here. If he goes with you to Bovey Tracey, he has such an eye for plants that it will surprise me if he does not find some which have been missed.

"He has such stores of books, and herbaria, private and public, and living plants in the Botanic Garden, such a public and private collection of fossil plants to refer to at Zurich, that I have no doubt that it will be best to send to him at once all the specimens you can, and all your drawings. He will get the additional drawings done cheaply, such as may be necessary.

"If he makes out what subdivision of the Lower Miocene Bovey belongs to, it will indeed be a great step; already it seems to be, as Gaudin said, Lower Miocene.

"As soon as he gets the specimens, he may communicate such conclusions as may enable you to draw up your application of the botany to the geology.

"I was afraid that Heer's numerous academical and publishing engagements would have made his visit to England impossible; but, fortunately, his 'Tertiary Flora' is finished.

"The *Aspidium* led two geologists into that astounding blunder of identifying the Carboniferous and Tertiary flora.

"When you have quite done with Heer's letter, I shall be glad of it again.

"Do you not think Miss Coutts should see it? . . .

"I should be inclined to send off at once by post a small box of minute fossil seeds of Bovey, that he may see them before he leaves Zurich for his tour, and may write to you, and perhaps make suggestions."

Pengelly to his Wife.

"*Torquay, August* 19, 1861.— . . . I am just back from Exeter, and having an hour before bedtime will occupy at least a part of it in a narrative to you. This morning I went to Exeter by first train, my travelling companions being Barnes and Wolfe, the last on his way to Ireland, the former off to Switzerland. At Exeter I met R. Dymond, who introduced me to the Devon and Exeter Institution, where I found a copy of Lyson's 'Magna Britannia,' and made a copy of the account of the Bovey lignite which it contains. Whilst there I encountered Mr. W. Vicary, who took me to see the gravel deposit near the Nursery Garden at St. Thomas's, remarkable as a geological formation, and still more since very recently ROMAN *pottery* has been found in it, *eight feet below the surface ! ! !* What changes this river plain must have undergone within even the historic period ! I do earnestly hope that this matter will be followed up; it is a fertile subject. Next, Vicary took me to his house to dine; but before dinner he showed me a lot of fine fossils, found in the pebbles on the beach at Budleigh Salterton; also a very splendid series from the Greensand of Haldon; then a series of Beekites from the red conglomerate of North Tawton, sufficiently like those of Torbay to show that they are Beekites, and sufficiently unlike them to show that the conditions could not have been identical. Lastly, and best of all the good things, he showed me unquestionable pebbles of the Dartmoor Porphyritic granite, found by himself in the red conglomerate of Haldon. I hope to visit the locality with him on Wednesday to get some specimens, and then prepare a paper on the geological age of the Dartmoor granite. Why, it is really a jolly go!! We can now limit the age of the granite on both the ancient and the modern side. It is not so old as the Carboniferous age, since it has sent veins into rocks of that period; it is more ancient than the red conglomerate, *i.e.* Triassic probably, otherwise it is Permian, since it sent pebbles to help to form the said conglomerate. Hence between the Carboniferous and Triassic (if it be Triassic), that is, during the Permian age, by no means supposed to be one of our long periods, there was time enough for the granite to be formed and the rocks which MUST have covered it, probably several miles thick, to be stripped off, so that the granite was exposed at the surface; or if the red rocks be Permian, then between it and the Carboniferous era a vast period of time must have elapsed, and this time is totally unrecognized in the chronological series of the geologist. What an astounding, an overwhelming value it sets on geological units in even the first case! I must bring this matter before the scientific world, and must do justice to Vicary in the case.

"Well, then we dined, and next to the Guildhall to see the Mayor and Corporation receive the [Archæological] Association. First came the Mace-bearers, then the Sword-bearer with a marvellous hat presented to the City by Henry VII., then the Mayor shook hands with Sir Stafford Northcote the President, and Mr. Pettigrew the Treasurer, then he asked us to take refreshment, which we did in the Council Chamber, after which we went in a body to the Subscription Rooms, and Sir Stafford delivered an excellent extempore address. This over, we went round the City to see the fragments of the City Wall still in existence. I fraternized with Pettigrew and Wright the Antiquary, whom I had met before. I had to reach home that evening, so could not attend the evening meeting, which I much regretted. . . ."

Pengelly to his Wife.

"*Lamorna, Torquay, August* 22, 1861.— . . . Yesterday morning I took first train to Exeter, found Vicary and his carriage awaiting me at the station, drove to Haldon, found and extracted granitic pebbles in the red conglomerates, studied the greensand that caps the hill until my heart ached to think of the thousand thousand questions which forced themselves before me, and which I felt sure I shall never live to answer, and my mental eyes ached at looking so far into the abyss of antiquity. Drove back to Exeter to dinner with Vicary. Took a stroll in Veitch's garden and then home, to find a letter from Lyell, inclosing one from Heer, in French, which states that Bovey has yielded forty-five distinct species (hip! hip! hurrah!! Again! again! again!!

Three cheers more ! ! For he's a jolly good fellow), decidedly Miocene.[*]
This morning I received a letter from Wright the Antiquary, proposing
that I should accompany him to Brixham Cavern. I put off several
lessons, then to the station just in time to see the train go off. So I
came home to work at my paper, and then at Tor Abbey to meet the
Archæologists, got there at half-past two, and after waiting an hour they
arrived, but so much after time that the Abbey had to be scamped ;
down came the rain. Then home to work, and the Archæologists to
the Hotel to dine. . . ."

Sir Charles Lyell to Pengelly.

" *August* 21, 1861.— . . . I send you Heer's most interesting and
satisfactory dispatch, which I shall be glad to have again when you
have digested its contents. Not that I mean to forestall him and you,
for I shall have only room for a sentence or two about Bovey, but there
are several points in answer to queries of mine which I must again refer
to. I only got Heer's letter this morning, and I sent an abstract of the
leading results to Miss Coutts, thinking it right that she should know, not
only how fruitful your labours have been, but also that Heer, following
our instructions, has employed his artists largely on the forty-five species
(!) already made out. The *Sequoia Couttsiæ* is a good hit, as it is so
abundant, and furnished the lignite.

" I congratulate you on the prospect of Heer's visit to Torquay in
the middle of next month. You see, he will be here 31st August, and
stay here ten or twelve days. . . ."

Pengelly to his Wife.

" *Lamorna, August* 26, 1861.— . . . I hasten to acknowledge the
receipt of yours just to hand, I seem to be always writing, and cannot
see my way to a moment's leisure, hence I fear my letters to you have
probably a hurried aspect. I begin to doubt whether I shall ever over-
take my work. . . . Well, well, it will all be over some day, and some
other person will be puzzled with the problem which puzzles me, to wit,
' is there any real advantage in having a restless, active mind ? ' . . ."

Sir Charles Lyell to Pengelly.

" *August* 26, 1861.— . . . Many thanks for returning Heer, to
whom I must write to-day at *poste-restante*, Paris. I see by the papers
that Miss Coutts is gone to the Continent. . . . .

" Next to finding fossils to show whether the red conglomerate is
Permian or Trias, the granite pebbles are valuable. You remember
I inquired whether you had seen any. . . ."

Pengelly to his Wife.

" *Torquay, August* 29, 1861.— . . . I saw the case of the Swiss
Guides some days ago ; it is very interesting, and proves that Forbes

---

[*] The important fact that these species were later on determined to be Eocene,
by Mr. S. Gardner, is mentioned at the beginning of this Chapter.

(James, not Edward, remember) has real knowledge respecting the laws, if not the cause, of Glacial Motion. We have knowledge when we can predict, but not else, I think. The fossils are just back from Zurich. I have not opened the box, and do not think of doing so before I get back from Manchester. 'For Better for Worse' is finished and most charmingly. 'Philip' is going on well under Thackeray's unmistakable guidance."

During September, 1861, the British Association met at Manchester. Pengelly attended the meeting as usual, and had the pleasure of being accompanied by his wife. He read the following papers at the Geological Section : "A New Bone-cave at Brixham," "The Recent Encroachments of the Sea on the Shores of Torbay," "The Relative Age of the Petherwin and Barnstaple Beds," "The Age of the Granites at Dartmoor."

Section " C " was that year ably presided over by Sir Roderick Murchison.

Sir Charles Lyell to Pengelly.

"*September* 4, 1861.— . . . I spoke to Professor Heer about Miss Coutts' message. . . .

"He has arranged with Sir. R. I. Murchison that the drawers of mull plants should be open to him, though the Jermyn St. Museum is closed, and he is to visit that and the British Museum to-day and to-morrow. He has plenty to do, and will, I expect, find among the fruits and seeds in the Museum at Kew, some which will throw light on the fossils. Dr. Hooker has told me when he can see them.

" He will be much more prepared by his stay here to do the Bovey business well.

" I am sorry to say Heer has a cold, and must take great care of himself. He has always had a consumptive tendency, and for that reason went to Madeira, as I think I told you. Heer's address is 'Swiss House Hotel, Golden Square, London.' When you know on what day you will join him, pray write to him. . . ."

Sir Charles Lyell to Pengelly.

"*September* 22, 1861.— . . . I confess I was surprised to hear that Professor Heer could be two hours in your collection and find no additional species. It shows how well you chose the set you sent to Zurich, and how good an eye you had acquired for nice botanical distinctions.

" You will be glad to hear that Dr. Hooker is much struck with the work which Heer has done in the Bovey Coal plants. He pronounced quite an *éloge* on it.

" Will you be so good as to give me notice when Heer will be in town, and tell him Dr. Hooker wishes him to come again to Kew. He (Dr. H.) has also sent me some specimens of the seeds of *Platanus orientalis*, and *Platanus acerifolia*, as bearing on a point discussed with Heer, which I want to show him, and talk over.   Please mention this.

"I have heard from M. Gaudin from Bex.   He was to return to Lausanne in time to see Miss Coutts.

"I hope that Professor Heer's health has not suffered, and that the cold which he took away with him from London has not continued to plague him. . . ."

Sir Charles Lyell to Pengelly.

"*September* 28, 1861.— . . . It is very remarkable that Professor Heer failed to detect any new species in your collection, which you had certainly mastered the contents of very thoroughly.

"I am glad you advanced the money which you allude to.

"As to reading a paper, I know of no way but writing to the Secretary, Dr. Sharpey ; you may say I recommended you to do so, and to ask when you can have an evening, or part of one.   As to Heer not being ready, it will do if he sends in such sketches as will enable them to make rough estimates of the cost, and then the plates can be engraved at Zurich, and more correct drawings used.

"Most of Heer's paper will never be read, and might remain untranslated till later.

"You could not have had three more eminent men to show your rocks to than the three Swiss * who were with you.

"If you could enable me to write to Professor Heer, I should be glad of an address, to send to him a message from Dr. Hooker before he gets here ; but if you do not know, you need not write. . . ."

Sir Charles Lyell to Pengelly.

"*October* 9, 1861.— . . . I have this day sent you the plates and manuscript of Professor Heer's paper, which he gave me charge of when he left London, and begged me to send it to you immediately, and to say that a small part of the translation he had not time to add in his handwriting, but you will find it given in Mr. Earle's manuscript, which is sent.

"I need not say that I shall be honoured by having to communicate such memoirs.   I am truly glad it is to come on so soon.   I meant to be at Barton at Sir C. Bunbury's, but must arrange to stay here till 21st, so you must accept their offer and gain time.

"As soon as it is printed it may be distributed privately before the volume is out. . . .

"Instead of fifteen to twenty species Heer has described—

"Forty-nine Miocene,

"Four Post-pliocene. . . .

"Mr. Key of Newton Abbott has sent in his paper, with numerous detailed sections, which I have communicated to the Geological Society.   They are very good, and will probably show some details different from yours.

"I invited him to contribute his information to you and Heer, but this he declined. . . ."

* Oswald Heer, Escher-von-der-Linth, and Peter Merian.

I

Sir Charles Lyell to Pengelly.

"*October* 13, 1861.— . . . I mentioned to you in a former letter how much Dr. Hooker has been struck with the able manner in which Professor Heer had executed his task, in getting drawings and descriptions made of the Bovey Tracey fossils. The plates are certainly beautiful, so admirably arranged and instructive. Dr. Hooker went so far as to say that it would be well for us, after the publication of Heer's paper, to consider whether we might not at the Geological Society award the Wollaston Medal to Heer, for having so clearly settled the age of the Bovey lignite, and given so good a botanical account of the British flora of that Older Miocene epoch. We must, of course, say nothing about the medal at present, but I shall not forget the hint.

"When I was last with Heer at Kew, Dr. Thomson, who has had charge of the Government Botanical Garden at Calcutta, and is the author of important works on the Indian flora, assisted us in comparing the plants of the rich herbarium at Kew with Heer's fossils, and Thomson told me he was much delighted with the knowledge of living plants which Heer showed. Sir William Hooker also looked over the twenty-one plates on the Bovey coal flora, and Dr. Booth, the botanist, has seen Sir William since, who spoke in great praise of the drawings and of Heer. His whole journey has been very successful. . . .

"It would certainly be more convenient to me if your paper and Heer's were read one week later than the day you mention. If you can so arrange it with Mr. Stokes, please to let me hear from you, and I will make a point of attending at the Royal Society 28th November. . . ."

Mrs. Pengelly to her Mother.

"*October* 26, 1861.— . . . William is gone over to Bovey this afternoon with the two Savans. Professor Heer speaks very little English. He found a few small leaves new to him, but had not time to go down into the pit. One of the leaves was myrtle. He has found nearly fifty species in the fossils William sent him, some very interesting ones. He is accompanied by a clergyman named Earle, from Bath, a friend of his, and an excellent German scholar, having also a profound knowledge of Anglo-Saxon.

"On Saturday Professor Escher dined with us (as well as Professor Heer and Mr. Earle). I enjoyed his company extremely. He gave us a great deal of interesting information respecting the Lake-dwellings in Switzerland, to which he has been devoting himself with much ardour. He drew me a plan of them, and also drew me some of the flint implements. Another day the two professors, with the addition of Professor Merian, all came to spend the day with us. . . . They took leave with innumerable bows, thanks, and protestations; they laugh and say they are 'Land-rats.' William says he thought he should never have got them away from 'Hope's Nose,' they were so astonished and delighted with everything they saw. William is very much engaged getting his paper on the Bovey Coal ready to read before the Royal Society in November. . . ."

Sir Charles Lyell to Pengelly.

"*November* 5, 1861.— . . . I have answered all the queries in the annexed except No. 6. I cannot offer to make the abstract, being much driven for time, and I am in the press and must be out by a certain month, or miss the season and a year. But if you will send up any part of Heer's MS. which you have any difficulty with, it shall be immediately returned with the passages written out as I understand them. My wife is accustomed to Heer's writing in French, German, and English, and will help.

"I will also help in any way I can, on points where you feel responsibility. . . ."

Mrs. Pengelly to her Mother.

"*November* 30th.— . . . William read his paper before the Royal Society on the Bovey Explorations, and it was very well received. I wish you could have seen some of the drawings, they were so beautifully done. One beetle's wing was discovered.

"We had a delightful letter from Professor Heer a week or two since, enclosing a photograph, in which the three professors are depicted in a group, and underneath the following lines, which amused us very much, and showed more knowledge of English than we expected—

> "'See, my good friend Lamornian,[*]
> How Escher, Heer, and Merian,
> United strong in heart and hand,
> Go travelling to Britain's land.'

"William is delighted with it, and so is Sir Charles Lyell, who says he shall not rest till he gets one. . . ."

Mrs. Pengelly to her Mother.

"*November*, 1861.— . . . We had a delightful call a few days since from Sheridan Knowles, who sat a good while chatting and telling us many interesting incidents of his past life. He is an old friend of William's, and is looking for a house here, on account of the climate, as he has become exceedingly infirm. He is very serious. He told me he was offered £500 lately to write a tale for a Magazine; but he refused, thinking 'that, having put his hand to the plough, he ought not to look back.' Speaking of his Plays, he said, 'there is something very good in the Public after all, for that sentiment (which he read us) on Procrastination has never yet been repeated in the Theatre without bringing down thunders of applause;' but you should have heard him read it, it was very fine. . . ."

Pengelly continued to enjoy taking geological expeditions from time to time, and thus relates some of the adventures which he encountered in the course of his rambles.

---

[*] In reference to the name of Pengelly's house, "Lamorna."

"It is unnecessary to say that geologists are frequently trespassers on other men's lands. Sometimes they remain in happy ignorance of the fact; but, when it is made known to them, they generally find the simple statement that they are geologists and strangers sufficient to secure a free passage. Occasionally, however, the battle is not so easily won; but, if it is ever lost, it may, in all probability, be ascribed to defective tactics.

"A tempting cliff having once detained a companion and myself, so long as to render it improbable that we should reach a neighbouring railway station in time for the last train to the town whither we were going, we committed the trespass of walking on the railway, by which the distance would be shortened by fully one-half. When within sight of the station our way was barred by a stop-gate, at a point where the common road crossed the rails. The gate-keeper who presented himself, possessed a countenance so far from assuring as to satisfy me that he would, at least, turn us back. Resolved, however, to make a push for it, I addressed him thus—

"'Of course, you have the power to turn us back, if you like to do so; and, though we shall lose the train and be put to great inconvenience, we will retrace our steps at once, if you say we must. If, however, I can read faces, you are much too good-natured a fellow to do anything of the kind. Which shall it be?'

"'Well, sir,' he replied, 'I'll open the gate for you this time; but don't trespass again. And let me say that, though I like a little *butter*, I hate *grease*.'

"'Thank you,' said I. And we passed through.

"'I think you're checkmated, old fellow,' said my companion.

"'Never mind that. Whether *butter* or *grease*, it did the work I intended.'

"A friend and I once spent a good deal of time, in studying a very long and fine cliff section of the *Keuper*, or Upper New Red Sandstone. We had proceeded in the direction of the *Dip*, until we had reason to believe that the famous *Bone Bed* was so near at hand that a short distance farther would bring it to the level of the beach, so that we should be able to investigate it easily. Unfortunately, however, before this point was reached, the entire section was concealed by the *debris* of a great and famous landslip, which extended a considerable distance along the coast. There was nothing for it, but to ascend the cliff at the first point at which a path could be extemporized, and to seek the outcrop of the bed at the summit. Having gained the top of the cliff, we found it necessary to cross a hedge, on which I accordingly got, and was about to descend on the other side, when a gentleman standing just below me, and whom we had not previously seen, said—

"'You can't come here!'

"'Why not?'

"'This is my property; and I allow no trespassing.'

"'Is the land on this side your property also?'

"'No; that belongs to ——.'

"'Well, I'm very sorry; but it can't be helped.'

"Then, turning to my companion, I remarked—

"'We must give up the search, that's all.'

"And I jumped back to the ground I had just left—intending, nevertheless, to get permission to cross the hedge, and, if possible, to find the stratum we were seeking.

"The owner of the adjoining land walked leisurely away from the cliff, keeping near the hedge which separated us; and we did the same thing on the other side.

"At length I ventured to say to him—

"'Allow me, sir, to congratulate you on your property; and pardon my adding that I really envy you—as you are the fortunate proprietor of the *Bone Bed*.'

"'What *Bone Bed?*'

"The question was asked in a tone and manner that showed a desire for information on it; and I proceeded to explain the leading characteristics of the stratum, its position in the geological series, and the chief fossils it yielded. It was obvious that our new acquaintance had some knowledge of geology, and that he was interested in the statements to which he had listened. We accordingly felt that he was disarmed, and would speedily strike. Having put a few pertinent questions on the subject, he pointed out a comparatively low part of the hedge, and said—

"'I think you can cross there, without doing any harm. I wish you good luck in your search for the *Bone Bed*. Good day.'

"'Good day, and thank you.'

"With this he left us. We returned to the cliff, were very soon on the *Bone Bed*, and extracted a large number of fossils from it.

"On one occasion, the discovery of fossils of a remarkable and interesting character in a new locality, tempted me to prolong my search to a later hour than I intended. At length, just before sunset, I started to walk to my temporary home—fully eight miles distant. Being familiar with the country, I knew that by crossing a couple of fields, at least a mile would be saved. That this had been frequently done, a well-worn path assured me; and that it was a trespass was rendered equally clear by an announcement to that effect on a board erected on a pole, at the point where I diverged from the highway. I had almost cleared the distance, when, to my dismay, the farmer who occupied the land—a thorough John Bull—was standing in the path awaiting me. Putting a bold face on the matter, I marched on, as if his presence in no way affected me, until well within earshot, when he roared—

"'You must go back!'

"'Go back! Why?'

"'You're trespassing.'

"'Trespassing! I'm extremely sorry.'

"'Sorry! Yes, I reckon. You know you're trespassing. Sorry, eh!'

"'What makes you say so?'

"'Dedn't 'ee zee the board back there?'

"'I saw the board on the pole, if you mean that.'

"'Ees, I do mean that. I know'd you a zid en safe enough. Ded 'ee read what's upon en?'

"'My dear sir, pardon my saying so, but are you not going too fast? Should you not first prove that I *can* read?'

"Oh! oh!—that's good, that es! A man like you not able to read! Oh! oh!—that's uncommon good. Beats cock-fighting all to fits. Oh! oh!'—and his sides shook with laughter.

"Having succeeded in making him laugh, I knew he would not turn me back; so I said—

"'I have to go to L—— to-night; and that, as you know, is a long step. Nevertheless, I'll go back at once if you insist on it; but if you'll allow me to go on, I shall feel much obliged.'

"'Well, I don't s'pose you'll do much harm, zo you may go on now you've got zo var; but 'tez uncommon hard to have a lot of trespassers 'pon your ground day arter day. Ees, you may go on now.'

"'Thank you very much. Good evening.'

"When I had got some distance from him, he shouted after me—

"'Holloa! I say!'

"'What is it?'

"'B'ant you a Methoday passon?'

"'Oh dear, no. You flatter me too much.'

"I presume that he felt he had lost the battle, and had sent his question after me as a parting shot."

When on these rambles, Pengelly often cultivated his chance companions on the road, in the hope of obtaining insight into local beliefs and superstitions. He thus describes one of his conversations—

"During one of my visits to the famous granite pile known as the Cheesering, near Liskeard in Cornwall, I remarked to a man at work hard by—

"'The Cheesering's very wonderful. Does anybody in the district know how it came here, and got piled up, in that strange way?'

"'Oh, by all accounts, 'twas washed there by the flood.'

"I thought, but didn't say, 'Oh, you ill-used, over-worked flood, what labours are assigned to you!'"

In spite of much healthy out-of-door life, Pengelly was never at any time a good sleeper, but he bore this inconvenience with his customary cheerfulness, and even professed to have found a remedy for it. A friend who knew him intimately sent the biographer the following recipe against insomnia in Pengelly's own words.

"One day I was introduced to young De Morgan, son of the well-known Professor De Morgan. I said to him—

"'Mr. De Morgan, I am delighted to make your acquaintance, for I am so much indebted to your father for his book on "Formal Logic."'

"I noticed that the young man seemed confused and puzzled what to say. At last he replied—

THE CHEESERING, NEAR LISKEARD.

[To face p. 118.

" ' Well, Mr. Pengelly, to tell you the truth, I have never read my father's book on " Formal Logic." '

" ' Neither have I,' was my answer; 'but the facts of the case are these.   I am sometimes troubled with sleeplessness.   I keep your father's book on a shelf in my bedroom, and when I am restless at night, I get it down and begin to study it.   Before I have got through five pages I am fast asleep.   So I may well consider myself indebted to your father for that book.' "

CHAPTER IX.

GEOLOGICAL LECTURES AT NORWICH ; THE FOUNDATION OF THE DEVONSHIRE ASSOCIATION.

EARLY PART OF 1862.

DURING the winter holidays, January, 1862, Pengelly delivered a course of Geological Lectures at Norwich, of which he gives some account in his home letters.

Pengelly to his Wife.

" *The Close, Norwich, January* 15, 1862.—The journey here was in no way remarkable, nor the country interesting. The only thing which struck me was Ely Cathedral, which is a striking object, and stands well. The lecture was largely attended. I do not think I was very successful, and the audience by no means uproarious in their applause. A party to supper very pleasant. To-day I give to seeing the town. I hope you will not have any great trouble about sending off the box of specimens to Heer at Zurich."

Pengelly to his Wife.

" 16*th.*—Yesterday Mr. Compton called and took Mrs. Crowther and myself to the Museum, which is a good though not a local one. The collection of birds from every part of the world—a hobby of J. H. Gurney—is excellent in every way, all but perfect. The collection of mammalian, especially elephantine, remains, is capital. In the afternoon I went on a voyage of exploration through the town, and wrote to Heer."

Pengelly to his Wife.

" *The Close, Norwich, January* 18, 1862.— . . . Yesterday I had a second nice ramble in the neighbourhood. Tell Trotty I saw thirteen great windmills all working away at once. We had a party here last night before the lecture, which brought me an invitation from a Mr. Jessopp * (head master of the Grammar School, of which Mr. Crowther,

* The Rev. Dr. Jessopp, author of " The Coming of the Friars," and other works.

with whom I am now staying, is the second master) to stay at his house during my second week, and from Mr. Field for my third week.

"The lecture hall last night was densely packed. I was listened to with great attention, and all seemed greatly pleased. They are not an applausive people, but so pleased were they, that they talk of asking me to give twenty-four lectures; but of course I can do nothing of the kind! I think I lectured well; but I also think I have lectured better. I am getting very lazy, not up until nine in the morning. It is very cold."

Pengelly to his Wife.

"*The Close, Norwich, January* 19th.— . . . I could not very con-veniently get off a letter to you this morning, hence I have two days' journal to write. Yesterday, in the thick of breakfast, came my unshaven friend I mentioned in a former letter, to take me for a walk, etc. Mr. Crowther had previously arranged for me to call on a clergyman who had promised to show me some of the chalk-pits in his neighbourhood; this being communicated to my friend B——, he volunteered to accom-pany me, and we accordingly started. The clergyman joined us, and I saw several good 'sandpipes' and 'potstones,' both of which puzzled me much. We, the trio, then started under B——'s (the unshaven one's) guidance to see some of the principal antiquities in the place; they are interesting, but not pictorial in any way. The town has no architectural pretensions of any kind, and is, indeed, of a mean appear-ance. We then started for Caistor Castle, a fine old Roman ruin; it must have been a large and strong place. Nothing now remains but the outer walls, which are all but entirely covered by greensward. On the way I picked up what I believe to be a flint implement among a heap of flints, for road repairs. We returned to B——'s to tea, where we were joined by Mr. Miller, his wife and daughter. Having passed a pleasant evening, I returned to my quarters accompanied by my friend, who, though rough, is extremely kind and intelligent, as well as hospitable. . . . I suppose I shall go to Mr. Jessopp's on Tuesday. I have been extremely comfortable, and very much at home with Mr. and Mrs. Crowther, both of whom are extremely kind. . . ."

The flint implement mentioned in the last letter was submitted for examination to Mr. [now Sir John] Evans, F.R.S., etc., undoubtedly the highest authority on this subject. Two letters concerning it were received from him some months later, but for the sake of the continuity of the subject, they are given now.

John Evans, to Pengelly.

"*Nash Mills, Hemel Hempsted, June* 4, 1862.—It is some time since I saw a flint implement, which I was informed had been found by you on a heap of stones near Norwich; but my impression is that it was not shown me by Dr. Falconer. I should like to see it again before giving any decided opinion upon it; but as far as I remember (1) it certainly was an implement, but (2) not of the Drift period, but rather an unfinished or *un*ground celt of the so-called Stone period, of which

(3) specimens are found all over England, but about which (4) I should like to refresh my memory before making any very solemn affidavit. If it is in London, I would look at it again; or if not, you could perhaps send me a rough sketch of it. I am off into the north for a week or ten days on Friday, so do not be surprised at not receiving a very speedy answer to your letter, should you write. I hope to send you by this post an account of some of the further discoveries of the implements in the Drift, and also a few copies of a plate of their various forms, which I hope may be useful for distribution, so that people may know what to look out for. If ever I can be of the slightest use to you, pray don't scruple to write to me."

John Evans to Pengelly.

" *Nash Mills, Hemel Hempsted, June* 18, 1862.—I arrived at home last night, and take the first opportunity of giving you my opinion, *valeat quantum*, about the flint implement you found in Norfolk. I have examined it carefully, and the conclusion at which I arrive is that it does not belong to the Drift period, but that it must be classed among the implements of the so-called Stone period. The general form is very much that of the ordinary stone 'celt,' adapted for cutting at the broad end; a portion, however, of the edge has been broken or worn away. I am not sure whether there are not some traces of its having been ground on some parts of its surface, especially just below 'Caistor' on the label, where there seems to be a tongue of polished surface between the places where two chips have been struck off. Judging from the appearance, I should say that the 'celt' had been lying upon or near the surface for a considerable time in rather a sandy soil. It seems to be altered superficially to a considerable depth, and the numerous rusty marks upon it testify to its having frequently been brought into contact with the plough and harrow, whose rude assaults its tough constitution has enabled it to withstand. I have packed it up and sent it to London, to be forwarded by Great Western Rail to Torquay, and hope it will reach you safely. Some time, when you are coming up to London, I wish you would arrange to run down here for a night. I have several things that I think would interest you, and my collection of the Drift implements is now very extensive, to say nothing of those of the later Stone period. With many thanks for the sight of your specimen."

Pengelly to his Wife.

" *The Close, Norwich, January* 21st. . . . Yesterday I went to breakfast with a Mr. Crompton, once a Unitarian Minister, a brother-in-law of George Dawson's. Mr. and Mrs. Crompton took me a long walk to a village named Thorpe (taking an artesian well by the way), where I had an opportunity of seeing the Norwich Crag for the first time. It is just a bed of millions of shells, most of them recent species. I thought of making a collection, but the remembrance of over-gorged drawers at home flashed before me. I am glad, nevertheless, to have seen them. We dropped in at a charming place and took luncheon, as we quite intended to do. . . . I am very happy here, but shall be very glad to get home. . . ."

Pengelly to his Wife.

"*Rev. A. Jessopp's, Cathedral Close, Norwich, January 22, 1862.*— ... I have now passed my first day here, and am quite at home. My stories help me amazingly. I have done but little to-day. Yesterday I left a card on Sedgwick, who is Canon of this Cathedral; to-day I have received a note from him stating that he was unable to call on me, as he had to leave by an early train. In the afternoon I took Mr. and Mrs. Jessopp to the spot where I found my flint implement, which is really making a sensation, but we had not the good luck to find another. This evening Mr. Firth, a leading surgeon here whom I had previously met, called on me to offer to take me to Cromer in his carriage, in order to see the cliffs. I do not know how it will eventuate, as I have scarcely a day open for it. Mr. Firth and some others subsequently came in to spend the evening, and a merry one we certainly had. I really never saw anything so truly hospitable as the Norwich people are."

Professor Sedgwick was now a great invalid, as the following extract from one of his letters will show.

"*Wednesday, 7 a.m., January 22, 1862.*— ... I am grieved much that I cannot call on you, but I am packing, and about to start by an early train for Cambridge. Some one told me that you are about to give lectures here. Had I remained I could not have attended them in consequence of the condition of my head. Thank God, by complete rest I am much better; but I am going back to attend an examination, which I greatly dread. On your way back you will, I hope, make a halt at Cambridge, and I shall be very glad to show you my museum. . . ."

Pengelly to his Wife.

"*Rev. A. Jessopp's, Norwich, January 22, 1862.*— ... I have done next to nothing to-day besides delivering my third lecture; the audience very large, and my lecture of two hours' duration was listened to with very marked attention. Mr. Gunn,* a clergyman of this district, well known as a geologist, called to-day and has arranged to take me home with him, some ten miles off, after my lecture next Friday, and to keep me there until Tuesday, when I return for my fourth lecture. . . ."

Pengelly to his Wife.

"*The Close, Norwich, January 24, 1862.*— ... This morning I went to Yarmouth, and saw that dear fellow 'the Sea.' I was delighted to see him, and he capered and bounded right rampantly. My audience to-night was an enormous one. Mr. Gunn and Mr. King were both there. Mr. Firth, the surgeon, takes me over to Cromer to-morrow, where Mr. Gunn joins us, and on Monday Mr. King is to join us also. . . . Nothing can be kinder than the Jessopps. Excuse haste, it is near midnight, and I have to be up at six. . . ."

---

* The Rev. John Gunn, M.A., who died May 28, 1890, at the age of 88.

Pengelly to his Wife.

"*Cromer, Norfolk, January* 26, 1862.— . . . Dr. Firth and his son took me from Norwich yesterday about nine, and by aid of their fine pair of horses brought me here soon after one. As soon as possible we took another pair of horses and got to Weybourne, where one of the Ocean Telegraphs plunges into the sea; but what shall I say of the interminable beach of flints? What an awful amount of time must have been spent in denuding the vast body of chalk in which the now liberated flints formerly reposed. We walked under the cliff about four miles and saw some of the finest sections in the world, sections of 'Drift' containing mountains of fragments of chalk transported from afar, yet quite angular. It was really overwhelming in the questions which it suggested. We then returned here to a late dinner, and, that meal over, we had a visit from a blind Captain Wyndham, brother of the General,* a Mr. Birch surgeon here, and a Captain King of the Coast Guard. We remain here to-night, and all being well, reach Norwich to-morrow night. This must be a charming place in the summer. . . ."

Pengelly to his Wife.

"*Norwich, January* 27, 1862.— . . . Yesterday we had a very pleasant walk in the neighbourhood of Cromer, and saw much geological fact which will, I think, long live in my memory. It is scarcely possible to conceive of the all but endless number of merchant ships constantly passing along the coast. I think I never had so great an idea of Britain's Commercial Marine. This morning we left about ten for Mundsley, a village on the coast, where we spent an hour; then on to Happisburgh, where we remained four hours; in this period we walked to Eccles to see the remnant of a church which the sea has taken possession of.

"Next we dined, and then drove home, Mr. Firth taking me to his house to lodge. I have very greatly enjoyed my turn out, indeed it is one of the most prominent of the many pleasing things with which this lecture engagement has been associated, but I shall be delighted to get home again. . . ."

Pengelly to his Wife.

"*Mr. Field's, Surrey Street, Norwich, January* 28, 1862.— . . . On going, to-day, to Mr. Jessopp's I found a letter from Alfred. He gives a good account of himself. At one o'clock I attended the annual meeting of the Norfolk Archæological Society, and was drawn out to make a statement about the Brixham Cavern. On going to Mr. Jessopp's for a dinner-party given in my honour I found your welcome letter and enclosure from Heer. I am glad the parcel has come from Heer. We had Mr. Gunn and Mr. King at dinner, with some others. There was a great crowd at my lecture on the Antiquity of the Earth. It excited much interest, and I was greatly cheered : the subject seems entirely new to them. After the lecture I came here (Mr. Field's) for

---

* An old friend.

the first time.   I never saw people so hospitable as they are here ; they never seem to think they have done enough for one.   I conclude now, as I have very little time, it being near midnight, and I have to be up very early. . . ."

Pengelly to his Wife.

"*Norwich, January* 29, 1862.— . . . This morning Mr. Field and I were up early, got some coffee, and drove off to breakfast with Mr. King at Saxlingham, where we arrived about 9.30, in time to see the drawing-room fire lighted, and to welcome the family down as they successively descended from their dormitories. When all assembled, there were Mr. and Mrs. King, and their daughter, and Mr. Walpole. Mrs. King is as enthusiastic a geologist as her husband, as is their daughter also, a girl about twelve years old. Mr. Walpole is the brother of the Earl of Orford. We spent the greater part of the day looking over Mr. King's capital collection of Norfolk fossils, in which are some unique mammalian remains. After luncheon we went to see a few chalk pits, and then home to dinner. In the evening there was a party and a good deal of pleasant chat. I am getting very desirous of returning home, which really seems ungrateful, as nothing can be kinder than the people are to me ; but still home is home, and I hope to see it and all its dear inmates, in about seventy-two hours from this ; it is now about midnight. . . ."

The last letter is good evidence that, in the midst of congenial scenes, hospitable entertainment, and the pressure of continuous work, Pengelly's thoughts and longings turned constantly homewards. Although extremely fond of society, he was not of that temperament which causes a man to find one place as good as another. The scientific meetings in London attracted him strongly, but in a letter to his wife he speaks of being glad that he has not to live there, as, in that case, he fears he would be less master of his own time, and thereby debarred from her society. When away, scarcely anything was allowed to interfere with his daily letter home. His aged mother (now a widow) paid him and his wife long visits every year. Although she was naturally very proud of her son's scientific work and attainments, she felt too nervous ever to go and hear him lecture at Torquay.

The following letter from Babbage, gives an example of the unfortunate position, in which a scientific man is placed, when he has a reason to believe that his discoveries are unjustly claimed by or assigned to others.

C. Babbage to Pengelly.

"*Dorset Street, Manchester Square, May* 27, 1862.— . . . I enclose copy of the abstract of my papers on the 'Action of Ocean Currents.'

"You will perceive that I have *not* raised the question of the correctness of the 'geological doctrine of outliers,' but that I have shown that another admitted geological cause may '*sometimes*' (page 3) produce appearances which have been attributed to subsequent denudation.

"Outliers may either be produced during the deposition of a stratum—or long subsequently; but I have not attempted to point out cases of each kind.

"Geologists generally are but slightly acquainted with physical science.   Thus, when I published my theory of the doctrine of isothermal surfaces in the abstract of a paper on the Temple of Serapis examined by me in 1828, the geologists *ignored* the discovery. But when at a later period Sir John Herschel arrived at the same conclusions which I first published for him in the First Edition of The Ninth Bridgewater Treatise, the Geological Society republished a few days after in their abstracts that portion of his letter which contained his view of the subject, without *any reference* to my publication several years before in a former volume of their proceedings.

"This tendency first to ignore and then to transfer intellectual property from an unpopular to a popular author has met with considerable support from geologists.

"Sir Roderick Murchison, in his 'Siluria,' seems to wish to make it a joint discovery of mine and my friend's.

"Other geologists have followed in his track, and foreign writers have been misled; until at last I was myself present at a meeting of the Geological Society at which the theory of isothermal surfaces was assigned entirely to Herschel.   Neither the president nor any other member corrected the error, and it would so have appeared in the printed proceedings had I not mentioned the subject to the secretary, who took upon himself the responsibility of mentioning my name.

"I have added a note to Stephenson's opinion, which I wish to be inserted, with my name attached, if you wish it. . . ."

Pengelly's correspondence was now so large that it is marvellous how a man, busily occupied as he was, could keep it in hand.   Strangers wrote constantly, asking his views on every variety of subject.   That many of these letters were not of much interest may be judged from his remarking occasionally that the postmen had "brought him several *envelopes*, which did not deserve to be called letters."   In sending replies, he was greatly assisted by his wife, who also helped him in a variety of ways, especially in translating foreign scientific works and papers, and acting as interpreter with scientific foreigners whom they met at home and abroad, for he was no linguist.   He laughingly accounted for the inability of the French people to understand him, by asserting that in passing through the capital his accent had become too Parisian to be understood in the Provinces.

His love of fun was infectious, and made him a pleasant companion in every class of society. An inveterate punster, and endowed with a keen sense of the ridiculous, his humour was invariably kindly and genial.

Pengelly to his Wife.

"*Lamorna, June* 5, 1862. . . . Since I last wrote you I have had some letters from Dr. Falconer. I enclose them; they will tell their own story. Falconer's first was in reply to one I sent him, informing him that I had given up all thought of London for the present. It is most vexing about the plates,* but I confess I feared it from the first. I wished much to have been in town to have looked after my paper last night. I hope they treated me mercifully. I am progressing very satisfactorily with my collection. I have finished the Sponges, and am perhaps half-way through the Corals; my last entry was number 576. This post has brought me a letter from Falconer, and also one from Miss Coutts. I must send Falconer's to her to-day. Heer insists on seventeen plates. T. Hunton has been in to supper, and we have had a nice chat. . . ."

Pengelly to his Wife.

"*Lamorna, June* 18, 1862. . . . Here goes, I hope, for the last letter to you on this occasion. Be sure to write me, by return if possible, to say by what train I am to expect you. Tell Miss Forster as is, but who is to be Mrs. ——, that I observe I am not invited to the wedding, and that I am so far from being vindictive that I will do her two kind acts. If she will send me a telegram just to say at what moment the happy couple intend to tear themselves away from their sorrowing friends for their journey, I will throw one of my oldest slippers at my wheelbarrow. I would throw it at the carriage were I at hand, but I am not without hopes that she will be nearly as much benefited by the plan I propose. . . ."

Pengelly to his Wife.

"*Lamorna, June* 18, 1862.— . . . The party at Miss Hopperton's school went off well. There was a crowd; there was the 'Mademoiselle,' the 'Fraulein,' C. Fowler, and myself. The visitors included Mr. and Mrs. Pitcairn, Dr. Edersheim,† and lots of other folk, all very good and proper. Plenty of music, instrumental and vocal."

Pengelly to his Wife.

"*London, July* 3, 1862.— . . . I reached this duly yesterday. Found Dr. Falconer from home. Went on to Miss Coutts at once; found her cordial as ever, though in great bustle for her party in the evening. It is said, and I believe truly, that there were a thousand guests. The Duke d'Aumale was there, also Murchison, Falconer, Lankester,

---

* Illustrating Professor Heer's paper for the Royal Society.
† Rev. Alfred Edersheim, D.D., afterwards Greenfield lecturer at Oxford.

Gladstone, Bowring, Landseer, E. W. Cooke, Fowler, and many others I knew and had pleasant chats with. I slept in Stratton Street last night, and am to go on to Holly Lodge to-night. Miss Coutts wishes me to remain until Tuesday, which I shall probably do. I am in great haste now, and hope to write you a better letter to-morrow. . . ."

Pengelly to his Wife.

"*Holly Lodge, July* 4, 1862.— . . . Yesterday I spent the greater part of the day at Falconer's, where I breakfasted. We went thoroughly over my Bovey paper. I am to take it down to Torquay with me, and Heer's also, for I am to prepare both. In the afternoon I called on Dr. Skey, and finding that he was also going to Holly Lodge, I agreed to accompany him ; but before we set out I went to Jermyn Street and had a good chat with some of the men, chiefly Salter. I am sorry to find he is about to leave the Museum. . . . I hope to get home on Tuesday, but I doubt my being able to go to the 'Field Club.' I shall try to get to the Exhibition to-day. Yesterday was very wet ; this morning gives promise of a fine day, which I hope may be realized, as Miss Coutts is to have a great Horticultural Fête here. All the world is expected. . . ."

Pengelly to his Wife.

"*International Exhibition, July* 4, 1862.— . . . Yesterday, having received an invitation from my friend, E. W. Cooke (the Royal Academician), to dine with him, I left Holly Lodge as soon as the Flower Show opened, so as to secure a peep at it, and went to the Exhibition. At 5.30 I went to Cooke's, where I found every evidence of a successful artist and a man of great taste. You would enjoy going over his house greatly ; it is a perfect museum of everything old and interesting. Fossils, pictures, old furniture, antiquities generally ; his garden, too, is a gem, beautifully and expensively made the most of. He had a rather large party, among them Ward the botanist. I have given up all thought of the meeting on Haldon. . . ."

Pengelly to his Wife.

"*Holly Lodge, July* 8, 1862.— . . . This, in all probability, is to be my last letter to you on this occasion. On Saturday morning two carriages left this for the International Exhibition. The first contained Miss Coutts, the Bishop of Cape Town and his wife (Mrs. Gray) and myself; the second, Mr. St. John * (author of 'Life in the Forests of the Far East,' *i.e.* Borneo, etc.) and Mr. Johnson (nephew of Sir J. Brooke).

"The Exhibition opens on Saturdays at 12, and we got there at 11.30 so as to have a private view; this indulgence had been granted to Miss Coutts. She left early ; but I remained there until 5 p.m., believing it would be my last visit. Truly it is a splendid thing. I cannot

---

* Now Sir Spencer St. John, English Ambassador at Stockholm.

particularize further than that the machinery astounded and even awed me, and the Colonial Courts showed me the germs of future empires. I saw nothing in the Picture department which pleased me more than 'Eastward Ho.' I met many people I knew. I returned to this to dinner, where I met the Bishop of Oxford and his son; the former is the most able and agreeable man in company I ever met, the latter the most free-and-easy. Yesterday the Bishop preached here a missionary sermon, very clear, very learned, and eloquent in a very high degree, but over the heads of ordinary hearers. With this exception yesterday was a very quiet day. There is to be a great gathering of Antiquaries in Stratton Street to-night, hence I stay over until to-morrow. . . ."

During the summer of 1862 the first meeting of the Devonshire Association was held at Exeter. The idea of its formation had been originated by Pengelly, who received important assistance from his friends, Sir John Bowring, Mr. Spence Bate, and the Rev. W. Harpley. He had been for some time anxious to form a County Association for the promotion of Scientific and Literary objects, but at first received little encouragement even from some of those who afterwards became his colleagues. He was not, however, easily discouraged by difficulties, even though they might appear insurmountable to others. He worked and waited, and was rewarded by the eminently satisfactory character of the opening meeting at Exeter, under the able Presidency of Sir John Bowring. The gathering, though small, was distinguished by able and most interesting papers, and animated discussions, and the Association soon became recognized beyond the county of Devon as a centre of intellectual life and work.

Pengelly, besides contributing numerous papers, managed all the financial work with characteristic caution and success. It is almost needless to say that his connection with the Association, as with the other societies in which he was interested, was purely honorary, although his labours connected with it involved the sacrifice of a large portion of his time, inasmuch as they necessitated his attending to numerous details which, though apparently trifling in themselves, were indispensable to the success of each meeting. Many of his friends regretted the absorption of so much of his leisure, but he himself was always anxious to devote any spare moments to the promotion of scientific and literary objects in his adopted county.

At the first meeting he read a paper on " The Lignites and

Clays of Bovey Tracy," and "The Age of the Dartmoor Granites."

Pengelly's letters describing the Exeter Meeting, with accounts of the various papers read, are nearly all missing; but one, giving a sketch of the social character of the gathering, has been preserved.

Pengelly to his Wife.

"*Exeter.*— . . . Many of the papers were short, and elicited good discussions.   We sat until about half-past four.   The audience was small, as there were the more popular attractions of a Bazaar and Flower Show.   At 5.30 we dined together, and had an ample supply of food and fun. . . . After dinner there were some decent speeches; and at half-past eight we went in a goodly party to Lady Bowring's tea-table, where Sir John christened me Mr. *Pun*gelly.   Friday was so wet that we had to give up the excursions, and so I got home early in the afternoon.   I am happy to say mother is quite well now, though sorry to lose Alfred, who has been extremely good and attentive to her.   He left us this morning in good spirits. . . ."

The Rev. W. Harpley, the valued Honorary General Secretary, gives the following description of Pengelly's work in connection with the Association.[*]

"In 1862, he started the Devonshire Association for the Advancement of Science, Literature, and Art, of which he was President in 1867–8.   Until the last few years he was the best-known figure at the Annual Meetings of the Association, and for a considerable period he regularly contributed papers upon a variety of subjects.   Not only did the plan of a County Association, on the lines, to a certain extent, of the British Association, originate in his fertile brain, but it has been chiefly owing to his instrumentality and careful and judicious organization, that the Association has grown and prospered.   He managed it financially, until physical infirmities compelled him to relinquish the work."

Another of the members has kindly written an excellent account of the objects and scope of the Association.

" *A Reminiscence of the late William Pengelly, F.R.S., in his connection with the Devonshire Association : by a Member of the Association, of nearly thirty years' standing.*

"It is commonly understood that what is now known as "The Devonshire Association" owes its origin to a small group of men of scientific and literary culture, resident at Plymouth.   This is, in a sense,

<hr>

[*] *Transactions of the Devonshire Association,* July, 1894.

correct; but, beyond controversy, the first idea of the scheme emanated from Mr. Pengelly. At that time, however—and I am referring to the year 1861—the southern part of Devonshire was not unprepared for some such development of intellectual activity. Plymouth had its established local institution, publishing its *Transactions*. Exeter was distinctly a literary centre, although the atmosphere of a cathedral city was not then altogether favourable, it was supposed, to scientific investigation. And Torquay, with its leisured, if cosmopolite, circles had already its Natural History Society, of which Mr. Pengelly had been one of the founders.

"Some organization on a more comprehensive scale was now aimed at, and at the right moment Mr. Pengelly, a born administrator, whose scientific attainments had already been recognized on a wider field, and who had acquired a practical knowledge of the working of the British Association as one of the honorary secretaries of the Geological Section, conferred with Sir John Bowring and Mr. Spence Bate, who warmly seconded him; and the Devonshire Association, for the advancement of science, literature, and art, was fairly launched. There were preliminary discouragements, as of course; and Mr. Spence Bate had almost feared that the bantling, as he facetiously called it, which had been cradled in Plymouth, would never emerge to breathe the larger air of the county.

" The professed objects of the Association were : ' To give a stronger impulse and a more systematic direction to scientific inquiry in Devonshire, and to promote the intercourse of those who cultivate science, literature, or art in different parts of the county.' The form which the Association ultimately took, its aims and methods, from which it has since departed only in details, was a modest imitation of those of the British Association, only with the addition of literature and art to its objects, and the limitation of its sphere of action to the county of Devon. Science was to be at the forefront; but latterly the tendency has been rather towards historical and archæological subjects. This, however, has been probably due merely to a fluctuation of taste or thought, that is to be expected from time to time.

" Of the group of original promoters of the Association only a few, I believe, now survive, including W. Vicary, F.G.S., J. Brooking Rowe, F.L.S., and the Rev. William Harpley, from the beginning to the present time the General Honorary Secretary of the Association, who by his eminent services has secured and retained the esteem and confidence of the members generally.

"The first general meeting of the Association took place at Exeter in August, 1862, under the presidency of Sir John Bowring, a man of eminent ability, of broad sympathies, and of encyclopædic knowledge, with a reputation as a philologist almost European. I am not sure that the meeting was not looked upon somewhat askance by a few persons of light and leading in the city. Be that as it may, ten years later, amidst the same surroundings, the annual gathering of the members took place under the presidency of the bishop of the diocese.

"Six papers only were read at the first meeting, a contrast to the six-and-twenty which is now about the average number; but the promise of the development and success of the Association was assuring. In accordance with its migratory programme, the Association, in the following years, held its meetings in different towns in the county, gathering new members everywhere and fresh interest as to its proceedings. The influence of these meetings, while otherwise socially agreeable, has been most marked in stimulating researches connected with local history, archæology, or science, which would otherwise have been neglected, and in directing attention to objects of interest which would have been overlooked or lost. Such obligations are rarely acknowledged ; but, if all paid their due, many of us would have to account to the memory of William Pengelly for a new interest in life.

"Without any fixed rule, the president of the Association of the year has been usually selected on account of his recognized distinction in his own department, whether of science, literature, or art ; and it is to the credit of Devonshire that on several occasions the choice has fallen within the limits of the county. At the Barnstaple Meeting, in the year 1867, Mr. Pengelly, who had been recently elected a Fellow of the Royal Society, filled the office with considerable *éclat*. His inaugural address, being mainly a brilliant and lucid review of the then existing knowledge of the geology of Devonshire, was listened to, as the demonstration of a master, with unmistakable interest.

"In the year 1876 an alteration was made in one of the bye-laws of the Association, at the instance, I believe, of Mr. Pengelly, to which we had been rapidly drifting. The subjects of the papers to be offered to the Association were henceforth strictly limited to those relating to Devonshire. It might have been, and probably was, doubted by some not having the advantage of being Devonians, whether, with this restriction, the contributions to the paper-list were likely to be of sufficient volume to do credit to the Association. But the justification was the immediate advance that took place in the number of members from three hundred and fifty-six to four hundred and seventy-one within the next two years, and the obvious satisfaction with which the localization of the aims of the Association was received. Since that time nearly thirty original papers, including reports of committees, have been, on the average, annually read before the Association, all relating to Devonshire ; and there is, as yet, no sign of any diminution in the rate of their production.

"At the annual gathering of the members there was perhaps no gratification so much looked for, when Mr. Pengelly was present, than the discussions elicited by the reading of the several papers. A characteristic of Mr. Pengelly on these occasions will be at once remembered. There was no mistaking the evident zest with which, after the reading of a paper, he initiated, as he generally did, a discussion thereon. He took his part with unfailing geniality, and his views upon the value of facts, upon the importance of precision of language, and upon the folly of hasty generalizations, were pretty sure to come to the fore. Mentally I am disposed to bracket him with a famous Oxford tutor who lived to be a hundred years of age, and who, on being asked what oracular advice he could give to his pupils as a result of his long experience, replied, ' Verify your references.'

"An extra work at the Association which extended over a period of eight years, has been the translation, extension, and printing of the

Domesday record so far as it related to Devonshire.   Mr. Pengelly had grave misgivings as to the strain which this undertaking might have upon the finances of the Association.   But there can be no doubt that the Association has done nothing more creditable ; and it may be hoped that the great cost of producing the two handsome volumes of the Devonshire Domesday will be recuperated as the value and importance of the work—one of the bases of the history of our land and people— become better known.

"With regard to the quality of the papers contributed to, and subsequently printed in the *Transactions* of the Association, it is not perhaps too much to say that those of few local associations of a similar character possess a higher general level of ability or interest.   Notwithstanding the indulgent censorship of the Secretary, there are not many that can be said to sink below mediocrity.   It would be invidious in the present connection to specify the many of absolute excellence ; but there can be no question that the series of geological and palæontological papers which, during a period of more than twenty years, were contributed by Mr. Pengelly, are a monument to his accurate and recondite knowledge of his facts and of his peculiarly happy manner of treating and expounding them, and also a testimony of the permanent value of the work which he left behind him.   To this general estimate it may be added that the *Transactions* have been not infrequently quoted for proofs and evidences of the original research by some of our most eminent writers.

"In the last few years of Mr. Pengelly's active connection with the Association, he contributed a series of three papers on a subject that led him into an entirely new domain of study, that of comparative biography.   The papers were written with remarkable acumen and minute criticism which might have been expected from the writer, and were certainly read, and will continue to be read, by not a few with appreciative interest.

"There was, I am sure, only one feeling of regret among the members of the society with whom Mr. Pengelly had been for so many years associated, when he withdrew to the retirement which increasing years and infirmities imposed upon him.   He had finished his work.   Yet, to the last, he retained an almost pathetic interest in the Devonshire Association, which he had founded and for which he had done so much.

CHAPTER X.

ELECTED A FELLOW OF THE ROYAL SOCIETY.

SEPTEMBER 1862 AND 1863.

IN the autumn of 1862 Pengelly interested himself in the disposal of Mrs. Griffith's beautiful and valuable collection of sea-weeds, which Miss Coutts was about to present to Kew.

Later in the year he attended the British Association which met at Cambridge ; an additional interest was attached to this visit to the University, as his son Alfred was soon to begin his college life there.

In 1863 Pengelly was elected a Fellow of the Royal Society, and though he usually cared very little for honours and distinctions, was naturally gratified that his scientific services should have been recognized, by what Sir Joseph Hooker once admirably described as "so high an honour as Fellowship of the Royal Society, the only one of the kind in England that is limited as to the number annually elected, and selective in principle." [*]

At the close of July of this year the second annual meeting of the Devonshire Association was held at Plymouth, under the presidency of C. Spence Bate, F.R.S. Pengelly, who communicated a paper on "The Chronological Value of the Red Sandstones and Conglomerates of Devonshire," was greatly encouraged by the complete success of the gathering, and the evidences afforded of the interest in science which it had already fostered in the county.

Pengelly to his Wife.

" 1, *Stratton Street, September* 6, 1862.—Yesterday Miss Coutts took me to the banking house to see the sea-weeds, and having given them some attention, she returned home, and I went on to Tennant's, Somerset

---

[*] Presidential Address to the Royal Society, November 30, 1878.

House, and Jermyn Street; saw Ramsay at the last, and had a good chat with him. Then to Kew, to see Sir William Hooker about the sea-weeds, and there I remained until it was quite time to return to dress for dinner. Sir William was extremely kind, and took me through all the gardens, houses, and museums; it is a fine affair truly. Soon after I called, a gentleman, at the head of the hospital at Trinidad, called also; and we got on capitally. After dinner we went to see *Lord Dundreary*. The piece is stupid and absurd, but the part of Lord Dundreary is acted to perfection, and I think I never laughed more in my life."

Pengelly to his Wife.

"*London, September* 9, 1862.—Yesterday, after a late breakfast, I called on Lyell, and had a long chat with him. In his new book, he says he is 'going the "whole hog" both in the Antiquity of Man, and Darwinism, and if any man ever deserved excommunication, he thinks he certainly will.' I did not gather from him when the book will appear.

"I then went off to the British Museum, and whilst talking with the brothers Woodward, in their private room, Falconer came in; he was very pleasant, and we engaged to go together to Somerset House.

"My business at the museum was to take S. P. Woodward's opinion as to the best museum to which to send the collection of British shells made by Mrs. Griffiths and purchased by Miss Coutts. Woodward strongly desired to have them there, and referred me to Owen. I took my fish 'scale' with me, and got the opinion of Mr. Davies, a good ichthyologist, on it. He decided it to be a scale of *Phyllopeles concentricus*, a fish characteristic of the uppermost old red sandstone of Glenburnie in Scotland. The fact is a very important one in its bearings, and furnishes me with matter for a paper for the British Association. It is so important that Owen took a note of it at once. Owen also wishes to have the shells there, in the event of their getting a grant for the removal of the museum into a larger building. Falconer and I then started for Somerset House, where I got, through him, all the 'plans' of the Brixham cavern. Having arranged to call at Falconer's between four and five, I called at Tennant's to name some Devonshire corals, etc., for him. This done I started to see R. Godlee at his chambers. Then to Mudie's, where I bought Percy's 'Metallurgy.' Then to Falconer's, where I made the few alterations in my paper which I desired, and then back to Stratton Street. We dined at 6.30, and afterwards Miss Coutts and Mrs. Browne, Miss Savage and I went to Drury Lane to see the *Colleen Bawn*, which greatly delighted me, and then home to bed. . . ."

Pengelly to his Wife.

"*Cambridge, October* 6, 1862.—After breakfast yesterday, several of our Corpus party walked into the country, about three miles, to attend church. The building was extremely simple, the preacher a decidedly good man, but not a philosopher. He preached on angelic existences. We then walked back to hear, at St. Mary's, what may be called the British Association sermon, by a celebrated man whose name has escaped me. It was the first of a series of lectures on the Life of St. Paul, and was devoted to the consideration of the Apostle as a man of tact and presence of mind; it was extremely able, and was listened to by a large party of the Association men. Another stroll into the country brought the hour for dinner. I think I told you I was to dine at Potts'. There was a large gathering of ladies, Mrs. Fison, a cousin of Mrs. Potts', being amongst them; but besides Potts and myself there was only one other gentleman, a Dr. Heaton of Leeds. Mrs. Potts is beautiful, young, and clever, and talks admirably. Potts is elderly, and talks excellently. We had a good time. I scarcely think 'there is a better time coming.' Brixham was loudly called for, and made a decided impression. . . ."

To ameliorate in any small way the condition of the poor Irish fishermen was a most congenial task to Pengelly, the humane and serious side of whose character was well known to intimate friends. Any memoir would be imperfect which left unnoticed his strenuous efforts to improve the prospects of others, and his many acts of unostentatious kindness.

Mrs. Pengelly to her Sister.

"*January* 15, 1863.— . . . Please tell M——[*] that Mr. Crawfurd, whom she will remember as Chairman of the Ethnological Section at Manchester, is coming to-morrow on a visit to Miss Coutts, and William is going to dine with him to-morrow and the next day. He has been in correspondence with R. Were Fox, for Miss Coutts, about the Irish fishermen, as she is very desirous of doing something to improve them. . . ."

Surprise has often been expressed that a complete account of the results obtained by the Brixham Cavern Committee was so long in being given to the scientific world. Pengelly, having personally conducted the whole of the work himself, had lost no time in preparing his own report. The latter part of the following letter will show that he was in no way responsible for the delay which caused so much comment.

Pengelly to Dr. Falconer.†

"Lamorna, Torquay, December 16, 1862.

" . . . Of course I have not forgotten that 'the Brixham Cave exploration was carried on throughout under the Committee of the Geological Society,' seeing that I was a member of the committee. But, truth to tell, I had come to the conclusion that the committee had

---

* A married sister.

† The early part of this letter, which is omitted, refers exclusively to Professor Heer's work, and has no reference whatever to Brixham Cavern.

'died and made no sign,' since it had allowed three years and a half to elapse, since the exploration had closed, without anything in the shape of a report.

"Until receiving your last I was not aware that Mr. Prestwich was the secretary of the committee.

"Since I last wrote you I have decided to wait until I have had the opportunity of reading Sir C. Lyell's book, which, right or wrong, we are looking for daily here in the country. After that, since the committee is still alive, I shall, with great pleasure, be prepared to submit my paper, on the Cavern, to the committee, through Mr. Prestwich, the secretary; as soon as I hear from him that the other reports of which you speak—on the Bones, the Flints, and the Gravels—are also ready.

"I presume this will be the right course, since you think it doubtful 'whether the Royal Society would entertain a paper on an isolated part of the investigation.'

"I am very sorry to hear of Mrs. McCall's indisposition, both on her account and on yours. We men are but part of ourselves without the kind offices of a woman."

"P.S.—I will write to Mr. Prestwich, at once, to inform him that I have a paper on Brixham, and asking for information."

Sir Charles Lyell to Pengelly.

"*London, February* 18, 1863.— . . . I thank you much for the notes and corrections on the Torquay cave, all of which are adopted.

"Although the errata already amount to about forty, scarcely any one has hit on the same mistakes as another, even of the attentive readers.

"So when you have read more you will greatly oblige me by sending any remarks.

"The history of the obstacles put in the way of your publishing the Brixham results makes me somewhat indignant, and if I were not afraid of doing mischief I should take it up more vehemently, but I shall not forget it.

"I shall tell the President of the Royal Society how the matter stands, and how injurious I consider it to be to you personally. . . ."

The following letter received from Lyell tells its own tale :—

Sir Charles Lyell to Pengelly.

"53, *Harley St., London, Monday, April* 13, 1863.— . . . I have just returned to town and find your letter. I may say that, being a member of the Committee [Brixham Cave], I always understood that the idea of working it systematically had originated with the Nat. Hist. Soc. of Torquay. . . . that they were in treaty for a lease, had secured the refusal, and that they had caused the ransacking of the contents to be discontinued. . . . There can be no harm in my saying that you had previously studied caves, served on the Kent's Hole committee, and objected to former mode of working, etc. I may also say that Mr. Pengelly was the first geologist who visited the cave. . . ."

Notwithstanding the time occupied in scientific work and correspondence whilst in London during the summer of 1863, Pengelly had numerous social engagements, from which he derived great pleasure.

Pengelly to his Wife.

" 1, *Stratton Street, May 28, 1863.* Yesterday after breakfast I called on Sir C. Lyell and remained with him until about noon. Then to the British Museum to see Woodward about Mr. Vicary's[*] box of fossils. He could make nothing of them. Afterwards to South Kensington Flower Show. The azaleas and geraniums were quite gorgeous ; and the ladies many of them very beautiful, so it was not a great trial of one's self-denial to be there. I forgot to say that I called at Jermyn Street to see Salter about Mr. Vicary's fossils; but he was out, so I left the fossils, and saw Sir Roderick, who gave me a ticket for his gathering as President of the Geographical, telling me that Miss Coutts had written informing him of my being in town, and that he was that moment about to send off a card to Stratton Street, for me. At seven dined."

Pengelly to his Wife.

" 1, *Stratton Street, London, May 29, 1863.*— . . . I returned here about four o'clock, and found an arrangement had been made for me to go to the House of Commons, where I should meet John Abel Smith, who would take me into the House to hear a debate on the Dover Contract. I heard Mr. Walpole, Gladstone, Lord J. Manners, Lindsay, Lord R. Cecil, and Whiteside. The last I can scarcely say I heard, as the House was impatient to divide and made a great row. The division at length came, 191 to 205, *i.e.* 14 for Ministers. . . ."

Pengelly to his Wife.

(Date uncertain.)

". . . Next I called on Tennant, and then back to dinner. I knew most of the guests, to wit Dean and Mrs. Milman, Mr. Harness (author of Miss Mitford's Life and Letters), Miss Moore (niece of Sir John Moore), Miss Smith, etc., etc. After dinner came Crawfurd, Count Strelezski, and General Kmety, a Hungarian, who was the real defender of Kars, and so the evening passed off mighty pleasantly. The lecture seems to be the only real business I have in town.

"There appears to be some scheme afoot to bring me permanently to town. At any rate, J. A. Smith spoke to me on the subject, but I think it is no more than a vague and misty idea, and will probably melt away. . . ."

Pengelly to his Wife.

" *Stratton Street, June 2, 1863.* . . . You will see that I am really going off to-day. I am getting quite proud of my self-denial, for there

---

[*] William Vicary, Esq., F.G.S., of Exeter, an intimate and highly valued friend.

is much to tempt me to remain.   There is to be a good meeting of the Ethnological to-night, and to-morrow night the whole Abbeville case comes on at the Geological, yet I mean to go.   Yesterday I made a delightful call on my pupil, Mrs. Cavendish, then to see the Ghost at the Polytechnic, which is well worth seeing.   Then to the House of Commons with Captain Gordon, then with Miss Coutts and Mrs. Browne to Lady Lyell's party.   Lady Lyell very beautiful.   I met Murchison, Cooke, Sir P. Egerton, Bunbury, Babbage, etc."

Early in June Pengelly received a letter from Mr. J. W. Salter asking him to procure some Devonshire fossils, which Sir Roderick Murchison had long been desirous of securing.

J. W. Salter to Pengelly.

"*June* 2, 1863.— . . . I am sorry I was out, the more so as I hope to be down in your neighbourhood for a day or so in August, and should be very glad if you were to meet our party and give us the benefit of your local knowledge.   Perhaps we may meet?   At all events I shall drop you a line when we have made our day out, and take the chance.   As Austen and Pattison will probably be with us, you would not think the day ill given, I know.

"Now to business.   Those fossils, which I asked you three years back to procure, and which you promised to try for, are still *desiderata* in our cabinet.   I have Sir R.'s sanction for saying, that though we have no cash for a general collection of Plymouth fossils, he should feel *obliged* by your looking out for specimens of these—if they should fall in your way for us.   You know best where these *occur*, how they *occur*, and why they *occur*.   And it *occurs* to me, that if they *occur* to you, it may *occur* to the men to offer them to you, and we shall be all the better and happier and richer if you cause them to *occur* in our museum, and some of Sir R.'s spare cash in the men's pockets. Q.E.D.

"I was at Dudley at Whitsuntide.   Such fun!   Why not leave your box?   I would have sent them to you.   Will August do?"

The tie between Pengelly and many of his pupils was exceedingly strong, as will be seen by an extract of a letter from one of them, who had heard there was some prospect of his leaving Torquay.

"My first feeling on reading the latter part of your letter was one of such *intense selfishness*, that I would not let myself write for a few days, till I could say that *if you leave Torquay for your own advantage*, I shall be glad of it, though I shall miss you more than any friend you have there. . . . Tell me what to look for near Lewes in the Chalk. I mean to work very hard; can I get anything for you?   I don't care for Mr. Gosse or his book; or anything, till I hear whether we are to lose you."

Several well-known men were amongst the fifteen candidates admitted this year to the Royal Society; namely, Sir Henry Roscoe, Professor William Crookes, E. W. Cooke, R.A., Professor Daniel Oliver, Dr. Robert Harley, Dean Stanley, and the Rev. Dr. Salmon, Provost of Trinity College, Dublin. All the active work of Pengelly's candidature had been undertaken by Sir Charles Lyell, who wrote to congratulate him, as did numerous other friends.

Sir Charles Lyell to Pengelly.

" *London, May* 9, 1863.— . . . On my return to-day from Osborne, I am happy to find that you are one of the fifteen selected by the Council of the R.S., for election on the 4th of June as an F.R.S. Of course, until the ratification takes place on that day you will say nothing, but in truth all is now safe.

Pengelly to his Wife.

" *Lamorna, Torquay, June* 7, 1863.— . . . This is the eighth letter I have written to-day, so I opine it runs a risk of being short. Yesterday brought me a letter from the Royal Society, informing me of my election. . . . I have to-day received the first-fruits of my F.R.S. in the form of No. 55 of the 'Proceedings' of the Royal Society. It looks wonderfully dry; a few copies would be of immense value to a laundress. I wonder whether I shall ever get my work done? . . ."

Pengelly to his Wife.

" *Torquay, June* 11, 1863.— . . . I find I must go to town next Thursday, the 18th, to be presented ('admitted' is the right phrase) to the President of the Royal, or defer it to one or other of the two first meetings in November; failing these, my election is void. As there seems to be little to prevent my going up next week, I think of doing so. My intention is to go up on Thursday and back on Friday. Miss Coutts, finding that I must be in town, asked me to go there, and to be present at her ball on the 11th (to-night). I should have liked it; I have no doubt it will be a brilliant affair. The Princess Mary* and Duchess of Cambridge are to be there. Brave moral courage! Remember these facts! State in my epitaph that I was proof against the discussion on the Abbeville jaw and Miss Coutts' ball, yet that I could have enjoyed both. I am writing in the little parlour, all clean and tidy, and most sweet and comfortable, more especially as it smells villainously of Turpentine and Co., who have been introduced here by Mademoiselle New-broom.† I have received Mrs. R——'s and Mrs. W——'s accounts, and am now as rich as a Jew, and am thinking of setting up a carriage and pair."

---

* Now Duchess of Teck.   † A servant.

Pengelly to his Wife.

"*London, June 22,* 1863.— . . . On Saturday I spent the entire morning at Jermyn Street. In the evening Lady Beecher, formerly Miss O'Neill, dined here. . . .

"*June 23rd.*—I am sadly vexed to find in my pocket this morning this letter which should have been posted yesterday. I spent the morning in a visit to Miss Coutts' school, at the east end of London. After luncheon, Mrs. Browne and I went to a huge concert at 2, and about 3.30 Miss Coutts joined us; it was an enormous crowd, and all the vocal stars were there. Then home to dinner, and at 8.30 I started alone for the Geographical meeting, to hear the Nile explorers (Captains Speke and Grant) give an account of their travels. It was a great crush. Speke is a poor speaker, so the meeting was, on the whole, a failure. Grant spoke but little, being second in command."

The distance between London and Torquay often prevented Pengelly being present at meetings which it would have been a great pleasure to him to attend. It was a serious disappointment to him to miss the discussion on the "Abbeville Jaw," a subject frequently referred to in his letters at this time, when it was greatly interesting the geological world. The claims of the local societies which he assisted, and the difficulty of sparing much time from his numerous pupils, however, combined to keep him in Devonshire, although the absence of Mrs. Pengelly, who was staying with her widowed mother (now too great an invalid to come to Torquay) made his home less cheerful than usual.

Mrs. Pengelly to her Mother.

"*Torquay, June* 27, 1863.—William has returned, having much enjoyed his visit to London. He was at a very large party on Tuesday night, where, amongst others, he met Baron von Brunnow, the Russian Ambassador, with whom he had much interesting talk about his old pupils, the Russian princes, and he made the acquaintance of Whewell and several others. The Duke of Cambridge also was there. Since his return he is very busy with a cavern he is examining, and has got a wall made, and a second door in it; he is, as usual, very closely engaged."

At this time, and on many future occasions, he had the pleasure of accompanying his friend Mr. Vicary on short geological expeditions.

Pengelly to his Wife.

"*Ilfracombe, July* 4, 1863.— . . . We have very much enjoyed our visit here. On Thursday we went to Baggy Point and got some fossils, and saw a gloriously wild coast. Yesterday we went to Lynton, where we saw the Valley of Rocks, and the East and West Lyn, and found a few fossils. I have received your enclosures, and feel that I ought to be back to-day on account of Etheridge ; but as he cannot arrive before twelve on Monday, and probably not so soon, I have accepted Mr. Vicary's invitation to remain until Monday, when I hope to get home between two and three. . . ."

The cave-bones which Pengelly had found in Devonshire proved of great importance to Sir Charles Lyell in his investigations.

Sir Charles Lyell to Pengelly.

"53, *Harley Street, London, W., July* 16, 1863.—I was glad to receive your report on my return from a visit to the Museums of Paris and Chartres, as well as to the Drift containing *Elephas meridionalis* at St. Prest. I send you Desnoyers' two papers on the marked bones, of which I examined some hundred and fifty or more, and most interesting they were. If by any chance you possess Desnoyers' papers, please return them to me ; but, if not, I wish you to study them.

"From this time forth we shall want abundance of specimens of bones collected from caverns in which we are certain that man dwelt or took refuge. I am not sorry that you are working at a collection of remains of comparatively modern date.

" I think I can disprove Desnoyers' *glacial* strictures, or his ice-theory, but the human agency is more promising; but here we have a new language to learn. All the negative and positive observations of your cave-bones will acquire new importance. Lartet distinguishes at once between the marks of teeth of dogs (or wolves) and hyænas, or rodents and carnivora. There are cuts circling half round some bones which it is most difficult to refer to any action *yet known*, save human tools.

"An argument at Paris against certain marks indicating man's intervention was that there are too many of them at St. Prest ; but on counting the unscratched or uncut bones, I found them far more numerous in proportion than had been supposed. I must have seen two or three hundreds.

"Every one of your bones of the commonest animal acquire a new interest by these new theories. How many are free from all marks? How many exhibit scrapings, sawings, cuttings, fractures, etc., which are distinct from furrowing caused by organic structure and from teeth-marks of animals, and modern pickaxe blows and scratch of finger-nails in clearing?

" I shall be for four days (from July 20th to 24th) at Col. Wood's, Southall, Swansea, and shall be glad of a letter if, after reading Desnoyers, any queries or facts suggest themselves. I shall have my friend Symonds with me, and we shall go into some of the principal Glamorganshire caves and over Col. Wood's museum.

"No less than one hundred and twenty molars of *El. meridionalis* have been found in one large gravel-pit at St. Prest, unaccompanied by any other species of elephant !"

Sir Charles Lyell to Pengelly.

"53, *Harley Street, London, August* 6, 1863.—I returned to-day from a three weeks' geological tour through South and North Wales, with Rev. W. S. Symonds, Pendock Rectory, Tewkesbury, who is coming out with a second edition of his geological book, and would be well worthy of one of the six copies of the Bovey paper, which looks very handsome, and will, I am sure, read well when I can get a few hours to study it.   I should have replied to your letter before, but we had, what is almost unheard of in Wales, uninterrupted fine weather in July, so I never had the rainy day which I had determined to spend in answering letters. . . .

". . . I am glad you are persevering in the cave exploration.   I have not time to enter on the Gower caves to which we gave nearly a week.

" I collected arctic shells from the glacial drift of Moel Tryfan near Snowdon, at about 1400 ft. of elevation."

The meeting of the British Association at Newcastle-on-Tyne was a great success.

Pengelly to his Wife.

" *Newcastle-on-Tyne, August* 27, 1863.— . . . The opening meeting last night was in every way a success.   The number of persons present was beyond all precedent, they say 2850.   The President's address the best I ever heard, splendid in matter and excellent in manner.   Lots of my acquaintances here, amongst them Falconer ; Lyell and Owen to come on Monday.   I am happy to say I am well and happy, *i.e.* as happy as I can be when absent from the best of wives.   I fear I must conclude having no matter—or too much—or no time."

Pengelly to his Wife.

" *August* 30.—The dinner-party at Sir William Armstrong's last night was large, and the whole affair enjoyable.   Crawfurd, Harkness, Bate, Sorby, and I sat together.   In the midst of the dinner Sir Charles and Lady Lyell came in, having just arrived.   After dinner a huge concert was provided by the Mayor for the Association.   Altogether the Newcastle folk had eclipsed all known in the history of the Association. . . ."

Pengelly to his Wife.

" *Newcastle-on-Tyne, September* 1, 1863.— . . . We had a great day in Section ' C ' yesterday.   Afterwards we fixed the next meeting at Bath, with Lyell as President.   Hurrah ! . . ."

Sir Charles Lyell appears from the following letter to have left during the meeting.   He consulted Pengelly frequently at this period with reference to the new edition of the " Manual " which he was preparing.

Sir Charles Lyell to Pengelly.

"53, *Harley Street, London, September* 1, 1863.— . . . Mr. G. Austen tells me he is to come on with a paper on the Loess of the Rhine, and he told me the purport of it. He promised to send me any abstracts which may be given of it ; but I should consider it a great favour if you will order any newspaper or journal (*Literary Gazette*? or other) which may give reports of the section on this or other matters relating to the Association, as I cannot attend personally.

"I will repay you by postage stamps or if we meet in town. My chapter on the Loess has been in print this four months, and I hardly think I shall have to alter it, but should like to hear what is said on this or on any cave remains, or flint implements, or on the controversy between Owen and Huxley on Man and Ape.

"You know well what would interest and concern me, while I am rapidly passing my sheets through the press. The glacial period is largely treated of by me. Mr. King said he had thoughts of reading a paper on Scotch glacial clays, etc., to the section. I suppose he is in Cambridge, and therefore I do not hear from him in answer to my last letter. I had some other news to send him on the subject of his last to me, had I been sure where to address him. If you see him in the Geological Section, please tell him this.

"I know how precious moments are in the bustle of the meeting, so excuse my writing and asking you to order some papers to be sent to me. I shall not grudge a duplicate should Austen chance to send me the same as you. But his would probably be confined to his own subject, and I should like to see about things in general. I do not take in the *Athenæum* or *Literary Gazette*, so any paper that is really giving the notices would be welcome."

Sir Charles Lyell to Pengelly.

"53, *Harley Street, November* 2, 1863.— . . . I am sorry it would cost so much to do justice to Kent's Hole. We might get a grant of £200 or more from the Royal Society, and perhaps some from the British Association, but I do not see my way for the rest. I would join in a private subscription, but we could hardly raise enough. . . .

" In the Gibraltar cave there are human jaws of individuals of two races, and much pottery of two ages, and *below* the stalagmitic crust rhinoceros, ursus, leopard, zebra or small horse, hyæna crocuta, ox, deer, etc.

"The Bovey Tracey paper is very well done, and makes a handsome and instructive work. I hope soon to send a copy of 3rd Edition of 'Antiquity,' with additions in appendix."

Sir Charles Lyell to Pengelly.

"53, Harley Street, December 21, 1863.

" I find my wife is writing to you on behalf of a governess, which reminds me that when I read over my twenty-sixth Chapter of the 'Manual' or 'Elements,' which has required much re-casting in the Scotch part, I was rather wishing to have your criticism on pages 423 and 424, etc., on the South Devon Devonian. I am trying not to extend the text, both because I am pressed for time, as well as for space. My getting out the book will depend on my being able to leave a good deal of it unaltered, except where there are positive errors. But if a good writer like yourself could suggest a sentence or two by way of modification, improvement, or addition, it would be welcome and not cause delay. The pages I allude to struck me as rather dry, and might be enlivened by citing briefly your palæontological results on the corals. I shall not want it before a month hence. In a day or two I hope to send you the third edition of my 'Antiquity of Man' by post, in which you will see not a few of your suggestions adopted."

Pengelly to Sir Charles Lyell.

"Lamorna, Torquay, December 24, 1863.

"Many thanks for yours of the 21st inst. I need not inform you that though Sir R. Murchison regards the Slates, Grits, and Limestones of Devon and Cornwall as strictly contemporaneous with the Old Red Sandstones, and, indeed, places the Upper, Middle, and Lower divisions of the former on precisely the same horizons as the groups bearing the same names in the latter (see Siluria, 3rd edition, p. 433); and though Mr. Salter has recently endorsed this doctrine (see *Quar. Jour. Geol. Soc.* for November, 1863, pp. 474 to 496), there are many who do not subscribe to it.

"To pass by all other dissidents at present, I may mention that Mr. B. Jukes, knowing that Mr. Davidson is now engaged on his Monograph of British Devonian Brachiopoda, has recently been in correspondence with him on the subject. The latter has been so kind as to forward to me all the letters as they came in, so that I am pretty well acquainted with Mr. Jukes' present views. I say 'present' because he has recently taken them up.

"The first part—there will be three—of the 'Devonian Brachiopoda' will contain something—probably not much—on the question. It will appear early in 1864; it is hoped in January, say February. I wish you could have the advantage of seeing it before completing your corrections.

"The following passages will put you in possession of Mr. Jukes' opinions :—

"'The beds of North Devon are identical in mineral character with those of South Cork, and the fossils' (many of which he says are identical) 'occur in precisely the same positions, etc. But clearly the whole of our Carboniferous slate' (of South Cork) 'is above the top of the Old Red Sandstone, as may be seen in section after section for hundreds of miles, therefore it cannot be called Devonian anyhow. And if, as I believe, it is merely the muddy and sandy representative of the Carboniferous limestone, it follows that all the Marwood and Pilton beds of North Devon are so too. I am *perfectly* convinced that this is the true interpretation, and that in North Devon there is not a fossil that is not a genuine carboniferous one, and no such thing as a Devonian one at all. What is the case in South Devon I do not know . . . but I suspect all the so-called Devonians are merely geographical representatives of the carboniferous beds, and that Calceola and Stringocephalus, etc., are merely southern carboniferous forms, contemporaneous with the well-known carboniferous in Britain and Ireland, and not preceding them.

"'As to the Old Red Sandstone, it will have to be split into two if not three. The Cephalaspis beds are the top of the Upper Silurian, the Cocostens beds will probably form the base of the carboniferous. Perhaps there might be a middle group, which may be called *Devonian*, provided it can be proved to occur in Devonshire.'

"In writing Mr. Davidson I made the following remarks, which will give you my opinion on the question. 'Mr. Jukes appears to hold that the entire Siluro-Carboniferous interval is represented by the Old Red Sandstone. If he is correct in this, it will follow, I think, that our lower slates, *i.e.* those below the Torbay, Newton and Plymouth limestones, are the only true Devonian beds we have, all above them being Carboniferous.' (See my paper in *Geologist* for 1862, pp. 456–9.) 'Nay, if Mr. Jukes carries out his threat of handing over to the Carboniferous system the upper Old Red, our lower slates must go too, as they are, I think, on the same horizon. My impression, however, is that the Old Red Sandstone represents the lower, and the Devonshire or Devonian beds the upper part, of the Devonian period or Siluro-Carboniferous interval as in the following scheme.

Carboniferous.

		Petherwin.
	Damnonian.	Dartmouth, or Upper Slates.
Devonian.		Torquay, or Limestones.
	Old Red.	Meadfoot, or Lower Slates and Upper Old Red.
		Middle Old Red.
		Lower Old Red.

Silurian.

"'I believe the Pilton or Barnstaple group to be rather Carboniferous than Devonian, perhaps passage-beds between the two; hence they are omitted here.

"'The Dartmouth and Petherwin groups may be on the same horizon, but the former has yielded very few fossils. . . .

"'It is no doubt the truth that there are certain species common to Devonshire and to the Carboniferous system; but it is not the *whole* truth, for there are also some species common to Devonshire and the Silurian system, whilst by far the greater number are neither Silurian nor Carboniferous, but *intermediate* forms, that is, they represent an *intermediate* period, if it be possible for fossils to do so. There is no doubt that, both specifically and generically, the connection with the Carboniferous is closer than with the Silurian system; but this appears to prove merely that we have no lower Devonian rocks in this county.'

"I fear, Sir Charles, this long affair will have wearied you. I will only add that I am engaged in making an abstract of all that has been written on our Devonian rocks since 1836, and that you will find all I have written on them in the following papers, viz. 'On the Devonian Age of the World' (see *Geologist* for 1861, pp. 332–347), 'On the Geographical' (misprinted 'Geological') 'and Chronological Distribution of the Devonian Fossils of Devon and Cornwall' (see *Geologist* for 1862, pp. 10–31). This paper was printed more correctly in the Report of the Cornwall Geological Society. I think I sent you one of the reprints, 'On the Correlations of the Slates and Limestones of Devon and Cornwall with the Old Red Sandstones of Scotland' (see *Geologist* for 1862, pp. 456–459).

"I trust I need not say that I shall be delighted, and indeed proud, to write anything to be added to or cited in your Devonian chapter; but as all I can say on the fossils of this district will be found in the papers just named, you will, perhaps, be more likely to please yourself by boiling down to a sentence or two, all I have written in many. . . ."

Amongst the visitors to Torquay in the autumn were Dr. Day and Mr. D'Israeli. This was the commencement of an intimate friendship between Pengelly and Dr. Day which lasted till the death of the latter. Although closely occupied at this time, he paid very frequent visits to this invalid friend, endeavouring to cheer his sad and painful hours.

Mrs. Pengelly to her Mother.

"*November*, 27, 1863.—Yesterday I went to call on Dr. Day, late Professor of St. Andrews, and a friend of Professor Edward Forbes, who is come here in a very feeble state, from the effects of a fearful accident he met with some years ago on Helvellyn, falling down the shaft of a disused mine; he is almost confined to his bed. He is quite an intellectual man; his relative, Miss Otté, who lives with them, is a clever, interesting woman. She translated Humboldt's 'Cosmos.'"

Mrs. Pengelly to her Mother.

"*Torquay*, 1863.— . . . We have had several calls lately from Mr. Dillon Croker, son of Crofton Croker the author; he brought a letter of introduction to William from Mr. Wright the antiquary, whom he knows intimately. He tells us that Wright is often up at four in the morning at his writing, and gets through a vast amount of work. . . . Mr. Croker is also a friend of Halliwell, the Shakesperian writer, so he and William have much in common."

"*Torquay*, November 29, 1863.— . . . Dined at Mrs. Cosway's on Friday, meeting amongst others Sir John and Lady Harding; he is a lawyer, and had the chief settlement of the Trent question. D'Israeli is staying here at present, the old lady he used to come to see having just died—Mrs. Bridges Williams. She was over a hundred. It is more than eighty years since she was married. She lived near the Hacks, who knew her well and said she was very eccentric, keeping a whole colony of cats. She had no near relations, so some time ago wrote a letter to D'Israeli saying how much she admired him, and should like to make his acquaintance. When he got the letter, he was staying with the father of Monckton Milnes, and read the letter out at dinner, as a good joke; but a lady who was present told him she came from Torquay and knew Mrs. Bridges Williams, and advised him to answer it seriously; so he came to Torquay to visit her, and now she has left him £50,000. . . ."

Pengelly's geological rambles frequently landed him at nightfall in out-of-the-way districts. He describes, in the following words, the difficulties he sometimes experienced in finding a night's shelter :—

"I once spent a summer morning in a quarry of yellowish argillaceous deposits. The commencement of the day was fine, but not assured. Its beauty was somewhat enhanced by a suspicious indication of eventual rain, which was strengthened by the fact that several immediately preceding days had been very wet. About eleven o'clock it accordingly began to rain, but so gently as not to interfere seriously with my work, and as the sky for some time seemed not to have quite decided on its course of action I continued to seek and extract fossils. Soon after noon, however, all hesitation was abandoned ; the rain became so very decided and energetic that there was nothing for me but to seek a temporary home. The nearest town was several miles distant, but I strode rapidly on, through the heavy rain and abundant mud, and soon became thoroughly wet through, whilst my clothing failed not to testify to the colour of the deposits in the quarry where my morning had been spent. Had the question been put respecting my appearance, I must undoubtedly have replied that it was bedraggled, pitiable, and utterly unclean. My only thought, however, was that of reaching the town, in which, though an entire stranger, I knew there were plenty of inns. At length I stood at the bar of the principal hotel, but was told that they were quite full, and could not make up another bed. Application to the next inn produced the same result, and so on to the sixth. The case had now become serious; and at length the truth flashed upon me that my appearance was neither respectable nor assuring, and that my ability to pay was probably doubted. Acting under this idea I placed ten sovereigns on my palm, and with open and outstretched hand, proceeded to the next house which promised 'Good entertainment for man and beast,' and asked, 'Can I have a bed?' The effect was magical. 'Certainly, sir,' was the immediate response. Everything was done to make me comfortable; and in a short time I was enjoying an excellent meal, and laughing over my adventures."

On another occasion we find the following amusing account of a ramble near Modbury :—

"To Kingsbridge Road by train. Pleasant walk from station to Modbury. Lanes of the true Devonshire type. Ferns very numerous and luxuriant. Modbury a quiet old town. Walked on to Kingston. Found a comfortable inn—the Britannia—kept by Mr. Berry, who was my pig-killing host of the Jolly Sailor at Mothecombe. The Britannia is at the same time an inn and grocer's shop, and Berry was gone to Plymouth (twelve miles) to lay in a stock of ales, porters, and groceries. Ten o'clock at night having arrived without him, his wife became uneasy, but tried to console herself with the remark, which she frequently made, that the cart would be heavily laden, and the roads very bad. As time crept on, so did her anxiety, which at length became very serious; at last, however, just as the clock had struck eleven, the rumbling of cart wheels in the distance had a tranquillizing effect on her nerves; but when Berry entered the house, it was found he had lost his coat. He had not previously missed it, and thought it must have dropped from the cart not far back; so the tiny servant, only eleven years of age, was sent in search of the missing garment. I volunteered to go too, and at something less than half a mile we found the coat. On our return it appeared the unfortunate Berry had not paid due attention to the stocks of groceries required from Plymouth, and he was being very decidedly, and in no gentle terms, reminded of many such shortcomings on former occasions. His better-half had carefully treasured up all his little as well as his great peccadilloes, and with these, as a 'Cat-o'-hundred-tails,' she certainly did flagellate the poor offender, in the most merciless manner. Berry meekly bowed his head so as to allow the storm to pass with as little injury as possible, and when an auspicious lull came, he volunteered a story he had picked up, which proved to be a charming bit of gossip, that is, judging by the effect which it seemed to produce on the mind of the landlady."

CHAPTER XI.

COMMENCEMENT OF THE EXPLORATION OF KENT'S HOLE.

END OF 1863 TO DECEMBER 1865.

PENGELLY'S many-sided activity continued to be manifested by ever-increasing interest in geological, palæontological, and anthropological research. Some correspondence with Mr. J. W. Salter (who has been already mentioned) has been preserved, and is specially noteworthy, as Mr. Salter's name is known and respected wherever palæontological work has been carried on. Dr. H. Woodward, F.R.S., speaks appreciatively of his labours,* and especially mentions the work on British Trilobites to which the following letters refer :—

"J. W. Salter, Esq.," Dr. Woodward observes, "undertook a monograph on the British Trilobites for the Palæontological Society in 1864, of which four parts appeared—from 1864–1867. This work occupies two hundred and twenty-four pages of letterpress, illustrated by thirty-one quarto plates, and contains descriptions of one hundred and fourteen British species (leaving about two hundred more to be described). No one who takes up this fine work of our old friend can avoid a feeling of regret that Salter's valuable life and splendid palæontological knowledge should not have been longer spared to us, to carry on to its completion this most important service."

J. W. Salter to Pengelly.

" I only keep your *Cheirurus*, as they will come into an early plate, Nos. 948, 949, 957.

"But I have taken notes of the numbers and localities of all the others I shall want to see and describe some future day, so I hope your methodical collection will remain nearly as it is. You have some very choice specimens ; a new *Phillipsia* among the rest, and the only specimens I have yet seen that show the heads of the *Bronteus*—eye,

* See Anniversary Address delivered before the Geological Society of London in 1895.

etc. *Cyphaspis*, too, and other good things. May you prosper and increase! Many thanks for your prompt kindness in sending these. I thought you would like to have all back which were not in early use, and I take advantage of the opportunity to return them.

"Mr. Vicary and the others are extremely kind. I ought to have come down to see you from Exeter; but I could not do it. It was all I could do to get through my actual business there. What a wonderful shorthand report of my lecture, to be sure!"

J. W. Salter to Pengelly.

"Finchley, November 2, 1863.

"There are five tablets I discovered after I had written you all safe. Decade eleven is not out. But why ask me to send a list of Survey publications, I have o to do with it now. Reeks would send you one directly. On second thoughts I send you my own copy and will get another, that will be less trouble to you.

"Oh yes, I've thought about the Dodman! I believe they are the same set, and told Vicary so. Some I know are. Why should not those who have the B[udleigh] S[alterton] pebbles compare them with those in Cornwall?

"I've stated in my appendix about these Great Peraver fossils. Thank you for the hint and for all your good will."

Pengelly to J. W. Salter.

"*Torquay, January* 28, 1864.—Many thanks for your kind note of 25th inst. . . . But to the real business of your note. I can only send you localities for three out of the five species you have figured, namely *Phacops lævis*, Trappean Ash, Knowle Hill, Newton Bushell, S. Devon; *Phacops latifrons*, very deep down in the Pleurodictyum slates at Black Hall, near Totnes, S. Devon. *P. arachnoides*, very deep in the Pleurodictyum slates at St. Keyne Hill, near Liskeard, Cornwall. No other Torquay collector has anything worth your notice, I find. In our Museum we have Dr. Battersby's collection, which I should like you to see. If you wish I will apply to the Committee to have all the trilobites sent you. Let me hear from you on this point. I have forwarded your slip of figures to our friend Vicary, and have asked him to send it on to Mr. Valpy of Ilfracombe. Besides these I know of no collector in this district. I have no doubt there are some good specimens in the Geological Museum at Penzance, of which Saml. Higgs, jun., Esq., F.G.S., is secretary, and also in the Museum at Truro, about which Dr. Barham of Truro can give you information. I have no doubt an application from you, with a statement of the object, would bring you the specimens. If you write to either or both you can use my name if you wish. . . ."

J. W. Salter to Pengelly.

"*St. John's Wood, April* 22, 1864.— . . . I do not quite know the locality or name of the Museum at Penzance where Professor McCoy saw, and whence he described, the list of species occurring at Gorran

Haven and Great Peraver. But I wish much to examine all the trilobites from that locality, and should be glad through yourself to make a formal application for the loan of them to figure in the plates now executing for the Palæontographical Society. I am moreover describing the Budleigh fossils, and these documents would be valuable just now. McCoy describes *Homalonotus* and *Calymene* and *Phacops*, etc. I want to see the whole of the trilobites. Will you try to get them for me?"

Dr. Daubeny was at Torquay on several occasions this year, and was much interested in Pengelly's work.

Mrs. Pengelly to her Mother.

"*Torquay, January* 22, 1864.—Our little party was very pleasant. We had several friends to meet Dr. Daubeny and Professor Phillips, and they all seemed thoroughly to enjoy themselves, and there was no lack of conversation. Professor Phillips is a most agreeable man, every one liked him. He was very much pleased with some of William's fossils, and has given him the new edition of his last work. William has taken him and Dr. Daubeny to see the working at Bovey Tracey which much interested them. I forgot to tell you Professor Phillips was at William's lecture on Monday which was so crowded, that chairs had to be put up all the middle of the room and every spare corner. Some of our friends who came over on purpose to attend it from Plymouth, though only five minutes late, would have had to stand all the time but that more seats were with difficulty carried up for them."

Pengelly to his Wife.

"*Torquay, June* 30, 1864.— . . . On Monday I went to Newton and joined Vicary in a drive to Denbury and Ipplepen. On reaching home I found that Dr. Daubeny had left a card, with a message that he is here for a few days only. Tuesday Alf. and I called at Daubeny's; we had a long chat, amongst other things with regard to the evening Lectures at the British Association. He told me our friend —— almost insists on giving one—it is an immense blunder. . . . This morning my mother informs me that Jane * intends giving you warning, as soon as you return, as she is about to marry. The confidence of this young couple in each other is really most touching. Jane doesn't know what is John's employment, and John cannot get from Jane what her name is. She informs my mother that the business began thus; and in Holy Week. John came with butter on Monday. Quoth Jane: 'Be you a promised?' John: 'No, but I be a looking out.' Jane: 'So be I.' John: 'Shall I come on Good Friday?' Jane: 'I shan't be out then! you can come next Sunday if you like.' So John came; and now! Well, well; and all this in Holy Week! . . . I think our Cornish journey may take about a week. We start in a few days. . . ."

A project was on foot for exploring the limestone caverns

<hr>

* The cook.

of Sarawak, but Pengelly never thought of doing the work himself, though it would be gathered from the following letter that he had done so :—

Sir James Brooke to Pengelly.*

"Barraton, February 20, 1864.

"I enter heartily into the project mentioned by Sir Charles Lyell for exploring the limestone caverns of Sarawak, and beg you will assure him that any and every assistance shall be given to carry it through. I only wish the Government was in a position to defray the expenses under Sir Charles' direction. It will be *no easy task*, for the caves are of great and unknown extent, and our Dayaks not infrequently lose their lives in collecting the edible birds' nests found there. Every appliance for the examination should be considered and provided in England. There are fossil remains of shells, etc., found in the strata of the stream both in the right and left hand branches of the river. When *you* determine upon going, pray inform me, as I shall be tempted to become your companion! I am not sure whether Mr. Wallace visited these caverns when he was in Sarawak. . . ."

Pengelly was always greatly interested in those who could claim Keltic origin, and the Welsh and Bretons, as having an especial affinity with his native Cornish stock, particularly attracted him.

Mrs. Pengelly to her Sister.

"*Torquay, April* 4, 1864.— . . . William has much enjoyed his visit to London. He was a good deal with Sir Charles Lyell, who is very desirous for William to accompany him this summer to the South of France ; but he fears he will not be able to arrange it, though it would be a great pleasure to him to join Sir Charles, they have so much in common. He was also extremely interested in attending the Soirée at the Royal Society, which he speaks of as a very bright gathering ; he was introduced to a Monsieur Pengouilly from Brittany, so of course they fraternized. William says that Colenso, who was standing by listening to them, seemed much entertained with their endeavours to understand each other. . . ."

Pengelly was contemplating a short stay in Cornwall, to continue some of his investigations in the rocks of his native county. The following letter from Mr. C. W. Peach is in reply to a letter written earlier in the spring by Pengelly, asking some questions regarding localities he wished to examine :—

* Rajah of Sarawak.

C. W. Peach to Pengelly.

"Wick, N.B., March 18, 1864.

"Accept my very best thanks for your *four* papers. I hope to read them carefully, and thus again see, through your description, the rocks of Devon, etc. Bovey Tracey I have never visited; I *think* I once saw that spot at a distance. I shall, however, I am sure, have much pleasure in perusing the book and examining the drawings of the plants. I have ascertained this much, that the plates are beautifully done, and no doubt the papers equally well. Thanks, dear friend, thanks for them. How I wish I could go with you to the hard quartz rocks of Cornwall; not being able to do so, I will do my very best to give you directions. I did place some of the Silurian fossils in the Museum at Truro. . . . In the Geological Museum at Penzance *my best* fossils collected for my own collection are. They, as well as the Silurian fossils, are beautiful ones from *every locality* in Cornwall and Devon. Amongst these are two Ichthyodorulites from Polperro, which, I would stake a good deal on, are really fish defences. Probably you will be able to see them. There is one specimen from Polruan which I *now know* is a coprolite. I've seen so many in Scotland, that I can speak with confidence now. I should like to see the collection again, and hope yet to see it. St. Austell is the best spot to go to first—thence to Mevagissey, and so to Goran Haven. The spot I got the Silurian fossils first at is the great Cairn near Goran Haven. The quartz is the highest point in Great Peraver. . . . The fossiliferous blocks are at the foot of the *cliff*. When I left, the spot I got most at was partly covered with the *débris* from the cliff. Amongst the large blocks there, you will find rolled ones, and others in which you will find trilobites and *small shells;* the larger shells in the large blocks, which have not been disturbed. As well as the quartz rock, there is a blue gray softish sort of rock, in which curious black fossils may be got. I only wish I was amongst them now, for I am sure additions to the Cornish list may be made in them. These rocks are next the quartz towards Bodrigan. . . . The next locality for fossils (Silurian) is the quartz at the Diamond rock near Cayerhayes beach. . . . The blocks of quartz are the best to search; and as well as *Orthides* you will meet with a curious coral-like fossil. But only in the Cairn, Great Peraver, these occur. I ought to have mentioned this before. This curious fossil is *most abundant* in the quartz rocks of Assynt, Durness, or [elsewhere] in Sutherland. I was very much struck on seeing them there, and at once recognized them as like those in Cornwall. They are called by Mr. Salter 'Annelide bores.' I rejoice exceedingly to think that you are going to visit my old haunts. I am often there in fancy. By-the-by, I got on the top of the Great Cairn at Peraver a piece of quartz *beautifully polished and striated*—evidently by *glacial action*. I did not know then what I do now—after having seen acres of polished rocks —ah! *scores* of miles. Now, then, for my own work, should all be well this summer. By the same post that I got yours, I received an invitation from Mr. Gwyn Jeffreys of London to go with him on a dredging voyage for two months to Shetland. To start in May. I hope to go. I fear you will tire of my long yarn."

Pengelly to his Wife.

"*Torquay, July* 10, 1864.— . . . I got home safely last night after a pleasant, toilsome week in Cornwall. The following brief sketch will show you our movements.

"*Monday, 4th.*—Left by first train, and at Newton joined Scott and Vicary. We proceeded to Penzance without delay, which we reached soon after 3 p.m. Having secured rooms at the Queen's Hotel on the Esplanade, between Penzance and Newlyn, we went to the Geological Museum to see the Lower Silurian fossils found by Mr. Peach in the quartzites of Gorran Haven. There are numerous but indistinct specimens of few species. We could only identify one as belonging to the Budleigh Salterton species. This done we called on Henwood, who received us very pleasantly; we then returned to the hotel to a meat tea. Whilst we were discussing this, Mr. Henwood came in to take us to see sundry Elvan dykes; this completed, we went to see the lighthouse in course of preparation for the Wolf Rock—between Land's End and Scilly.

"*Tuesday, 5th.*—All to breakfast with Henwood, after which we drove to the Logan Stone, and thence to the Land's End. Had a capital view of the Scilly Isles, which remained visible all day. Walked to Sennen and Whitesand Bay. Much interested in the granite and blown-sand phenomena. Back to Penzance to a late dinner. Mr. Bolitho (my former pupil), having heard from Henwood of our being in Penzance, called and invited us to dine with him next day. After dinner Henwood came in for a chat.

"*Wednesday, 6th.*—Left for Marazion by 6.5 a.m. train, ordered breakfast at an inn at Marazion, and took a boat for the Mount. Went through the castle, and carefully inspected the granitic veins and joints, after which back to breakfast. At 11.15 left by 'bus for Helstone, where we overtook a trap for the Lizard and Kynance Cove. At the latter there were several holiday parties, amongst whom I found some old acquaintances. We also encountered young Cooke, son of the artist, rambling about solitarily; he is on a walking tour in Cornwall. We returned to a late tea at Helstone.

"*Thursday, 7th.*—Walked to Looe Pool, and at 10.30 left by 'bus for Falmouth, which we reached soon after twelve. Walked to Pendennis Castle and the Raised Beach. Called on R. Were Fox at Grove Hill, but found that he and his daughters were at Penjerrick. Met Alfred Fox and his daughter Mrs. Pease, and also Alfred Lloyd Fox and his brother. Dined at the Royal Hotel. Took train for Truro about four; where, having arrived, we went to the museum, with the same purpose, and with the same result, as at Penzance. Took train for St. Austell, and got there soon after eight.

"*Friday, 8th.*—Drove to Gorran Haven (nine miles), and after much search found Mr. Peach's fossiliferous bands; but, though we got several specimens, could not identify more than one with the Budleigh Salterton fossils. Returned through Mevagissey, which is more of a town than we had supposed.

"*Saturday, 9th.*—Visited, the Clay Works.   Left St. Austell by 2.50 train, and got home about 8.45, heartily tired, but very glad to find your letter. . . ."

Pengelly to Dr. Davidson.

"Lamorna, Torquay, February 1, 1865.

"Thank you very much for your kind letter of yesterday's date, and also for that of the 15th ult.   I have great pleasure in furnishing you with such information as I can (from memory) respecting the fossiliferous beds of my native place, Looe.   East and West Looe, in Cornwall, are two small towns on the opposite sides, and at the mouth, of the narrow tidal estuary of the river Looe, and are situated about fourteen miles, nearly due west, from Plymouth.   The rocks of the district are essentially bluish grey slates; the stratification is beautifully distinct, and the dip, both in amount and direction, is characterized by very considerable uniformity, through great vertical and horizontal spaces.   According to Professor Sedgwick, it is 'about 30° east of Line South at an angle of 40° (*Quar. Jour. Geol. Soc.*, vol. viii. p. 16).   In some places there is a considerable amount of inter-stratified schistose grit, and a few thin calcareous bands here and there present themselves.   What appears to be contemporary hornblendic ash is occasionally met with, and in some localities quartz veins are numerous.   Some of the less gritty beds are not infrequently ferruginous, in which case the newly exposed surfaces are of a yellowish-brown or reddish-brown colour; these are the principal, but by no means the only, depositories of organic remains.   All the Looe Brachiopoda which I sent you were from beds of this character.   Well-defined joints—most of them at (sensibly) right angles to the plane of the horizon, and also to that of stratification—are common, and such as have been some time exposed to the weather frequently disclose small orifices, which are trustworthy indications of fossils.   The remarkable coral *Pleurodictyum problematicum*—which, according to Murchison, is a characteristic fossil of the Lower Devonian Rocks (table, p. 433, Siluria, 3rd ed. 1859)—is very abundant in the same beds.   Some of the specimens are of considerable dimensions, measuring fully seven inches in diameter.   This coral occurs also in the slates of Meadfoot, Torquay; and Mr. Godwin-Austen speaks of it as 'ranging through the whole middle slate district of South Devon' (*Trans. Geol. Soc.*, 2nd series, vol. vi. part 2, p. 468).   The finer varieties of the Looe slates contain the fossils formerly known as the 'Polperro Fish-remains,' but which have been pronounced to be sponges by Messrs. McCoy and Carter, who founded the genus *Steganodictyum* for their reception.   These sponges extend from Looe, westward as far as Fowey, and eastward to the Rame Head, at the entrance of Plymouth Sound.   I have met with them also at Bedruthen Steps, on the north coast of Cornwall, a few miles south of Padstow harbour; and at Mudstone Bay, near Brixham in South Devon, in the slates which underlie the great limestones of Berry Head and Sharkham Point.   Like *Pleurodictyum*, they are confined to slate rocks.   I have troubled you with these particulars in order to indicate the range of some of the organisms that were undoubtedly contemporaries of the Looe Brachiopoda. I am glad, but not at all *surprised*, to hear that you are to receive the Gold Wollaston Medal. I know of no one who has more thoroughly earned it. I beg most cordially to congratulate you on the distinction, and the council on their decision on the question. May you live long and happily to enjoy this mark of the appreciation of your scientific friends and contemporaries. I am getting quite anxious to see your second instalment of your Devonian Monographs, especially your Tables of Distribution. I have great belief in *tables* for those who *geologize* as well as for those who *jollygize*. After that fearful pun I will close.

"P.S.—If I can give any further information on Devon and Cornwall, I shall be most happy to do so. Have you seen any of the Lower Silurian Brachiopoda from the quartzites of Gorran and the Great Peraver in Cornwall, besides the one or two I sent you?"

Pengelly to Dr. Davidson.

"Lamorna, Torquay, February 6, 1865.

"Thank you very much for your letter of the 3rd inst. I now, to the best of my ability, beg to send you replies to your various queries. I would 'locate the *Looe grits*' (more correctly slates) not in the *Middle* Devonians at all, but near the top of the Lower Devonians (I scarcely need say that I use the terms *Lower*, *Middle*, and *Upper* Devonians as terms of convenience merely, not as equivalents to *Lower*, *Middle*, and *Upper Old Red;* see pp. 44, 45 of the first part of your *Devonian Monograph*); and here also I would place all the slates of South-east Cornwall, as well as of Mudstone Bay near Brixham, Galmpton Creek on the Dart, and Meadfoot near Torquay; in fact, all the *Pleurodictyum* and *Steganodictyum* beds. In the first part of your *Devonian Monograph* you recognize the Looe beds as Lower Devonian (pp. 19, 40), and at page 4 you give, from me, a chronological scheme in which they are thus located. You are quite correct in supposing that I hold the Petherwin beds 'being, as to age, intermediate between the upper beds of the Middle Devonian and the Marwood ones.' I fear I cannot send you any more Upper Devonian localities in either Devonshire or Cornwall. We have no beds of that age in South Devon. Tintagel is certainly Upper Devonian (see Part I., *Devonian Monograph*, p. 4). Landlake (not 'Landlabe') is in Cornwall. You will find it in Sheet XXV. of the Ordnance Survey Map, a short mile nearly due east of South Petherwin, and barely two miles south of Launceston. It is, I believe, in the parish of South Petherwin, and is the chief fossil locality in the district. In the writings of geologists, Landlake and South Petherwin are synonyms. There are no fossils at the latter place. I am glad to find that Mr. Champernowne is so zealous. . . .

"Ramsleigh (not Ramsleugh) is situated between Ogwell and Woolborough; if we were sure of an unbroken sequence (which we very certainly are not), the Ramsleigh beds would be far above those of Ogwell and Bradley, and below those of Woolborough. Lithologically they resemble the Woolborough beds rather than those of Ogwell, but they have very few zoophytic fossils in common with either, whilst the Ogwell, Bradley, and Woolborough beds have a large number of corals and sponges in common. I shall return to this point. I observe that in your Table you put Linton and Ilfracombe together; they are fully twelve miles apart, and this distance is by no means in the direction of the strike of the beds; moreover, the rocks differ a good deal lithologically. Linton is undoubtedly at the base of the Devonian series in that part of Devonshire, and unless the beds there are Lower Devonian, there can be none of that age in the county. Murchison ('Siluria,' Table, p. 433, 1859), Lyell ('Elements,' Sixth Edition, p. 532, 1865), and Salter (*Quar. Jour. Geol. Soc.*, vol. xix. p. 489, 1864), unanimously place them on this horizon. Should you, however, decide otherwise, I shall be glad to find that you have given each of the two localities a separate column.

"You have done well to give Woolborough a column to itself, and there seems no objection to the union of Lummaton and Barton; the argument, however, is still greater in favour of Ogwell, Bradley, and Chircombe Bridge being united. In fact, there is no such fossil locality as Chircombe Bridge at all. It is simply a small bridge across the little river Lemon, a tributary of the Teign, which it joins at Newton. The Ogwell quarries (there are two, Westhill and Ivy Green) are on the right or south bank of the stream, and Bradley quarry is on the left bank. These quarries are almost within a stone-throw of one another and of Chircombe Bridge. When a geologist uses the words 'Chircombe Bridge,' he means Bradley or Ogwell, or both.* . . . At Bradley and Ogwell quarries the limestone beds dip about 20° towards S. 39° E., and therefore strike about S. 51 W. to N. 51° E. (true). . . . At the village of East Ogwell there are numerous interstratified, and therefore contemporary, beds of ash and slate, apparently conformably overlying the limestones just mentioned. These ash and slate beds are succeeded conformably by the Ramsleigh limestones; but in the quarry it is next to impossible to make out stratification at all. Woolborough quarry is in an *outlier* of limestone, and the ground between it and Ramsleigh is occupied with grits of carboniferous age which entirely conceal the Devonian beds. Moreover, it is quite impossible to make out stratification at Woolborough. To use Murchison's expression in October last, 'it is a charming piece of bedevilled limestone.' My advice is, that you unite your Bradley, Chircombe Bridge, and Ogwell columns into one, under the name of 'Chircombe Bridge,' with a footnote to say that it includes the two adjacent fossil localities of Bradley and Ogwell.

"P.S.—Instead of 'Meadfoot Sands' at the head of one of your columns, I would use the word Meadfoot simply. It is a sea beach, hence the word sands, which I find has led some strangers to suppose that the fossiliferous beds there are sands instead of slates, which they are in reality."

The important and striking results which had arisen from

---

* Here follows a roughly drawn ground-plan.

the workings in the Brixham Cavern induced many leading geologists to desire a systematic exploration of Kent's Hole. It was therefore decided that an application for funds for that purpose should be made to the British Association at the meeting at Bath. The result of which was the grant of £100 for the beginning of the work, Sir Charles Lyell, the President, taking an active interest in it.

This opened a new chapter in Pengelly's life, for he not only superintended the exploration of the Cavern, but undertook its entire management, throwing himself, heart and soul, into the numerous duties which it entailed. The labour was arduous, and severely taxed his energies for more than fifteen years ; but it was a congenial employment, and most faithfully performed. He was always happy in the midst of his constant and unremitting labour, which was in itself a sufficient recompense to one who worked, not for fame or reward, but to advance the sum of human knowledge.

Pengelly to Sir Charles Lyell.

"Lamorna, Torquay, April 2, 1864.

" . . . It is not unlikely that you have given up all thought of exploring Kent's Hole, nevertheless I wish it could be managed. . . . I cannot but think that there are reasons why an application for £100 to the British Association at the next meeting might be successful. You will be President, Professor Phillips (who is favourably disposed) will be President of the Geological Section, and I am to be one of the Secretaries. If you decide on the application, it would be well for you to see Sir L. Palk about it.

"The Duke of Argyll has spent a few days here. He was at my Lecture last Monday, and on Wednesday I went with him to Bovey, and in returning, to some of the Devonshire Limestone quarries near Newton. My wife unites with me in kind regards to Lady Lyell, and the expression of sympathy with her under her recent bereavement."

After undertaking the exploration, Pengelly became such an enthusiast in the progress made, that, when in Torquay, he never (unless prevented by illness) failed on a single week-day to visit the Cavern, while he devoted many hours at home to the examination of the specimens exhumed. He even abridged as much as possible his short holidays, and all idea of living in London was abandoned on this account. "It falls to the lot of but few men," writes a brother geologist,[*] " who have spent their lives in a provincial town, to attain to so eminent a

* Henry Woodward, LL.D., F.R.S.

position in science, and become so widely known and highly esteemed, as was the late William Pengelly, of Torquay."

But to return to the Bath meeting, which was interesting and important, though clouded by the sad fate of Speke, one of the discoverers of the Sources of the Nile, who was to have given his narrative in full on this occasion.

The next letter will show the generous manner in which Pengelly was supported by his colleagues, on the reading of his Paper entitled "Changes of Relative Level of Land and Sea in South-Eastern Devonshire in connection with the Antiquity of Mankind," and the pleasure that the favourable opinion of his views (bearing on this question) by such eminent scientific experts, naturally gave him.

Pengelly to his Wife.

"*Bath, September* 17, 1864.— . . . I have been very sadly negligent; but, in truth, I have worked extremely hard. I read my paper (Changes of Level, etc., and Antiquity of Man) on Thursday, to a densely packed house. The success was immense. Murchison complimented me on my 'eloquence and clearness.' Harkness declared I had made a 'great hit.' Etheridge said it was 'the best paper I had ever written.' Evans backed me up like a brick. Phillips, Warington Smyth, Symonds, Evans, and Boyd-Dawkins spoke in unqualified approval. Colenso, finding I was a Cornishman, almost shook my hand off. . . ."

Pengelly to his Wife.

"1, *Stratton Street, November* 23, 1864.— . . . Yesterday at breakfast I found who were staying in the house ; there were Mr. Gladstone, his wife and daughter, and Sir Stephen Glynne (Mrs. Gladstone's brother). Breakfast passed off very pleasantly ; Gladstone is a good talker. After the meal Miss Coutts, Miss Gladstone, and H. Wagner went, under my guidance, to Jermyn Street Museum, and I played the showman. Having seen the ladies off, I had a chat with Percy and also Etheridge, and then returned to luncheon, when Sir Charles and Lady Lyell, the Rajah,* and Mr. John Abel Smith were added to the party, and after the meal Crawfurd called, and we all did talk amain. I then went off to Somerset House to make arrangements about the meeting of the Kent's Hole Committee. . . ."

Pengelly to his Wife.

"*London, November* 25, 1864.— . . . I was glad to get your nice budget of letters yesterday. I called at the British Museum with my Rocombe Kitchen Midden under my arm, where I got S. P. Woodward

* Sir J. Brooke.

to name the shells, W. Davies the bones, and A. W. Franks the pottery, etc.; then to the Royal Society to call for the *Phil. Trans.* due to Dr. Day and myself; then to College of Surgeons to see Flower, respecting the Whale Vertebra; all very pleasant. At dinner we had the Gladstone party, Lord Harrowby, etc., etc., all fortifying themselves to hear and endure my lecture on the Arithmetic of Creation. The lecture was very largely attended. Sir Harry Verney, John A. Smith, and many other friends there."

Pengelly, with his friend Mr. Vivian, was now occupied with arrangements for the opening of the Kent's Cave work, which entailed much writing and thought, it being especially requisite to provide very careful and trustworthy workmen. He was disappointed in not being able to secure the services of his head workman at Brixham, Henry Keeping, an intelligent and most reliable man, who was now permanently engaged by Prof. Sedgwick in the Museum at Cambridge. His brother Charles Keeping, with a very steady assistant named Smerdon, was finally engaged, and the following extracts from Pengelly's Kent's Cavern Journal (in which for the succeeding fifteen years is recorded the daily work of the exploration) mark the beginning of operations :—

"*March the 27th* [1865].—Went to the cavern with Mr. Vivian, when all necessary instructions were given to C. Keeping, who attended us. Engaged Smerdon as a labourer to work under Keeping.

"*Tuesday, March 28th.*—To the cavern. The workmen, as directed, had broken ground outside the cavern, for the purpose of cutting a roadway through a talus of earth and stones which almost closed the southern (arched) entrance, which for the present is to be the entrance used exclusively by the superintendents and the workmen, the visitors and guide being confined to the northern entrance. The talus consists of fine earth and stones, popularly, and perhaps correctly, believed to have been thrown out of the cavern by the earlier explorers, etc., etc."

The following letter to Sir C. Lyell accompanied the first Monthly Report :—

Pengelly to Sir C. Lyell.

"Torquay, May 1, 1865.

"I enclose our First Report of Progress, and have no doubt that you will think we have made a good beginning, and that the British Association is not likely to throw away its money."

Mrs. Pengelly to her Sister.

"*Torquay, April,* 1865.— . . . I was very busy two days colouring a very large Diagram for William's lecture, so of course had a crowd of

M

callers, amongst others Mr. Gunn, an old clergyman from Norfolk, who remained a long time looking with intense delight at some of the Cavern bones; he has a splendid collection of fossil Elephant remains, is a good archæologist, and is brother-in-law to our friend the botanist, Sir William Hooker. Lady Hooker is spending the winter here; she is a fine old lady. The other day Miss Croome (Dr. Daubeny's niece) went to call upon her, and found her embroidering a frock for her great grand-child, who is just three months old. We have had delightful visits from Sir Wm. Hooker; he was very much pleased with some of our ferns."

Mrs. Pengelly to her Sister.

"*Torquay, April,* 1865.— . . . William is extremely occupied with Kent's Cavern just now; they have not got inside yet, but even on the outside have found a considerable number of shells and bones, not, it is supposed, of great antiquity. He went to Brixham Cavern yesterday with Mr. Gunn and a large party, who were all greatly interested. He has had a nice letter from his old pupil, the Princess Mary of the Netherlands.

"You will be pleased to hear that Alfred has got a Scholarship at Christ's College, Cambridge, which is very satisfactory."

Princess Mary of the Netherlands to Pengelly.

"*Huis de Parar near the Hague, April* 4, 1865.— . . . Princess Mary of the Netherlands thanks Mr. Pengelly for his letter and for the beautiful volume of Lyell's 'Geology,' which she has received through the agency of Mr. Murray. The Princess recalls with much pleasant recollection the delightful months which she spent at Torquay, and the many *geologizing* and *jollygizing* hours for which she was indebted to Mr. Pengelly. Miss von Doorn desires to be kindly remembered to him."

Pengelly to his Wife.

"*Torquay, June* 18, 1865.— . . . Your letter duly reached me yesterday. I am glad to find you *got* and *get* on so well. I am doing my best to imitate you. On Friday afternoon I took a friend to Kent's Cavern, and had the pleasure of finding that a splendid oval flint implement had been turned up; it was lying four feet deep and mixed up with teeth of the hyena. Yesterday a capital flake was found. Yesterday Alfred and I went to Hope's Nose, geologizing, and spent the evening at Mrs. Yorke's, all mighty agreeable."

Pengelly to his Wife.

"*Torquay, July* 5, 1865.— . . . In the Cavern we are at present removing huge blocks of fallen limestone, and consequently finding little or nothing. Vivian is now at St. Ives. He does not think he has much chance, but is satisfied that were the voters left at liberty he would beat Mr. Paull two to one. It appears there is great excitement

THE ENTRANCE TO KENT'S CAVERN.

[*To face p.* 162.

there. . . . I have just received a good volume from the Palæontographical Society. Davidson has figured a good many of my fossils, and has done me full justice."

Mrs. Pengelly to her Sister.

" *Torquay, November,* 1865.— . . . . Yesterday I was prevented finishing my letter by a visit from Sir John and Lady Lubbock, who came to see the fossils from Kent's Cavern, and as William was out I had to show them. Sir John seemed exceedingly interested in them, and sketched the Flint implements, making notes of them. William dined with them, and took them over to Brixham and through both the Caverns."

Mrs. Pengelly to her Sister.

"*November* 19, 1865.— . . . Yesterday we had a visit from Sir E. Lytton Bulwer,* who came to see the Kent's Cavern fossils, and remained for some time chatting, so we had a nice opportunity of making his acquaintance ; but he was very deaf unfortunately. He has lately come to live here."

The following passage in a letter from Sir James Simpson, whose name is so honourably and inseparably connected with the use of anæsthetics in surgical operations, refers to the Cave work at Torquay and elsewhere.

Sir James Simpson to Pengelly.

" *Edinburgh, October* 31, 1865.— . . . I took the liberty of sending to you yesterday a copy of the *London Medical Times,* with an article on 'Sculpture in Cave-halls,' marked ; and I did so, knowing—as all know—that you have worked more successfully on the archæological secrets of caves than any other man living or dead. If perchance any sculptures are ever found in the various caves near you, I should feel deeply obliged by any notice of them, however slight. I have found them now in four Fife caves. . . ."

During his rambles Pengelly had noticed signs of ice-action in Devonshire, which pointed to the probability that the climate had at one time been much colder than at present.

Pengelly to Professor J. B. Jukes.

"Lamorna, Torquay, October 6, 1865.

"I have just seen, in the October *Geol. Mag.,* your interesting note on Glaciation in Devonshire. Years ago, I was in the district you mention, walking from Bampton to Porlock ; when I observed a remarkable series of mouldings on an almost vertical rock surface,

* The celebrated novelist Lord Lytton.

adjacent to, and on the right-hand side of the road, just before reaching a wayside hostelry known, I think, as the 'Rock Inn.' This cannot be far from the spot you name. Is it the same? I have never seen it since, but it has frequently occurred to me as a probable case of glaciation. If you have five minutes to throw away, I shall be glad to know whether or not it is the same as the case you mention."

The following letters from Sir Charles Lyell, referring chiefly to St. Michael's Mount and the change of level in land and water on the Cornish and Devonshire Coasts, were received by Pengelly during the summer and autumn of 1865. His answers to the various queries in these letters are unfortunately missing in several cases.

Sir Charles Lyell to Pengelly.

"53, Harley Street, May 11, 1865.

"Referring to your letter of November 3, 1864, I find the question as to the date of my first mention of St. Michael's Mount, and whether it was formerly in a wood, etc., and you say that in your next address to the Nat. Hist. Society of Torquay you meant to allude to what Sir H. James had said on the subject.

"I am going over page 323 of the 'Principles,' and should be glad to see your address for 1864 (I have that of 1863), or perhaps, still better, if you would tell me whether you think what I have said should be altered or modified.

"I enclose the page of last edition, lest you should not have it by you, and beg you will return it.

"Have you not in some paper spoken of the submerged vegetable stratum at Torquay, in which the elephant's tooth was found? I cannot find it in the papers you have given me."

Pengelly to Sir Charles Lyell.

"Lamorna, Torquay, May 13, 1865.

"My address for 1864 to the Torquay Natural History Society was never printed. I send you by this post thirteen pages of the MS., in which you will find all I said about our submerged forests, the insulation of St. Michael's Mount, etc. I shall be glad to have my MS. again in a few days or a week. . . .

"The paper about which you inquire, in which I speak of the Torbay submerged forest containing the elephant's tooth, was read at Bath, and printed in the *Reader* for November 19, 1864, page 643. You will find the subject more fully treated in the MS. now sent. I need not say I shall be very happy if it can be made of service. I presume you are preparing a new edition of your 'Principles,' which I am very glad of. In looking over the paragraph on p. 323 (which I enclose), it appears to me that, since the submerged forests are more modern than the ossiferous caverns which are now admitted to contain evidence of the presence of man, it has ceased to be 'very remarkable' that 'there seems evidence of the submergence having been effected, in part at least, since the country was inhabited by man.' I think this, the last sentence of the paragraph, requires a slight modification. Perhaps all that is needed is to substitute 'interesting' for 'remarkable.'

"Before concluding, I trust you will excuse my calling your attention to a paper on 'Recent Encroachments of the Sea on the Shores of Torbay,' which I read in Section "C.," British Association, at Manchester, in 1861. It is printed *in extenso* in the *Geologist* for 1861, page 447, etc. I was not favoured with proofs by the printer, hence there are a few typographical errors, and Figs. 1 and 2 are atrocious."

Sir Charles Lyell to Pengelly.

"53, Harley Street, May 15, 1865.

"Your MS. has arrived, and I will return it by to-morrow's post. It is well worth printing, and some day I hope all these scattered papers of yours, which I value much, will be put together in a work on the geology and modern changes of the district. . . .

"This reminds me of the Brixham Cave meeting. A previous engagement made it impossible for me to attend it; my notice also was much too short in this busy time in London.*

"I think it possible that a low tract with wood may have been swept away at St. Michael's Mount; but it probably had nothing to do with the submerged forest, which, like that of Torbay, may have belonged to the mammoth era.

"How old do you imagine the Cornish language to have been? Professor Nilsson, who is a much higher authority than Sir G. Cornewall Lewis, believes that the Phœnicians had a tin trade with the Cassiterides (as argued by Dr. George Smith) twelve hundred years B.C., and that their trade lasted a thousand years.

"After reading your paper in the *Geologist*, which I shall cite on the encroachments of the sea in Torbay, one cannot help wondering that Ictis and St. Michael's Mount agree so well geographically, but they must have been the same; and it only gives one the more respect for the antiquity of the Torbay elephant, to say nothing of the beach of Hope's Nose, and the antecedent Kent's Hole and Brixham flint implements, and yours of the remoter glacial."

Sir Charles Lyell to Pengelly.

"53, Harley Street, May 22, 1865.

"I have no summons yet from the Brixham Cave,† which is strange.

"As you are going to St. Michael's Mount, I have determined to send you the two views given by Sir Henry James of the Mount at high and low water, which I was just putting into the hands of an artist to reduce them to half their present size, in order that they may serve as illustrations for the new edition of my 'Principles.'

---

* Amongst Pengelly's papers reference is made more than once to the impossibility of his attending these committee meetings on the same account.
† Committee.

"I shall employ a good artist, who will put the figures, to give an idea of different distances, out of his own head, and would make any other alteration which you might suggest, if you would kindly criticize the drawing on the spot. In the first place, I learn from Sir H. James that Plate I. was made from a small engraving sold at Penzance as a heading to notepaper, and Plate II. was produced by merely representing the water over the part which is overflowed at each tide.

"Now, if you could buy for me the original from which he took Plate I., it might be more nearly the size that I want, if not exactly. At any rate, it could not fail to be a great help to me. I should also be glad if you would tell me whether my friend Mr. Edward Bunbury is right, and that the isthmus is made of rock (query, granite or slate?), covered partially with sand and shingle.

"*Also*, Whether St. Michael's Mount is made of granite and clay-slate, the last invaded by granite veins.

"*Thirdly*, It is difficult to determine whether certain projections on the surface of the rock in the meridian A, B, are of stone, or meant, as I suppose, for bushes or trees.

"*Fourthly*, Is the great mass of bare rock under the castle granite or slate? Is there some greenstone?

"*Fifthly*, Does not the width of the isthmus here represented in Plate I. indicate very low water?

"*Sixthly*, How many feet of water may there be over the isthmus in Plate II. at ordinary and at highest tides?

"*Seventhly*, The port which we see is, I presume, the only one.

"Mr. Bunbury, who has lately been at St. Michael's Mount, and who is a good archæologist and scholar, is quite convinced that the mount is the Ictis of Diodorus; but he does not believe that in the last two or three thousand years there could have been trees here.

"As to the submerged forest in Mount's Bay, it may be as old as the Tor Abbey mammoth and *Bos longifrons*, and of higher antiquity than the Phœnician, even allowing that they traded with the Cassiterides a thousand years or more B.C.

"Please to buy freely anything that may help my two woodcuts, and send back the plates as soon as you can, and tell me what you have spent. Return them also, should anything prevent you going to St. Michael's Mount. I would not trouble you with so many queries if I did not think that the subject would interest you, and beg you will not go out of your way to answer them, as I can put my case tolerably, having seen the Mount long ago, even without the replies."

Sir Charles Lyell to Pengelly.

"53, Harley Street, June 1, 1865.

"I am very much obliged to you for the views and photographs, and am glad that I shall have your paper to refer to long before I print what I have to say. I mean freely to use for illustration the materials you sent me, including the small general view slightly clipt on the exterior. . . . Look at the fifth edition of Murray's 'Handbook of Devon and Cornwall,' in which there are some remarks on the waste of land in Mount's Bay, not all of it, I think, in the fourth edition.

"In all estimates respecting the rate of waste in past times, we are apt to err in not allowing for considerable pauses. Nature, having infinite time at her disposal, proceeds in a most leisurely way, taking up her operations with activity for a short spell, and then suspending them for ages. In going along a coast where waste has occurred here and there in the last five centuries, there would be long spaces where no work of destruction has been done. To strike an average you must take these areas of inaction into account."

Sir Charles Lyell to Pengelly.

"Munich, July 26, 1865.

" . . . I hear from Mr. John Carrick Moore that you have written an important paper about the Trade Winds, Gulf Stream, Sahara, etc. As you may not have had separate copies so as to give me one, I shall depend on your telling me in what journal I can buy it, for it is a subject which I am working at. Is it not singular that the hot water of the Tropical Indian Ocean should, as we are told, flow round the Cape of Good Hope across the Atlantic to Brazil, while the water of the Gulf of Mexico flows north-west towards Polar regions? If the Equatorial Sea north of the Line sends its hot water towards Arctic regions, the Equatorial Sea south of the Line ought to send its warm water towards the Antarctic latitudes. I suppose it is the geographical conformation of the land and bottom of the sea that causes this different behaviour of the southern and northern hot currents. If you have been studying the Trade Winds you can perhaps enlighten me. I presume that, if there were no such winds, the heated tropical waters expanding and becoming lighter would flow towards the north, and towards the south from the Equator, while cold undercurrents would be flowing in opposite directions."

Pengelly to Sir Charles Lyell.

"Lamorna, Torquay, August 6, 1865.

"I am afraid, from your remark, that Mr. John Moore attaches undue importance to my brief communication on the Sahara, etc. The facts are as follows. In the Quarterly Journal of Science for last April, there is a note from a Rev. I. H. Ward, on 'The connexion between the supposed Inland Sea of the Sahara and the Glacial Epoch;' in which the author thinks most geographers think with him, that the north-east trade wind is mainly caused by the Sahara. Believing this to be an error I sent to the editor a note to that effect, which was printed in the July number of the same journal. This is the note to which Mr. Moore refers. I am sorry to say that I have no reprints of it, as the proprietors object to allow any to be struck off. I am sometimes afraid that there may be a tendency to overrate the unquestionable influence of the Sahara on the Glaciers of the Alps. Can you, without great inconvenience, let me know who has written on the subject, and put me in a way to get a sight of these writings? I should like to know (1) what is the proof of the synchrony of the drying up of the Sahara and the diminution of the Alpine Glaciers, and (2) whether this proof is more conclusive than that of the synchrony of the Glacial ages in North America and in Europe.

"My opinion on oceanic currents is of little or no worth; but, so far as I understand the question, it appears to me that were our world entirely without dry land, and were the ocean everywhere of uniform depth, the excessive heat of the tropics would produce both excessive expansion and evaporation of the waters there; but that the evaporation would so much exceed the expansion, as to tend to empty the tropical seas. This would cause a constant flow of water in both hemispheres towards the equator, but in consequence of the earth's rotation, these currents would move towards the south-west and north-west in the northern and southern hemispheres respectively. The ascended vapour would pass poleward, with the trade wind counter currents, in north-easterly and south-easterly courses. But these effects would be not only confirmed but augmented by the trade winds. By the introduction of land—varying in outline, in height, in horizontal extension, and in thermal relations and qualities—and by the formation of inequalities in the sea bottom, the scheme would be so overlaid everywhere with modifications as to be scarcely recognizable. Nevertheless, all other things being the same, the modifications would be least complicated in the hemisphere having the least land, or, more correctly, least coast, hence we are entitled to expect, that in the southern hemisphere there will on the whole be a more marked movement of water towards the equator, than there is in the north. The Gulf of Mexico is so well represented by the Bay of Bengal and the Chinese Sea, that it may be expected that the thermal characters of the North Pacific and North Atlantic will be very similar, and, judging from the Isotherms, this is the fact as I have endeavoured to show in the *Quarterly Journal of Science* for January last. . . ."

Sir Charles Lyell to Pengelly.

"53, Harley Street, October 6, 1865.

" . . . I write to ask you a question respecting the age of what Mr. Godwin-Austen called New Red Sandstone in his paper on 'The Valley of the English Channel,' *Quart. Jour. Geol. Soc.*, vol. vi., 1850, p. 97. He says that subangular blocks of porphyry of large size show agency of floating ice. In conversation he now tells me that what he called New Red in Devonshire, in 1850, would probably now be more correctly referred to the Permian period; in which case it would help to confirm Ramsay's Permian glaciers. Do you think that the breccia he alludes to is of Permian age? Does it appear to you, whatever be its age, to have the characters of a glacial drift?

"I have read your paper in the *Quarterly Journal of Science* for July, which is very interesting. Is it admitted that the north-east trade wind by raising the Gulf of Mexico (Ward says thirty feet) gives origin to the Gulf Stream?

"As to what you said of evaporation in tropical seas causing a loss which currents from higher latitudes must supply, do not the heavy tropical rains, sometimes equal in a day or two to our whole annual rainfall, supply the loss by evaporation? The moment you pass beyond the tropics there is a rapid diminution of rainfall, so that I doubt whether currents from temperate regions are much required, if at all, on this score ; but, as it is a subject I have not studied so much as you have, I should be glad of your opinion."

Pengelly to Sir Charles Lyell.

"Lamorna, Torquay, October 9, 1865.

" In reply to your letter of 6th inst., I am happy to state, that the *whole* grant of £200 was voted for Kent's Cavern at Birmingham.

" I hold that the Breccias of which Mr. Godwin-Austen speaks are of Triassic, not Permian age.

"The reasons for this opinion are given in two of my papers—1st, 'The Red Sandstones and Conglomerates of Devonshire,' Part I.   Reprinted from the *Transactions of the Plymouth Institution*, 1861-2.   See pages 15 to 18.   (I hope and believe that I sent you a copy.   On page 18, line 3 from top, for 'unstratified' read 'stratified'.)   2nd, 'On the Age of the Dartmoor Granites.'   Pages 11 to 20 of the *Geologist* for 1893.   I had no reprints of this paper.   It was read before the British Association at Manchester, and printed in abstract in the Report for 1861, page 127, etc.

" I do not think Ice agency is required to, or would account for, the character of the breccia referred to.   I have treated of this in my *second* paper on 'The Red Sandstones, Conglomerates and Marls of Devonshire,' reprinted from the *Transactions Plymouth Institution* for 1862-3 (of this, too, I believe I sent you a copy).   See pages 16 and 17, where you will find that I notice the large masses of porphyritic trap to which Mr. Godwin-Austen refers.   Pardon my saying that he does not, as you appear to believe, speak of them as being 'sub-angular.'   So far as my observations have gone, however, he is wrong in stating that they are 'included in sands and marls;' they are found only in very coarse beds.

" I may remark here that in his memoir on the 'Geology of the South-east of Devonshire,' *Trans. Geol. Soc.*, 2nd series, vol. vi., part 2, page 454, he says, 'No masses occur in the New Red Conglomerate which exceed in size such as, during every gale, are removed by the waves on our own coasts.   The largest porphyritic blocks which fall from the cliffs east of Teignmouth are soon transported away.'

" In the foregoing papers I have supposed *all* the red rocks of Devonshire to be of the age of not only the Trias, but of the Bunter.   In a *third* paper on these rocks, now being printed at Plymouth, I state why I think this should be modified.   I fear I shall not get any reprints of it for several weeks, but I send you, by this post, a corrected 'rough proof' of some of the sheets, which I have just found in my wastepaper basket, and which will show you what I say on the point.   See pages 37 to 39.

" With reference to the origin of the Gulf Stream, Lieut. Maury, in his 'Physical Geography of the Sea' (1857), combats the opinion that the trade winds are the cause of the Stream, but ascribes it to the difference of density arising from difference of temperature between the equatorial and polar waters.   See chapter i.   Sir J. Herschel says ''The dynamics of the Gulf Stream have of late, in the work of Lieut. Maury already mentioned, been made a subject of much (we cannot

but think misplaced) wonder, as if there could be any possible ground
for doubting that it owes its origin entirely to the trade winds.' See
' Ency. Britannica,' 8th edit. (1859), vol. xvii., page 578, paragraphs 57 to
60, or better still, the article, 'Physical Geography,' corrected and
reprinted as a separate work. There can be no doubt that the Gulf
Stream is at least mainly due to the Trade Winds. Though I do not
think the time has yet come when it would be possible to write the
Thermal History of the Earth, I am glad to find you are grappling with
the question."

Sir Charles Lyell to Pengelly.

"53, Harley Street, December 20, 1865.

" I have just been reading over again my references to your papers
on Torbay and St. Michael's Mount for my new edition, and referring
to a newspaper account or abstract of your Birmingham paper on the
Mount. I suppose that no detailed and authorized version of what
you communicated to the British Association has yet been printed. If
so, please let me know. The drift of your argument, as I understood
you, was that the known rate of the waste of the coast was far too
slow to enable us to explain how the Mount could have been in the
midst of a wood within such a period as that in which the old Cornish
language was spoken. Therefore you concluded that a forest tract
which surrounded the Mount before the time of Diodorus Siculus must
have been submerged. In favour of the fact or probability of such a
sinking is the submarine stratum of vegetable matter with the stumps
of trees which borders the promontory of St. Michael's Mount. This
subsidence may have occurred shortly before the time of Diodorus,
whereas the other hypothesis of the waste of land by the waves of the
sea would demand twenty thousand years. . . .

" There have been many changes of level in Post-pliocene times on
this coast since the human period began, and the last of them may
have been shortly before the time of Diodorus; and the same land as
that on which the Torbay mammoth lived, may have continued above
water long after the extinction of the mammoth, for most probably
people speaking the old Cornish language had no more acquaintance
with the mammoth than the lake-dwellers of Switzerland in the age of
stone, whose fauna did not include any of the extinct mammalia.

"St. Michael's Mount appears to me most valuable, as showing that
in a region where the monuments of Post-pliocene change are so rife,
and the proofs of oscillations of level so various, including the Torbay
coast as part of the evidence, there has nevertheless been no important
geographical change for nearly nineteen centuries. This does not
surprise you or me, because we are prepared to allow tens of thousands
of years for post-elephantine times. If any one could tell us that five
thousand or ten thousand years hence St. Michael's Mount would answer
to the description of Diodorus, we should not think that it implied a
suspension of those causes of subterranean movement or of waste which
in the course of ages have so often modified our south-western littoral
region.

" My chief desire is to know what you have done in the way of publication on this subject, and whether I understand correctly the conclusions you announced at Birmingham.

"I am glad to see you are to have a Friday evening at the Royal Institution.   Dr. Bence Jones has, I think, obtained an unusally select and good set of Friday evening lecturers."

Sir Charles Lyell to Pengelly.

"53, Harley Street, December 27, 1865.

"I return you your MS., which I have read with interest.   I quite agree with the reasoning as to the vast period to which we should have to go back in order to restore a tract of low land in Mount's Bay, surrounding St. Michael's Mount.   It seems to me also, that long before the time of Diodorus, the island was only rendered useful to the old navigators because of its isolation, and I am unwilling to give a late date to the submergence of the Newlyn and other submarine forests. . . . I was glad to have your Torbay forest paper and the other three papers, which I shall read, and probably refer to on a future occasion."

CHAPTER XII.

PROGRESS OF EXPLORATIONS.

1866 TO 1868.

IN the spring of 1866 Pengelly had the pleasure of a visit from his friend Professor Harkness. In the following July he visited the scene of the marks of glaciation mentioned by Professor Jukes in a previous letter, and found that these "glacial traces" were nothing of the kind.

Professor Robert Harkness to Pengelly.

"Queen's College, Cork, April 22, 1866.

"After I left you I had an excellent day for seeing the country between Dartmouth and Torcross. Plenty of South dips in the slates which continue nearly to Slapton. I found your fossiliferous grit near Beasands, and have no doubt of its being in the Middle Devonian shales. I was not more fortunate than yourself as regards fossils, for on the whole, mine were more disturbed by cleavage than your specimens. I have no faith in the Metamorphic rocks of Devonshire. Those of Start Point and the neighbourhood, are, I believe, nothing more than Middle Devonian schists which have been terribly contorted and fearfully smashed up, sometimes along cleavage and sometimes along bedding planes ; and which have become perfectly saturated with quartz veins. From this conclusion it follows that the oldest rocks in Devonshire are those of the Lynmouth axis. I should very much have liked to have seen the Cornish rocks of Veryan Bay and the neighbourhood, for something interesting must occur there showing the mode in which the Devonians overlie the Carodoc sandstones. If it be that Middle Devonians occur here, then the Devonian base has yet to be made out. I must see Cornwall. Try to get the British Association either to Plymouth or Exeter as soon as possible.

"Nothing new here in the way of geology. In about six weeks I shall be again at work in the Lake Country."

Pengelly to his Wife.

"*Torquay, July* 6, 1866.— . . . I was very glad to get your nice letter this morning. You will be glad to hear, leastways you ought to be, that I have been enjoying myself very much.   Judge by the following narrative.

"*Tuesday.*—Reached St. David's Station, Exeter, at 3.15.   Found Vicary there.   We took North Devon train to Crediton.   Walked to Yeoton and Pàsbury to see the Traps (*i.e.* Volcanic rocks).   Very fine sections, conclusively showing the Feldspathic traps of Devon to be of strictly Triassic age.   Plenty of rain and mud.   Got back to Inn at Crediton Station.   Took tea there, returned to Exeter.

"*Wednesday.*—Scott called.   We rejoiced together over the resignation of Ministers.   Cause why, we shall have a more thorough Reform Bill, by waiting a year or two.   Vicary and I started by the 9.45 train for Tiverton.   Drove thence to Bampton to see the lime-quarries there. Drove thence to Rock Inn to see the marks of Glaciation mentioned by Jukes in *Geol. Mag.* in October last.   You will remember that it was at the Rock Inn I was offered by the landlord board and lodging for nothing, if I would talk to the men who would be attracted by my blarney.   This happened years ago.   I inquired tenderly after the said landlord, but he has gone away.   Well, Jukes's 'Glacial traces' are nothing of the kind, that's perfectly clear.   What are they, then?   Why, nothing but slickensides.   Really and truly nothing else in the world. Well, but what are slickensides.   To tell you the truth, I don't know. Oh dear! oh dear! 'tis very sad to have one's faith in everything and everybody oozing away.   Well, no, not everybody.   There's my wife left.   We drove back to Tiverton, eighteen miles, by the side of the Exe, a glorious drive, you ought to have been there.

"*Thursday.*—Took trap and drove to Slantycoombe, to see Trias Outlier mentioned by De la Beche.   Could find no trace of it.   Quite clear that De la Beche made a great blunder.   At any rate, we said so, until an old man, whom we casually met, showed us the precise locality! Thence we drove to Westleigh, to examine the extensive limestone quarries there.   These quarries are distinctly seen, and are at no great distance from the Bristol and Exeter Railway between Tiverton Road and the long tunnel, and on the right of the road.   This done we drove back to Tiverton Road, where we took train for Exeter, which we reached about seven.   After tea came a rest and a chat, and at ten I started for home, where I arrived about twelve.

"I have just had an invitation from Samuel Morley to be his guest during the meeting of the British Association at Nottingham. . . ."

During this meeting, Pengelly received the following amusing petition from Mr. Salter, imploring him to do justice to a Report which he and Mr. Hicks were sending in on their latest labours.

J. W. Salter to Pengelly.

"St. David's, August 18, 1866.

"We have tried to get Harkness to read our condensed Report (with map and section) of Hicks's latest labours.   Don't let Harkness murder it, or abbreviate it, or read it to half a room—as the life of the undersigned—of Mr. Hicks, of Mr. Lightbody, of the section, and the whole civilized world depends upon and is based upon the Menevian and Arenig groups.

"Indeed, I think you may put all your own bones and caves aside, in order to read this with effect. It has been strained three times, and ought to have no dregs left. So do it justice, or justice shall be done upon you! Look at the map! Only think what it cost to make it! It is full of *faults*, but they are the *faults* of St. David's Head, and *not of Hicks or J. W. Salter.*

"Do try to see Harkness and know if he will read it. He has a special liking for Skiddaw rocks. If not, do you, please. And Mr. Lightbody will, we know, unpack the fossils, and see they are packed again for Jermyn Street."

The exploration of the cavern was going on satisfactorily, and sufficient funds were now in hand to carry on the work for another year.

Pengelly to Sir Charles Lyell.

"Torquay, Oct. 1, 1866.

"Herewith I send you the Sixteenth Report of Progress, from which you will find there is very little to communicate. I cannot help thinking, however, that the paucity—almost total absence—of Bones in that part of the Cavern adjacent to, and lying immediately between, the two external entrances is a remarkable and interesting fact. It would have been very discouraging, however, had it presented itself at the commencement of our researches. The Report I read at Nottingham was well received and excited a great amount of interest. It has been printed *in extenso* in one of the Torquay newspapers, and a few reprints have been struck off, of which I send you a copy by this post. At Nottingham Mr. Busk was added to the Committee, and a further grant of £100 was voted by the General Committee. Of the former grant about £75 remain, so that we shall have sufficient funds to carry us through another year.

"The application made by Messrs. Boyd Dawkins and W. A. Sanford was referred to Mr. Busk.

"I propose to send up to Mr. Busk, with as little delay as possible, all the identifiable bones I have by me, so that we may hope that our Report next year will contain a list of all the animals whose remains we have met with."

The Chair of Geology at Glasgow being at this time vacant, Pengelly was urged by some of his friends to become a candidate. Finding from his friend Professor Joseph Lister,[*] however, that Zoology was also included, he renounced the idea, and wrote as follows to Sir Charles Lyell in 1866:—"I at once decided, of course, not to become a candidate, and, truth to tell, I should

* Now Lord Lister.

regret having to leave my studies in Devonshire Geology. I wish the Government would endow a Chair (perhaps a camp-stool would be more suitable) of Vagabondage in this county, and appoint me to it."

Pengelly was often amused at the different hypotheses suggested by visitors to the Cavern, as to how it had become tenanted by its various occupants. The following extract from a letter from the late Martin Farquhar Tupper, who was desirous to visit the Cavern under the explorer's own guidance, shows his ideas on the subject such as were perhaps at that time not very uncommon :—

" . . . I lunch with Mr. Wollaston on Saturday, and I'll see if I can induce him to join us for a Monday visit to Kent's Hole. I want to verify how far there can be room in the entrances for wild beasts, other than thin hyenas, to have got in bodily. Probably the elephants and rhinoceroses, etc., were pulled in piecemeal to be eaten—relics of the flood. . . ."

Between the years 1864 and 1869 there were fine displays of the Leonid Meteors, the maximum showers occurring in 1866.

Mrs. Pengelly to her Sister.

"*November* 14, 1866.— . . . We are all so excited about the Meteors, we can talk of nothing else—last night was brilliantly clear, I saw several, but nothing very striking till eleven o'clock, when there was a pretty constant succession, many of them with beautiful trains, one really magnificent, of a deep blue colour, like a brilliant lamp, with a glorious comet-like tail.

" I suppose, however, that I did not see the finest part of the shower, for Mr. Vivian came up, and would have William go down with him at twelve o'clock, to a capital spot on Walden Hill, where he had tea provided, and they had a grand time watching the splendid spectacle. William came back in ecstasies a little after four o'clock. He thinks they must have seen about four a second, on an average, and not less than fifteen thousand during the time they were observing; many were very beautiful meteors—the train of one was visible for ten minutes. The grand shower seems to have come later in the night than was expected. Mr. Richards was their companion—a good local astronomer—and they all agreed, should they be living at the next occurrence of the shower in thirty-three years, to meet at the same spot.* William gave a lecture on the subject last Monday, and great has been the surprise and wonder with many that his predictions have been so wonderfully verified. I suppose if it had been a wet or cloudy night, he would not have gained so much credit. Our friend and neighbour, Miss Otté, was much amused by her gardener saying to her this

---

* All three have passed away before the return of the shower looked for in 1899.

morning, 'Oh, ma'am, did Mr. Pengelly make all those stars come last night?' He had heard William had foretold the shower, and thought that was the way of accounting for the phenomenon. . . ."

Sir Charles Lyell to Pengelly.

"Harley Street, London, W., December 7, 1866.

". . . If you really think that any case has been made out to invalidate the conclusion that St. Michael's Mount is the true Ictis of Diodorus, please tell me when you next write. Not that it will be of any use to me now, as my volume is published. But it will be a satisfaction to know something about the pretensions of any other spot on the coast to such a claim. I suppose you will allude to it in your lectures, for the subject belongs to the theme which you have chosen.

"We are very much interested in your letter to Miss Coutts on the meteoric shower, by far the best account we have seen."

The following letter will show how gladly Pengelly welcomed discriminating criticism :—

Pengelly to J. Enys.

"Lamorna, Torquay, December 5, 1866.

"Thank you very much for the copy of your paper which you were so good as to send me.

"Those of us who hold (what may be called) the prevalent opinion respecting 'implements' and 'flakes' of flint, are much indebted to those who will print such objections as they may entertain. We shall observe and reason all the more accurately from a knowledge that the able and critical eyes of an opponent are upon us.

"I have sometimes thought that the vast difference between an 'implement' and a 'flake' is not sufficiently borne in mind. The existence of the former, whether polished or not, is a clear indication of the existence of the latter; since a polished implement must have first been chipped into shape, and in this process flakes, larger or smaller, must have been struck off. The converse proposition is not necessarily true, since Nature can and does form flakes. I do not enter into the question, whether or not it is possible to distinguish between natural and artificial flakes.

"Artificial flakes, in themselves, do not appear to me to possess any chronological value. They do not define any period. It is well known that man, in various stages of civilization, makes flint implements, and in so doing necessarily produces flakes. The former, so to speak, bear the impress of his individual mental culture; the flakes do not. Hence I see no reason why in Britain, flakes may not be of any age, from the advent of man on her soil, up to or even far beyond the Roman invasion. . . ."

The question of the Antiquity of Man was now exercising the minds of theologians as well as men of science, and to this

Sir John Bowring alludes in the postscript of the following letter :—

Sir John Bowring to Pengelly.

"Claremont, Exeter, December 25, 1866.

". . . I have written to Mr. Harpley . . . about my copies of the Paper on Devonshire Dialects. As soon as I get them, I shall have very great pleasure in sending one to Mr. Earle, gratified that he deems it worthy of his notice.

"I am sorry that I cannot be at Torquay on the 1st, when your working people have asked me to preside; but it is our Quarter Sessions, and I had another engagement (this may have a new rendering of the old teaching. 'To wish more *virtue* is to gain;' I say, to wish more *freedom* is to gain). The *wish* is father to the thought, and to the *certainty* of success.

"P.S.—Is it not amusing to see the bishops so complaisantly and so effectually knocking one another down? Oh you geologists! Great are your responsibilities, you turbulent troublers of ecclesiastical serenities!"

The Cavern was now yielding a large quantity of teeth, bones, and other interesting remains. Thus the Report of February, 1867, after mentioning that 165 Flint Flakes and Chips had been found during the preceding month ; and that amongst the bones there was one that had been fashioned into a "Harpoon," thus continues—

"In the stalagmitic floor there was found, on January 3rd, part of a human upper jaw with four teeth (right side), and one loose tooth ('Find 1930'). Identifiable bones and teeth of the ordinary cave mammals, though by no means very numerous, have been met with in the red cave-earth. The most remarkable object, however, which the red deposit (cave-earth) has yielded is a well-finished bone pin. . . . This interesting object was found in the fourth foot-level below the granular stalagmitic floor, which was twenty inches thick, and extended continuously in every direction, to considerable distances. It was found on January the 3rd, and was lying with an unworn molar of *Rhinoceros tichorhinus.* It is not uninteresting to observe again that in the Black Band, four feet immediately above this specimen, there were remains of the hyæna and other common cave mammals. . . ."

Mrs. Pengelly to her Sister.

"*Torquay, April* 25, 1867.— . . . We had a delightful visit a few days since from Dr. Tait, Bishop of London.[*] He was accompanied by Mrs. Tait and their son—and we had a deeply interesting discussion on the Antiquity of Man question. The bishop listened to all the information William gave him with marked attention. He has visited

<hr>

[*] Afterwards Archbishop of Canterbury.

N

the cavern with William, besides taking some other geological rambles with him, all of which appear to have much pleased him, as well as viewing the fossils at our house.   Both he and Mrs. Tait pressed us warmly to visit them in London.

"Last evening Miss Coutts gave a dinner-party for him at the Imperial Hotel, to which many were invited, and we saw a good deal of Dr. and Mrs. Tait.   We had a short but very pleasant visit yesterday from Captain Douglas Galton,* Mr. Godwin-Austen, Mr. Gwyn Jeffreys, and Mr. Prestwich † to view the cavern.   They were extremely interested with all they saw.   Several remarkable things have been found lately."

During the spring of 1867 Pengelly delivered a course of lectures at the Royal Institution.

Pengelly to his Wife.

"*London, 20, Northumberland Street, April 5, 1867.*— . . . I have just finished my third lecture.   I satisfied myself.   The audience was large and well pleased, I think.   This morning Tennant took Vicary and me to the Zoological Gardens.   Tell dear Trottie that we gave a leg bone to the striped hyæna to see how he would break it.   The keeper pretended to take it from him, and he laughed fearfully.   We saw lots of monkeys, swinging about on ropes, amongst them a Chimpanzee and an Orang Outang, and in the nursery we saw a little baby Orang.   We saw several pretty kangaroos carrying their little ones about, and a huge hippopotamus swimming about in its pond, and a seal in another."

Sir Charles Lyell to Pengelly.

"73, Harley Street, May 29, 1867.

"I am much obliged to you for the copies of your lectures, which are to me particularly interesting, and I rejoice you are to reprint them under another title.

"From some of the verbal reports made to me of what you said in your lectures, I gathered that you objected to something in my nomenclature of the Tertiaries—in regard to Pleistocene, Post-pliocene, and Recent.   As I am by no means satisfied myself on these matters, I should be truly glad of any criticism from a friendly quarter.   You have, of course, read what I have said in explanation, at pages 5 and 6, 'Antiquity of Man,' and page 108, 'Elements,' 6th edition, and note to that last page—how that I adopt Lubbock's Palæolithic and Neolithic ('Principles of Geology,' 10th ed., p. 176 and note), and that the Reindeer period intervenes (see p. 176, *ibid.*), and that I speak of Glacial and Post-glacial periods.   I am aware that, if asked what I mean by 'Recent,' I may not be able to give a very clear answer.

"I have, however, carefully avoided the use of Pleistocene in all my writings almost from the day I first started it, in order not to render the confusion greater.

* Now Sir Douglas Galton.   † Sir Joseph.

"I shall be glad to know what terminology you find to be most practically useful, as you have been working so well in these modern divisions of time."

Pengelly to Sir Charles Lyell.

"Lamorna, Torquay, June 3, 1867.

"Thank you very much for your kind letter of 29th ult. I remember that, on two occasions in my lectures, I said a word or two respecting the Nomenclature of the Tertiary and Quaternary deposits. On one occasion I stated that I used 'Cainozoic' in the sense in which Professor Phillips used it, as embracing both the Tertiaries and Quaternaries, and that I preferred this to the more restricted sense in which you used it, being as I thought more consonant with its etymology. The other occasion had reference to the word 'Pleistocene,' when I expressed the wish that Messrs. Dawkins and Sanford had in their 'Pleistocene Mammalia' abstained from the use of the word altogether, in accordance with your suggestion. I believe the foregoing is the substance of what I stated. I am somewhat inclined to hesitate before adopting Lartet's 'Reindeer Period.' From the evidence found in this district, the mammoth was living during the growth of the forests now submerged, and the reindeer during the much earlier time of Brixham Cavern. Lubbock's 'Palæolithic' and 'Neolithic' appear to me to be singularly happy. If our terms were to apply to our own and higher North latitudes only, or if the whole world had been glaciated, I at present incline to the thought that all present and probable requirements would be met by the terms Iron Age, Bronze Age, Neolithic Age, Palæolithic Age, Glacial Age, Newer Pliocene, etc."

In 1867 Pengelly was invited to become President of the Devonshire Association, in succession to Lord John Russell, and was followed by the well-known Devonian, Lord Coleridge, in 1868. The meeting over which he presided was held at Barnstaple, and proved a very successful gathering. His address was chiefly devoted to the Geology of Devonshire, and opened with the following paragraphs :—

". . . . It is somewhat usual—perhaps desirable—on occasions like the present, for the opening address to contain a summary of the prominent facts in the history of Science, Literature, and Art during the preceding twelve months. It would be easy for me to follow this practice, for the period since we met last has been by no means unproductive of important scientific events. Not only has the problem of laying an electric cable across the Atlantic been brilliantly solved, but it has been shown that a cable which has been lost a year, in an ocean upwards of two miles deep, can be recovered, carried to its destination, and rendered perfectly available for the purpose for which it was originally intended.

"Less than four centuries ago America was discovered, after a voyage of seventy days from Europe—a voyage, be it remembered, undertaken by a scientific man, and an enthusiast, who, by almost all the respectabilities, was denounced as a madman or a knave. Thanks to Science the voyage can now be performed in ten days, and we can send a thought across the Atlantic in a few seconds.

"And by what step-by-step process have the sciences which commercial enterprise has thus enlisted in her service reached their lofty positions! The Utilitarian may with advantage remember that truths which he has applied to eminently useful purposes, have frequently had a very protracted infancy. The Chaldean shepherd detected a few wandering bodies amongst the stellar hosts thousands of years before Astronomy was capable of presenting to the navigator the priceless gift of a method of determining his longitude by lunar distances. It was discovered in early times that a force existed which was capable of making amber attract light substances; but a hundred generations of men had to pass away before it was ascertained that this same force could carry a message round the world with a speed outstripping that of light. That steam could move a toy, was known when our British ancestors were savages; but it was not until the time of our own generation that it was found to be equal to the propulsion of sea-going ships. Within the quadrangle of the British Museum, there formerly lay a fine example of the ship of the aborigines of this island—the trunk of a tree, hollowed out probably with the aid of fire and flint implements; the application of scientific principles has transformed her into the *Great Eastern.* During their growth and development, these principles and truths were but lightly esteemed, and their votaries were sometimes allowed to starve; but without them the Atlantic cable would never have been heard of.

"Though we ardently admire, and are eminently proud of the application of scientific principles to purposes of general utility, especially in a world where, in the vast majority of cases, the *business* of life is to secure the *means* of life, it is probable that, notwithstanding its fascinating and important achievements in telegraphy, 1866 will be chiefly remembered as the year of the great meteoric shower. Those who were so fortunate as to witness the gorgeous spectacle displayed on the night of the 13th–14th of November must have been deeply impressed, not only with the splendour of the scene, but with the universality of law, the dignity of science, and the existence of faculties, aspirations, and cravings which lie beyond the reach of mere utilitarianism.

"Attractive as are the topics I have named, as well as many others contained in the budget of the last twelve months, I have decided to give my address a completely local character, and to aim at nothing more than a statement of the present position of opinion respecting the Geology of Devonshire. In making this decision I may have been unwise, but a people's history depends so largely on their mental development, and this is so closely connected with their avocations, which in their turn so distinctly hinge on the nature of the soil, that I have been unable to persuade myself that to any one likely to attend such a meeting as the present, the theme I have selected would prove utterly uninteresting. Whether the dwellers in a district were to be farmers, miners, manufacturers, or caterers for the comforts and pleasures of visitors, was predetermined by the agents which, at various periods of the remote past, produced the geological characteristics by which they are surrounded. To a large extent their history was pre-written on their rocks. . . ."

After a lengthened review of the various geological phenomena of the county, the address concludes thus—

" It must be unnecessary to remark that the time has by no means arrived when the Devonshire geologists can suspend their labours. There remain many unsolved problems within our borders. We still ask, ' What is the age of the Crystalline Schists at the southern angle of our county? What is the precise chronology of our Limestones and associated rocks? Is there, east of Exmouth, a break in the Red rocks? Whence come the Budleigh Salterton pebbles? Whence also the Porphyritic Trap nodules so abundant in the Trias? Are our Green-sands really of the age of the Gault? Whence the flints so numerous on our existing beaches? What is the history of our Superficial Gravels? Are there any indications of Glaciation in Devonshire? To what race did our Cave Men belong?' The solution of, at least, many of these questions must be reserved for another generation of inquirers, and to the young men of the present day I earnestly commend them."

In 1867 the British Association met at Dundee, where Pengelly was the guest of Mr. and Mrs. Walker, to whose kindness he often referred as making the visit a most agreeable one.

In the Report on the explorations of Kent's Cavern for this year, which he read before the meeting, he says—

"The committee venture to entertain the opinion that the evidence which the last twelve months have put into their possession renders it impossible for any one to doubt that man occupied Devonshire when it was also the home of the extinct lion, hyæna, bear, rhinoceros, mammoth, and their contemporaries.

"Of the tools alluded to, two have already been mentioned—the bone awl and the ' harpoon ' found in the Black Band, beneath the stalagmitic floor, in the Vestibule. As has been stated, in this same thin band there occurred, with the implements just mentioned, teeth of rhinoceros, hyæna, and other of the common cave mammals ; and the story they tell is at once clear and resistless. These, however, are neither the only, nor the best, bone implements which have been ex-humed. Two others have been met with, and both of them in the Red Cave-earth, below the Black Band. One is a portion of a highly finished ' harpoon,' two and a quarter inches in length, and differing from that previously mentioned, in the form of its point, and in being barbed on two sides. To use a botanical term the barbs are ' oppo-site,' not ' alternate,' as is the case with many of the doubly-barbed implements of the kind found in certain French caverns. It is worthy of remark that whilst in France the same cavern has rarely, if ever, yielded both singly and doubly barbed 'harpoons,' an example of each kind has been found in Kent's Hole. This implement was met with on March 18, 1867, in the Vestibule, in the second foot-level of Red Cave-earth. Vertically above these two feet of loam, there lay the Black Band about three inches thick, and containing flint flakes and remains of extinct mammals; over this again came the stalagmitic floor, eighteen inches thick, granular towards its base, crystalline and laminated towards the upper surface, continuous in all directions, unquestionably intact, and without fracture or crevice of any kind; and superposed on this was the ordinary Black Mould, with Romano-British potsherds. Like all bones found in the Cave-earth, the 'harpoon,' when applied to the tongue, firmly adheres to it. It has the condition which, from the spot it occupies, might have been looked for."

A bone needle, partially covered with stalagmite, was also found during the year's exploration, 1866–7. [See Rep. Brit. Assoc., 1867.]

A fracture may be observed in the eye of the bone needle, the history of which is somewhat remarkable. When discovered it was perfect. The news of the finding of so extraordinary an object created very considerable interest, and Pengelly was asked, by a lady, to exhibit this great curiosity to her guests at an "At Home." With his usual urbanity, he consented, and was at much pains during the evening in showing and explaining his treasure. When curiosity had been exhausted, and the needle was again safely in his pocket, his hostess came up suddenly, with, "Oh, Mr. Pengelly, would you let me have the bone needle for a few minutes to show to Lord Lytton, who has just arrived?" With characteristic confidence and good nature, Pengelly gave his jewel into the lady's hands. In the course of ten minutes it was restored to him, torn from the card on which it had been gummed down, threaded through the card, pin-wise, and the eye broken off and missing. Remonstrance or scolding he felt would be futile, and for the short time he remained in the room, Pengelly had to conceal his mortification and distress as well as he might. As he would relate the story, "I went home, lay awake all night, and took counsel with one whose wit rarely failed to be of use to me in any difficulty—my wife." Her advice was that he should make his way to the house ere the family were astir, seek out the head-chambermaid, and, explaining to her what was missing, should offer a handsome gratuity for its recovery. This was done, and, his mission of explanation accomplished, he took an anxious half-hour's

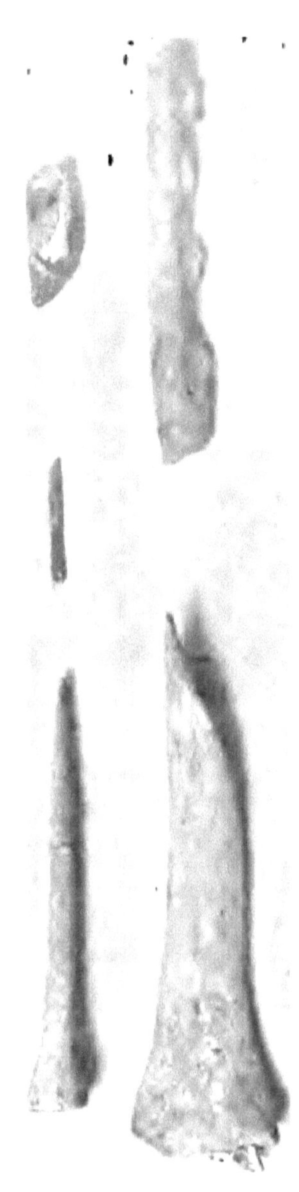

stroll by the sea.   On his return to the house, his eager enquiry was met by the production of the fragment, which he joyfully changed for a half-sovereign.   But for this happy recovery more than half the interest of ·one of the most important discoveries in Kent's Cavern would have been lost, for it would have been useless to explain that it had once been a needle with an eyelet.

The following letter from his old and valued friend Robert Chambers, reached Pengelly during his visit to Dundee, and shows that Dr. Chambers' last illness was then beginning.

Dr. Robert Chambers to Pengelly.

"6, Gillespie Terrace, St. Andrews, September 3, 1867.

"If, as is likely, you join the excursion party to this city on Saturday, please to become my guest here till the Monday morning, and join me in a drive to Dura Den on the Sunday afternoon.

"I am not strong enough in health to go into the turmoil of the B.A. at Dundee, but am alive enough for the proposed hospitality. A little paper about an *Esker* at St. Fort, near Newport, is herewith enclosed, with a request that you will read it."

In acknowledging the receipt of some papers sent to him by Pengelly, Professor Beete Jukes states his views as to the distribution of fossils.

Prof. J. Beete Jukes to Pengelly.

"Geological Survey of Ireland, Dublin, October 29, 1867.

"Many thanks for your packet of papers.   The one on the distribution of fossils will be useful to me now.   You have, however, one little imperfection in your table, viz. putting the word Coomhola, to represent all our carbonif. slate ; this would be tantamount to putting the word 'Marwood' to represent all the Devonian.   *Cyrtina heteroclita*, for instance, on which Davidson had no doubt, till he heard it occurred in the same bed with *Phillipsia pustulata*, does not occur in the Coomhola grits, but at least three thousand feet above them, in the black slates and calc. bands which doubtless represent your Torbay beds, and the Pilton, and the Ilfracombe.   Coomhola grits are merely scattered beds of sandstone, up and down in the carboniferous slate, but more at bottom than elsewhere, sometimes twenty feet thick only ; that is, the carb. slate, where it is three thousand or four thousand feet thick, will only have one bed of brown sandstone full of the Marwood cucullæas and five or six other beds of similar rock, but with no fossils, above and below it.   But in following the strike of those beds, other beds of grit, grey and brown, will come in above and below, and gradually they will get so numerous as to form a great feature, chiefly grits, two thousand or three thousand feet thick, with cucullæas, etc., scattered up and down them, but interstratified with black slates, and having two hundred feet of black slates below them, full of encrinites and a lot of other fossils of the same species as those in the slates five thousand feet higher.

"Touching fossils, will you favour me with putting side by side Davidson's descriptions of *Spirifera striata* [and *Spirifera disjuncta?* Read them out aloud sentence by sentence, first one and then the other, picking the sentences in the Devonian part, so as to bring the descriptions of similar parts in the same order.

"Will you then tell me the amount of specific difference you can extract from these descriptions, of those parts which are described in both?

"After that will you take the figures, and, comparing the differences among the five figures of *Sp. striata* and those among the twenty figures of *Sp. disjuncta*, will you tell me whether any greater difference is discernible in comparing the figures of the two *species*, than is discernible in the figures of either one?

"The only constant character I can discern in *Sp. disjuncta* to distinguish it from *Sp. striata* is that the former seems more finely *striated* than the latter. Is that worth making a specific difference? Is not *Sp. verneuilii* or *disjuncta* just a variety *Sp. striata?*

"Can you appreciate any difference between *Strophalosia caperata* or *productoides* and *Producta scrabicula?* I can't, neither can a good many people.

"These are but hints of the modifications of the palæontological facts, which will, I believe, be the result of the application of the true stratigraphical interpretation.

"Upper, Middle, and Lower Devonian are all bosh!

"There is but one fossiliferous group, the species being scattered irregularly and capriciously as they are in carboniferous limestone, Upper Silurian, etc., etc. ; certain species, however, being only found in particular kinds of rock or in particular localities, just as certain living shells are now.

"My recent examination of South Devon has swept away all my doubts and hesitation.

"The Old Red Sandstone lies under all your fossiliferous Devonian, coming up here and there, through faults or inverted folds, and over-lapped occasionally by the carboniferous slate, which stretched across it with a ridge of Silurian slate round Veryan Bay, which has been tilted up and *inverted* on to the Devonians by the very same line of inversion which runs from Dartmouth, through Plymouth Harbour, to the Dodman and thereabouts. The southern borders of the Plymouth limestones are inverted, and dip at the beds which lie under them—our Coomhola grits, etc."

In January of 1868 Pengelly delivered two lectures at Newcastle-on-Tyne.

Pengelly to his Wife.

"*Newcastle, January* 23, 1868.— . . . My second lecture is over. On Tuesday I studied this good town somewhat, and among other things I saw the *old* castle, which when *new* gave a name to the town.

It contains a very large collection of antiquities, mainly derived from the old Roman wall.   In the evening my host's sister, Miss Richardson, had a rather large party, of which I was a fraction.   The evening was very pleasant.   Yesterday I accompanied my kind host, D. Richardson, to see a large collection of local fossils, made by, and the property of, a Mr. Astley, a small country shopkeeper.   It proved to be a really splendid, probably unique, series of carboniferous fish, many of which induced me to believe that some of the so-called Polperro 'sponges' may be fish remains.   Next we went to a coal-pit, but did not go down. Then we travelled on an engine for several miles, in order to keep an appointment to dine with Mr. R. C. Clapham, one of the secretaries of the Newcastle Society.   Yesterday I got a letter from Sir W. Armstrong, asking me to spend a day and night at his house.   My time, however, is too much engaged and too limited to permit this, and so, when I met him at the lecture last night, we arranged that I should take luncheon with him on Friday.

"This evening Dr. Brady gave a party in my honour. . . ."

Pengelly to his Wife.

"*Stratton Street, January* 25, 1868.— . . . I am this moment come in, having left Newcastle two hours and a half late.   I am all right, and am going out for the rest of the day.   Yesterday I took luncheon at Sir W. Armstrong's, and spent a very pleasant afternoon ; indeed, my visit from first to last has been most enjoyable.   Everybody as kind as they could be ; nothing could surpass the kindness of my host D. Richardson and his wife.   Lady Armstrong showed me over her splendid fernery.   Sir William is so much interested in Kent's Cavern that he declares he and Lady Armstrong will come down to see it.   I purpose leaving this about noon on Monday, and expect to reach Southampton about 4.30.*   I shall be very glad to see you all once more.   I wish you could go with me everywhere. . . ."

Professor Huxley and Sir Charles Lyell were greatly interested in the discovery to which the following letters refer.

Rev. W. S. Symonds to Pengelly.

"Pendock Rectory, Tewkesbury, March 23, 1868.

"I enclose a note from Leonard Lyell,† from which you will see, if he has not already written to you, that you have discovered *Pteraspis* in the Devonian proper ; and a capital find it is, as being an undoubted Old Red fish of both Siluria and Scotland.

"Of course, it is a question whether the large species (which, as I detected its existence in your cabinet, I may venture to claim a right to call *P. Pengellii*) may not range into far higher beds than our lower zones of the Old Red of Herefordshire, than the *P. rostratus* or *Lewisii*. I do not know where your Plymouth beds lie in the Devonians, but I think you said near the base of the system.

---

* Where he was to deliver a lecture.
† Now Sir Leonard Lyell, M.P.

"I have a letter from Sir C. Lyell, saying that he thinks the argument of the nearly total change of species and genera of mollusca between the Upper Silurians of Siluria and the Lowest Devonians a very important point, and it is one to be carefully considered on attempting to correlate the Old Red with the Devonian.

"I shall not easily forget the pleasant days and instructive time I passed in Devonshire with you, or the kind hospitality with which you and Mrs. Pengelly welcomed me and my many friends. I look forward to seeing you both here, and to showing you some of our *Pteraspis*-bearing rocks before the summer is over. I promised you a photograph of my Old Red figure, so enclose it with kind regards to yourself and Mrs. Pengelly."

Leonard Lyell to Pengelly.

"42, Regent's Park Road, N.W., March 24th.

"When I took your cigar-box the other day to Jermyn Street and showed Mr. Huxley the specimens, he declared the larger slab to be unmistakably *Pteraspis*, and remarked on its large size, and the number of individuals jammed one on the top of another. Professor Huxley also suggested the propriety of your giving these beds at Looe a thorough working, to obtain perfect specimens of the *Pteraspis*, and of your sending to town a set of these fossil remains. As for the remaining specimens, he considered them to be portions of fish, but too small to determine.

"When I was leaving his room, and was looking about in case of any specimen being overlooked, Mr. Huxley assured me, with almost amusing gravity, that all the specimens were in the box, and that he had not withheld one. Then I began to understand your scruples concerning the morality of London palæontologists! I have since delayed returning to you the box only that my uncle might have an opportunity of seeing the *Pteraspis*.

"With many thanks to you for the pleasant recollections I have of the expeditions to Brixham and Kent's Hole."

Professor J. Beete Jukes to Pengelly.

"Dublin, April 4, 1868.

"I've just heard from Huxley about your *Pteraspis*, found at Meadfoot, 'between Torquay and Plymouth'—he says that is your description of the place; but surely Meadfoot is that place *in* Torquay, is it not? or is there another Meadfoot?

"It is a grand find, and goes against my views, I admit; still, it is *not conclusive*, any more than species of Silurian genera of trilobites make the Devonian rocks Silurian; so I shall stand by my carboniferous colours till they are battered down by stratigraphical as well as palæontological evidence.

"I've a paper on South Devon in the press; but have been quite knocked up this winter, with all sorts of botheration—had to go to Gully of Malvern, etc., etc."

Jonathan Couch to Pengelly.

"Polperro, June 15, 1868.

"I can confidently assure you that the fossils to which you refer were discovered by myself, and I have a lively remembrance of the circumstances attending the discovery, which was made as I was climbing upon some steep rocks at a place near what is called Chapel.

"But after this I engaged an individual of the Coast Guard to extend the inquiry, which he did with much intelligence and perseverance. His name is William Loughrun, now superannuated from the Coast Guard, and at present engaged with Mr. J. Gwyn Jeffreys in a dredging excursion among the Shetland Islands. He preserves fish exceedingly well, and supplies the British Museum with them. Our friend Peach was always persuaded that the fossils referred to were fish—which I never believed; but I once saw a small stone which bore the marks of skeletons of real fishes—*Pleuranectidæ.* I was not able to obtain it, and I believe it was finally lost."

Another interesting discovery was that of the remains of a whale.

Dr. J. E. Gray to Pengelly.

"British Museum, May 17, 1868.

"Thanks for the notice of the second vertebra of the whale from Babbacombe. Could I see the specimen, or a photograph of it? I am sorry to say that I have no separate copy yet of the account of it. The Proceedings of the Geological Society do not send the separate copies until the part containing the paper is out; as soon as I get one you shall have one. The discovery of this whale is most interesting, as there was only a single imperfect specimen of it known before, found on the coast of Sweden. I have had a facsimile of the vertebra of the original specimen sent to me, it and yours are nearly identical."

In the spring of 1868 Pengelly had the pleasure of a visit from Mr. C. W. Peach, who had been spending a short time in Cornwall with the object of reviewing and making notes on his geological collections, brought together many years before and presented on leaving for Scotland to the Penzance and Truro Museums. After leaving Torquay, Mr. Peach visited London on his way home, and the following extract from a letter to Pengelly relates the opinions formed of some of his specimens, by Geologists in Town.

"I brought with me from the Penzance Museum," he writes, "a few specimens from my collection. I thought them *Lingulæ.* It was pleasant to find Salter in the museum;[*] he was there for examination of Trilobites for Cambridge folk, for comparison. I showed him bits, and at once he said *Lingulæ;* and on Etheridge seeing them he said

[*] Jermyn Street.

the same ; and as they are the first noticed from Cornish rocks, I am glad to go ahead. I shall, I hope, one day say more about these ; at present, beyond going to Davidson, the thing must rest. I found Sir Roderick at the museum, and spoke to him, and told him about them. The old chief laughed, and told me about the *Land plants* of the Cambrian lately found, and that, since they were got, true *Lingulæ* have been found in the same rocks, and these said plants prove on examination to be *Sponges.* I hope these sponges will be more genuine than Mr. McCoy's. The veteran was in fine feather about this decision, and was on the top ropes about the meeting and dinner of the Geographical Society. He was looking well after the fatigue. They say he acquitted himself well, indeed surprised everybody. . . ."

At the British Association meeting, which was this year, 1868, held at Norwich, Pengelly read his Fourth Annual Report on the Kent's Cavern Exploration, in which are mentioned among other interesting "Finds" in the overlying Black Mould, pieces of Pottery, a spindle-whorl, a roughly shapen piece of New Red Sandstone, a portion of a bone comb, marine shells, and "part of a human upper jaw with eight teeth, of which four were still in their sockets." He also read a Paper "On the condition of some of the bones found in the Cavern"—in which he remarks . . . "The third class consisted of bones broken with an oblique fracture, and precisely resembled the larger remnants left by Hyænas, as the author had found by a series of experiments, which he had made at the Zoological Gardens, London."

Rev. Canon H. B. Tristram to Pengelly.

"Greatham Vicarage, Stockton-on-Tees, September 2, 1868.

"I have never stated in any of my works that any caverns I had visited are tenanted alternately by man and wild beasts. But I mentioned in some fugitive paper or other on Tunis and its interior, that several of the old Roman cisterns and crypts in the south of that region are used by the Arabs for shelter and for cattle-folds during their sojourn in the locality, and that when they have cleared off the pasturage and gone, the hyænas return and take up their quarters in these dens. I may add that at Rabbath Ammon (now Ammon) in Gilead, east of Jordan, I found plenty of the well-known droppings of hyænas in the vomitaria of the theatres, in places which are covered with the manure of the beasts, which the Arabs stable there during their sojourn every spring in the place. When we were there the Arab cattle had gone, but only a few days before, and we found no wild beasts."

In the autumn of 1868 Professor Boyd Dawkins arranged to visit Torquay for the purpose of identifying the bones found in the Cavern.

Professor Boyd Dawkins to Pengelly.

"Romford, September 8, 1868.

"Can you help me to the knowledge of the man who owns the lithograph stones of the plate of *Machairodus* tooth found by Mac-Enery, and published by E. Vivian in 1859? I write if possible to borrow it for Palæont. Society Monograph on Felis. Frank Buckland writes me that he knows nothing about it. Of course you know. Item—concerning bones; when will it be convenient for me to begin the task? I wish to finish them as soon as I can; for delay with me is a synonym for laziness. If possible I should like to get the task done before the year's end. . . . Hoping that you are digging away, etc."

Pengelly to Professor Boyd Dawkins.

"Torquay, September 21, 1868.

"I have delayed answering your note until I could meet with Mr. Vivian, as he alone can give information about the stones of the plate of *Machairodus*. I have just seen him (that is Vivian, not Machairodus), and he says 'the plates were lithographed by Scharf, on stones found in the stores of Hullmandel & Co., London, and printed by them for Mr. F. Buckland, and given to him, E. Vivian.' I can tell you no more on this point.

"I am busily engaged writing numbers on the Kent's Cavern bones, so as to facilitate your work when you arrive. I ought to have a good start before you begin, in order that I may be able to keep ahead of you. Will it suit you to fix your visit for the beginning of November? I shall have a large number ready by that time."

In the Monthly Report on Kent's Cavern for October, 1868, is thus noted the discovery of a fine bone needle—

"Before closing this Report it may be interesting to state that Mr. Boyd Dawkins, having arranged to visit Torquay shortly for the purpose of identifying the Bones and Teeth found in the Cavern, the Secretary has commenced a preliminary inspection in order to facilitate the heavy task. While thus engaged, on the 24th ult., he found among the contents of the box labelled '1847' what appeared at first to be a very small Bone having one end covered with stalagmite. On being touched the stalagmite fell off—a thing very common in the case of specimens which, like this, have been washed and dried—and the Bone proved to be a portion of a needle, having a well-drilled eye, which the stalagmite had previously concealed. It is slightly taper; its section is sub-elliptical, resembling that of a bodkin, rather than of a needle, and it has lost its point. It is about 0·85 inch long, its greatest diameter at the larger end is about 0·075 inch, and at the smaller end 0·05 inch. There are numerous fine longitudinal striæ on its surface, as if it had been scraped into shape. The Secretary's Journal shows that it was found, December 4, 1866, in the Black Band below the (Granular) Stalagmite

Floor, which was described in detail in the Third Report of the Committee, read at Dundee in 1867. (See Report British Association for 1867, p. 29)."

Professor Boyd Dawkins to Pengelly.

"*Romford, November* 2, 1868.—"I am preparing myself to wrestle with the Kent's Hole collection. The best plan of attack is, I fancy, to open the boxes according to their numbers. . . . In this way the work will progress swiftly, and we can do some thousand per diem. I know all the species at sight, except Grizzly and Brown Bear, and these I am getting up. Thank heaven, *F. Spelæa* is done for aye and aye ! . . . Don't trouble about lists or a catalogue ; I have it all sketched out, and all the names of the beasts are down—all that we shall find. . . ."

Another extract from Pengelly's Journal during the same month (November) records an interesting find.

"*Thursday, November* 26.—While engaged to-day in the preliminary investigation of the Cavern specimens at my house, I found in the 'find 2206' a well-formed 'Harpoon,' barbed on one side only. When I took it out of the box it was completely invested with stalagmite, a part of which fell off in my hand, and disclosed some of the barbs. The tool is not perfect, but another piece of bone, apparently an implement also, is not improbably a portion of the harpoon. (See Evans' 'Ancient Stone Implements,' p. 460, Fig. 404.) In the same 'find' there is a piece of bone with an artificial cut on it."

Pengelly to Sir Charles Lyell.

"Torquay, November 11, 1868.

" I beg to call your attention to the following minutes. . . .

" P.S.—Mr. Boyd Dawkins, assisted by Mr. A. Sanford, commenced the examination of the Cavern fossils at my house yesterday. You will be interested in hearing that they have detected remains of Beaver amongst them."

The Queen of Holland soon after this visited Torquay, and was much interested in Pengelly's Geological discoveries.

Sir Charles Lyell to Pengelly.

"73, Harley Street, London, November 26, 1868.

" I am glad to have copies of the five Memoirs on the Caverns and Ichthyology of Devonshire, as well as the Meteorology of your county, which attest your scientific activity in the present year.

" Miss Coutts invited us last week to meet the Queen of Holland at a luncheon party at her house ; and, having the honour to sit next her Majesty, she told me a good deal of her visit to Torquay, of which she had a lively recollection, especially on those points of the geology to which you had served as a guide. She said she had promised you the skull of an orang outang, which had been sent to her, and which she was told was a valuable specimen.   I happened to say, ' He will perhaps give it to the Torquay Museum.'   She said, 'Why should he do that ? I meant him to consider it entirely for himself.'

" I was glad to hear of the Beaver, but shall not be satisfied if Mr. Boyd Dawkins finds nothing new except that animal ; although if such should be the case, it would prove how well you have been observing all the osteological details so that scarcely anything had escaped you.

" Leonard will be pleased to read your notice of the *Pteraspis*.   The recognition of it was a good hit of Symonds."

Pengelly had this year the pleasure of showing Kent's Cavern, and explaining the work in hand, to Professor Tyndall, John Bright, the great orator, and other friends.

CHAPTER XIII.

RICH DISCOVERIES IN KENT'S HOLE.

1869 TO 1871.

AMONGST Pengelly's scientific friends at this period may be especially mentioned Charles Kingsley and the late Mr. W. Froude, naval engineer * (brother of Richard Hurrell Froude, so well known in connexion with the Tractarian Movement, and of James Anthony Froude the historian), who was now residing at Cockington near Torquay, and was conducting, at the wish of the Government, many interesting and important experiments on the displacement of ships, on a small piece of water artificially formed in his grounds. He and Pengelly had many interests in common, as will be seen from a few extracts from Froude's letters. Whether written in a playful vein, or on abstruse mathematical subjects, his letters were ever welcome, as his conversation, in like manner, always afforded pleasure.

IV. Froude to Pengelly.

"Chelston Cross, 11.59 p.m. (that is to say after the 11th hour).

"Sir Thomas and Lady E. are coming to dine with us to-morrow, rather on a 'grand hop.' I think it is likely that you know him; and if so, you will be the better able to judge whether it would be pleasant or a bore to you to meet them. He seems to me a very pleasing, intelligent, open-minded man (perhaps my reason for thinking him such is that he seems to like me!), 'and one who likes to know about things,' and who does know about many things in a sort of general way, without, however, having any definite pursuit. Now, if your cold is well enough, and if you can spare the time, and it isn't a bore to you so to spare it, it would give us and him pleasure if you would join us at dinner to-morrow (you see by this time it is to-day!) at 7.30 p.m. 'Don't hesitate to say no if you'd rather not,' but make up (in that case) some agreeable excuse, such as that the bottom had

---

* He died in Simons Town, South Africa, whither he had gone partly for his health and partly to carry on some scientific experiments, on May 6th, 1879.

fallen out of Kent's Cavern, or that the earth contained in it is in apogee, or that you are in opposition, or something more pleasant even if less true."

This spring Pengelly had the agreeable satisfaction of initiating and carrying to a successful issue Mr. Froude's candidature for the Fellowship of the Royal Society, and amongst other letters received on the subject was one from the late Professor Tyndall.

" I should gladly comply with any request of yours . . . the signing goes for nothing with the Council—what you want is a member of the Council to speak for your friend. If Mr. Froude has published in the *Phil. Trans* , I will sign his Certificate. . . ."

W. Froude to Pengelly.

" Chelston Cross, March 4, 1869.

"This is the third time I have been baulked of my purpose of calling on you, to thank you for the very great and effectual trouble you have taken on my behalf in reference to my F.R.S.-ship ambition. An interruption which I could not shirk having each time come most inopportunely. So let me now thank you on paper at least. You are kind enough to make light of it ; but I know what a tax it is on the time of a man who occupies his time fully, to write a lot of letters, and this tax you have paid for me without stint. I have received from the President an invitation to an evening at Burlington House on the 6th inst. and on the 24th April. I suppose they have Candidates up to look at them. I hope to go in April, but on the 6th I cannot go."

W. Froude to Pengelly.

" Chelston Cross, Torquay, June 22, 1869.

" You perhaps have seen the request I wrote to you the other day on behalf of Capt. Noble. Like the Sibyl in Roman fable, I become more exacting in proportion to my disappointments.

" Captain Noble has been talking of the Cave to the ' Distinguished Officers ' who are conducting the artillery trials on Dartmoor near the Prison. (It is a pity they can't have the Convicts to try the merits of ' Shrapnel *v.* Segment Shell ' upon. It would be more life-like.)

" Well, the said officers are very anxious to see the interior of the Cave, and to talk with you on your results (General Dickson is the name of the Boss) ; and as Saturday is the holiday, they would come over here next Saturday, so as to avail themselves of any part of the day you might have at your disposal to show them what is to be seen there.

" Seriously I feel that this sort of thing must be a really great exaction on any man whose time is so really filled up as yours.

" I explained this ; and you must not on any account hesitate to say ' no,' unless you can bring it within the ordinary limits of self-sacrifice, which I know you make full wide.

O

" I should have come to see you, but I have been laid up this week with the gout.   I am now afloat again, but not in trim.

" I will send over to-morrow noon to see if there is an answer."

IV. Froude to Pengelly.

" Chelston Cross, Torquay, August 22, 1869.

" I return your book, with many thanks; I have read with much interest the papers to which you called my attention. The more so, as I had on various occasions heard the views which the paper states comprehensively and compactly, crudely and loosely stated in conversation, and had been attracted by this.   The authority on which they come indeed is sufficiently good to oblige an outsider to adopt them so far as he need decidedly adopt any on the points in question, and besides that, so far as my weak geological knowledge enables me to follow them, they seem to be conclusively worked out—if indeed I except one point—my doubts about which I state with much hesitation. The difficulty is this : From principles involved in the circumstance of the Earth's rotation, I feel it difficult to understand how an oceanic current can combine a westerly element as it flows northward above the Equator. The Gulf Stream in its westerly course before it reaches the Equator, is acting in due accord with the principles in question, and no less so as it again trends eastward across the North Atlantic.   That it might be driven westward to some degree, by the combination of its northerly impulse and the pressure of an intercepting continent, is of course possible; but that impulse must become spent by degrees, namely, as soon as the excess of easterly velocity due to its Equatorial rotation, when transferred to the lesser velocity of rotation belonging to the higher latitudes, had become equal to its original velocity as a current.   This at least is a difficulty, the solution of which I do not see, though the difficulty seems real and obvious—but then it is one which the writer of the paper is certainly not likely to have overlooked—so I shall bottle up the doubt to serve as the subject of a conversation when next I meet you, and when the chances are you will be able at once to set me right."

Rev. Canon Kingsley to Pengelly.

" Eversley, Drychfield, March 15, 1869.

" I have been reading—I need not say with what pleasure—certain tracts of yours which I had not ere now time to study. I shall not intrude compliments on you, but come to a question. Among the ' Raised Beaches in Barnstaple Bay,' you take no notice of Northam Pebble Ridge.   I have long considered this as a raised beach, because—

" 1. It is high above high-water mark.

" 2. I could never find any sign of accretion to it, the sea-bottom outside being all smooth fine sand.

" 3. Because a similar pebble ridge, as it seems to me, is forming, or has been formed, at Buckish Gore, running out far to sea northward, to the westward of the ridge (four miles to the west of and intercepting any stones which may fall from the cliffs at least between Bucks and Hartland Point).

"4. Because beneath the pebble ridge at low tides there are exposed, beneath the sand, beds of blue clay and peat, seemingly homologous with the other sunken forests of W. England and W. Wales. Now this bears on your Presidential Address, page 26, where you say that 'In no instance are the subaerial portions of the forests overlain by marine deposits beyond the reach of the waves at the existing level.' Of course all depends on what you think the pebble ridge to be. I have looked at it long, and have come to the same conclusion as (I think) Phillips came to. But that it is of the same era as the raised bedded beach of the North side—Braunton and Lamerton (which I used to puzzle over as a boy, and which you so well vindicated against Spence Bate)—I do not say. It seems to me rather of the same era as certain raised shell beaches which I could show you about Hunstanton, in the North Coast of Norfolk, which certainly seem to me later than the submerged Post-pleiocene forests of Brauncaster, etc.

"Pardon my daring to differ from you in opinion."

Pengelly to the Rev. Canon Kingsley.

"Lamorna, Torquay, March 20, 1869.

"I am very sorry that I have not been able to answer your kind and interesting letter before. Herewith I send you a small parcel of my papers, one of which is on 'The Submerged Forest and the Pebble Ridge of Barnstaple Bay.' There appears to be good evidence that the Ridge marches slowly landward (the pebbles having an occasional game at leap-frog), and it is certain that, during heavy gales, vast bodies of water are thrown over it at spring-tide high-water. With these facts in view, it does not appear to me requisite to suppose that when the ridge was formed, the level of the land was lower than it is at present. Indeed, with such an unresisting plain landwards of it, I doubt very much whether, if the land were lower, the Ridge would long retain its present position, or stop short of the cliff which bounds the plain. You will find that whilst I believe the Raised Beaches of Braunton, Hope's Nose, etc., are contemporary with one another, and older than the Submerged Forests of Northam, Torbay, etc., I incline to the opinion that there have been changes of level since that which carried down the forests.

"If you will kindly let me know what papers of mine you have by you, I will, with your permission, send you copies of all you have not, as far as I can do so."

Rev. Canon Kingsley to Pengelly.

"Eversley Rectory, Winchfield.

"I have been reading your interesting paper on Beekites of 1858.

"One thing always struck me about them, and the beds in which they are found, viz. the trace of *active* volcanic agency. I always suspect volcanic springs where I find trace of water containing silex in solution. I *suspect* flows of hot water, holding silex in solution, may have caused our chalk flints.

"But there are (to me) distinct proofs of the conglomerates of Torquay having been formed, some of them under active volcanic agency. Froude the historian (who is no geologist) first pointed it out to me, when bathing off the Beekite beds at the Thunderhole. "See," he said, "that every fragment of these older rocks is angular. They have not been rolled on a sea beach. Have they not been blasted out of a volcano?" At once there occurred to me the great similarity between them and the dust and gravel beds of the Eifel, which I know well; and where, round each crater of explosion, you have vast (recent) layers of dust and little angular bits of the Devonian strata—rasped by steam off the lips of the crater.

"Do think over this action—unless you know all about it, and more, already. And tell me where I can find information about the 'traps' of S. Devon and their age."

The British Association met at Exeter in the autumn of 1869. Though not a large meeting, it was an interesting one. Being little more than an hour's journey from Exeter, many of the men of science gathered there took the opportunity of visiting Torquay and its neighbourhood.

Pengelly to Sir Walter Trevelyan.

"Lamorna, Torquay, July 19, 1866.

"When, upwards of two years ago, I had the pleasure of being introduced to you in Kent's Hole, by my colleague Mr. Vivian of this town, we had some conversation on the alleged occurrence, in the cavern, of *Machairodus latidens*, formerly known as *Ursus cultridens*. I am preparing a paper on the subject for the British Association, and shall be greatly obliged if you will be so good as to favour me with replies to the following queries with permission to use them publicly on your authority.

"1. Were you present when Mr. MacEnery found the canines of Machairodus?

"2. Did you obtain from him one or more of the canines?

"3. If so, have you it, or them, in your collection at present?

"4. If not in your collection, do you know where they are?"

Mrs. Pengelly to her Sister.

"*Exeter, August* 20.— . . . The soirée last night was delightful, but so crowded. I saw many I knew. William introduced me to Babbage, Professor J. Couch Adams, and several others. I had a very nice talk with Sir Charles Wheatstone, also Professor Huxley, which is always a treat, Busk, Balfour, etc., and a chat with Miss Becker, who was walking about with our friend Mr. Edgeworth. William read his Report on Kent's Cavern to a full house, Boyd Dawkins following. Professor Phillips's lecture was very good."

It was for the Red Lion Dinner at Exeter that a parody of

Gray's Elegy was written. The last two verses of which are thus mentioned by Dr. Woodward in his Presidential Address, at the Anniversary Meeting of the Geological Society, 1895. At the conclusion of his obituary notice of Pengelly, he says: "But few men write their own epitaphs; here, however, is the epitaph written by William Pengelly for himself, at the British Association, Exeter, 1869.

EPITAPH.

Here rests his head on balls of *album græcum,*
    A youth who loved Cave-earth and stalagmite;
If fossil bones they held, he'd keenly seek 'em;
    Exhume and name them with supreme delight.

His hammer, chisels, compass lie beside him;
    His friends have o'er him piled this heap of stones.
Alas! alas! poor fellow! woe betide him
    If, in the other world, there are no bones.

That his parody amused some of his friends is shown by the following letter from Sir Benjamin Ward Richardson, "Pray send me another copy or two of your wonderful elegy. I have learnt it already, and shall recite it at dinner to-night."

Mrs. Pengelly to her Sister.

"*Torquay, September* 5.— . . . To-day we had a very pleasant call from the Macmillans, who are staying here now. William knew rather intimately the brother who died many years since, and whom we liked exceedingly. He spent one or two winters here, and was the founder of their large business. Alfred R. Wallace, the traveller, is staying with them, and I was very pleased to be introduced to him and have a nice talk when I went to visit them. William has taken them all to the Cavern. Yesterday, we had a charming visit from the President of the British Association, Mr. Stokes;[*] he was accompanied by Dr. Robinson of Belfast and his wife. The latter is a sister of Maria Edgeworth. We much enjoyed showing them the fossils, etc., and they were so pleased and interested with all they saw. Dr. Robinson, who is Astronomer Royal for Ireland, is a delightful old man. William is reading Dean Milman's work on St. Paul's Cathedral now with much pleasure; knowing him well makes it more interesting.

"*September* 26.—The old Bishop of Exeter, Dr. Phillpotts, was buried yesterday in the beautiful little churchyard at St. Mary Church. Mr. Barnes the vicar (and Examining Chaplain to the Bishop) sent a note to William saying the family would be gratified by his attendance, so of course he went. There were a great many people there, but the funeral was very simply conducted. On Tuesday we spent a very

* Now Sir G. G. Stokes.

pleasant evening at Miss Coutts', to meet Sir Harry Verney and his charming daughter. Sir Harry is a very old friend of William's, and we saw much of Miss Verney when she was here a few years since, so it was very pleasant to meet them again. She tells me Miss Zitter, her companion when here before, and who left her to become Secretary to the Crown Princess of Prussia, is now teaching the little Princess of Nassau. If you remember, she was a friend of Mrs. Tennyson.* The next day Sir Harry and Miss Verney came for us, and we drove with them to the Cavern, where I left them for the Macmillans. They wanted William to dine with them on Thursday, to have more of Mr. Wallace's company; but he was unable to do so. He is going to Sir Wm. Tite's to dinner this evening, the architect, who is wintering here, and of whom we see a great deal."

Mrs. Pengelly to her Sister.

" *Torquay, November* 16, 1869.— . . . Dined at Lady Brownlow's last night, to meet the Countess of Mount-Edgcumbe and Lady Ernestine, and had a very pleasant evening. Sir Edward and Lady Malet were there; he was formerly our representative at Frankfort, and they are great friends of the Queen of Holland."

Sir Charles Lyell to Pengelly.

"Drumkilbo, Meigle, September 18, 1869.

"I have just returned from a tour in Sutherlandshire, where I have been studying with my nephew the relations of the Laurentian, Cambrian, and Lower Silurian rocks, the geology of which Murchison has so well made out. The scenery of that region is very peculiar, and more grand and picturesque than any part of the British islands I have before seen. We have had six weeks of uninterrupted fine weather, and got home just before the rain.

"I am afraid I cannot be of any use to you. Mr. Busk has my copy of *Schmerling;* but it is, I believe, just what you describe. There is a paper a few years old by Mr. Malaise, on some discoveries of the Liége Caverns, which I could look out if I were in town; and M. Dupont, to whom the Belgian Government entrusted the exploration of their Caverns and the placing the produce of them in a public museum, has sent me several reports, which, no doubt, I could hunt up if I were in London, if you thought they would be useful to you. I expect to be in town early next month.

"The British Association Meeting seems to have been very successful. I am glad you got a fresh grant, the vouchers for which have been sent me."

Professor Phillips to Pengelly.

" November 19, 1869.

" . . . I thank you heartily for the gift of the second part of Kent's Cavern Literature—very conscientiously and judiciously done. The

* Now Lady.

good old Prêtre * was really more worthy of a place among geological inquirers, than that which has usually been accorded to him. I have hope to find the first part among the many valued gifts of like nature for which I am indebted to you; and in that case I shall bind the researches concerning Kent's Hole; for a high place (within reach) in my Geological Library. You have written much and well, and I trust many years of health and good work are before you in the county which you have made famous."

Shortly after leaving Torquay, Mr. Alexander Macmillan wrote to Pengelly, requesting him to furnish an article on Kent's Cavern, for the Magazine published by his firm. He says in his letter—

"I cannot forget your kindness to us at Torquay, and the interest you added to our pleasant visit to your pleasant town, of many hills and *one* cave. I hope when you come to London you will come and see me here, and also at my house at Tooting, where, though there are neither hills nor caves, there is pretty enough country, and there will certainly be to you a kindly welcome."

Among the people of celebrity who visited the Cavern under Pengelly's guidance this year may be mentioned the Rev. Frederick Denison Maurice, Lord Talbot de Malahide, Sir J. K. Shuttleworth, Sir Harry Verney, and General Lefroy.

Sir James Kay Shuttleworth had become Chairman of a Committee for exploring the Settle Caves in Yorkshire, and was thus especially interested in the work.

W. Froude to Pengelly.

"Chelston Cross, Torquay, September 23, 1869.

"Many thanks for conveying to me Miss Burdett Coutts' message, which I shall act on.

"I was very glad to observe you dispense your 'Colourless Exegesis' to the Torquay (and other) public on the subject of Mr. ——'s threatened deluge. (As to ——, whoever he may be . . . his name has figured in so many foolish sham science prognostications, that he ought to have his exegesis, by no means colourless.) I was amused to observe how, while you allow—or rather oblige, your readers to feel that they are swallowing plain common sense, which will approve itself as such to any reader of ordinary intelligence, you oblige them at the same time to swallow a lot of hard words which will rather puzzle them, such as Anomalistic year, etc., etc., as a penalty for having gobbled down ——'s nonsense, just because it was so flavoured as to give them the notion they were 'being scientific' in accepting it. As a regular

* MacEnery.

doctor will often flavour his wholesome physic with a little extra nastiness, when he finds his patient has been taking the advice of a quack.

"It is a curious psychological fact that people will listen in the name of science to any quack who talks sham science, but are disposed to think that such men as the Astronomer Royal and his establishment, are ignorant or inattentive to their business.

"I remember an old stage-coachman of my acquaintance, who once listened with an uneasy patience to a narrative of some great cruelty which some one had been practising on a dog. My friend was fond of dogs, and when the story came to an end his indignation overflowed. Referring to the perpetrator of the act, he said, 'Well! if the Devil don't get that fellow, there ain't much use in keeping of a Devil (or having of a Devil—I forget which was the word used)—not as I sees.'

"So if we can't trust to the Greenwich establishment to keep us informed as to all the known or knowable results of usual astronomical combination, we had better leave off maintaining it.

"This sort of folly would hardly thrive so, if Education were what it ought to be.

"But I suppose things will mend by degrees—and indeed are mending. Only ——s ought to be abolished : they help to discredit real science in public opinion, whether the chance shots come right or fail. If they hit the mark by a fluke, the Public say, Why didn't any one tell us this? if they miss it, half the world won't see the failure—the other half set the humbug down as a scientific failure."

The mammalian remains found in Kent's Cavern brought Pengelly, from this time forward, into correspondence with Professor Owen,* who was always most willing to assist him with regard to Books, Plates, etc.

Professor Owen to Pengelly.

"British Museum, November 23, 1869.

"I applied the first leisure at my command on my return to London to the reply to your inquiry relating to *Schmerling*, which reached me in Wales. Our library possesses the 4to text (Liége, 1833), etc., and 4to text, 1846. Our Librarian knows not of any other publication, since 1846, by Schmerling, and I conclude that the volumes of that date were the last under his name. But I have further to remark, that the vols. of 1846 are not merely reprints, but the unsold parts of the impression of both text and plates of the edition of 1833 and 1834. With new title pages ! 'Premier Volume' of 1833 is 'Tome Premier' of 1846. 'Second Volume' of 1834 is 'Tome Second' of 1846. *Gollardin* vends the 1833-4 impression, *Oudart* vends the vampt-up edition of 1846. Voilà toute la différence ! As far as collation has gone, there is not an error corrected, or any alteration ; it appears to be the same impression with a new title.

* Afterwards Sir Richard Owen.

"Now let me thank you for the 'brochures' you were kind enough to send me.   MacEnery's is very suggestive.   What a pest the fixed idea of the Mosaic Deluge becomes, when a good observer puts that blinker over his eyes!"

How close the friendship between Pengelly and Mr. W. Froude had become is clearly shown by the following letter:—

W. Froude to Pengelly.

"Chelston Cross, Torquay, January 10, 1870.

" MY DEAR PENGELLY,

"Or does that sound, as a boatman of mine used to phrase it, 'too —— familiar'?   But the fact is, I don't go in much for Mistering. . . . It should by rights be the elder of the two who initiates that familiarity, and I waited for you as the senior to begin; but when I found how much stronger your hand is than mine, I began with grief to feel that it was I who was really the older, and I take the first free shot.

"I wanted to say a few words about the moon, and the evaporation and the warmth or cold which she causes on the earth, in reference to the few words we had on that subject the other night.

"Is not Tyndall's proposition, that a given thickness of water intercepts the same amount of obscure rays, whether coherent as water, or as in the shape of vapour?   So far, therefore, as that principle goes (if I state it correctly), the cloud would intercept as much obscure heat after it was turned into transparent vapour as before, while it was cloud.

"It may be, however, that the globular particles of *water* of which a cloud consists reflect obscure rays as they reflect luminous rays, and the effect of cloud in preventing the formation of dew would be not by radiating back the obscure heat which the earth has radiated to it, but by reflecting it back.

"This couldn't interfere with your proposition or paradox, that the moon's warmth *may* make us colder *sometimes;* it would only shift the basis of it."

In March, 1870, the Queen of Holland, Sophia of Würtemburg, called by some writers "La Reine Rouge," from her liberal tendencies, again visited Torquay, and was present at one of Pengelly's lectures.

Mrs. Pengelly to her Sister.

" *Torquay, March* 8, 1870.—As you express a wish to hear what we have seen of the Queen of Holland, I intend, if I have time, to give you a full, true, and particular account.   I think I told you William was asked to meet her at afternoon tea at Miss Coutts' the day after her arrival.   She talked a good deal to him, and expressed a wish to call on Thursday, which she did, with her suite.   When I was introduced to her she shook hands cordially, desired me to be seated, and said how pleased she was to make my acquaintance; she took much notice of little Hettie (Lydia, being at school, missed seeing her), asking her questions and petting her. We were greatly pleased with her visit, and also with the ladies and gentlemen of the suite, particularly with the Baroness de Dedan* and the Baron de Simonshaven. The Queen had visited the cavern when here for a few days last November, and had invited William to spend the evening with her at the hotel. She speaks English very well, and William says seemed thoroughly up in English matters, discussing who would be appointed Archbishop. Also she talked well on the origin of man, of Huxley's and Darwin's views, etc., and has given William the skull of an orang outang which she had, and thought he would value.

"On Monday she expressed a wish to attend William's lecture at the Museum—one of a geological course he is delivering there. Miss Coutts, who always attends them, came and met her at the door, sitting next her; the Vice-President also met her, and presented a bouquet. The first row of chairs was reserved for the party, the Queen sitting in the middle; she looked very much interested in it all, and when the lecture was over crossed over to tell William how pleased she had been, but said it was too short. Miss Coutts told me afterwards how much interested the Queen had been. (It is very amusing what a number of people have called to ask if the Queen would be at William's next lecture.) The Baroness de Dedan and all the suite, too, were most friendly, both then and in the evening, when we met at Miss Coutts', where a brilliant party was assembled. The dresses and jewels were magnificent, but the crowd was so great we could scarcely move. She talked a good deal to William about a hasty journey he had arranged for her into Cornwall, and which she found very satisfactory. She also conversed with me, and I had much interesting talk with the Baron and others of the suite on their journey into Cornwall, etc. The Queen is delighted with Torquay and her reception here, and says she shall come again; and every one is charmed with her. William went with some other of her friends to the station to see her off. She seemed much pleased to see him, and when stepping into the carriage, said, 'Don't forget me, Mr. Pengelly.' . . ."

The following two letters from the Rev. Charles Kingsley refer to the Presidency of the Devonshire Association, which he had been asked to accept, and which, after some difficulties were settled as to the time when it was to be held, he filled most ably.

Rev. Canon Kingsley to Pengelly.

"Eversley Rectory, Winchfield, March 13, 1870.

"Between business, and the enormous cold I, my daughter, and my son caught instantly on landing on these dark and dreary shores, I have overlooked your letter till now. Pray forgive me. I have written to Mr. Harpley to say that I should like the post above

* Now wife of Mr. Lecky, M.P. for Dublin University.

all temporary honours I could wish for.   But that my canonry keeps
me at Chester till the end of July; and it will then be impossible for
me to accept, if the meeting is as early as it is this year.   I shall be
at liberty the first of August, but not before; and of course I can't
expect the Association to wait my time.

"Alas! if I accept it will be with a heavy heart on one score.   The
Fanes of Clovelly were to have taken me in, if the presidency were
offered me; and now they are both dead, man and wife, in the prime
of their years.

"I should like much to see you.   I have many things to say about
the geology of the West Indies.   If you come to town, let me know."

Rev. Canon Kingsley to Pengelly.

"Eversley Rectory, Winchfield, April 15, 1870.

"Many thanks.   I accept joyfully the honour which is offered
me, and the date thereof.   I only feel a dread at so great a pleasure,
so far off, and at what may happen meanwhile.   For 'Life is uncertain,'
say fools.   'Life is certain,' say I, because God is educating us thereby.
But this process of education is so far above our sight that it looks
often uncertain, and utterly lawless.   Wherefore fools (with M. Comte)
conceive that there is no living God, because they cannot condense
His formulas into their small smelling-bottles.

"I am just sending off my eldest son, who has learnt his trade well
at Cirencester, and in the River Plate, to try his own manhood in
Colorado, U.S.   You will understand, therefore, that it is somewhat
important to me just now, whether the world be ruled by a just and
wise God, or by o.

"P.S.—It is also an important question to me, with regard to my
own boy's future, whether what is said to have happened to-morrow
(Good Friday) be true or false.   But I am old-fashioned, and super-
stitious, and unworthy of the year 1870."

Pengelly's time was now almost wholly devoted to the exploration of Kent's Hole, but he visited London in July.

John Evans* to Pengelly.

"Nash Mills, Hemel Hempstead, May 6, 1870.

"Prepare for a series of questions!   How are you, what are you
doing, and when are you coming to London, and (what is of much
more vital importance) when are you coming here?   You have been
due any time the last four years, but now your visit has become
imperative, for I have a heap of things here that I ought to return to
your safe keeping, and I have a heap of questions to ask you about
them.   So please tell me that you are coming here some time this
month, as when once June sets in I don't know where I shall be.   I
am just at work upon the Cave part of my book, and have been studying your reports; one of the results is that I find I ought to engrave

* Now Sir John Evans, F.R.S., etc.

several more of the stone things, and notably No. 4155, and possibly No. 3918, and not improbably you may know of some others. I also find that I ought to figure the bone harpoons, needle, pin, etc. What do you say to this? In any case will you try if you can pay me a visit some time this month, and bring anything out of the common from the cave with you? If Mrs. Pengelly can accompany you so much the better. Have you a spare copy of your third and fifth reports? I have all the rest. And where were Nos. 117, 286, and 2183 found? So much for questions. I have been away this Easter in France, partly in search of Tertiary Man, whom I have *not* found, and partly of Quaternary, whom I have. You will be pleased with some of the implements from Poitou, which approximate in character with those from Kent's Cavern."

Pengelly to John Evans.

"Lamorna, Torquay, May 7, 1870.

"Prepare for a series of answers to your questions of 4th inst. I have a bad cold, and am daily oscillating between this and the cavern. I have no prospect (worse luck) of visiting London or Hemel Hempstead. Nos. 4155 and 3918, and indeed all the implements mentioned in the fifth report, as well as a fine one found since, shall be sent you. Since the minute of the committee of the meeting held at Norwich, August 20, 1868, gives you permission to figure any of the flint implements, *or other archæological specimens*, in your forthcoming work, all the bone tools shall be sent you, also copies of the third and fifth reports on Kent's Hole are sent you by this post. No. 117 was found May 20, 1865, in the Great Chamber, fourteen feet within the south or arched entrance, in the second foot-level of cave-earth. No. 286 was found June 16, 1865, in the Great Chamber, twenty-two feet within the south entrance in the fourth foot-level of cave-earth; but the ground had been previously broken there, so that the position cannot be relied on. I am going to Truro on the 17th inst. I cannot, therefore, send the flints, etc., until I return. It is essential to my peace of mind that I floor the heretic surrounded by his own kith and kin. If you would send me the best ovoid flint tool from the cavern, I could cut him down at a stroke."

John Evans to Pengelly.

"Nash Mills, Hemel Hempstead, May 12, 1870.

"Many thanks for your answers, though I wish one of them had been to the effect that you were coming here. You must arrange for doing so next time you come to London. Would you kindly send the specimens, after you return from Truro, to Messrs. Dickinson and Co., 65, Old Bailey. I am going into Scotland at the end of the month, and should like to get the engraver at work during my absence. I hope you may succeed in converting Mr. ——, but it is rather like trying to wash a blackamoor white. He would not accept a flint as artificial if he saw you make it. Try."

Pengelly to his Wife.

" 1, *Stratton Street, London, July* 16.— . . . On Thursday I left cards on Mr. Prestwich and Sir Wm. Tite, but did not see either of them, the former being from home and the latter ill. In the afternoon I walked along a large part of the Thames Embankment, and after dining went to the House of Commons, where I saw a good many of the Members I knew—to wit, Sir K. Shuttleworth, Sir John Lubbock, J. W. Pease, etc. The debate was very interesting, as it turned on the question, should the School Boards in London be elected by ballot or not. I heard Lord J. Manners, Mr. B. Hope, Sir J. Packington, Mr. Gathorne Hardy, W. E. Forster, Gladstone, and others. Yesterday I met Scott and his son by appointment. We proceeded to see the South Kensington Museum, and afterwards went to Jermyn St. Museum. Then to a ladies' meeting (where a few gentlemen were admitted), with Miss Coutts, for the Prevention of Cruelty to Animals. Then Miss Coutts wished me to go with her, or rather to meet her at the House of Commons, as she wished to see Mr. W. E. Forster. Thither we went, and after a good deal of trouble I succeeded in bringing the two magnates together. We visited the House of Lords, and were there when, in reply to Lord Malmesbury, Lord Granville stated that he had no reason to doubt, though no official information had been received on it, that France had declared war against Prussia. Whilst there I saw Lord Talbot de Malahide, with whom I had a nice talk. I forgot to say that on Thursday I called at the Indian Office to see the Duke of Argyll by appointment."

The following letter from the late Mr. Kenrick of York,[*] is in answer to inquiries respecting some valuable fossils from Kent's Cavern in the York Museum.

" *York, October* 17, 1870.— . . . I have received the papers which I sent you from 'the archives of the York P. S.'[†] I have no doubt that the person to whom McEnery's letter was addressed was the President, the Rev. W. V. Harcourt, but 'Mr. Strickland' was not Hugh. The Record stands thus in the Report of 1826: " July 4th. Account of Fossil bones discovered in Kent's Hole Cavern, Torquay, by the Rev. J. McEnery, with notices by Baron Cuvier and Dr. Buckland (communicated by G. Strickland, Esq., M.W.S. and Y.P.S.)." He was *uncle* to Hugh Strickland the geologist. Several of the family were devoted to different branches of Natural History; one of them, Arthur, who resided many years near Bridlington Quay, had a noble collection of birds, especially of sea-birds, which has lately been acquired by the Y.P.S. I see no Strickland's name occurs in McEnery's mention of visitors to Kent's Hole ('Cavern Researches,' p. 37), nor do I know how Mr. G[eorge] S[trickland] came to be the medium of communication of the bones to our Museum. They are thus mentioned in the list of Donations : 'Twenty-eight specimens and casts of teeth and bones of

<hr>

* Author of the " History of the Phœnicians."
† Philosophical Society probably.

Bear, Hyæna, Tiger, Horse, Rhinoceros, Ox, Deer, Elk, etc., from Kent's Hole Cavern, Torquay.' In the Report drawn up by Mr. Harcourt they are thus spoken of: 'The remains of antediluvian quadrupeds from Torbay were accompanied by an interesting communication from the donor, who, having placed a similar collection in the hands of M. Cuvier, had obtained his opinion upon them. That eminent naturalist found one of the specimens, a cast of which is in the Society's Museum, to be the canine tooth of that species of bear, which he has named *Ursus Cultridens*, an animal of which no remains had been previously known, except a specimen of an entire skull found in Val d'Arno, and deposited in the Museum at Florence. The similarity of fracture which prevails in the bones found in this cave is noticed by Mr. McEnery, and the marks of teeth upon them are particularly remarked by M. Cuvier, who states that these may be more distinctly traced in the English specimens than in any others which he has seen. . . ."

Canon Kingsley followed up his acceptance of the Presidency of the Devonshire Association by consulting Pengelly as to his address.

Rev. Canon Kingsley to Pengelly.

"Chester, July 22, 1871.

"Can you tell me anything of the probable science papers at the Bideford meeting of the Association?

"Can you also tell me where I can find the state of geological opinion as to the supposed Mariven Fault in the North Devon bed? I read a good deal about it in the Geological Society's *Transactions* last year. Also any hints on geological problems, *e.g.* the sunken forest below the pebble ridge at Northam, and the flint implements said to have been found in it. My poor friend Dech, who found them, I think, is just dead.

"On the whole, anything that you can send me to post me up for my address, in any direction, will be most thankfully received.

"I have had a preposterous request from the printers, through M—— the Secretary, that I should send them the MS. of my address by the 4th. Do they think a man has nothing to do but to serve them? I want a whole fortnight after the 1st to write my address, and have two lectures and a scientific conversazione to get done between now and then. Pray protect me from the sharks, or slugs, if you are concerned in the matter."

During the meeting of the British Association at Edinburgh in 1871, Pengelly writes to his wife—

"I was so very busy yesterday as to be unable to write to you. On Monday evening the lions fed. It was not a very great success, still by no means a failure. After dinner I went to a huge party at the Misses Stevenson's. Yesterday I lent a hand in sections "C" and "A," and then went to the Committee of Recommendations, where without any difficulty I got another grant (£100) for Kent's Cavern.   After that to dine with a Mr. Smith, where I met Harkness and a lot of other men, some strangers to me.   Then to the Conversazione, and finally to an 'At Home' at Lord Neave's, where I met Miss Dundas (formerly my pupil at Torquay) and Mr. Shuttleworth and his bride.   Mrs. Prestwich invited me to dine to-night (Wednesday), but I was engaged.   I received an invitation to dine with Mr. Cowan on Friday next ; but that is out of the question, as I am to leave for home to-night. . . ."

Professor J. W. Dawson to Pengelly.

" McGill College, Montreal, July 3, 1871.

"I have recently been writing some popular articles on geology, and have arrived at the crucial point of the tacking on of geological to human *time*.   In doing so, I propose to take your explorations of Kent's Cavern as one of the best and most instructive examples, and almost the only one deserving of much confidence.   As I cannot be at the British Association meeting, I shall regard it as a very great favour if you will kindly send me any full report of what has been most recently done (I have not seen as yet the Report for 1870, except in an abstract). . . . If you have time to answer this you will much oblige."

Pengelly to Dr. Dawson, F.R.S.

" Lamorna, Torquay, August 29, 1871.

"Yours of July 3rd found me very busy preparing for the British Association, and with no more leisure than just to allow me to send you copies of such Kent's Cavern papers as I had by me, and appeared not to be in your possession.   I trust they reached you safely. . . . I hope to be able to send you a copy of our Seventh Report, read at Edinburgh, in a few days.   I shall read your article, in which you make the attempt to 'tack on geological to human time,' with great interest."

The Chair of Section "C" was occupied this year by Professor Geikie, F.R.S,* whose vast geological knowledge, and special interest in his native country, rendered the choice a particularly happy one.   In the Seventh Report on Kent's Cavern, presented at this meeting, Pengelly writes thus :—

"On the completion of the work in the Sloping Chamber on July 11, 1871, the excavation of the 'Wolf's Den,' which opens out of its northern side, was begun.   It was in this den that Mr. MacEnery found the canines of *Machairodus latidens*, which have excited so much attention.   No such specimens have been met with during the present investigation up to this time."

* Now Sir Archibald Geikie, Director-General of the Geological Surveys of the United Kingdom.

What pleasure it would have given the keenly watchful explorer of Kent's Cavern had he known that in the next report he would be able to announce the discovery of a tooth of this rare species !

Besides the Yearly Report on the Cave, Pengelly read a paper before Section " A," on " The Influence of the Moon on the Rainfall." He had for some time taken considerable interest in the subject of the Rainfall, especially that of Devonshire, and for many years kept careful meteorological statistics at his residence in Torquay. The following were among the conclusions with which the paper closed :—

" No indication of the moon's influence on the rainfall can be detected in the data furnished by an isolated *lunation*, or by even a few successive *lunations*. Though it may be doubted whether the rainfall statistics of a period shorter than that in which the moon's nodes complete a revolution, or of a solitary locality, would justify general inferences, the data under discussion appear to indicate that, in the long run, the moon does somewhat influence the rainfall ; that on the average the dry period of a *lunation* extends from the first day before full moon to the first day before the third quarter, and the wet period from the day of the first quarter to the second day before the full moon ; that the moon's influence on the number of wet days is less marked, and that the rainfalls are, on the whole rather, least heavy when the moon has north declination, and when she is in perigee, all indications harmonizing well with physical considerations."

When presenting his Annual Reports on the Cavern at the meetings, Pengelly usually exhibited some of the specimens found during the year. These, gelatinized and securely stitched down upon separate trays, proved of much interest to the public, though their charge during the journeys involved no inconsiderable amount of anxiety to the exhibitor.

One day when the cavern exploration had been in progress about six years, a young lady of his acquaintance called, and said, " Mr. Pengelly, you remember that our cook once lived with you ?" " Yes." " Well, yesterday she and the nurse were heard having the following discussion. Said the cook, ' Mr. Pengelly calls the bones what he finds to Kent's Cavern 'Possil's bones, but I say how can he know the bones of the 'Possils from the bones of other men ? ' ' Well,' said the nurse, ' I've heard say as he is uncommon clever, besides nobody knows where the Garden of Eden was, and, if so, why shouldn't it be here, and if 'twas here, where else should the bones of the Apostles be ? ' " It was evidently thought by these two eminent

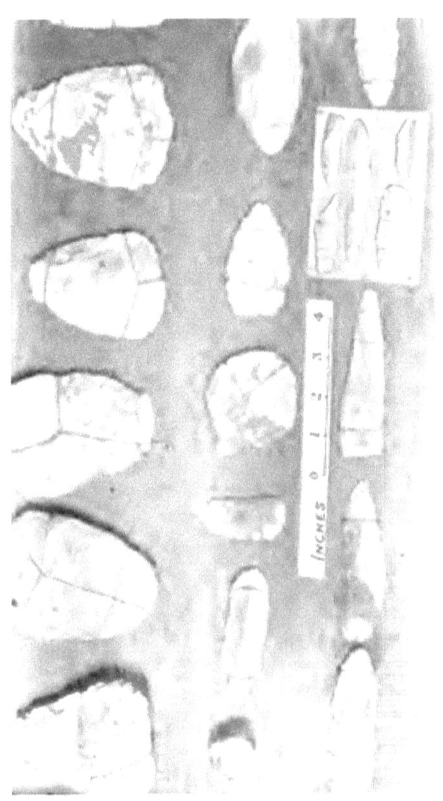
INCHES

theologians that the word *fossil* was synonymous with *Apostle*, or as they called it '*Possil.*

The Cavern was still yielding many fine specimens. In the Monthly Report for September, 1871, Pengelly states that they had entered and commenced work in the "Wolf's Cave," where MacEnery had found the five teeth of *Machairodus latidens.* Though much of the material had been broken up and searched by MacEnery, considerable portions of the deposit remained intact, especially beneath and between large masses of limestone which had fallen from the roof.

" Without reckoning the numerous specimens found, as usual, in the broken ground, we had found in the Wolf's Cave, up to the end of August, twenty-six teeth of hyæna, thirty-two of horse, fifteen of rhinoceros, six of deer, five of bear, one of lion, and one of elephant, portions of five antlers, numerous bones and bone fragments, amongst which those of rhinoceros greatly preponderated, but no trace of Machairodus. The fallen masses of limestone, many of them several tons in weight, were all completely buried in the cave-earth ; but between them at the eastern side, and near the entrance of the ' Cave,' there were occasional cavities or interspaces, having little or no deposit, but in some instances containing a few comparatively modern bones. In others there were Pecten shells, some of them of great size, and amounting altogether to about twenty-five. Most of them were quite perfect, some had Serpulæ attached to their inner surfaces, and many of them were thickly encrusted with carbonate of lime, containing traces of charcoal. In one instance two, and in another five shells were found fitted neatly one in another, and firmly cemented, leaving no doubt that Man had placed them in the cavities in which they were found."

In the October Report for the same year, after enumerating the number of specimens found during September, it is mentioned that—

" Many of the teeth are in portions of jaws, and some are very fine specimens. We may specially mention the left lower jaw of rhinoceros with a small part of the right jaw attached to it. Unlike the Cavern jaws in general, its lower border is entire, but its hinder or articulating end is gone. It contains four consecutive molars, and is quite the finest specimen of the kind we have met with. . . . One of the elephants' teeth has belonged to an adult animal, and the upper surface of the crown is six inches long."

During the autumn of this year, Pengelly stayed with some friends at Harrogate. He was much interested with the various places which he visited in that neighbourhood, more especially with the Dripping Well at Knaresborough.

Pengelly to his Wife.

"*Harrogate, September* 3, 1871.—Here I am, safe and sound, after a pleasant journey to, at least, Leeds. We were half an hour late in leaving Leeds, and nearly as much more in getting here. Such a rough lot of passengers from Leeds! Smoking everywhere.* Third-class passengers going where they liked! (Saturday night.) And when I got here, there was no fly to be had, and no porter, so had to wait a full quarter of an hour till a chance fly drove by, which I secured, the driver being so drunk as to be scarcely able to keep his seat. At the door he fell off on his head, which I hope was very thick. The ladies were still up, and gave me such a warm greeting. We are just going to church. Mr. Jervoise, General and Mrs. Gascoigne, the Bishop of Chester, are here, and I shall see them all, no doubt. I hope the work is going on well."

The ex-Emperor Napoleon, with the Prince Imperial, came to Torquay during the month of September. In the following month they visited Kent's Cavern, under the guidance of Pengelly, and seemed greatly impressed and interested, giving careful attention to all that was pointed out and explained.

Professor Roemer to Pengelly.

"Breslau, September 22, 1871.

"I safely came back to Breslau, and soon afterwards had here the meeting of the German Geological Society, which was very successful and attended by nearly all our best men in the Geological departments. The last day of the meeting was spent in a very interesting excursion to our Silesian Mountain range, the Riesengebirge.

"Mr. Fraas, of Stuttgart, who has explored with marked success the ossiferous caverns of Würtemberg, and who might be called the German Pengelly, was among the attendants of the meeting. These days of excitement and of much trouble to me having passed away, my first business shall be to write to you, and repeat to you my very best thanks for the kindness and hospitality which you have shown me during my stay at Torquay. I shall always remember these days as the most pleasant and instructive ones of my journey. Our excursion to Hope's Nose was particularly interesting to me. Not less my visit to Kent's Cavern, for the careful and systematic exploration of which the scientific world is chiefly indebted to you. The rumour of the ex-Emperor Napoleon's coming to Torquay, which was current when I was there, has since become a reality. The ex-Emperor, although he committed in these last years some considerable blunders, shows by his selection of Torquay that he is still a man of taste. I have no doubt that he will soon try to make the acquaintance of the man who deserves most to be known at Torquay, and who will be particularly valuable to *him,* because he probably wants a refreshment of his humour. Pay my

---

* Smoking in railway carriages was always a great trial to Pengelly, who, even as a sailor boy, could never endure the smell of tobacco.

respects to Mrs. Pengelly, and express to her, if you please, my best thanks for the pleasant hours spent at your house. . . ."

Mrs. Pengelly to a Friend.

" *Torquay, September* 20, 1871.— . . . William called by invitation on the ex-Emperor Napoleon to-day (he has been staying here for some time with his son). He was extremely pleasant, and anxious to hear all about the cavern. . . ."

Mrs. Pengelly to a Friend.

" *Torquay, October* 2.— . . . The Emperor, accompanied by the Prince Imperial, Prince Achille Murat, Dr. Conneau and his son, and several members of the suite, called on us to-day, to see the fossils, etc. It was a very informal visit. He introduced his son, a nice bright, intelligent-looking boy, who seemed to take a lively interest in his father's conversation with William, relative to the various objects found in the cavern. Speaking of the habitats of various animals, the Emperor mentioned that the rat, which had entered Paris with the Allies, had quite destroyed the old rats, and supplanted them there. The party remained for some time, talking and examining the various remains. . . ."

Mrs. Pengelly to her Sister.

" *Torquay, October.*— . . . Colonel Krupp,* his wife and only son (who is very delicate), the doctor and tutor, are all staying here now. They, too, have been to the cavern, and also paid us a very pleasant visit. They invited William and me to join them in a party to spend the day at Brixham, but we were not able to go. It must be rather galling to the Emperor to be constantly meeting the man whose invention has been so fatal to his country and himself."

Before leaving Torquay the Emperor sent the following autograph letter to Pengelly :—

Napoleon III. to Pengelly.

"Torquay, le 17 October, 1871.

" Je lirai, monsieur, avec un vif intérêt les livres que vous avez bien voulu m'envoyer, et qui renferment les résultats importans de vos scientifiques recherches. Je saisis cette occasion de vous remercier de l'obligeance que vous m'avez temoignée, et je vous prie de recevoir mes sentimens distingués.

" NAPOLEON.

" Je vous prie de faire également mes remerciments à votre ami, M. Vivian."

* Inventor of the new gun.

W. Froude to Pengelly.

"Chelston Cross, October 11, 1871.

"Shall you, in the natural course of events, be at the cavern to-day, and, if so, will it inconvenience you (well, of course it is sure to do that to a man whose time is always filled up with work; but will it inconvenience you *too much*) to have time enough in hand to talk to two ignoramuses who wish to learn,* one of whom (I answer for myself) is very glad whenever he feels bold enough or entitled to say of himself in praise, what St. Paul mentioned as the proof of the special wickedness of the Egyptian magicians, that he is 'ever learning and never able to arrive at a knowledge of the truth'? (For I think that to be 'ever learning' is something, and I don't believe that the wisest of us can feel that he has quite found it all out completely and perfectly.)

"My brother, who is the older of the two, has a better memory, and is better deserving of being told things than I am, and would specially like to see the cave under your guidance.

"If you will not be at the cavern, and if you will be to be found at home, shall you be visible there . . . or is nothing less than an emperor receivable at Lamorna. (I suppose the Emperor now may think himself capable of sitting to a landscape painter for a view of the *Lamorna Cove*.)† But if you will be probably visible at home, let me know, please, and we will be down on you there."

W. Froude to Pengelly.

"Chelston Cross, November 16, 1871.

"I am ashamed (*but some people don't mend when they are ashamed*) to think what trouble I may be giving you, in asking you to let friends go round the cavern with you in your daily visitation, which anyhow must be a great tax on your time. If you would once whisper in my ear really it *is* an undue absorption of time, I could always say I know it to be so. But if you are so good-natured that even if entitled to 'curse with your heart' you only 'give good words with your mouth and manner——'

"Well, after this preamble, I will say that my brother-in-law, Mr. J. Holdsworth (revising barrister in *north district*, so look out for the conservation of your vote), Sir W. Topham, a friend of ours, and young Mr. Waldegrave (son of Lady Chewton, whom I think you met a day or two since, and whom if she asked the favour herself you could not refuse, her manner and expression are so pleasing), and perhaps my daughter would like *pace tuâ*, but perhaps not at your pace, to see the interior of the cavern at your usual hour.

"May they come? If they come will you austerely fossilize them by sternness of manner, or will you mollify towards them, as the rocks were mollified by Hannibal's vinegar?

"Please say at what hour you will be at the cavern. I wish I also could come; but I fear I cannot."

* William Froude himself, and his brother J. A. Froude.
† Pengelly's house was named after the Cove of "Lamorna," near the Land's End, so this pun was frequently made.

Professor Owen to Pengelly.

"British Museum, December 20, 1871.

"Accept my thanks for the 'Third Part' of your instructive and exhaustive history of Kent's Hole. As F.R.S. you receive your *Transactions*, and therefore I don't trouble you with duplicates therefrom. But seeking about for what might in any way seem an approach to equivalency for your Christmas gift to me, I lit on an address which includes some passing thoughts of medicine as a science, and to which I add a communication on the sense in which classificatory characters are expressed and ought to be understood.

"I benefited so much by my last winter's sojourn on the Nile that I thought I might try a winter at home, having work I wished to finish. But the first frosty morning brought back my bronchitis. The change to mildness has taken away the sharper symptoms, but if we have a return to ice and snow, I may be ordered to some milder region in England than Upper Sheen. In that case I may ask your good offices to recommend a sitting-room and bedroom at Torquay."

The following extract from a letter will show the generous testimony which Pengelly always bore to MacEnery's labours in Kent's Cavern. He paid so little attention to the recognition of his own work there that the article which was asked for by James Anthony Froude in the following letter was never written :—

". . . Mr. MacEnery deserves all the honour which we can do to him. I am afraid, however, that his personality was so little known beyond Torquay and the neighbourhood that the readers of a general magazine would turn away from an In Memoriam devoted to him without caring to read it. If you would yourself erect a monument to him in your own words by giving us a paper on Kent's Hole and the discoveries there, I need not say how gladly I would accept it. Cannot I persuade you to do this? It would be but a recast of the same materials. MacEnery has been dead so long, and the investigations in the cavern have been carried so much further in subsequent years, that by taking his part of the business for the limit you lose the strongest claim on the reader's interest. I shall perhaps be at Torquay for a day or two in the winter, when I shall hope to renew my acquaintance with you. . . ."

CHAPTER XIV.

THE MENTONE CAVERNS.

1872.

A FEW lectures in the North occupied part of the holidays during the winter of 1871 to 1872, and Pengelly thus writes home :—

"*Kendal, January*, 1872.— . . . On Friday morning Mr. Taylor took me over his mill (cotton spinning), and thereby greatly interested me. I then took a look at the town of Bolton, saw a monument to, and the grave of, Crompton. Then to luncheon with Mr. Worthington, Secretary of the Bolton Lecture Society. My lecture was a success, the people say. I began by stating that so far as I knew I was unknown to every one in the room, but funnily enough, when the vote of thanks was proposed to me, a young man rose to support it, and said that he knew me very well, that he had frequently been in Kent's Cavern, and that he was a native of Torquay. I left Bolton for this at three, but didn't get here till after seven, the trains being, as usual on Saturdays, very late. I found waiting me a letter from Bishop Ryan, now vicar of Bradford, asking me to be his guest, during my stay at Bradford. I fancy I shall very much enjoy my stay here."

Pengelly to his Wife.

"*The Vicarage, Bradford, January* 26, 1872.—Here I am, the guest of the good Bishop Ryan, and am to remain in that capacity until to-morrow morning, when I start for Leicester. We had a very pleasant time at Keighley on Wednesday, where Mr. Callaway, the Secretary of the Bradford Phil. Soc., handed me dear Trot's welcome letter and enclosures. I remained with Mr. Brigg until yesterday, when he brought me here, and placed me in the hands of the Bishop. Bradford is now in a state of great political excitement, and there was a large political meeting last night, at the very moment I was lecturing, hence my audience was small; nevertheless it was a most satisfactory gathering. I am glad to think that four out of my six lectures have now been given ; my voice has not been affected in the least. I am going to Saltaire to-day, the Bishop having secured me one of the Mr.

THE CAVE AT MENTONE.

[To face p. 214

Salts to be my guide through the great workshops there. Though I
have been most kindly received everywhere, I shall be delighted when
I find myself home again."

Notwithstanding his geological labours, Pengelly found time
to devote to astronomy, in which he took much interest.

Pengelly to Professor J. Couch Adams.

"Torquay, January 12, 1872.

"I trust you will pardon my intrusion, and my attempt to pick your
brains. The books tell me that at present the obliquity of the ecliptic
is diminishing at the rate of about forty-eight seconds per century, and
that there is a limit to this diminution. Will you be so good as to inform
me what, according to the present state of astronomy, are the maximum
and minimum values of the obliquity?"

Professor J. C. Adams to Pengelly.

"Observatory, Cambridge, January 30, 1872.

"I hope you will pardon me for not having written before in reply
to your letter. It reached me at Bath, when I was away from my
books and papers, and since my return home I have been too busy to
make the search required to enable me to give an answer to your
question. I am not aware that any trustworthy results respecting the
greatest and least values of the obliquity of the ecliptic have been
published, but I believe that, several years ago, I worked out the
problem for my own satisfaction, and obtained results which were
fairly approximate. I will make a search among my papers, and if
I can find the calculations I will with much pleasure send you the
result."

Though, as already stated, Pengelly paid little attention to
the recognition of his own work, he was glad of the opportunity
to correct inaccurate statements as to his labours. The following extract is taken from a letter written by him to the author
of a geological book, the proof-sheets of which had been submitted to him for revision.

"Torquay, February 9, 1872.

"I have gone carefully over the proofs, so far as they relate to
Kent's and Brixham Caverns, and have made a few unimportant corrections. . . . You say 'the Exploration of (Brixham) cave in the manner
suggested by Dr. Falconer.' In the most unqualified way I state that
the *manner* was suggested by me only, and have so corrected it. . . .
"And now, let me say, I look forward with great interest to the
forthcoming of your book."

In writing to the Rev. W. S. Symonds, Pengelly throws light

upon the physical geography of the Polperro fish beds, and shows that there is no evidence of the occurrence of hippopotamus in Kent's Cavern, as mentioned incidentally by Professor Owen.

Pengelly to Rev. W. S. Symonds.

"Torquay, March 17, 1872.

"I have traced the Polperro fish bed all the way from the River Fowey to the Rame Head at the entrance to Plymouth Sound. Mr. Loughrun knows the fish bed near Polperro of course, but east of that he has no acquaintance with it. The key to the succession of beds about Polperro, Pencarrow Head, etc., is to be seen in the cliff about a mile west of my native place Looe. In passing from Liskeard to Looe, we have a continuous ascending series, which is continued beyond the latter place to Port Nadler—the spot in the cliff just mentioned. Here there is a synclinal axis, and beyond, *i.e.* south-west of it, we get, by continuing along the road, an entire reversal of the dip, and successively lower and lower beds, instead of as before higher and higher. In short we get beds we had passed between Looe and Port Nadler repeated, the bone bed is directly above the *Pleurodictyum* slates, and directly below the Plymouth limestones, *i.e.* the place of the slates of Mudstone Bay, in which I have also found the Polperro fish. If, however, there is not a great fault in Whitesand Bay by which these slates are brought up again at the Rame Head, the fish remains must occupy the slates above the limestones as well as those below them. When next I am in your neighbourhood, you and Holl and I must meet and talk this matter over. When at Plymouth did you see the tusk of hippopotamus? and what is the evidence that it was found in a cave there? I see no *a priori* objection to its having been so found, but in all these cases perfectly trustworthy evidence is required. Owen incidentally mentions the occurrence of hippopotamus in Kent's Cavern; Bellamy speaks of it at Oreston, near Plymouth; and an anonymous writer gives Chudleigh cavern, about 12 miles from this, as one of its localities. I have shown in a printed paper that there is no evidence in the first case. About the second and third I can say nothing. Busk says the Oreston rhinoceros was the *leptorhine*, or great southern form, not the *tichorhine*. The hippopotamus would be a similar companion. Some years ago, Ormerod bought, at a shop at Teignmouth, teeth said by the dealer to be found in Kent's Cavern. I identified them as molars of hippopotamus, and this was confirmed by Boyd Dawkins. I demanded proof of their having been found in Kent's Cavern. Ormerod went thoroughly into the question, and came out of it with the avowal that there was no evidence whatever. Buckland mentions hippopotamus teeth amongst the remains found in Kirkdale Cave, and I see Boyd Dawkins places him there (the hippopotamus, not Buckland) as well as in the caverns of Cefn, Durdham Down, Difont Den (Gower), and Ravenscliff (Gower). There seems no reason, therefore, why he should not turn up in some of the Devonshire caverns. I shall be glad to hear of the results of your investigations in your Wye Cavern."

Rev. W. S. Symonds to Pengelly.

"Pendock, Tuesday.

"Thanks for your note and explanations respecting the physical geography of the Polperro fish beds. I thought there must be a fault at Whitesand Bay. I wrote a short letter to the *Geological Magazine*, and sent it two days ago, calling the attention of amateurs to the Polperro rocks and their fish beds. It is a thousand pities they are not worked out by quarrying on purpose for specimens. At Lantivet Bay I am sure they would turn out treasures for those who have time to work them. I went with Mrs. Symonds to Oreston, and there we saw a Mr. Hodge, who has a collection of bones from Oreston, and who read a paper on them at Aberdeen; he showed us a number stowed away in a box, and on my coming to a tusk of hippopotamus he informed me that he obtained it from a cave at *Plymouth Hoe* and not from Oreston. . . ."

In the spring of 1872 considerable interest was caused by the announcement of the discovery, in a cavern at Mentone, of what was supposed to be a fossilized skeleton of a palæolithic or neolithic man. Sir William Tite, who was Pengelly's intimate friend, and had greatly enjoyed attending his lectures during winter visits at Torquay, was very desirous that the case should be investigated, and wrote asking him to undertake the journey to Mentone for this purpose, offering to provide the needful funds. Pengelly feared that the case might not prove sufficiently clear to repay the trouble and expense; but he was quite willing to undertake the expedition, should it be likely to be of scientific value. Sir William, in reply, kindly said, " Even if the cave offers but few attractions, the thorough change of scene and climate will do you both a world of good.[*] All which is a mere acknowledgment on my part, if you will allow me to put it so, of the many hours of infinite pleasure and information which you have given me at Torquay." The journey was accordingly undertaken, and proved of much interest.

A few extracts from "Notes on the Mentone Cavern," sent by Pengelly shortly afterwards to Sir Charles Lyell, give a brief outline of the Cavern and its contents:—

"Upwards of a mile east of Mentone, and about a furlong on the Italian side of the gorge separating Italy from France, in a vertical red cliff of Jurassic limestone, there are several small caverns which for some years have attracted the attention of men of science. . . . In 1872 Dr. Rivière, who, having been charged with a scientific mission, was

<hr>

[*] He had kindly included Mrs. Pengelly in the mission.

engaged in exploring the quarries and caverns in the environs of Nice and Mentone, discovered in that known as *la Berma du Cavillon*, bones of a human foot, and after the continuous and careful labour of eight days, disclosed an entire human skeleton. The full daylight reaches the inner end of the cavern, and thus enabled Dr. Rivière to have an excellent photograph of the skeleton taken *in situ*. The body lay in the longitudinal direction of the cavern, near the right or east wall, and about twenty feet within the entrance. The skull was of a red colour, and covered with numerous perforated marine shells, all of one species, *Nessa Neritra*, and twenty-two perforated canines of stag ; the whole having probably been a chaplet. Near the left tibia forty-one perforated shells of the same species were found, the remains, it is supposed, of an anklet. A bone instrument, pointed at one end, lay across the forehead. The skull was very dolichocephalic, and the facial angle, though not capable of being accurately measured, amounted to from 80° to 85°. The forearm had been broken and healed during life. The attitude indicated that the man died in his sleep, in the place where he was found. Surrounding and above the body, were fifty unpolished flint 'points,' scrapers and flakes ; a fragment of a small bone needle ; shells of *Patella ferruginea, Pectunculus glycimeris, Cardium rusticum, Cardium edule, Mytilus edulis, Pecten jacobeus*, the last containing traces of charcoal, and many others ; and the remains of the following mammals, in determining which Dr. Sénéchal had assisted : *Felis spelœa, Ursus spelœus, Ursus arctos, Canis lupus* of great size, *Erinaceus, Rhinoceros tichorhinus, Sus scrofa, Bos primigenius, Cervus alces, Cervus elaphus, Cervus canadensis, Cervus capreolus, Capra primigenia* Gervais, *Antilope rupicapra* and *Lepus*. Dr. Rivière is of opinion that the Cave lion, Cave bear, and rhinoceros, found near the skeleton, and on a superior level, indicate the epoch of the man. The skeleton has been taken to Paris and lodged temporarily in the *Jardin des Plantes*, where it was investigated by Mr. Vivian and myself, and we afterwards proceeded to Mentone to inspect the Cavern."

A short time afterwards, in answer to a question from Sir Charles Lyell, Pengelly writes :—"In reply to your question, I say very confidently that there was not a single *polished* flint implement lying near the skeleton, nor in the room where the skeleton lay, when I saw it at the Jardin des Plantes in Paris, but there was a vast number of *unpolished* flakes, etc., and I was assured by Rivière that not a single polished implement had been found."

During July, 1872, the Devonshire Association met at Exeter, under the able chairmanship of the Bishop of the Diocese, Dr. Temple, whose sterling qualities and breadth of view had always been admired by Pengelly, and who was already warmly appreciated in the county where he had been received at first with some feelings of apprehension. In making arrangements for the meeting, Sir John Bowring assisted Pengelly with his

THE MENTONE SKELETON.

[To face p. 218.

usual energy, and in writing to him speaks of the Bishop's interest in the meeting, and concludes with the following remarks :—

". . . I have just left the Bishop. He will suggest two or three of the scientific clergy for vice-presidents. I suggest they are *raræ aves* in our woods.

"He wishes to have a set of our *Transactions*. . . ."

Pengelly received from Mr. Edward Tylor some interesting facts which threw some light upon his theory as to the human skeleton found in the cavern near Mentone.

Pengelly to Edward Tylor.[*]

"Torquay, June 11, 1872.

"Thank you very much for your kind and interesting letter of the 9th, which reached me this morning. The South American tribes, who bury their dead in their huts, and still continue to live in them, are my prime favourites at this moment. The fact is that, in thinking on the circumstances connected with the human skeleton recently found in the Cavern near Mentone, it seemed that they rendered it necessary to suppose that his (or hers, as the case may be) friends buried him in the cave which still continued to be their home, and I was anxious to find some justification for such an idea.

"Any further facts that you may meet with, and will kindly communicate at your leisure, will be gratefully received and acknowledged."

Pengelly's extreme accuracy in describing facts was recognized by all those who knew him well. The charge, sometimes made against reviewers, of reading only such portions of the volumes they criticize as are to be got at without cutting, could never apply to him, for when asked to review a book, he always read it through from end to end two or three times, and even then had misgivings lest he should fail in doing full justice to the author's meaning.

It was not only in the domain of science, that this striking accuracy was shown, as some extracts from the following Paper, written by him, and entitled † "Is it a Fact ? " will prove. After some preliminary remarks, he writes :—

"The discrepancies in the narratives of a dozen eye-witnesses of the same event are sometimes very startling. Here, however, other sources of error besides defective memory come into play. Every person's narrative is necessarily, to some extent, subjective. There

---

* Now Professor Tylor.
† Read before the Meeting of the Devonshire Association at Exeter in 1872.

were things in the event to which his mind was keenly alive, and which he watched almost to the exclusion of other points equally important; whilst these, in their turn, took almost exclusive hold of another observer, and so on.

"Further, observers frequently make themselves partisans, and sometimes without being able to account for it. In their narratives they unintentionally soften or suppress certain facts, and give undue prominence or a strong colouring to others.

"It may be well to state thus early that, in the course of this paper, some illustrative cases which have occurred within my own experience will be given. They will be stated with the most scrupulous regard to accuracy, with the single exception that, where it seems desirable, the names of persons and places will be fictitious.

"Not long ago I was informed by a gentleman, whom I will call *Mr. Lopp*,* that *Miss Pontoon*, a friend of his, had seen at Westward Ho, North Devon, a man from Birmingham converting the flints he found on the strand into knives, which he sold to various museums at a great price; and that he visited the place every summer, as the flints found there were of a superior quality for the purpose of his trade. There was much in the story calculated to inspire one with doubt; and as it was supposed, by both the lady from whom it had come, and the gentleman who told it me, to be fatal to the doctrine of the great antiquity of man, I expressed a wish to examine it thoroughly. *Miss Pontoon* was readily induced to give me permission to make the investigation, and to publish the result. In order to render all the assistance in her power, she sent me, through *Mr. Lopp*, the following written statement—

"'About the beginning of August, 1866, we were at Westward Ho, and one day calling at '*Horsa*,' we were shown into one of the lower sitting-rooms to wait; and the apology made to us for the litter of the room, which was a good deal strewn with stones, etc., was that they were the property of a gentleman who came generally every year to collect them from the pebble ridge and make them into the knives which we saw partly finished. The woman said he came from Birmingham, and was very clever, and made a great deal of money out of them, as they wanted them at the Museum.

"'(Signed)   *M. Pontoon*.'

"It will be seen that already the case has become slightly shrunken. The lady had not *seen* the Birmingham gentleman make the knives; she had been *told*, apparently by a servant girl, that he made them.

"On the day the foregoing statement reached me, I addressed the following letter—

"'To the Lady who keeps the Lodging-house known as *Horsa*,
Westward Ho.

"'Lamorna, Torquay, February 2, 1869.

"'A statement, of which I enclose a copy, has just reached me from *Miss M. Pontoon* of this town, respecting a gentleman who

* Throughout this paper fictitious names are printed in italics.

appears to have lodged at your house in 1866 and some previous years. Will you be so good as to favour me with the gentleman's address, as I am desirous of writing him respecting the knives he makes? Pardon the trouble I give you.'

" As soon as the post could bring it, I received the following reply :—

" ' *Horsa* House, Westward Ho, February 4, 1869.

" ' In answer to your note, which I received this morning, I beg to state that I have no recollection of *Miss Pontoon* calling at *Horsa* in August, 1866 ; but about that time there was a gentleman from *Widrinker* (not from Birmingham) who was collecting flint-stones, which he dug out of the sands when the tide was out. He has been here every year since *Horsa* was opened, and is coming again this summer. He has collected a great number, and, I believe, presents them to the Museum ; but I don't think he makes them into knives. Some of them are indeed the shape or form of knives, therefore your friend's mistake. The gentleman's name is *Mr. Henry Sanderson, Widrinker.* In fact, he is this year the Mayor of *Widrinker ;* therefore perhaps you know him.

" ' There have been other gentlemen stopping at my house who have made collections, but none to the extent that *Mr. Sanderson* has made.'

" Such was, no doubt, the genuine story of the Westward Ho flint knives, which, it may be stated, proved to be precisely what I expected, as the case was well known to me from the beginning. It may not be uninteresting to note the metamorphoses the story had undergone in its passage through one single person, who, though she no doubt had a decided bias, was highly educated, well-informed, and utterly incapable of intentional misrepresentation. The gentleman was not from Birmingham, but *Widrinker ;* did not make, but found, the knives ; not in the pebble ridge, but in the sands ; and did not sell, but presented, them to the Museum.

" Unfortunately, moreover, a tendency to prevarication is among the defects of human nature. I refer not so much to the bolder and more audacious falsehood, as to untruthfulness in what are regarded as small things—the minor details of a narrative. Memory, perhaps, was a little at fault, or one or two links in the chain were not carefully noted, and what appeared to be the probabilities, or, if the expression may be used, the inevitabilities, were called in to supply the defects. Thus, in some instances, a story is rendered more complete by him who narrates it ; and this not with any desire of, or indifference to, exaggeration. On being told him, it suggested one or two things, perhaps, which were recalled on repeating it ; and, forgetting that they had really nothing to do with it, he annexed them to the story.

" Not long ago I stated on a public occasion that no one knew anything about the origin of the name of Kent's Cavern, near Torquay, that, indeed, there was not even a tradition or legend respecting it. In the course of the evening, the late Mr. Charles Babbage, who had heard the remark, told me what had once been given to him as the origin of the name.   This story I, a day or two after, related at a dinner table, precisely, I believed, as it had been told to me.   Within a week after it was told me, a lady, who had heard the story on the occasion last mentioned, related it to an evening party; when Mr. Babbage and I were present.   The following is the story as she told it:—

" ' It is said that a dog, which was lost in the cavern, was some time after found in the county of Kent, wriggling up through a hole, and having all its hairs turned perfectly white.   From this it was concluded that there was a subterranean passage from Devonshire to Kent, and hence the name of the cavern.'   On being appealed to by the narrator I remarked that, with the exception of the statement respecting the colour of the dog's hair, which was quite new, the story was precisely what Mr. Babbage had told me.   ' Indeed it is not,' said he ; ' I simply said the dog, lost in the cavern, was afterwards found in Kent, but not a word about its wriggling up through a hole.'   There was just as much difficulty in convincing the lady that she had ' improved ' the story, as in satisfying me that I had achieved the same thing.

" Not long afterward, I was accompanied to the cavern by a distinguished American writer, and on the way I told him the story just related, as it is given above.   Subsequently it appeared in *Harper's New Monthly Magazine.*   The following is the American New Version :—

" ' The legend as to its name is, that a traveller went in there with his dog ; the traveller was never again heard of, but the dog was found in a weak condition in the county of Kent, about one hundred and seventy miles distance.' *   From this we learn, what we did not know before, that the dog was taken to the cavern by a man and a traveller, who was lost, and that the dog was found in a weak condition.

" Whilst, so far as I am aware, this is the most modern form this story has assumed, the following passage in the late Mr. MacEnery's Manuscript, ' Cavern Researches,' apparently takes us back to its pre-canine stage.   ' As indicating,' he says, ' the popular [notion] of the indefinite range of the cave, may be noticed a tradition which is seriously told and believed.   It is related that Sir George Cary, an ancestor of the present proprietor of the neighbouring abbey, despatched a hawk with billet and bells, in the hope of discovering its furthermost outlet towards the sea.   The hawk was taken on the coast of Kent, from which circumstance it is gravely affirmed it takes its name.† . . .'

" Those who have favourite, but slenderly supported, hypotheses are greatly in danger of giving a new circulation and an increased tenacity of life to untrustworthy statements.   Every alleged fact which can be made useful is hastily pressed into their service, and whatever men may think respecting that which it is made to bolster up, the statement itself attracts attention, and, thanks to the indolence too common amongst us, is not unfrequently accepted as an unquestionable fact. . . .

" The duty of verification is not at all times easy of accomplishment. Some time ago I had occasion to allude in a paper to a great gale of

---

* *Harper's New Monthly Magazine,* No. ccxiii., December, 1868, Vol. xxxviii. p. 31.

† See *Trans. Devon. Assoc.,* vol. iii. p. 460 (1869.)

November, 1824, so fearfully destructive of life and property, especially at Plymouth. At the time of this memorable storm, I was a sailor boy, and rode out the tempest in one of the branches of Plymouth harbour. Though the only damage we sustained was the loss of our bowsprit, the fact that it was my first winter at sea, and my first great gale, enabled it to produce an ineffaceable impression on my mind. I believed the date to be burnt in on my brain, and never doubted that the storm commenced on the evening of November 24th, and culminated early in the morning of the 25th. In order, however, to be accurate, I wrote to two friends at Plymouth, who perfectly remembered the storm, and had no doubt of their ability to determine the exact date.

"The first reply informed me that 'the great gale of November, 1824, commenced on the 24th and continued three days." This, so far as the date was concerned, agreed with my own belief, and had my second friend remained silent I should have taken no further pains in the matter. His reply, however, arrived in a few days, and stated that ' the wind began to rise between nine and ten o'clock on the evening of the 23rd of November, and increased in violence until between two and three o'clock on the morning of the 24th, when the gale reached its height. It then began to ease a little, and finally dropt almost suddenly about half-past three, with a dreadful crash of thunder. By eleven o'clock the Sound was like a mill-pond.'

"It will be seen that the foregoing accounts differ both as to the date and duration of the tempest. My belief is that neither of them is correct in the latter particular. Unless I am greatly in error, the gale did not last twenty-four hours, and I am confident that, instead of being ' like a mill-pond,' the Sound was exposed to a heavy swell for more than a week.

"As the discordance of the replies had rendered the date uncertain, I requested a friend to consult such county newspapers as were filed in the Library of the Devon and Exeter Institution, and in a few days he sent me three paragraphs respecting the gale, copied from Trewman's *Exeter Flying Post*, of Thursday, November 25, 1824.

"The first stated that ' the storm began Monday, November 22, 1824, at Exeter, early in the afternoon, and continued with little interruption for twenty-four hours.'

"The second, dated Plymouth, November 24, 1824, recorded that 'the wind last evening, at the south, increased to a hurricane, and continued with unabated violence during the night; and it being spring tide, the lowest parts of the town were inundated.'

"The writer of the third paragraph, dated Plymouth, November 23, 1824, said, 'We have been visited with one of the most tremendous storms that ever was experienced here—perhaps the *most* violent. It began to blow hard yesterday at the turn of the tide, and continued increasing in violence the whole night.'

"Up to this point, five statements had come to hand, of which one made the gale begin on the 24th, two on the 23rd, and two on the 22nd, and to add to the amusing discordance, the three paragraphs from the same newspaper did not agree.

"As the inquiry could not be allowed to stop here, I requested a friend to examine the local newspapers filed in the Cornwall County

Library at Truro. He promptly forwarded extracts from the *Cornwall Gazette* of November 27, 1824, descriptive of the storm and its ravages at Penzance, Falmouth, Fowey, and Polperro, in each of which it was stated to have begun on November 22nd.

"At this stage I remember that the Religious Tract Society had published a description of this very storm. On application at the depôt, I readily obtained a copy of it, and found that it made the storm begin on the 22nd. Beyond this I made no inquiry, being willing to accept the 22nd as the correct date, and to believe that, respecting a great event whose progress I had painfully watched, I had for upwards of forty years unwaveringly held an opinion that was *not* a fact.

"I have often thought that every teller of 'good things' must frequently be in a state of great apprehensiveness when relating some choice anecdote, epigram, or *bon mot*, lest some candid and kind friend should remark, 'Oh! that's a very old Joe! It was first told of So and So. . . .'

"There formerly lived in a Cornish town, two ministers of religion, each having the same name, let us say 'Jones,' and each a Doctor of Divinity, but one a member of the Church of England, the other a Dissenter. It will be readily foreseen that letters and parcels frequently went to the wrong house. On one occasion, so runs the story, the clergyman of the Establishment received and opened a letter intended for the eye of his namesake only. Perceiving the error, he reclosed the letter and sent it to him for whom it was intended, and with it the following laconic note:—'Sir, if you had not taken to yourself a title to which you have no claim this mistake would not have occurred. I am, etc.' Some time after, the Nonconforming Doctor received a parcel, which proved to be a series of manuscript sermons intended for the Churchman. On detecting the mistake he forwarded the parcel to its destination, accompanied by the following note:—'Sir, if you had not entered an office for which you are apparently not qualified, this mistake could not have happened. I am, etc.'

"Having heard this story several times, I once availed myself of what seemed a satisfactory opportunity for ascertaining whether it were a fact. I was once introduced to a brother of the dissenting Doctor, himself a Nonconformist minister, and asked him whether the story were a truth or a fiction. He replied that it was unquestionably and literally a fact. Thus endorsed, I had frequently told it until I was informed by a friend that he had often heard the same story of two Reverend Doctors, of the name of 'Brown,' we will suppose, who resided in the same town in Sussex.

"It would be easy to enlarge this budget of untrustworthy statements which usually pass as facts, but probably enough has been said to show the necessity and duty of verification.

"In conclusion, I may allude to the numerous slanders which, from time to time, appear in the public prints respecting many of our most eminent men. It is true they have generally been disposed of in the most satisfactory manner, and as soon as they have presented themselves; but it is also true that they follow one another so rapidly as to induce one to ask, Is it a Fact that the public pay no attention to the continued cry of 'Wolf'?"

Sir Charles Lyell was now about to set to work on a new edition of the "Antiquity of Man"; owing to increasing trouble, from the state of his eyesight, he was unable to work for long at a time.

Pengelly to Sir Charles Lyell.

"Torquay, June 8, 1872.

"Though I am afraid you greatly over-estimate my strength in the question of Human Antiquity, and though I have no prospect of such leisure, it will afford me great pleasure to devote such time as I can command to the work you propose. . . ."

Sir Charles Lyell to Pengelly.

"73, Harley Street, July 2, 1872.

" . . . I am much obliged to you for the notes which I received this morning, and which are just exactly what I want.

"I may have to ask you about the change of level at Pentewan, for I am rather puzzled as to the period when it took place. I see you are not inclined readily to admit post-Roman changes of level, and I expect that I shall have to declare against them entirely, as regards that part of Scotland where Geikie thought there was a change of twenty-five feet.

"My correspondence on this subject with Mr. Milne Home, and the sub-curator Young, of the Glasgow Museum, is becoming so interesting that I think by-and-by of sending you the letters. The antiquaries have recently found a new Roman inscription, which shows that the legion which finished the building of the wall, left off a few yards from where they would now, from the present shore, and only a few feet above the present level of the sea. It will, I think, bear upon the changes at St. Michael's Mount, etc."

From Sir Charles Lyell's Amanuensis to Pengelly.

"73, *Harley Street, London, W., July* 5, 1872.— . . . Sir Charles Lyell has just returned from a tour in France, where he has been visiting the caves and learning much about the work being done there. He is now about to set to work on a new edition of the Antiquity of Man, which is required, and finds that in the ten years since the last edition, such an immense amount has been written on the subject that it will be very difficult to review it, especially as he is obliged to work very little at a time now.

"He thinks that if you could find time to read through the Antiquity, and make notes as to the parts which seem to you to require revision, and points on which you know good papers have been written, it would be a very great help to him. . . .

"He will keep the book in its present form, and enlarge it as little as possible—if possible not at all, leaving everything that still remains true, and making room, by omitting any doubtful statements, for any new facts that are absolutely necessary—as, for instance, the carvings and sculptures on bones which are all new since the last edition, and of which new ones were found even when Sir Charles was in France. . . ."

Towards the end of July in this year (1872), Pengelly had the great satisfaction of discovering in Kent's Hole Cavern, an incisor tooth of the *Machairodus latidens*, for which he had long and anxiously searched. He thus announces his find at the close of his Annual Report of the Kent's Cavern Committee, read to the British Association at Brighton in August, 1872.

". . . The other specimen is a well-marked incisor of *Machairodus latidens*, found July 29, 1872, with the left lower jaw of bear containing one molar in the first or uppermost foot-level of cave-earth, having over it the granular stalagmitic floor two to five feet thick. It answers admirably to the following description given by MacEnery of the incisor he found: 'The internal face of the enamel is fringed with a serrated border. This tooth is distinguished further by two tubercles or protuberances, at the base of the enamel from which the serration springs, and describes a pointed arch on the internal surface . . . the body of the tooth in this specimen is not compressed, but rounded.' He adds, 'Whether this belongs to an inferior species of *U. Cultridens*, or [is] simply the incisor anterior to the canine of the larger species of *U. Cultridens*, I am not able to pronounce with certainty. If merely the incisor, it is still interesting, as it serves to show that the serrated character is not confined to the canines, and that the rest of the teeth, and consequently the frame, are marked by a peculiar conformation.' A glance at the new specimen suffices to explain why Mr. MacEnery was uncertain respecting the canine or incisive character. Indeed the workmen sent it to the secretary of the committee, under the belief that it was the canine of a wolf, it being partially covered with cave-earth, and its true character was detected whilst it was being washed, August 5, 1872.

"MacEnery states that his incisor, which unfortunately cannot be traced, was 'about an inch long'—the expression in all probability of a rough guess, and not of actual measurement. The incisor from the cavern (doubtless that discovered and described by MacEnery) figured by Professor Owen in his 'History of British Fossil Mammals, etc.,' very nearly corresponds in size with its homologue just found; the new specimen is slightly longer in the crown, and somewhat thicker in the fang. . . .

". . . One of the hopes of the cavern committee, in commencing their researches, was that they might find some traces of *Machairodus*. This they have never abandoned, though year after year passed away without success; and they cannot but express their gratitude to the body, whose patience and liberality has enabled them to continue their labours until this hope was realized. The greater part of the report was written before the discovery was made; and had the work ceased on July 28, 1872, those who always declined to believe that *Machairodus*

INCISORS OF HYÆNA, MACHAIRODUS LATIDENS, AND WOLF.
(*From photograph by A. R. Hunt, Esq.*)

[To face p. 226

had ever been found in Kent's Cavern would have been able to urge, as an additional argument, the fact that the consecutive, systematic, and careful daily labours of seven years and four months had failed to show that their scepticism was unreasonable. This great accumulation of negative evidence has been for ever set aside, and all doubt of Mr. MacEnery's accuracy for ever removed, by the discovery the committee have now had the pleasure to announce. They can now announce also that *Machairodus latidens* and man were contemporaries in Britain; for even if, notwithstanding the great array of facts to the contrary, the former should prove to have belonged to the era of the breccia, and not to that later time represented by the cave-earth, the two flint implements found in the breccia, to which attention was called in a previous part of the report, as well as that produced and described at Exeter in 1869, take man back to that earlier period also. . . ."

Mr. Harpley, in his valuable obituary notice of Pengelly, mentions the following incident which occurred during the reading of the Report.

"He had the pleasure of being Mr. Pengelly's companion at the meeting of the British Association at Brighton in 1872. While returning from the railway station, whither they had gone together to see after the safe transit of the boxes containing the bones, implements, etc., collected during the previous year's exploration of Kent's Cavern, Mr. Pengelly was suddenly seized with hemorrhage in the throat; this produced a fainting fit, from which he speedily recovered, but great weakness of the throat succeeded. Mr. Pengelly was induced by medical advice to abstain as much as possible from using his voice during the meeting, and the writer undertook to read his report for him. On reaching that portion which referred to the discovery of the 'Tooth,' Mr. Pengelly, with his characteristic enthusiasm and impulsiveness, seized the manuscript, and said, 'Oh, I must read this at all hazards!' and finished the reading, in spite of the pain he suffered, amid the cheers and acclamations of the Savans assembled in Section 'C.'"

Professor Owen to Pengelly.

"Sheen Lodge, Richmond Park, December 28, 1872.

"Accept my best thanks for your additional elucidation of one of our rarest and most interesting British fossils—*Machairodus;* and your valuable summary of the literature of the Oreston Caverns.

"I hope to be able to make some return in kind, when I am back to work in spring, for, notwithstanding the rare mildness of this December, I have had so obstinate and severe a cough that I am ordered off again to Alexandria."

CHAPTER XV.

LECTURES IN THE NORTH; RECOGNITION OF HIS WORK IN KENT'S HOLE.

JANUARY, 1873, TO DECEMBER, 1874.

AT the meeting of the Devonshire Association in 1873, Pengelly read a paper entitled the "Literature of the Cavern at Ansty's Cove, near Torquay." This cavern was examined by Mr. MacEnery, and is well known, as it is situated in one of the most lovely parts of Devon. The exploration had yielded some important results. At this meeting he also read papers, on the "Caves of Buckfastleigh and Chudleigh," and on some "Implements found in Kent's Cavern."

In January of this year he visited some of the large towns in the North to fulfil lecture engagements. He thus writes home from Hull :—

Pengelly to his daughter Lydia.

"*January* 15, 1873.—You will all be glad to hear that my lecture was largely attended last night, and apparently gave great satisfaction, and that I am none the worse for it; still, it was a wise course to stipulate for a clear evening between two evening lectures. I have written to Mr. McK. Hughes,* declining his invitation to visit him and the caves near St. Asaph, though the temptation is a strong one.

"I am sorry to have missed Admiral Spratt, whom I know pretty well. He was captain of the ship-of-war in which the late Professor Edward Forbes made his natural history researches in the Ægean Sea, and through Forbes he no doubt knew our friend Dr. Day.

"After the lecture a good many friends dropped in at Mrs. King's; amongst them were several I knew, and a pleasant evening was spent. In this way I made the acquaintance of Mr. Staniland Wake, who, though in practice as a lawyer here, frequently attends the meetings of the Anthropological Institute in London, and occasionally reads papers there.

* Now Professor of Geology at Cambridge.

"Yesterday was very fine and mild here, and I walked about all day, chiefly on the outer wall of the docks, where I at once commanded a view of the enormous number of ships (for this is the third port in England), the Humber, and of the opposite or Lincolnshire coast. This is likely to be a fine day also, so as soon as my letters are disposed of I shall start for another walk, if all be well."

A letter of Darwin's in *Nature*, on "Perception in the Lower Animals," attracted Pengelly's attention. The well-authenticated stories alluded to in the following letters were verified with much care, and were included in a paper read by Pengelly before the Torquay Natural History Society, under the title of "Notes on the Sagacity of the Infra-Human Animals."

Pengelly to Charles Darwin.

"Lamorna, Torquay, March 17, 1873.

"Your letter on 'Perception in the Lower Animals' in *Nature* of the 13th has induced me to send you the enclosed slip. I trust you will pardon this intrusion by an almost entire stranger."

"THE HOTEL DOG.—(Copy of a letter from Mr. R. Fry, formerly of Woodgate, now of Exeter.)

"Woodgate, near Wellington, 12th mo. 8, 1859.

"There is a very pretty light tawny-coloured dog, with a fine bushy tail, at the Queen's Hotel, Exeter, that has attracted my attention by his sagacity as well as his beauty.

"I watched his contrivance a week or two ago to get out of the coffee-room. The door is a double swinging door, opening either way, but so stiffly that the dog has not strength enough to put it open with his nose. He therefore walked back several yards, and ran against the door. This manœuvre opened the door, but not wide enough to please him ; he therefore repeated the act, taking a longer run than the first, and having acquired a greater impetus. This done, he opened the door wider, and then passed through.

"On speaking to his owner about the cleverness of the dog, he said the dog had learnt by experience that it was unsafe to attempt to pass through if the door was not pretty far opened, for he had twice had his tail caught and pinched from the door falling fast before he was completely through. Is not the above an exhibition of something more than instinct?"

"THE ISLE OF WIGHT DOG.—(Copy of two letters from Mr. Kirkpatrick, Banker, Honiton.)

"Honiton, November 19, 1868.

"In compliance with your wish expressed by you when I had the pleasure of meeting you in the train on Tuesday last, I will now recapitulate the little anecdote I told you about the terrier dog belonging to my late father, Joseph Kirkpatrick, of St. Cross, Isle of Wight.

"About the commencement of the present century, before the days of quick coaches and railways, my father crossed from Cowes to Southampton with his horse and terrier, and rode to London *via* Basingstoke. On reaching town he put up his horse at an inn in Westminster, and, as he was going into the city, directed the ostler to tie up, and take care of, his dog.

"When he returned from the city, he found the dog had broken loose and disappeared. Exactly twenty-four hours afterwards the dog arrived at St. Cross.

"About a month after this my father was at Cowes with the dog, and on meeting Captain Stevens of the *Fox* cutter, which plied as a passage vessel between Cowes and *Portsmouth*, Stevens remarked, 'Is that your dog, sir?' 'Yes,' was the reply. Stevens then added, 'He was my passenger a few weeks ago from Portsmouth to this place' (Cowes), 'and on the vessel sailing into Cowes harbour, without waiting to get into the boat, jumped overboard and swam ashore.'

"This is the story I have often heard my father relate."

"Honiton, November 20, 1868.

"I quite forgot to tell you in my note of yesterday that the terrier to which I referred was born in the Isle of Wight, and had never been out of the isle till the day my father rode to London by Southampton."

Charles Darwin to Pengelly.

"Down, Beckenham, Kent, March 19, 1873.

"I am much obliged to you for so kindly sending me the very curious account of the sagacity of dogs. I can believe almost anything about them. You must forgive me for differing from you on one point, when you call yourself 'an almost entire stranger,' for I, at least, have a lively and very pleasant remembrance of seeing you some dozen years ago at Torquay."

It will have been seen that Pengelly, who was always desirous to benefit all classes of the community by the dissemination of scientific knowledge, found some of his most interested hearers amongst the skilled artisans of the manufacturing towns, the shrewd Scottish people, and the miners of his native county of Cornwall. He writes on one occasion :—

"I have frequently been much pleased at the interest manifested by working men—especially miners—in geological questions and discussions. With a geological friend, I once left a large mine accompanied by the captain or chief superintendent—a well informed, thoughtful man, who had risen from the ranks. He had shown us over the works, and was walking with us to the neighbouring town, about four miles distant. Our road lay through a district of considerable interest, displaying, amongst other things, elvan dikes traversing the stratified rocks; whilst on the surface of the country there were several large boulders of distant derivation.   These naturally formed the subjects of our conversatoin, and we stopped from time to time to note the phenomena more carefully.   A party of miners who had ' just come to grass '—in other words, had come up from their work underground—left the mine very soon after us, and were observed, when they overtook us, to regulate their pace so as to keep within hearing.   About two miles from the mine the road divided—one branch leading to the town, whilst the other and less important led to the miners' cottages.   Instead, however, of turning off there, as they ordinarily did, they followed at our heels; and this fact seemed to annoy the captain, as he feared they were going to the town, and might be tempted to some public-house. He accordingly turned and said—

"' I hope you are not going to the town?'

" And one of them replied—

"' No, sir; but we want to hear what you've got to say 'bout elvan courses and that; and, as it won't take us much further, we're going on to the next lane end—about half a mile further on.'

" The reply was, of course, more than satisfactory: and we induced them to join us, and join in the conversation.

" I once requested an innkeeper in a small hamlet, to get me a guide to a point on the coast said to be of great interest, but difficult to hit. He very soon brought me his ' brother John '—a fine stalwart young fellow, the occupier of a small adjacent farm—who offered to be my companion to the cliffs.   The distance was about two miles, over a fine table of moorland, and commanding an excellent view of the sea.   Of course we beguiled the way with talk, which John thus opened—

"' I've heerd that people think a good deal of the scenery hereabout, especially where we're going; and many strangers come from distant parts, quite a good way up the country, to zee it.   I s'pose that's what makes you wish to go there?'

"' Well, the scenery is spoken very highly of, and I quite expect to be much delighted with it; but my main object is to examine the rocks, to see what they are, how they lie, and whether they contain any fossils—as I quite expect they will.'

"' Oh!'

" This last word was obviously pronounced in order to avoid saying nothing; but John's puzzled look was much more significant, as it unmistakably told me that he had no idea of what I had been speaking. During the rest of the walk out, we talked of the weather, and the state of the crops; and he pointed out such objects as he thought likely to interest me.   At length we found ourselves at the foot of the cliff; and almost immediately a black patch in the bluish-grey slate presented itself, and as I expected, proved to be a fragment of the well-known Devonian fossil, *Steganodictyum*—now known to be fish.   The moment its true character was disclosed, I was down on my knees, with hammer and chisel endeavouring to extract it; whilst John exclaimed—

"' Why, what be about?'

"' Do you see this black patch?'

"' Ees, I zee it plain enough.'

" 'Well, that's a fossil, and I'm trying to get it out.'

" 'Oh, that's a fossil, is it? what is a fossil?'

" 'Sit down, John, and I'll try to explain. Do you suppose there are any dead shells, or fish bones, lying on the bottom of the sea yonder?'

" 'Of course there is.'

" 'What is the state of the river, in yonder beautiful valley, after heavy rain?'

" 'Why, very muddy.'

" 'When there's a very heavy gale, throwing violent waves on this cliff, does the cliff ever give way?'

" 'Oh yes ; there's always some part or other of it wasting.'

" 'Very well. Now, the mud which the river brings down from the country, as well as that which the waves tear from the cliffs, finds its way to the sea, as you know, and sooner or later it settles on the bottom of the sea, and buries up such remains of dead animals or vegetables, as may be lying there, and forms a new sea bottom ; on which, by-and-by, other shells, and things of that nature, will find their way ; and these will be buried in their turn.   Now, if this work goes on for a very long time, the mud and sand carried into the sea will form a very thick mass ; and if you can suppose it to become more or less hard, it will be a rock, with remains of animals in it. And if it should from any cause get raised above the sea, the waves would begin to break it up, little by little, just as they break up the rock on which we are sitting ; and after a while any person who carefully looked for them would be able to see the shells, and fish bones, and so on, that had been buried very long before, and he would call them fossils.'

" 'But do you mean to say that that's the way that black thing got into the rock?'

" 'Yes ; that's what I mean to say.'

" 'Was this rock mud once?'

" 'Yes.'

" 'Not made when the world was made?'

" 'Oh, dear no ! It was made very long since. There are rocks of very great thickness in other parts of the world, made in the same way, and some of them are much older, and others much newer, than this.'

" 'Well, you *have* opened my eyes.   I'll tell 'ee what 'tis—I've lived longer this morning than in all the years of my life before. So that's a fossil, is it?   Was it a shell or a fish bone?'

" 'There's a difference of opinion about it at present. None of them are very perfect ; and some say it's a piece of sponge, whilst others think it's part of a fish.'

" 'Well, never mind ! 'Tis a fossil ; let me look at 'en, and then I'll try to find some.'

" He accordingly proceeded to inspect the rocks, and in a few minutes cried out—

" 'Here's one.   Here's another,' and, in a short time, detected several good specimens.

" On our journey back, John asked me numerous questions, most of them very pertinent, and some of them by no means easy to answer. At the inn I betook myself to the 'parlour' in order to greater quietude for writing.   John felt himself happier in the kitchen; but, as the one room opened out of the other, I frequently heard my zealous disciple repeat to the villagers who came in from time to time—though with sundry modifications and some errors—the lecture he had heard in the morning; the invariable peroration being—

"'I'll tell 'ee what 'tis—I've lived longer this morning than ever I lived all the years of my life before.'"

It was a real pleasure to Pengelly to receive letters such as the following from working men :—

W. G. Cove to Pengelly.

" Westminster, March 8, 1873.

" I suppose you will be surprised to receive a letter from me, but if I have never written to you, it is not because you are not thought of, for often when talking of days long past I cannot help feeling gratitude, mingled with great pleasure, for the lasting happiness you were so anxious and constant to impart to us young men, during the 'Young Men's Society,' and afterwards at the Mechanics' Institute, which existed by way of diffusing knowledge amongst us, and although I have been a teetotaller now thirty-three years, I don't forget that it was to you I owe with thankfulness the first gleam of light on the subject when answering a question at the Young Men's Society Meeting.

"I think it stood thus, 'Is Drunkenness curable? If so, what is the most efficient cure?' and you undertook to answer it, which you did by advocating entire abstinence from intoxicating drinks, which at the time I did not clearly see. I hope not to tire you with too lengthy a letter, so will pass over a great number of pleasing circumstances in connection with the Young Men's Society, and Mechanics' Institute days, in which I derived much information on many subjects from you, which as I before stated affords me lasting pleasure; and I have often felt and said I owe more gratitude for the small amount of knowledge I possess, to Mr. Pengelly of Torquay, than to any living man, and I think there are a few now in Torquay who might truly say so too. I did not intend to say so much, but having honestly stated my convictions, I now come to the intended purport of my letter. An acquaintance of mine will be taking a holiday this month, and wishes to go into Cornwall to see some of its beauties. Now, as you are well acquainted with what such a person should see there, I thought you would be kind enough (as he is passing through Torquay) to direct him an interesting route thither; for the late Robert Ash and myself were favoured once by you as to what we ought to see, when planning to go there, and greatly pleased we were. I think that was in the summer of 1841. If convenient also I think he would feel interested in knowing a little of famous Kent's Cavern."

From a " Manchester man."

" Manchester, December 15th.

"You will, I hope, pardon the liberty of a plain uneducated working man addressing you on this occasion, who makes no pretension whatever to any literary ability, neither received any education beyond the three R's, and that in a country village school, in my school-boy days before either the last or the present educational code was introduced.

"I beg respectfully to intimate that I take a great interest in scientific subjects, but more particularly in that of Geology, having been employed at a mine for eight and a half years; hence geology has been my favourite study ever since.

"During my leisure hours, for sheer innocent amusement therein, I have written a kind of sixes and sevens or 'patchwork' description of one of our public parks (Peel Park), wherein I have introduced a Section on Science, including a little on geology on twenty-seventh page, wherein I took the liberty of introducing your name in a footnote therein (being copied verbatim from a newspaper paragraph which I came across) in reference to your scientific contents of Kent's Cavern, and also being the subject of your lecture to-night, which I intend to avail myself of the very great pleasure in hearing you on this exceedingly interesting subject. . . ."

The following notice of the second of Pengelly's lectures in the "Science Series for the People," given at Manchester on December 17, 1873, contains some account of the discourse :—

"The lecture of Wednesday night was delivered by Mr. W. Pengelly, its subject being "The Time that has elapsed since the era of the Cave Men of Devonshire." It may be remembered that Mr. Pengelly delivered a lecture in the last series on the same subject, consequently, lecturer and audience met as old friends, and were clearly on the very best terms with each other. . . .

"Mr. Pengelly's style is most attractive. It is incisive, clear, and at times there are touches of humour. His perfect knowledge of his subject, combined with his intense earnestness, clothed his lecture with genuine eloquence. No one who heard him but regretted the unusually speedy termination of the orthodox hour, or who did not wish to have the time prolonged. We have heard many excellent lectures in the Hulme Town Hall, but have never listened to a better or an abler one than that of Wednesday night."

The answer to the following letter is unfortunately missing.

Pengelly to Edward A. Freeman.

"Lamorna, September 8, 1873.

". . . I infer from passages in your paper on 'The Place of Exeter in English History' (*Macmillan's Mag.*, Sept., 1873, p. 476), which I have read with the greatest interest, that the Bishoprics of Cornwall and Devonshire were first joined in the time of Edward the Confessor; that on the junction being made Exeter became the See; and that Leofric was the first Bishop of the united dioceses. I had previously believed, solely on the authority of Carew (Survey of Cornwall, pp. 81, 109, 124, ed. 1769), that the Danes having burnt the Church and Palace of the Bishop of Cornwall, at Bodmin, the See was removed thence to St. Germans in the same county ; that in the time of Canute the two bishoprics were joined at the instance of Livingius, Bishop of Crediton, who became Bishop of the united dioceses, and had his See at Crediton ; and the See was subsequently translated to Exeter. Without questioning your correctness, I should be gratified if, without much trouble, you would kindly refer me to authorities on the points raised."

In March, 1874, Pengelly was the recipient of a very handsome testimonial in recognition of his nine years' work in Kent's Cavern. The presentation was made by Professor Phillips, who most kindly took a special journey from Oxford to Torquay for the occasion. Professor Phillips opened the proceedings with an eloquent scientific address. He said—

"The purpose of their meeting was to commemorate the successful progress of a great geological work which had been undertaken in this neighbourhood at the suggestion of the British Association for the advancement of Science, and especially of the Geological Section of that body, namely, the excavation of Kent's Cavern. They had a second duty, to express—on the part of the Geological section of the British Association, and very many members of the Geological Society, and of every member of the committee appointed by the Association to direct the operations in Kent's Cavern—their affectionate admiration and gratitude for the great amount of labour, long continued and of a highly scientific character, that has been performed at the request of the Association by one of their townsmen, Mr. Pengelly. A few words only were required to place them in possession of some of the reasons why the geologists of this country had felt so great an interest in the excavation of Kent's Cavern, and in having the work directed with the extraordinary degree of minute and careful attention which had characterized the proceedings. Mr. Pengelly had not only shown a rare carefulness and scrupulosity in collecting and preserving interesting specimens ; but he had literally inspected and examined the work of exploration from day to day, giving a large portion of most precious time to examining the stuff as it was dug up, taking home the fossils, washing and labelling them, putting them in a catalogue, and writing notices respecting them. Mr. Pengelly had, in fact, turned his own residence into a substitute for Kent's Cavern, and his house must be full of bones. Out of regard for him, however, he hoped Torquay would be able to preserve a very fine collection, the largest and most perfect, of these remains, and that it would be for a long time the principal feature of the Museum of the Natural History Society. In undertaking such a duty, however, it should be remembered that it was not sufficient merely to place these bones in drawers and to say they were safe there ; what was wanted for them was that they should be so placed as to instruct all who had sufficient interest in the history of mankind and in the nature and extent of these discoveries. These remains afforded evidence which carried them back to the first occupation of this country, to a period much earlier than was generally supposed, when the reindeer and early races of deer lived with the elephant. For the minute examination of which these discoveries were the result they were especially indebted to the extraordinary scientific acumen and untiring zeal of Mr. Pengelly, and they should be performing a great act of injustice, now that the Geological Section of the British Association was coming near to the end of its most prosperous work in connection with Kent's Cavern, if they were simply to accept the results and give Mr. Pengelly an ordinary expression of thanks. He thought they should take the opportunity now afforded them to express to Mr. Pengelly, in the presence of his personal friends in his own town, amongst those who knew his personal worth and were aware of his high scientific attainments, to offer him publicly an expression of the affectionate regard and the profound respect entertained for him by persons in this country who devoted themselves to geological inquiry of a high order, and by all persons in the least degree interested in the most important historical inquiry which related to the occupation of the northern parts of Europe by races of inferiorly educated men.

Mr. J. E. Lee (the treasurer of the testimonial fund), said—

" Though he entertained a dislike generally to testimonials, yet there were exceptions to every rule ; and, if there was an exception which it was proper to make to a rule, it was in the present case of Mr. Pengelly. He had no hesitation in saying that there was no professional man living who had worked harder and more freely, and more successfully, without the slightest idea of remuneration, than Mr. Pengelly. No one who knew Torquay could deny that if they wanted to meet Mr. Pengelly at a certain hour they had only to put themselves on the Babbacombe Road between four and five o'clock in the afternoon, and Mr. Pengelly would be sure to be met either going to or returning from Kent's Cavern."

At the proposal of Mr. Guyer, Mr. Pengelly was also to be presented with an illuminated parchment, containing the names of the subscribers, and setting forth the object of the testimonial as follows :—

" The undermentioned members of the British Association and other friends beg to present to Wm. Pengelly, Esq., F.R.S., etc., etc., this testimonial in recognition of his long and valued services to science in general and more especially for the exploration of Kent's Cavern, Torquay. March 17, 1874."

Mr. Vivian, in asking Professor Phillips to make the presentation, expressed his indebtedness to Mr. Pengelly for the amount of geological teaching he had received from him.

Professor Phillips then presented the testimonial to Mr. Pengelly.

" As a mark of the high appreciation of his services by the Geological Section in particular, and the members of the British Association very generally, and every member of the Kent's Cavern Committee, of which he was the secretary.   In making the presentation, he would only add these words in regard to Mr. Pengelly—

> ". . . cui
> Gratia, fama, valetudo contingat abunde,
> Et mundus victus, non deficiente crumena."

The professor then handed to Mr. Pengelly the illuminated address and a cheque.

The recipient acknowledged the honour paid him in a characteristic speech, beginning in the playful and humorous style for which he was so well known.   He went on to say that—

" He had done this work in connection with Kent's Cavern simply because he liked it.   He was, however, utterly unable to give expression to the gratification which he felt at their kindness, and the kindness of his friends throughout the country generally, unless he could coin his heart into words, which was beyond him.   It had been very pleasant to him to do the work in Kent's Cavern day by day for now nearly nine years, it having been begun on March 28, 1865.   He had endeavoured to husband the means at his disposal as if the money were his own.   He had had the pleasure of spending five hours a day, taking one day with another, for the past nine years on Kent's Cavern work ; and, whilst his work in the Cavern had been considerable, that at home had often carried him into the morning hours.   But he had experienced intense pleasure in it ; and he could assure them that, on his finding a *Machairodus latidens*, after seven years and a half exploration, the discovery of that one tooth, in his opinion, was worth all the money that had been spent in the exploration of the Cavern.   It was particularly pleasurable for him to receive this testimonial at the hands of Professor Phillips, for he could not forget that he represented geologically the great University of Oxford, he being the Professor of Geology in that university, and that to the reading of one of Professor Phillips' works he owed more of his geological knowledge than to any other man.   It was also pleasurable, to find in the list of subscribers every member of the Kent's Cavern Exploration Committee ; * also the names of the president of the Geological Society and of the two presidents before him, and those of both professors of geology at the universities of Oxford and Cambridge, and friends whose names he hardly expected to have seen there, but which gave him a great deal of pleasure.   Reference had been made to the possible inconvenience of his having to keep the fossils in his own house.   He had only 6320 boxes of bones there. He hoped to devote a portion of the money presented to him in building an additional room in which he might put the large private collection

---

* The Committee now consisted of the following members : Sir Charles Lyell, Bart., F.R.S. ; Sir John Lubbock, Bart, F.R.S. ; John Evans, F.R.S. ; Edward Vivian, M.A. ; George Busk, F.R.S. ; William Boyd Dawkins, F.R.S. ; William Ayshford Sanford, F.G.S. ; John Edward Lee, F.G.S. ; and W. Pengelly.

of Devonshire fossils he had collected, so as to enable his friends to study them. He thanked Mr. Lee for the kindness and delicacy he had displayed in the matter. He did not wish for one moment to speak slightingly of the pecuniary value of the testimonial, but let it be understood, once for all, that their appreciation of his services, such as they had been, was the thing which he valued chiefly in this matter. . . ."

A few days later the following article appeared in connection with the Testimonial :—

"There are those who receive testimonials and those who deserve testimonials. The world is full of one class, whilst only a comparative few belong to the other. Mr. Pengelly is one of the few. The whole geological world is indebted to him for the results which have attended his careful and energetic exploration of Kent's Cavern, and the country up and down is under compliment to him for his contributions to science, whilst Torquay owes a double meed of gratitude to him for his lucid exposition of scientific and social truths during a generation, and for lending it the distinction of his name. Geologists generally have been afforded the opportunity of acknowledging their obligations to and appreciation of Mr. Pengelly by permission to subscribe to a testimonial ; but the Torquay townsfolk, and particularly those who years ago derived advantage from Mr. Pengelly's lectures, and to whom testimonial circulars would not be sent, have a right to complain that sufficient publicity was not given to an intended public compliment. By confining the knowledge of the Committee's intentions to those who were likely to give large sums, the very appearance, that of paying in coin rather than in expression of feeling, which Mr. Pengelly, as well as the Committee, would wish to avoid, was given to the testimonial. The sixpences of the working men, who have derived advantage from Mr. Pengelly's private and public instruction, would be more acceptable to him than the pounds of more wealthy subscribers contributed as a reward. These, and others who knew nothing of the testimonial, have a right to complain at the somewhat exclusive character of the compliment."

The kindly feeling shown in this paragraph calls for no comment. It is, I trust, unnecessary to say that Pengelly was altogether unaware of the manner in which the funds of the testimonial had been raised. Most highly would he have valued a tribute of esteem from the working men of Torquay, whose appreciation of his labours was most grateful to him. To have seen their signatures in the list of subscribers, would have been to him quite as great a pleasure as the recognition of names so illustrious in different branches of science as those of Sir Charles Lyell, Sir John Lubbock, Charles Darwin, Sir William Armstrong, and Sir John Hawkshaw, or others so eminent in the social world, as the Dukes of Argyll, Devonshire, and Somerset, the Baroness Burdett-Coutts, and Sir Wm. Tite, then in his last illness. The following letter from an intimate friend of the eminent architect, bears touching testimony to his constant attachment to Pengelly :—

"March 20, 1874.

"In the Torquay paper, which I receive weekly, I have just read a very pleasant column, on which you must please let me congratulate you very sincerely! It is a most delightful thing to see an act of justice and kindness done, and especially so when one has the added satisfaction of knowing the recipient.

"I am sure one little circumstance I can tell you, will contribute to your appreciation of the Testimonial. The *last* time poor Sir William ever signed his name, was to the cheque by which he paid his tribute to the Testimonial. This was two days after his final illness had assailed him, and was the closing act of business and of kindness! After dictating a letter concerning this matter he never again *asked* for letters, or made the least effort to transact business of any sort."

Criticisms on scientific work and information as to the scientific mode of investigating caves were frequently solicited from, and always most cordially given, by Pengelly. Readers of "The Life of Sir Charles Lyell" will call to mind an appeal made to Pengelly by that great geologist, concerning the exploration of caverns in Borneo, which came within the jurisdiction of Pengelly's friend, the Rajah Brooke, whose good offices Sir Charles was anxious to enlist. "No one," he writes, "could better explain, than you, the interest of such an inquiry."

Pengelly to Sir Charles Lyell.

"Torquay, March 22, 1874.

"What a busy man you are! I had no idea that a second edition of your 'Student's Elements' was in the press, and lo! the postman hands me a presentation copy of the said new edition. Be so good as to accept my warm thanks for it, and the assurance that it is most gratifying to be thus remembered by you. Have you seen a letter by —— published for March on the *Eoozoon Canadense*? . . . In substance it is this: He is silent on the question of the mineral or organic character of Eoozoon, declines to give an opinion on the mineral hypothesis by King and Co., but states that the structure is most certainly not that of Foraminifera. I trust you will see the article. Pardon my calling your attention to what is, in all probability, an error in the useful diagramatic Table of British Fossils at the end of your new edition. In the Group *Trilobita*, page 630, the families '*Phacopidæ*,' '*Cheirudidæ*,' and '*Cyphuspidæ*' are represented as not extending into the Devonshire formation, whereas in Salter's monograph, *Pal. Soc.*, Part I., the following species occur in the Devonians of Devon and Cornwall : (1) *Phacops granulates*, (2) *Ph. lævis*, (3) *Ph. cryptoptophatinus*,

(4) *Ph. latifrons*, (5) *Ph. perniclatus*, and (6) *Cheirocurus articulatus*. Indeed your text and figure of *Ph. latifrons*, page 446, establish the extension of the *Phacopidæ*. When poor Salter was preparing his monograph, I sent him all my Devonshire Trilobites from Devon and Cornwall, and when they came back, I found them all named by him, and they are still in my cabinet, with his handwriting on the tablets. I have all the species named above, with the exception of the third only, and in addition a specimen of *cyphaspis*, but without a specific name attached, found in the middle Devonian limestone of Newton Bushel. This specimen has not been described, but it establishes the extension of the Cyphaspidæ into middle Devonian times."

Professor A. Newton, F.R.S., to Pengelly.

"Magdalene College, Cambridge, May 9, 1874.

"Will you kindly inform me whether you have any work going on now in Kent's Cavern or elsewhere? My object in asking is that a young friend of mine has just been selected as one of the naturalists to the Rodriguez Transit Expedition, and in that island are some very interesting caves which will have to be explored by him. Consequently I should like him to see, if possible, your admirable method in practice, for, though he has had some experience in cave-hunting, it would be well for him to be acquainted with all the latest improvements—the more so since he will have only half-savages to dig for him instead of intelligent men.

"Perhaps if there is nothing going on with you, you may know where people may be at work in the proper manner, and if so I would ask you kindly to use your good offices so that my friend may be able to see and avail himself of the process. I don't yet know when he will have to leave England, but most likely not till July or August.

"I have just found a grand prize in a magnificent *Bos primigenius*, almost perfect, dug up near this place within the last few weeks."

Mr. Slater, the friend alluded to in Professor Newton's letter, paid a short visit to Torquay, when he daily took advantage of the opportunity of studying cave exploration as exemplified in Kent's Cavern under Pengelly's guidance and instruction.

In several letters subsequently received from Mr. Slater he expressed his indebtedness for the valuable aid given him, as well as for the hearty kindness with which he had been received.

The following letter from Mr. Froude relates to the chairmanship of a local Scientific Society, which his friend was anxious he should undertake :—

W. Froude to Pengelly.

"Chelston Cross, Torquay, July 2, 1874.

"What a man you are : what a way you have !

"I hate to disoblige kind friends, who I know are seeking to express their goodwill towards me, and appreciation of me, in making the request you have conveyed to me. And if I only could know for certain that I should be dead by the time at which the assent would have to take effect, I would assent most cordially.

"But if a man at sixty-four does not know the duties he is *unfit*, for he is a fool, and is fit for little; and really, I know so well that I am not the right man in the right place if I sit in the chair to which you invite me, that so far as the fitness of things is concerned I should be courting it, in accepting the invitation. I know very well how kindly you value me, *over*valuing me in many ways, and especially not knowing of some of my particular defects.

"I grant, or rather I am vain enough to assert, that I know a great deal about some particular subjects, and have an intelligent apprehension of the elementary ideas belonging to other subjects.

"Yet in dealing with one of the subjects I understand best, to put together into a readable, still more into a preachable form, an exposition of the things I want to say and know are worth saying, is to me a burden and an anxiety which wears and tears me. . . .

"You who have such astonishing power of work, and do your work so clean and well out of hand, will hardly understand the difficulty I am trying to describe.

"My brother, who though not a man of science is a man full of philosophical ideas, has the readiness of mind and pen which make his task easy for him; and there are many men who without being philosophers, as he is, have a general acquaintance with science and a facility of composition, that enables them to get through the work both interestingly and instructively. I should be both a failure and a bore.

"If, then, you can get me off, without my appearing a graceless curmudgeon for refusing a proposal which I know has been meant so kindly, I hope you will do so. But if I am putting you in a disagreeable dilemma by being reported as recusant, I will forego my objection; for I am sure if, after what I have said, you desire me to accept, it will be for some reason which I could not rightly disregard. If you can get me off, *do*; if you can't, don't!"

During this summer, whilst his wife went with her daughters to spend the holidays from school at Budleigh Salterton, Pengelly visited Ireland, and attended the meeting of the British Association at Belfast, returning directly after the dispersion of the gathering to Devonshire.

Pengelly to his youngest child Hester.

"Lamorna, Torquay, before breakfast, September 11, 1874.

"I am beginning this letter to you with the present intention of sending it off not to-day, but to-morrow. Just after taking my tea yesterday, a note came from the Baroness,[*] stating that they were to have a small party, and as I had been obliged to refuse the dinner,

---

[*] Burdett-Coutts.

asking me to drop in, not late. I accordingly went, and found the drawing-room pretty well filled with ladies, including Lady Erskine, Mrs. Fortescue, Miss Dyott, and many others. In due time came in March Phillips, Vivian, Dr. Ramsay, Sir George Macgregor, Mr. Fortescue and others. . . . Your very nicely written letter of yesterday has arrived. I am glad to find you are all enjoying your walks, games, and blackberries (I mustn't forget them), and glad too that you saw so much of the regatta. I am getting on with 'Romola,' which seems a sad story. The kitten came back on Tuesday evening, and seems to have had proper care. She is frisking about at this moment as madly as ever. . . .

"The 'snake'* has not been used, it being utterly unnecessary, as there has been rain every day this week so far, and in no limited amount.

"There, now I think I have disposed of your letter. Saturday, September 12th. Lydia's letter has come to-day; be so good as to thank her for it, for me, and, if you can trust me for so much, you may give her a kiss. Tell her that no respectable female will be able to get into the new Chamber in Kent's Hole until at least three months' work has been spent on it, and that I am not sure that so much will ever be done, for we are finding nothing now to encourage us to do so. . . . I go into the garden nearly every day and pick and eat two or three pears, but it is so fearfully wet among the bushes, that we cannot pick up the fallen fruit."

How much Pengelly's time, ever burdened with serious work, was encroached upon by strangers and casual acquaintance wishing to visit the cavern under his guidance, the following letter, selected from many of a similar character, will testify.

Pengelly to his Wife.

"*Lamorna, Torquay, September* 18, 1874.—I have just reached home from the Cavern, where I had to act guide to Miss T——, her aunt and two other relatives, and this has occupied more of my time than it is pleasant to think of, though I must say the dear old maids were all very nice, and Miss —— kindly allowed the idea to peep out that they were doing me a kindness to visit my cavern under my guidance. All this to tell you that I have but little time, and that you must put up with a short letter. I yesterday had a call from Mr. W—— of Liverpool, whom I have seen at the Brit. Assoc. Meeting, but did not know. He was at Belfast, but not being able to get to hear my '*Lecture* on Kent's Cavern,' he had called to ask where, if anywhere, it had been or was to be printed; he being much interested in Cavern researches and kindred topics. I told him the Report was printed *in extenso* in this week's Directory, and would be in large abstract in *Nature*, probably of this week. On which he said, *Nature*, what *Nature*? And then it came out that this man, a

---

* His child's name for the water-hose.

resident in Liverpool, interested in cavern researches, and I blush to add, a Cornishman, was ignorant of the serial called *Nature*. At the Cavern yesterday, I found two men from Halifax, waiting for me with a letter of introduction from Mr. D. of Halifax. The funny thing is that I know no Mr. D. of Halifax. Be this as it may, I took them into the Cavern, and they were well pleased. This afternoon I found three ladies (?) waiting at the Cavern for me; but I handed them over to Smerdon,* much to his, and perhaps not to their satisfaction. On my return C. Parker waylaid me, and in the most pathetic manner besought me to go home to tea with him."

* The chief workman who was allowed to take visitors over that part of the Cavern not in course of exploration.

CHAPTER XVI.

LOSS OF FRIENDS.

A VARIETY of untoward circumstances and events combined to make the opening of the year 1875 a period of singular discomfort, anxiety, and depression for Pengelly. The season was one of extreme severity, and being far from robust in health at the time, he suffered greatly from the cold in the fulfilment of his engagements to lecture at Gloucester and other towns ; while sickness in his own household made it difficult for him to leave home, and caused him great uneasiness during his absence. In January he was much affected by the intelligence of the death of his valued friend Canon Kingsley, whose warm-hearted enthusiasm in the cause of popular education, and the deep interest he took in furthering the well-being of the working-classes, had greatly endeared him to Pengelly as a kindred spirit and fellow-worker in the cause he had so constantly at heart. This severe blow was followed by another that he felt no less keenly. As his human sympathies were engaged by the noble character of Canon Kingsley, it may be readily understood how his scientific life and studies had been intertwined and bound up with the work of the great geologist Sir Charles Lyell, his intimate friend and constant correspondent, whose death occurred in February of this year. Though he had been in failing health since the decease of Lady Lyell, in 1873, his last illness and death came as a sudden shock, and had an effect on Pengelly which even his buoyant nature did not enable him to recover from for a considerable period. The void which his death caused in the world of science was not greater than that which it left in the heart of his friend.

In February, 1877, Pengelly was the second recipient of the recently established Lyell Fund, which was presented to him

—as the President of the Geological Society remarked—by the unanimous wish of the Council, "as evidence of his untiring devotion to the great task of extending scientific knowledge relating to the Antiquity of Man. . . ." In the spring he had the pleasure of welcoming home, on long leave, his son Alfred, who was now a Deputy Commissioner in the Forest Department of the Indian Civil Service.

Pengelly had been a member of the "Boulder" Committee of the British Association for some years, and numerous letters relating to the work for the furtherance of which it was appointed, are found among his papers. It was a subject that had special attractions for him.

In a letter written during the previous year he thus describes the origin and labours of the Committee :—

Pengelly to the Editor of the Western Morning News.

" . . . The British Association first appointed a Boulder Committee in 1871, at the instance of D. Milne Hume, Esq., whose labours in connection with the Scotch boulders are well known; and it has been annually re-appointed. No report was made in 1872, but one, read at Bradford in 1873, will appear in the annual volume of the Association, which it may be presumed will shortly be published. It may be well to state, in order to prevent a loss of labour, that the Report in 1873, contains a description of the famous granite boulder on the northern shore of Barnstaple Bay, and arrangements have been made for including in the Report for 1874 an account of the numerous boulders in the 'Head' of Bovey Heathfield and the adjacent districts. It is hoped that no one will describe any specimens from mere hearsay, as a careful inspection alone can secure the accuracy essential to science. I shall be happy to send copies of the printed questions on which the Committee are desirous of information to any one wishing to have them, or they can be obtained from the Rev. H. W. Crosskey, F.G.S., Hon. Sec. Boulder Committee.

"It is to be hoped that the boulders on Dartmoor will not be utterly neglected, even though they may be of the granite of the district, partly because Dr. Otto Torell of Lund, an eminent authority on the question, has expressed the opinion, after a careful personal study of the district with G. W. Ormerod, Esq., F.G.S., that glacial Moraines exist on the Moor; and also because the Committee are desirous of recording all legends and superstitions connected with any particular boulders.

"Observers intending to assist the Committee will do well to study the first report of the Committee on Boulders appointed by the Royal Society of Edinburgh, drawn up by D. M. Hume, Esq., and published in the *Proceedings* of the Society, vol. vii., 1871–2."

The following letter from the Secretary of the Committee,

the late Rev. H. W. Crosskey, refers to a contribution to the Report for 1875.

Rev. H. W. Crosskey to Pengelly.

"Birmingham, July 14, 1875.

"I am delighted to return the 'Hail fellow, well met' involved in dispensing with 'Rev.' and 'Mr.' and 'Sir.' Many thanks—the Report will do admirably—please let the Boulder Committee have the privilege of printing it—and not the Devonshire Association. It is precisely what is wanted for each district."

In response to a request from Professor Rolleston, Pengelly read a paper before the Anthropological Section of the British Association, which met at Bristol, in 1875.

Professor Rolleston to Pengelly.

"Oxford, July 20, 1875.

" . . . I have to preside over the Anthropological Section of the Bristol British Association meeting, and I write to ask if you can give us something out of your ample stores. Mr. John Evans, who has just been staying with me, encouraged me to ask you, and, acting upon this advice, I do so. Anything which you can give we shall be glad of, and I do not presume to suggest any particular line to you. Except so far as I may say that probably we shall have some foreign anthropologists at the meeting, and that they might be disappointed if they did not get some *viva voce* discourse from you on the points with which they have learnt from print to connect your name."

Pengelly to Professor Rolleston, F.R S.

"Lamorna, Torquay, July 21, 1875.

"The only subject on which I have any special knowledge is Kent's Cavern. If you care to have a summary of all that has been done there, under some such title as 'The Anthropological (? Archæological) Discoveries in Kent's Cavern, Devonshire,' I shall be most happy to comply with your flattering request, if all be well.

"I purpose reading the Eleventh Report of the Kent's Cavern Committee to the Geological Section, which no doubt will be fixed for the orthodox time of eleven o'clock, Friday, August 27, and I would rather not encounter another Section the same day, as my throat is not very strong. I therefore suggest Monday, the 30th.

"Be so good as to favour me with a line just to say, 1st, Whether you approve the topic and the title.

"2nd, Whether you prefer that I should *speak*, or write and *read*, what I have to say.

"3rd, What amount of time you would wish me to occupy."

Professor Rolleston to Pengelly.

"Oxford, Thursday, July, 1875.

"I have been away from Oxford exploring, with Colonel Lane Fox, the flint mines which the early British excavated at Cissbury as other people did at Spienne. Otherwise your note would have been answered, as I hope you will have imagined, before this.

"As regards your questions, I would say in short, that we shall be glad of anything you will give, with whatever title, and whether written or spoken, and the longer the better. However, to answer in detail, I should think the title would be 'Anthropological (rather than Archæological) Discoveries in Kent's Cavern.'

"As to reading the MS., I should think if you had a short abstract such as would do for the volume, and gave us *viva voce* the details, that would be as well for all parties.

"As to time to be occupied, you could give us forty minutes, if that is not too much."

Before going to the meeting, Pengelly attended the Devonshire Association at Torrington, and afterwards joined his wife in a family gathering at the marriage of one of her nieces, Mrs. Burgess.

Pengelly to his Wife.

"Lamorna, July 31, 1875.

"Here I am, having just breakfasted and read your letter. We have been lucky indeed in the weather. . . . Now for a brief account of our meeting at Torrington. The President's address was admirable. I enclose a copy. The next day the reading of the papers was well attended, the only drawback was that the President was a little too indulgent in the precious matter of time. At six our dinner began, when nearly eighty sat down. I had my old Toast of 'The New Members.' It was over by nine, when we went to the Concert of which you know already. C. Fowler played charmingly. Thursday the papers as before. The meeting over, about thirty of us went off to see Wear Gifford Hall and Frithelstock Priory. It was a very pleasant drive, but the day was too far done for us to see much of the Priory ruins. Friday morning I went to the Vicarage to breakfast, where, besides Mr. and Mrs. Buckland (the vicar and Vicaress), the former the half brother of the famous Dr. Buckland, I met our President and some others, and 'the fun grew fast and furious.' Happily there was a little ballast, as every now and then the point of a joke had to be shown to Mr. G—— and sometimes he got a faint view of it. About one o'clock Mr. Wren, owner of some clay pits, drove in from his place, in his break and four, and drove a lot of us out to his pits about five miles off. We got back just in time to get a chop and catch the train to Exeter, and the meeting at Torrington began to fade away to join its older brothers somewhere in the mighty past. . . ."

Amongst those in search of information about the discoveries made in Devonshire caverns were Dr. Dawson, F.R.S.,[*] and Mr. G. H. Kinahan.

Pengelly to Dr. Dawson, M.A., F.R.S.[*]

"Lamorna, Torquay, January 3, 1876.

"First let me wish you in British fashion a 'Happy New Year,' and then thank you for your letters of 7th and 13th ult.

"I have not the least doubt that the 'cave-earth' was introduced in small instalments, at very protracted intervals by a small stream, which heavy rains occasionally swelled, but which ordinarily flowed tranquilly through the valley immediately in front of, and but little below the cavern entrances, instead of, as now, about seventy feet below them.

"I incline to the opinion that the 'breccia' is at least of interglacial age, but more probably preglacial; though I have not been able to detect any signs of ice action.

"Some of the bears' bones and implements in it may have been rolled, but probably not many of either series. The bear's leg, of which you have heard, was found in Brixham, not Kent's Cavern. There is much error afloat concerning it. By this post I send for your kind acceptance a few of my papers, which will perhaps answer all your questions better than I can in a letter. I need not say that I shall have great pleasure in giving any further information I can, as I am sure that though we may differ, we both desire to know and teach the truth.

"P.S.—Though we have broken all the pieces of stalagmite embedded in the breccia, we have found no organic remains in them. W.P."

Pengelly to G. H. Kinahan, Geological Survey, Wexford, Ireland.

"*Lamorna, January* 21, 1876.—In reply to yours of the 9th inst. I have to state that we find in Kent's Hole skulls of sheep in the 'Black Mould,' or uppermost deposit only—some of them horned, and some hornless, but none of them having more than two horns to the best of my recollection. Sheep and goats are easily confounded with one another, I believe."

This summer Pengelly visited Scotland again, and, whilst there, attended the British Association Meeting at Glasgow. He had lectured in Scotland in December, 1875, and did so again in the early part of 1877 at Glasgow and Dundee.

Nowhere were his lectures and papers more warmly received than North of the Tweed. The Duke of Argyll, writing to him in 1876, says, "I have never heard a clearer lecturer, nor one with so much enthusiasm for his subject."

---

[*] Principal of McGill College, Montreal, Canada; now Sir William Dawson.

Pengelly to his Wife.

"*Glasgow, September* 11, 1876.— . . . On Saturday, Harkness dined with my host and hostess, and we spent a bright, merry evening, which every one seemed to enjoy. On Sunday I went to hear the sermon announced in the enclosed, which was simply magnificent, though it had one or two errors in it. The sight of fully four thousand people (as I judge) hanging on the lips of one man, was a grand one (I was on the platform and could command the whole); and the singing—congregational as well as trained—was truly superb, and made me vibrate from top to toe. I then rambled about, took a light dinner, and at 6.30 found myself in a 'Hall of Free Thought,' of the Holyoake stamp and probably foundation. There were one hundred and fifty people present (as I judge). A good discourse—not cultivated—was delivered, though it is not what is called Christian, and there were some curious scenes of which I may tell you. . . ."

Pengelly to his daughter Lydia.

"*Glasgow, January* 25, 1877.—Thank you heaps upon heaps of times for your nice letter. . . . And now for the events in my history since I wrote yesterday. We duly dined at Sir James Watson's, where I met Sir William Thomson,* Dr. Allen Thomson, and several other folk. The gathering was a most pleasant one. The lecture audience was much larger than that last year, and my reception very flattering. It would have done your heart good to have heard some of the laughs. My new diagram, the printed one, was, and is, an undoubted success. It is not a bit too large. I am beginning to feel jubilant as the back of my work is broken, and I shall soon be speeding southwards, if all be well. . . ."

Towards the close of the year 1876, Pengelly paid a visit to Sir Samuel Baker.

Mrs. Pengelly to her Sister.

"*Lamorna, Torquay, December* 25, 1876.— . . . William returned yesterday from his visit to Sir Samuel Baker, which he has greatly enjoyed. The Duke of Somerset, who lives near Sir Samuel, came in on Sunday with the duchess. William says she is still a most charming woman. She was a Sheridan, and a sister of Mrs. Norton whom we met when she was in Torquay. Sandford Orleigh, the Bakers' house, is full of curiosities ; they have brought home numbers of heads, and horns, and skins of animals shot by himself. He told William that his tale for boys, 'The Castaways,' brings him in quite a little fortune. Unfortunately Mr. Froude, who had been asked, with the duke, to meet William, could not come. . . ."

Mrs. Pengelly to her Sister.

"*Torquay, April* 5, 1877.— . . . We dined lately with the Hunts to meet Lord and Lady Rayleigh. They were on their way home

* Now Lord Kelvin.

from Madeira.   Mr. Froude was there, and he and Lord Rayleigh (who was Senior Wrangler) would talk mathematics.   Lord Rayleigh took me in to dinner, and I found his conversation very interesting. We greatly enjoyed our evening.   Both he and his wife are much occupied in scientific questions.   She is, as I expect you know, a niece of the Marquis of Salisbury. . . ."

In April, 1877, Pengelly's friend and fellow-worker at the Museum, the Rev. T. R. R. Stebbing,* who had for some years resided at Torquay, left that place for Tunbridge Wells, and his congenial companionship was much missed by him.

The Rev. T. R. R. Stebbing to Pengelly.

"Tunbridge Wells, May 28, 1877.

"We are now definitely settled here.   For a long time we had a sort of vague feeling that we were only here on a visit, and that when the holidays were over we should return to the Warberry Hill, and this feeling was heightened by my receiving notices from time to time of important meetings of the Natural History Society.   The natural impulse is still at times very strong upon me of an afternoon, when there is nothing else in particular to be done, to wander down to the Museum. . . .

"Who are the comparative anatomists that confounded a bear's fibula with that of a man ?   That sort of slip gives great occasion to the unscientific to scoff at wisdom and research."

Pengelly's exhaustive treatment of the Geology of Devonshire is thus amusingly described by his friend Archdeacon Earle, now Bishop of Marlborough, when enumerating the difficulties in choosing a subject for his Presidential Address, before the Kingsbridge Meeting of the Devonshire Association :—†

"First I turned my mind naturally enough to the geology of Devon, and thought (as is evidently the duty of a local president to direct attention to local objects of interest; and in this I felt some small comfort, because a very bad bit of timber may make a very decent directing post) of a local paper on the Thurlestone Rock, and the submerged forest under Milton Sands, which are two of the principal objects of geological interest in the neighbourhood.   But I found that not only had Mr. Pengelly been before me in this particular subject, but that he would be before me when the address would be read.   The idea of reading a geological paper in the presence of the father of Devonshire geology was absolutely fossilizing, and I felt that I would sooner sit out the remainder of my existence in the remotest darkness of Kent's Cavern, with the absolute certainty of becoming an interesting

* Author of " The Challenger Amphipoda," and " History of Crustacea," etc.
† President's Address, Trans. Devon. Association, 1877.

addition to the human remains in that solemn crypt of scientific mystery, than attempt such an impertinence as to speak of geology in his presence. So I left Thurlestone and its geology to him."

In August, 1877, Pengelly presided over the Geological Section of the British Association, held at Plymouth; taking for the subject of the address, " The History of Cavern Exploration in Devonshire."

Professor Harkness to Pengelly.

"Penrith, Cumberland, August 3, 1877.

"I am glad to find you are to be President of Section 'C' at Plymouth. Being a Cornish man, you will be able to give me some information about the country where the Silurians occur in the county. I think Veryan Bay is a place on the shore where they are seen, and that there is a section here which has been described by Sedgwick. I have read Sedgwick's paper, and from it I gather that his time and the weather were not favourable for a proper examination.

"Is not St. Austell the best place to stop at to see the Silurians? How far is the coast section which shows them from this? After I have seen them, I must try to see the Serpentines, which I think are best exhibited at the Lizard. I also want to look at the Granites, and I wish also to obtain some minerals. Bonney read a paper on the Serpentines of Cornwall at the Geological Society a short time ago. I have not seen it, and perhaps it is not yet printed. If it be, I must try and get a copy from him."

Not only was he warmly supported by his brother geologists, but the public were attracted by the Chairmanship of one who had taken a leading part in establishing, on a scientific basis, the belief in the Antiquity of Man. His old friend Mr. Crosskey was unable to be present, and wrote as follows :—" To my very great disappointment, engagements, I find myself unable to alter, will prevent me from reaching Plymouth. I know well how first-rate the *Geological* gathering will be, in especial under your happy Presidency, and all the heartiness which will be thrown into the Wisdom; but the Fates are against me."

Mrs. Pengelly to her Sister.

"Plymouth, August 18, 1877.

". . . It is not a large meeting, but many of the Papers are interesting. I enjoyed one to-day by Professor Rolleston exceedingly. The subject was, ' The Flora and Fauna of Prehistoric Times.' He also made some very good remarks on the various objects of interest in the Plymouth Museum, brought here for exhibition. Professor Rolleston is a delightfully bright speaker, and Professor Newton almost equally so. Yesterday we dined at Mr. and Mrs. Fox's, to meet the President, Professor Allen Thomson, and his party, Dr. Beddoe, Mr. John Evans, and many others. The pictures are a most interesting feature of the Exhibition : two Holbeins, a splendid landscape of St. Michael's Mount, and another of the Mill near Capel Curig by Leader, a charming study of wallflowers by Mrs. Leader, etc., etc. Of course Sir Joshua Reynolds, Opie, and other Devonshire artists were represented. We had a very pleasant day in Cornwall. Mr. E. W. Cooke the marine artist accompanied us, as he wanted to see that part of the coast which was new to him. He was delighted with everything, each fern and flower, as well as the lovely sea views. He made a few charming little sketches while we were at Looe. Every time we see him he says, 'Wasn't that a delightful day we had in Cornwall.' He is a very old friend of William's, and they always seem happy together, and enjoy each other's society extremely. William tried to put himself into the old Pillory at Looe to amuse us, and Mr. Cooke was so much entertained that he made a sketch on the spot. A Mr. Ashley, an artist who was staying at Looe, finding out who Mr. Cooke and William were, gave them each an engraving of the Pillory adjoining the curious little old Guildhall. . . ."

Mrs. Pengelly to her Sister.

"Plymouth, August 24, 1877.

". . . On Thursday William went to act as guide to the Torquay excursion party of the British Association, Kent's Cavern, of course, being one of the attractions. He says they had a most enjoyable day, and that when they reached Panorama hill, they all sat down to rest, while Professor John Couch Adams gave them an account of the two satellites of Mars just discovered in America.

" To-day William and several other members of the Association are gone to attend a curious old ceremony, held by the Corporation every year in commemoration of Sir Francis Drake having brought in the water here from the moor, then and ever since an immense boon to the people of Plymouth. The ceremony is held about nine miles from here. It consists in first drinking to the memory of Sir Francis Drake in water, and then comes the Toast, 'May the descendants of him who gave us water never want wine.' The first dish served always consists of fish caught in the Leat."

Professor Rolleston to Pengelly.

"33, Clifton Place, Plymouth.

" Do you happen to have any separate copies of your papers on De Rivière's Mentone Man, which were published in the transactions of the Devonshire Society? I have got the volumes out of the library, but should be very glad to have the papers available to my hand. The same, I need not say, applies to any papers you may have of your own. But I must refer to your papers on the Mentone Man in a part of a book I'm engaged upon just now."

Professor Rolleston to Pengelly.

"Oxford, September 4, 1877.

" I am very much obliged to you for the papers you have sent me. I wish very much I had anything of corresponding value or interest to send to you in return.   I do send two small publications of mine which may show you, at any rate, how very heterogeneous my field of activity here is.   I took the opportunity of reading a considerable number of your papers whilst I was at Plymouth, having borrowed the *Transactions of the Devonshire Association* from the library.   I do not, if I can avoid it, go out to dinners at Association or other times, and hence I get quiet evenings for the purpose.   But I am very glad to have the papers for myself, and I thank you very sincerely for them.   I have referred to them for one or two points in a part of a book which Greenwell and I are bringing out.

" I see that Dawkins enumerates the rabbit among the Prehistoric Mammalia.   I still doubt it, and I think you do too, from what you say of the finding of it and of the pig in the Mentone Cave.   But there is, of course, as the skull of the pig you showed me and many others, abundant evidence for the pig having been in England and even domesticated in the Neolithic times.

" It would be, as it has always been, a pleasure to me to see you here or elsewhere."

Notwithstanding his unremitting attention to geology, Pengelly took a considerable interest in folk-lore, dialect, and kindred subjects, and amongst his correspondents were Professor Skeat and other eminent authorities.

The Paignton meeting of the Devonshire Association in 1878 occupied his time to a greater extent than usual ; for in addition to the fact that it was held in the immediate neighbourhood of his residence, the President-elect, Mr. William Froude, was almost at the last moment prevented from fulfilling his engagement, owing to the death of his wife.   Fortunately Sir Samuel Baker was prevailed on to fill the vacant place, which he did most successfully.

Pengelly to his Wife.

" Lamorna, Torquay, June 16, 1878.

" . . . I have written the rough copy of my paper on the Geology of Paignton, but instead of embracing the whole Parish, it is confined to the Cliff from Torquay Gas Works to Col. Smith's odd looking house.   Two books have recently arrived from the *English Dialect Society ;* and one of them is dear old delightful Thomas Tusser's ' Five Hundred Points of Good Husbandrie.'   It seems a work to be issued by the *Early English Text Society* rather than *English Dialect Society*, but I don't care whence it comes, so glad am I to get it. . ."

C. W. Peach to Pengelly.

"30, *Haddington Place, Edinburgh, July* 3, 1878.— . . . I have again the pleasure of handing you a Lady's Ticket for the Meeting of the Devonshire Association at Paignton. I confess to feeling sorrow at not being able to be with you there. I have the farther regret that I have nothing to send you to be read. Perhaps you know that I lived at Paignton for a year or more, and although I had commenced collecting—principally sea-weeds—I did no more, and have no records to refer to. I have, however, faint recollections of the Rocks and Madrepores, the Pholades in the Red Sandstones, and of getting, in what was then Paignton harbour, *Defromoia purpurea* (under a flagstone I tore up)—several of them. They were such very fine ones, Mr. Jeffreys begged two of me when writing his work on shells, believing them to be a good variety *Philberti* or *Laviæ* of *Masavinga*. See Jeffreys, British Conchology, vol. iv. page 374, where he mentions my find as belonging to Var. 1.

"I also remember the Beach being thickly covered with a beautiful cardium, etc., etc., in such abundance they became a nuisance. Also I remember seeing a seine drawn in upon the beach, with lots of *Maia squinado*, 'Gaverok' of the fisherman of Cornwall—plentiful there—wanting on the east coast of Scotland. These were all soft, having exuviated. Unfortunately I did not note whether male or female—this I have often regretted, so little being known about them when in this state. I ought to be whipped for it. I fancy they were males, because it is a well-known fact that, when the female is exuviating, the male always attends to protect her, and his shell is then hard. *Maia squinado* was one of Charles Kingsley's pets, see 'Glaucus,' p. 133. I *do* so regret not being able to visit Paignton; after nearly fifty years leaving it, who would know me? I have wept as I walked up the street of my native village, no one knowing me to say, ' Charles, how do you do?'"

After attending the meeting, Pengelly spent his summer holiday in Ireland, combining pleasure with business by being present at the British Association at Dublin, where, besides the usual Report on the Cavern, he read a paper, entitled, "The Raised Beaches and Submerged Forests of Torbay," before the Geological Section.

Pengelly to his Wife.

"*British Association, Dublin, August* 17, 1878.— . . . I dined in ' Hall' at Trinity College last night, as Haughton's guest, where I met Roscoe, W. Adams, and a lot of other men I knew, and had 'a good time.' After that I went to the evening lecture on ' Animal Intelligence,' by Mr. Romanes. It was *very* clever, but unfortunately I had to leave before it was over to catch the 9.45 train to Bray. To-night Mr. Findlater * and I dine with the Lord Mayor to meet the Lord Lieutenant. We agreed to apply for £100 to continue the Kent's Cavern work. . . ."

* His host at Bray.

During a visit to Dartmouth in the following month, some difficulty was experienced by Pengelly and his friends as to viewing the interior of the chancel of the fine old parish church. The Rev. Prof. Haughton, who was particularly anxious to see the finely carved screen, was much annoyed, and said to the caretaker, "I am a clergyman, and you may tell your Vicar that he has no right to close this to visitors," adding some very forcible language to his message. On the next occasion when Pengelly visited the church, he asked the custodian if she remembered his having come there with a clergyman who wanted to see the chancel. "Oh yes, sir," was the immediate reply; "he told me to tell the Vicar that he ought to be d——d for closing it." "Hardly so strongly worded as that," was Pengelly's amused answer.

Pengelly to his daughter Lydia.

"Lamorna, Torquay, September 6, 1878.

". . . I throw myself on your mercy and admit that I have neglected to write you ever since you have been on the borders of Taffy's Land;* but, on the other hand, I claim your full and deep gratitude for having brewed you so large a barrel of most admirable weather, wherewith to enjoy your excursions, picnics, etc. . . . Dr. and Mrs. Boycott are here; they called yesterday. Professor Haughton of Dublin and his son (home from Ceylon) came to see me on Wednesday. I took them to the Museum, to Kent's Cavern, and to Dartmouth, where we called on Mr. George Bidder, and oddly enough, two Miss Bidders called here the same day. . . ."

---

* His daughter was staying with friends in Monmouthshire.

CHAPTER XVII.

COMPLETION OF THE EXPLORATION OF KENT'S HOLE.

1879 TO JULY, 1883.

THE exploration of Kent's Cavern terminated on June 19, 1880, and Pengelly's work is thus referred to by an eminent geologist,* who, having been engaged in similar work, was fully competent to give a just estimate of its value.

"Day by day, except when the work was stopped, he visited the cave, and recorded on maps and plans the exact spot where each specimen was found, for no less than sixteen years. The vast collection of palæolithic implements and fossil bones, each of which bears traces of his handiwork, is represented in most of the museums in this country, and the annual reports, listened to with so much pleasure by crowds at the meetings of the British Association, are the most complete that have ever been published. It may be objected that the accumulation of so much evidence of the existence of man in the Pleistocene age in the south of England was unnecessary. It was, however, necessary to sweep away the mass of prejudice, and this could best be done by repeating the evidence. Had this not been done man would not occupy the recognized position which he now holds in the annals of geology. The rest of Pengelly's life was mainly given up to the researches in the other caves in Devonshire. In estimating his scientific work, it must not be forgotten that it was done in addition to the daily task of bread winning."

The completion of the excavation ended the last important geological work undertaken by Pengelly. It was a fitting close to his long and energetic career, which was characterized by a past President of the Geological Society, as leaving "a record equalled by few and surpassed by none."

Professor Boyd Dawkins to Pengelly.

"*En route*—London, February 5, 1879.

"I am writing under difficulties, in an express, to ask you to be kind enough to allow a friend of mine, Mr. Barlow (who is of a geological

---

* See Obituary Notices of the *Proceedings of the Royal Society*, vol. lix.

turn), to enter the hallowed precincts of Kent's Hole.   And I introduce him to you.

"I hope that you and yours are none the worse for this Arctic weather—and that you have beaten me in caves. I have just lately scored Hip. and R. leptorhinus along with man, of your breccia age.

"P.S.—Do you know of any small dark Cornishmen of the same sort as the dark Welsh? Stephen Hawker alludes to a small village near him which *may* be what I want to discover."

In April, the Rev. Canon Greenwell, of Durham, to whom all those who are interested in Pre-historic Archæology are so greatly indebted, visited Torquay.   It is hardly necessary to say with what pleasure Pengelly received one whose studies and pursuits were so entirely in accord with his own.   Soon afterwards the distinguished archæologist wrote, in the following terms :—

The Rev. Canon Greenwell, D.C.L., F.R.S., to Pengelly.

"April 9, 1879.

"You will not, I am sure, think it impertinent in me when I express my obligation for the most careful, patient, and scientific way in which you have conducted the exploration of Kent's Cavern.   Though I was aware how thoroughly it had been done, I certainly did not rightly appreciate the wonderful effort of patience it must have been to go on year after year and inch by inch.   Few persons could have put such a restraint upon themselves as you must have done, and have worked with such a singleness of purpose.   Pre-historic archæology owes you a deep debt of gratitude.

"Since I saw you I have been as far as the Land's End, seeing a few early remains in Cornwall, amongst them a most curious assemblage of dwelling places at Chysawster near Penzance. To-day I was at Wookey Hole, where there is, I should think, a valuable field for exploration. The small cave which has been worked at appears to be still, to some extent, unexplored.   To-morrow I go to Stonehenge, which I have not seen for some years past, and then to town for a few days before I return home."

Amongst the visitors to the Kent's Cavern during the year before the exploration was terminated were the Prince of Wales's sons, accompanied by their tutor, Mr. Dalton.

Mrs. Pengelly to her Sister.

"Lamorna, Torquay, July 21, 1879.

". . . Yesterday, while William was giving young Harrison his lesson, before leaving for the Devonshire Association Meeting at Ilfracombe, we received a visit from the two sons of the Prince of Wales with their tutor, Mr. Dalton, who had come over from the *Britannia* at Dartmouth. They called to ask William to accompany them to the

Cavern, but would not hear of his delaying his departure on their account, as he wished to do. They were most pleasant, asking many questions about the fossils, corals, etc., in William's museum; but the skeleton leaves, in the case in the drawing-room, particularly charmed Prince George, who is very bright and pleasant looking, much shorter than his brother, though I believe only about a year younger. The elder is very like his mother, and will make a very good-looking man. The bones gnawed by the hyænas, both ancient and modern, seemed to amuse them very much.

"We could not possibly have had a better opportunity of seeing them. Their midshipman's dress was very becoming to them; they looked very happy natural boys. When William was showing them a rough flint implement, Mr. Dalton, their tutor, reminded them that they had seen similar ones in the museum at Copenhagen. Mr. Dalton seems fond of science, and is very easy to get on with. He preached a farewell sermon on board the *Britannia* on Sunday; he is to accompany the Princes on the *Bacchante*. As they leave Dartmouth the day after to-morrow, they had no opportunity of coming, or they would have done so, in order to get William to accompany them to the Cavern; so they went there with the guide after leaving us. I could not help being reminded of the poor Prince Imperial who was so much the same age and size as Prince Edward, when we saw him in the same room a few years ago, and he was so pleasant and friendly when he accompanied his father * on his visit to us, when you were staying with us, and we were all so interested in wondering what his future would be. . . ."

The meeting at Ilfracombe, mentioned in the last letter, passed off well under the Chairmanship of Sir Robert Collier.†

That held the next year at Totnes was equally successful, and was presided over by Dr. (now Sir Henry) Acland, of Oxford, whose charming address was listened to with marked attention.

Just before the meeting Pengelly received a letter from Dr. Acland, then staying at Winchester, in which he says:—
". . . I cannot help writing a line to say I am coming towards you. I am looking forward to your meeting with deep interest."

In later years, when Pengelly had become a confirmed invalid, Dr. Acland was much at Torquay, and afforded his old friend much pleasure by the frequent visits he paid him.

Pengelly naturally felt considerable regret at the loss of an occupation which had for many years engrossed a large portion of his time and thoughts. It is characteristic of his solicitude for the well-being of others that, in concluding his final Report on the Kent's Cavern explorations, read at the Swansea meeting

* The Ex-Emperor Napoleon III.   † Lord Monkswell.

of the British Association, in August, 1880, he dwelt particularly upon the careful manner in which the workmen had performed their task, and made a special appeal on behalf of George Smerdon, of whom he says that "he had been continuously engaged on the work, and for thirteen years he was the foreman. During the entire period he not merely discharged his duties in a most faithful manner, but he never had a misunderstanding with the Superintendents."

On leaving the Geological Section, after reading this Report, a telegram was put into Pengelly's hand, urgently summoning him to Torquay. Arriving at home long after midnight, he was met by the sad intelligence of the death of his only surviving son, Alfred, whose promising career had been cut short by an accident encountered in the pursuit of big game in India. The shock of this sudden bereavement was acutely felt by Pengelly, though the sympathy of friends, and the tenderness of feeling shown to him on all sides, relieved, in some measure, the poignancy of grief. "Your departure, and its cause," wrote one of his friends from Swansea, "have cast a gloom on this meeting which nothing can dispel."

At the Geological Section in particular this kindly feeling of sympathy was especially strong, as evinced by the following letter :—

W. Whitaker, F.G.S., to Pengelly.

"British Association for the Advancement of Science, August 30, 1880.

" I write on behalf of the President and Committee of Section ' C,' to express our heartfelt sympathy with you in the sad loss of your son, a loss which we feel may affect you the more from his absence from home and from the suddenness of its occurrence.

" We trust, however, that the affection of the other members of your family may in some measure soften the sorrow which they share.

"On behalf of all the geologists here, I beg you will accept our condolence."

This melancholy bereavement rendered it necessary that all geological and other work should for a short time be laid aside. The first thing which revived Pengelly's interest in daily affairs was his desire to help in the collection for the "Smerdon Fund."

He had experienced too much trouble himself, and was, moreover, too considerate by nature, ever to be indifferent to the anxieties and needs of others. The claims of his valued workman—like himself a sufferer from rheumatism brought on by labouring in the damp cavern—were advocated by him so ably that a sufficient sum was collected to purchase for the old man a small annuity.

During the spring of 1881 Pengelly had the pleasure of again meeting Sir James Watson and Sir Henry Cooper at Torquay. The latter remained there for some time, and took many rambles with his old friend, who was still a good walker, in earlier years having been able to manage forty miles a day with ease.

In July Pengelly paid a most pleasant visit to the Rev. Richard and Mrs. Barham of Dawlish, to attend the Devonshire Association Meeting. His host, a son of the author of the " Ingoldsby Legends," and himself a man of fine literary taste, was a most bright and genial companion. Just before the meeting, he wrote to Pengelly concerning a paper on which he was engaged.

Rev. R. H. D. Barham to Pengelly.

"West Cliff, Dawlish, July 4, 1881.

" My dear Mr. Pengelly,

" . . . My paper is not ready for the press, as one or two points remain to be made clear. Let me thank you, however, very heartily, for the friendly interest you have shown in it. But the fact is I have been ill, very ill part of the time, or the article would have been completed. . . . We have trouble before us anent our ' Barrow,' which Mr. Hutchinson proposes to open. The money wanted was voted *nem. con. ;* but the proprietor talks of his wife's feelings !—regards it as a family mausoleum—would like to be present when it is opened, but can't—expects to find his great grandfather there—if not, can't guess where he can be, etc., etc. Clearly a shuffler and jibber—not, I fear, to be driven or coaxed. Baker, however, fancies he has got another dish of the same sort to set before the Association. Once more let me thank you for all your kindness."

Pengelly read two or three papers at the Devonshire Association. An enthusiastic friend who had contributed a paper with which Pengelly was much pleased, wrote to him afterwards thus modestly, " My small contribution savoured of Solomon's cargoes, apes and peacocks among gold and ivory. . . . You need not fear that I shall desert the Association as long as you are with it."

It had been suggested by a large circle of Torquay friends, in the beginning of 1881, that Pengelly should be presented with his portrait. The proposition met with a hearty response both in the neighbourhood and elsewhere, and in the summer of the same year the well-known portrait-painter, Mr. Arthur S. Cope, was commissioned to undertake the work ; so Pengelly left Dawlish for London, in order to begin the sittings for his portrait.   In the meetings of the Medical Congress he found a pleasant relief from the monotony of sitting.

Pengelly to his Wife.

"Surbiton, Surrey, August 10, 1881.

" Monday brought me a letter from the best of wives, and to this I proceed in the first instance.   I read to Mr. Cope the passage, ' I hope he will not put you too much colour, as it is not natural to you to have very much.'   He received the hint charmingly.   In fact he is a most agreeable fellow.   He told me a day or two ago that he believed the portrait would be the best he had done.

" Now for such news as I have in my budget.   Last Monday Wilberforce Bryant * and I went to the gathering of the ' Medicos ' at Holly Lodge.   It was very wet, and the crowd and packing were very great.   I met many old friends—Dr. Leith Adams, Gwyn Jeffreys, Dr. Gladstone, Tomlinson, Mr. Johnson (nephew of Rajah Brooke), Mr. Critchett, and others. . . .

" Yesterday on leaving Cope I went to the Physiological Section of the Medical Congress, and was in time to hear the President of the Section, Dr. Michael Foster, close the Section, which he did in a very eloquent speech.   MacAlister was there, and we chatted a little. The final meeting of the Congress was held at two, in St. James's Hall, when Huxley delivered a lecture on Medicine and the Biological Sciences.   The meeting was very large, but he was not heard well. The lecture will no doubt appear in an early number of *Nature.*   After the lecture, the ' Butter ' [concluding] meeting, which was well managed. Amongst the audience were Dr. Henry Acland, Dr. Carpenter, Dr. Boycott, Bowman (oculist), Allen Thomson, Joseph Lister, and several others I knew.   I sat by Mac Alister, Prof. of Zoology at Dublin. . . . "

The Jubilee Meeting of the British Association in 1881 was appropriately held at York, the cradle of the Association. An unusually large number of old members attended, and Pengelly had the pleasure of again meeting Alfred Russell Wallace, Sir Joseph Hooker, Professor Owen, Sir William Armstrong, Professor Huxley, Sir Andrew Ramsay, and many other friends.   He also made the acquaintance of Dr. Asa Gray, the distinguished American botanist, who was a guest at the same house in which he was staying.

A friendship sprang up at once between the two scientists, and Dr. and Mrs. Asa Gray visited Torquay, before leaving for America.

* A former favourite pupil, and now his very kind host at Surbiton.

Pengelly's portrait was completed in the winter, and the day before it was presented he thus wrote to his wife's invalid sister, for whom he entertained the highest regard :—

"*Lamorna, Torquay, January* 18, 1882.— . . . Time has invested me with authority to congratulate my relatives and friends whenever an anniversary of their birthday occurs. Such an anniversary is to happen to your history to-morrow, if all be well, and the note I am now writing is intended to convey to you my very warm congratulations on the event. I am using no mere words of custom or civility when I say that I am—that we are—thankful, very thankful, that you have been spared to us; and I am thankful, too, that I am still among those who can offer you congratulations. When I occasionally look over my correspondence, the fact that most of my friends are already gone, comes vividly, painfully before me ; and a few minutes ago, when looking over the list of subscribers to my portrait, I was struck with the fact that, though the list was opened no longer ago than last May, eight of the names are those of friends who have since passed to the unseen world. 'On this side, and on that, men see their friends drop off, like leaves in autumn.' The portrait just mentioned was to have been presented on the 12th inst., my birthday ; but being inconvenient to the secretary of the committee, the day was changed to the 19th, to-morrow, your birthday instead of mine. The portrait arrived yesterday, but has not yet been unpacked. The artist (Mr. A. S. Cope) is to reach Torquay to-night, and take up his abode with Mr. Lavers until Friday morning, when he returns to town. We are to meet him to-morrow at dinner (Thursday evening), and there are to be no other guests. . . ."

The following notice of Pengelly, which appeared shortly after the presentation, shows that, in spite of his long residence in Devonshire, it was never forgotten that he was a Cornishman, and it also bears testimony to the sincere regard entertained towards him in the West Country.

"Mr. Pengelly, F.R.S., is a link binding Cornwall to Devon. Born at Looe, and being a thorough Cornishman in sympathy and in social characteristics, he has become a naturalized Devonian by a residence of forty-six years at Torquay. The time has not yet come, happily— and we hope is far distant—for reviewing Mr. Pengelly's work as a whole. He has yet, we trust, much useful work to do, much pleasure to impart, and much happiness to enjoy. But he has long since, by his genius and industry combined, become famous alike as a geologist, a lecturer, a humorist, and a public man of very varied attainments and multifarious work. To know him well is to esteem him highly, and to be admitted to his society is a profitable privilege. It is not surprising, therefore, that Mr. Pengelly's fellow-townsmen should make him an exception to the proverbial rule, and do honour to the prophet in their midst. The admirable portrait of himself, presented to Mr. Pengelly on

Thursday, the arrangements being made by the committee of the local Natural History Society, is a well-merited tribute of admiration, respect, and regard. By doing honour to Mr. Pengelly, reflected honour has been shed upon the committee which originated and carried out the proposal."

For a year or two after the completion of the excavation, Pengelly had the full intention of giving to the scientific world the results of his conclusions, in a more complete form than could be found in his scattered papers to various societies.   In 1882 he writes thus to an American correspondent :—

" . . . I have no reason whatever to change my opinions respecting the stalagmites of Kent's Cavern, namely, first, that they are of very slow accumulation ; second, that they are not necessarily definite or trustworthy chronometers.   I have not abandoned the idea of publishing a book on Kent's Cavern : but I am an old man, having my hands full of work."

Gradually, however, the conclusion forced itself upon him that the task must be given up, seeing how entirely his time was occupied with gratuitous work for local societies.   In 1884 he wrote to a correspondent : "I have more writing on my hands than I shall ever get through."   Had the book which he contemplated been written, it might have proved a really important contribution to geological literature.   It is not, of course, for the present writer to estimate the loss caused to the scientific world by the abandonment of the scheme ; but knowing how congenial the work would have been to him who alone could have executed it, she cannot but regret that its accomplishment remained for ever an unfulfilled desire.

In March, 1882, Pengelly received a volume entitled, 'Addresses and Sermons," by the Rev. E. E. Jenkins, M.A.,* who was his assistant teacher, when he was conducting his school at Torquay.

Rev. E. E. Jenkins to Pengelly.

"3, The Paragon, Blackheath, S.E., March 14, 1882.

"I am sending you a copy of a volume which I hope you will do me the favour to accept for 'Auld Lang Syne.'   I have now a long past of memories, but none of them are more distinctly traced or more agreeably recalled than the scenes of our association now many years ago.   Our vocations have called us to tread different paths, but

* President of the Wesleyan Methodist Conference in 1880.

I believe both have been honest seekers after truth ; and I pray that the great Author and Redeemer of our mind may permit us to find light and rest in Himself."

Pengelly was Vice-President of Section "C" of the British Association, which met at Southampton in 1882.

Pengelly to his Wife.

"*Southampton, British Association, August* 23, 1882.— . . . Got here safely yesterday afternoon. Professor W. G. Adams and I lunched together at Salisbury, saw cathedral and Blackmore Museum, and travelled thence together. At the station found Harpley and son. He had secured lodgings for me, if I chose to have them. Went to Reception Room with them; found that every hotel of every kind was full and had 'turned hundreds away.' Went with Harpley to said lodgings—close to the sea, of which a fine view. No extra charge for 'insects.' I had to get up between one and two, and after sundry experiments and failures slept, if I did sleep, on the floor. Professor W. G. Adams, not having a Harpley here, had got no lodgings when I saw him about eight last night. 3.30 p.m.—Have seen lots of friends. Don't think there will be a newspaper worth sending. No daily paper in this town. I am again a vice-president of 'C,' and a member of the Committee of Recommendations. My paper is to be read in 'C' to-morrow (Thursday), and in Anthropology another day. . . ."

Pengelly to his Wife.

"Southampton, August 29, 1882.

". . . Sir William Thomson's lecture on the Tides, which was given to a large audience, was good for all who understood it. But Thomson himself was splendid ; he danced about the platform in all directions, with a huge pointer in his hand ; he shook in every fibre with delighted excitement, and the audience were as delighted as he. I sat next Prestwich, J. C. Adams, and W. G. Adams. On Sunday, in the afternoon, I took a delightful walk on the left bank of the river up to the village of Millbrook, whence I walked back to Southampton. In the evening I went to church and heard the rector of All Saints preach, in his own pulpit, a capital sermon on the words, 'What shall I do to be saved?' He is a brother of the new Dean of Westminster, and happily neither patted Science on the back, nor took up the question of 'Science *versus* Theology.' I was glad I went. Yesterday I read my paper to the 'Anthropops,' where it was well received. Evans and Dawkins spoke on it.

". . . In the evening Professor Mosely gave a capital lecture on ' Pelagic Life,' which, pardon the impertinence, means strictly, ' Life on the Surface of the Ocean, distant from Land.' It was well delivered and well illustrated. Thanks were proposed by Professor Gamgee, and seconded by the Bishop of Winchester, the scholarly Harold Browne, whilom a rector near Truro, and who married a Truro lady. I was glad to see him.   There has been a long discussion in our Section to-day anent the Channel Tunnel, and we have been popular. . . . "

In the autumn of 1882, a Temperance Mission, conducted by Canon Wilberforce and other eloquent speakers, was held at Torquay.   In the midst of scientific activity, the busy geologist found time to attend these meetings, which appealed warmly to his sympathies as a means of raising the moral standard of the people and conducing to their happiness and well-being.   He wrote thus of the mission :—

"Lamorna, Torquay, October 4, 1882.

". . . The Temperance Mission was a remarkable affair.   The final figures are that 2509 new pledges have been taken, and 4290 blue ribbons accepted.   Of course there are many children, who, like some of riper years, may change their minds ; nevertheless a very large amount of good has no doubt been done.   Blue ribbons meet the eye everywhere, worn by persons of all ages and all ranks, from the old magistrate to the small errand boys, and including some rough loafers.   I made use of the ' blue flag' yesterday.   Several small boys were teasing, almost beyond endurance, the ' mad woman ' who comes about sometimes.   As I passed the group I observed that two of the boys wore the blue, and I at once appealed to them not to disgrace the ribbon by their cowardly cruelty.   The appeal had the desired effect.   This month's *Fraser* contains the following announcement, ' With the present number the publication of *Fraser's Magazine* will cease.   On November 1st the first number will be published of *Longmans' Magazine*, which will be continued monthly.'   Thus dear old *Fraser* died with the issue of No. 634, which signifies an age of fifty-two years and ten months ; and it makes me sad.   The fact is significant.   Longmans—the publishers in each case—hope to reap a better harvest by cultivating readers who can pay 6*d*. monthly, than those who pay 2*s*. 6*d*. monthly.   In short, the masses have become readers ; there's a text for you. . . ."

Pengelly's enthusiasm in the cause of science first drew Mr. H. H. Howorth's [*] thoughts to the study of Eastern ethnology.

H. H. Howorth to Pengelly.

"Eccles, May 23, 1883.

"It was a gleam of sunshine to receive a letter from you. I am buried elbow deep in Eastern ethnology, and receive heaps of letters from all kinds of Eastern sages, but from none whose acquaintance I hold more dear than the famous Troglodyte of Devonshire, whose enthusiasm first, I believe, stirred me to think of these subjects.   Will you send me your photograph to add to my so-called menagerie? "I expect to have a whole posse of geological hammers on my

* Now Sir Henry Howorth, M.P., K.C.I.E., F.R.S., etc.

head before I have done; but I mean to go on, for no chickens are hatched until some shell is broken, and if mine prove addled, well, the sitting will not have been altogether thrown away, and you, who used to love fighting, will forgive me.

"May you live for ever ; and if any chance brings you this way, come and see me. I am afraid I shall not be at Southport; a congress of Eastern people at Leyden will have greater attractions for a Mongol like me. Many thanks for the note about the Lemming, which I will take care shall be used."

The following letter from Pengelly is in reply to another from Mr. Howorth, which is unfortunately missing :—

Pengelly to H. H. Howorth.

"Torquay, July 9, 1883.

"Thank you for yours of the 6th inst. I read Dawkins' letter in the *Geo. Mag.* for July, and had no doubt that you would reply. When you say, ' There are no Scotch caves,' I presume you mean none that have yielded remains of mammoth. The *Proc.* Society of Antiquarians of Scotland (vol. x., 1875) contains a Paper, by Messrs. Corrie, Bruce-Clarke, and Hunt, descriptive of a cave they explored in Kirkcudbrightshire. They begin with a long notice of caves previously explored near Montrose, at Wemyss, near North Berwick, in Banffshire, at Oban, and at Duntroon, in Argyleshire. None of them appear to have any bearing on your question.

"The following passage occurs in Leith Adam's British Fossil Elephants (*Pal. Soc.*, p. 174): 'I can now have no hesitation in admitting the Mammoth among the pre-Glacial Mammals of the British Isles.' I think Mr. Newton takes this view in his ' Vertebrata of the Forest Bed.'

"Here's the photo, such as it is. . . . I am sorry you are not to be at Southport."

It was in the summer of this year that Professor Huxley was elected President of the Royal Society, and Pengelly, who greatly admired his splendid services to science, and also enjoyed his personal friendship, wrote warm congratulations on the occasion. The following extract from a letter in response shows how much the Professor appreciated the pleasure which the appointment gave to his large circle of friends :—

Professor Huxley to Pengelly.

"July, 1883.

"I am a very bad correspondent, but not so bad as to think of leaving a kind letter like yours without acknowledgment. . . . I think the best part of the business is the multitude of kind expressions which have reached me in consequence of it."

Later in July Pengelly, according to his invariable custom, attended the meeting of the Devonshire Association, which was held this year at Exmouth, under the Presidency of the well-known historian, Dr. Merivale, Dean of Ely.

It will be readily understood that Pengelly, in common with most men whose scientific work has attracted general attention, was continually asked to furnish a sketch of his life and labours for periodical publications and biographical notices ; nor did he escape frequent applications for a conference from "interviewers." He had, however, the strongest objection to say or write anything that might savour of self-seeking notoriety or advertisement, and his replies, though always courteous, were sufficiently decided to stay further correspondence.   The following may be taken as an example of the numerous letters of a similar kind he had to write :—

"Lamorna, Torquay.

"I beg to acknowledge receipt of your kind letter and to thank you, as well as the Editor of ——, for your gratifying proposal.   I can only say in reply that it has always appeared to me undesirable to print a biographical sketch of a living person, and undesirable that any one should write his own biography.

"I trust you will not think me churlish in abiding by the aforesaid opinions."

CHAPTER XVIII.

MISCELLANEOUS WORK.

SEPTEMBER, 1883, TO OCTOBER, 1887.

IN September, 1883, Pengelly, having been elected President of the Anthropological Department of the British Association at Southport, took for the subject of his address, "The Bone Caves of Devonshire." * He had lately devoted much of his time to the work of distributing duplicate specimens of the fossils found during the excavations at Kent's Hole amongst various museums, and his next letter refers to some of his work, before leaving home.

Pengelly to his youngest daughter, Hester.

"Lamorna, Torquay, September, 1883.

". . . I trust you may have a safe and pleasant journey—that the Watsons will be most kind, I am sure. Please time your journey down from Scotland † so as to reach Southport on the 18th as early as you can. . . . I was hard at work all last week, as indeed for some time before, arranging Kent's Cavern specimens for exhibition in our Museum; almost as fast as I arrange them Mr. Else ‡ fastens them in their places. I am anxious to complete the arranging before leaving for Southport, so that Else may complete his part by the time I return, if all be well. We shall then be able to get the room ready for the lectures. Else works capitally; but it will tax him to the uttermost to get ready in time. I had quite a foretaste of the British Association yesterday. The post brought me a letter from Bonney about my address. Also a letter from Spence Bate, to the effect that he was not going to Southport, but intended to attend the Canada Meeting next year; he wishes to go as some sort of official.

* See Chapter VII.

† His daughter was for the first time visiting the Western Highlands with Sir James and Miss Watson.

‡ Mr. Else, the Curator of the Torquay Natural History Society, who for many years was invaluable in carrying out all the arrangements at the Museum, in a most efficient manner.

" While at the Museum, two youths, sons of Professor Balfour Stewart, called, bringing cards of introduction from their father and Boyd Dawkins. They had scarcely sat down, when Mr. Francis Galton,* whom you no doubt remember, called on me, and I did what was civil to the trio, and dismissed them. Galton and his wife are in lodgings here. Next came Mr. George Griffith (whom you also remember), his wife and some friends, and once more I had to be civil. . . . Sunday. About 1.45 I started for Oddicombe beach, and walked thence under the cliff to Babbacombe, and then home. My object being to see whether the Teign Naturalist Field Club, which I am to conduct on Tuesday, all being well, would be prevented by the tide from getting along under the cliff. The result was ' they will not.'

" I got home just in time to enter the door with J. E. Lee,† and our old friend, Professor Roemer of Breslau. The Professor with his Professoress, is on a visit to Mr. Lee. They all intend to go to Southport."

Pengelly to his daughter Hester.

" Lamorna, Torquay, October, 1883.

" Your letter arrived yesterday, and I may safely say it was welcome. I have never seen Whalley Abbey, but Ingleborough Cave I have seen. . . . You no doubt remember that in my Address ‡ I stated that no trace of hyæna had been found in the Forest Bed of Cromer. Since my return Mrs. Colman of Norwich, wife of the M.P. of that city, has written me stating that hyænas' teeth, now in her possession, were found recently in the Forest Bed, and are to be figured and described in the *Geological Magazine* shortly.

" On Sunday, Mr. —— preached on the following lines—

<blockquote>
' God leads to joy through suffering,
To quietness through strife,
Through yielding unto conquest,
Through death to endless life.'
</blockquote>

Who is the author? The preacher spoke well and at some length, professedly by way of exposition; but, like many expositors, he found more in the lines than the author intended probably.

" Did I tell you that my old friend and co-worker, Professor Heer of Zurich, was dead? I saw by the journals last night that Barrande is dead. I will tell you who and what he was when you return, if you wish."

In the following summer a party of excursionists belonging to the " Geologists' Association " of London visited Devonshire, making Plymouth their head-quarters, and Pengelly was asked to arrange a geological day's excursion for them at Torquay.

---

* Francis Galton, D.C.L., F.R.S., etc.
† John Edward Lee, F.S.A., F.G.S. Author of " Isca Silurum." Translator of Dr. F. Keller's " Lake Dwellings."
‡ Delivered at Southport to the Anthropological Department of the British Association.

Pengelly to W. H. Huddlestone, F.G.S.

" Lamorna, Torquay, May 27, 1884.

" Your letter of the 24th duly arrived yesterday. I know of nothing at present to render 21st July or 4th August an unsuitable day. It will be high water about 4.45 on each date, and as the party will no doubt travel by the train leaving Plymouth at 8.35, and due here at 10.6, that will suit fairly, not perfectly well. The following is my programme :— I meet you at Torquay Station, and conduct you along the coast to Hope's Nose—the northern horn of Torquay—pointing out the Submerged Forest on Torre Abbey Sands, the place of junction of the Trias and the Devonian Limestone, the contortions in the Torquay Limestone, the Slaty Cleavage at Meadfoot, the Raised Beach at Hope's Nose, and the contorted and Cleaved Limestone near it. This will be quite as much as we can accomplish, if we proceed on foot ; but the best plan, on every account, would be to take boats at Torquay, and to land at points of great interest (not otherwise accessible) on the way to Hope's Nose. In this case we might be able to reach the fine junction of the Trias and Devonian in Babbacombe Bay, touching, perhaps, at the Trap of the Black Head on our way. I will inform Mr. Champernowne of my proposed programme, but it will not in all probability clash with his. A month of hard work would give but a superficial acquaintance with the geology between the Teign and the Dart. . . ."

It was about this time that Pengelly was introduced to Mr. F. S. Ellis,* who had lately come to reside in the neighbourhood of Torquay. The acquaintance soon ripened into friendship, and was a source of great pleasure to them both. Mr. Ellis, writing after Pengelly's death, says : " His was one of those wonderful personalities towards which one feels at once attracted, and with which one is more charmed by recurring intercourse. Alas ! that such men must share the common lot ; but his memory will sweetly live while one person survives who knew him."

Pengelly attended all the meetings of the British Association, from 1856 to 1889 inclusive, with the exception of that held at Montreal in 1884. From the time when the visit to Canada was first mooted, he had strenuously opposed the suggestion, not only because of the increased expense to the members, but mainly because he thought it impossible for many of the leading scientists to spare the time requisite for such an expedition. Notwithstanding this protest it was suggested by some people, that, being such a regular attendant, he would certainly be seen at the meeting. Any one entertaining such an idea for a moment

---

* F. S. Ellis, author of the "Shelley Concordance," and editor of the Chaucer and numerous other books for the Kelmscott Press.

must have understood his character very little, for he was the last man in the world to change his mind, without good and sufficient cause. The time he might, perhaps, have spared, and the expense was not an objection (for his wife's private means had now become sufficiently ample to save him all anxiety on the score of cost), but his decision remained unaltered. There is abundant evidence, in letters he received from eminent members of the Association, to prove that he was by no means isolated in his opinion on this matter.

This summer Pengelly, accompanied by his family, made a long tour in Cornwall.

The following letter, received from a medical friend who shared his antiquarian tastes, and love of Cornwall, greatly pleased Pengelly :—

"Auray, South Brittany, Sunday, June 15, 1884.

"I have been thinking of you so much to-day, and wishing so much you were with me as counsellor, companion, and friend, that I have determined to have my say to you on paper.

"On this bright summer's day, with a cool wind, I started for Carnac, and the country all there about, to see the Megaliths and the Cromlechs, and I have seen so many that I am *blasé* with them. It is a grand sight. I have been in the land of the great forgotten, I have been in the tombs of the mighty dead, I have moralized among avenues of Megaliths that in the distance seem coming over the hills like a pack of hounds in full cry, and I have spent two hours in small local museums which have made me take in learning by the pores, and I have longed for you. The French Government (vive la République) protect their historic monuments. They have set up a great number of the stones on their bases again, they have run a narrow trench each side of the avenues, and have put up what look like milestones, and thereon inscribed 'propriété de l'état,' with a caution against mischief-makers. Every Cromlech is protected by a light rail or hurdle with the same stone, and at the junction of the roads are iron finger-posts directing the traveller where to go and what to see. 'They manage these things better in France,' says Yorick, in the 'Sentimental Journey,' and they do.

"That most glorious of all mediæval monuments, St. Michael's Mount, visited by me last Wednesday, is also protected and very *well* restored by the Government.

"There are three sets of monuments here : tumuli, dolmens, and menhirs. In the tumuli are found human remains, pottery, glass beads, gold collars and bracelets, bronze implements. In the dolmens, parts of human skeletons, in one case a complete skeleton lying on his side, which I have seen, and, with or without these remains, flint implements, beautifully shaped barbed arrow heads, a few with some polished neolithic ornaments, and crystals or crystal pebbles and mother-of-pearl shells, and chalcedony, pierced for ornaments, but underneath the megalithic menhirs nothing is found but palæolithic chipped spear heads, etc., of the usual type. I took a long time questioning the curator of a museum on this point, and I touched each article separately and said menhir, tumulus, and so on to the end, and then he told me that no polished tool had ever been found under a menhir, nothing but rough chipped flints. I questioned him particularly as to whether it was only a chance find, whether it were only one found here and there, but he said positively that they were found in numbers under the few that had been undermined, and he showed me a drawing to corroborate his statement. Now, if this be so, it is a most remarkable fact, because it connects the erection of these menhirs with the old flint chippers, as much as the money put under the foundation stone of a modern building connects the building with its modern founders.

"Brittany is French Cornwall. It is Cornwall all over. I cannot imagine at times I am out of England. The rail is like the Cornish rail—runs along the tops of hills, then suddenly comes upon a deep valley and you shoot over it on a lofty viaduct—one a hundred and sixty feet high. Then a town I was at (Concarnea) yesterday, is supported on, and stinks of, pilchards. Well, I could stand all that. If God sends them pilchards, and they are nasty enough to eat them, it is no sin; but when I found they had stolen a Cornish saint and rechristened him, I was angry. Why, in the church at Landerneau, there is an enormous painting of an old saint crossing to Brittany on a big flat stone pushed by angels. Now *we* know that it was St. Piran who came to Cornwall, from Ireland, on a grindstone, and these pirates have boned the idea and the credit."

From Falmouth Mrs. Pengelly wrote to her sister :—

"*August* 13, 1884.— . . . We are much enjoying ourselves, the sea is splendid and the harbour very fine. On our way here we visited Lostwithiel, an interesting quaint old town, with an exquisite lantern spire on the church; from there we walked to Restormel Castle, a ruin, more beautiful though not so extensive as Berry Pomeroy. We then went on to Truro, where we paid a visit to the new Cathedral, and were astonished to find it so far advanced. It will be very beautiful when the tower is finished. At twelve next day we went to the Polytechnic Hall, and soon met Anna Maria Fox, who at once engaged us to go to Pengerrick in the afternoon. It was so nice to see her again; she starts for Canada to-morrow to attend the British Association. The Bolithos, and many others we met, all seemed delighted to see William down in his native county, and he was speedily pounced upon to second the vote of thanks to Lord Mount Edgcumbe for laying the foundation stone of the new Observatory.

"We all attended the ceremony in the afternoon. Archdeacon Phillpotts read a suitable prayer; he is very like his father the old bishop. William spoke after Mr. T. Bolitho. We then started for Pengerrick; there were only a few invited (as Anna Maria Fox was starting so soon). Mrs. Warrington Smyth and a few others. The place, as you will imagine, looked delightful, the trees and shrubs magnificent; many subtropical. Palms in abundance, though not large. A Tree-fern seemed most flourishing, as well as a Camphor tree, and some rare specimens from California and other warm countries. The birds would have delighted you. In the evening we returned to see a torchlight procession of boats round the harbour. The Polytechnic Exhibition was a very good one—especially the pictures. Those of Napier Hemy (who lives here) were decidedly interesting."

On returning home at the end of August, Pengelly received a letter from his friend Dr. Percy, Professor of Metallurgy, introducing Mr. Woolner, the sculptor and poet, who had long wished to make his acquaintance. Mr. Woolner had prolonged his stay at Torquay that he might be able to visit Kent's Cavern under such able guidance. Immediately after reaching London he sent Pengelly a copy of his poem, " Silenus," with a letter of hearty thanks expressing the extreme interest he had found in witnessing the evidences of pre-historic life under such favourable circumstances.

Later in the autumn Sir Henry Thompson, the eminent surgeon, visited Devonshire, and was most enthusiastic in his appreciation of the wonders of Kent's Cavern and the collection of specimens disinterred from it, as arranged in the Museum of the Natural History Society. He wrote of his visit to the Cavern as "one of the most delightful treats ever enjoyed," and was very anxious to induce Pengelly to lecture once more at the Royal Institution. He was, however, unable to accede to the request, and wrote as follows to Sir William Bowman :—

Pengelly to Sir William Bowman.

" Torquay, November 26, 1884.

" Thank you very much for your kind proposal that I should give two lectures on Kent's Cavern at the Royal Institution next February. I have thought the matter over, and have come to the conclusion that the topic has become a little stale.

" Most people are satisfied that Man's advent was not later than Pleistocene times, and are now considering whether it was not earlier ; and on this part of the question I have little or nothing to say.

" Moreover, all the Cavern specimens having been distributed to various museums, I have nothing whatever to *show* an audience.

" On the whole, therefore, I feel under the necessity of declining your kind proposal.

" While recently on a visit here, Sir Henry Thompson went to the Cavern, and to the Museum of the Torquay Natural History Society, with me, and was greatly interested ; but unfortunately I cannot take the Cavern, or the Museum into your lecture theatre."

T

He had now given up all professional work, even the teaching for which he had so great a love and so remarkable an aptitude. It has already been mentioned that he had a great power of winning the affection of those he taught, and an old pupil, the well-known novelist "Q" (A. T. Quiller Couch), who attended the lectures he gave some years before at Newton College, writes thus appreciatively :—

"Your father's visits to Newton are among the pleasantest recollections of my school life there, and I think he was particularly kind to me for the sake of my ' haveage.' I know he once tried to persuade the Head Master (Mr. Warner) to let me have a whole holiday with him in Kent's Cavern—unluckily without success. But what kindness on the part of such a man, towards an urchin of twelve !

"He was, I think, the most inspiriting lecturer I have ever met. He simply compelled one to attend. But it is rather as a friend that— with all the difference of years—I presume to remember him."

His last pupil was the present writer.

The year 1885 was mainly occupied by miscellaneous work. Amongst the visitors of note to Torquay during the winter was the traveller, Mr. im Thurm.

Mrs. Pengelly to her Sister.

"Lamorna, Torquay, December 29, 1885.

" . . . The traveller you ask about who is staying here, is Mr. im Thurm, of British Guiana, the first explorer who has ever ascended the very remarkable mountain there, called Roraima. He found some very curious plants on his expedition, and showed us some striking photographs of the vegetation there. William has been greatly interested by his descriptions of the natives and their customs, and hopes to get him to give a lecture on them. Mr. and Miss im Thurm brought home from British Guiana a squirrel monkey, which they have given to the Zoological Society of London. He told us that when he went there the other day it twined round him most affectionately, though he had never taken much notice of it, as it belonged to his sister ; this certainly shows that it had a wonderful memory. Poor Sir Walter Medhurst, whom we had seen so much of since he came to live here lately, was seized with a most alarming attack on Wednesday, after taking a cold bath, and died a few days afterwards, to our great regret. Did I tell you that he had been a great deal in China, and gave us an excellent lecture on 'The Chinaman at home,' only a month ago ? He had promised us another on Japan. We have quite a good course of lectures coming on. Our friend, Lady Low, takes a great deal of interest in them, and is a most wonderful woman for her age. She has a great knowledge of Indian affairs, her husband, Sir John Low, having been a very experienced soldier. Her brother, Sir Richmond Shakespeare, was the young officer who so bravely rescued the English prisoners from the Afghans in 1842. She has given William an account her brother wrote of one of his earlier expeditions, which quite delighted him. She often tells us amusing tales about Thackeray, who was her first cousin. . . ."

Early in the year 1886 Pengelly received a visit from a deputation of the Falmouth Polytechnic, asking him to become President in succession to Lord Mount Edgcumbe. This he was obliged to decline, though it would have been a great satisfaction to him to be so closely connected with one of the Associations of his native county.

The winter was a bitterly cold one, even in Devonshire. In February Principal Tulloch died at Torquay, where he had been staying for some time. Pengelly was one of the very few people he had been able to see during his illness, and, in common with all who knew him, much regretted his loss.

On the 18th of February, Pengelly went up to London and was presented on the following day with the "Lyell Medal" of the Geological Society. He received many warm congratulations on the occasion, and much enjoyed seeing several of his old colleagues. The President concluded his speech with the following words : " There is a peculiar fitness in the award to you of this medal, as a memorial of the fearless and illustrious author of 'The Principles of Geology' and 'The Antiquity of Man.'" Pengelly, in reply, spoke of the gratification which this award afforded him, especially as it bore the name of an old and well loved friend, with whom he had worked much and earnestly.

Soon after returning he had the pleasure of meeting Sir William Gull, who was paying a short visit at Torquay, and in April his old friends, Sir Joseph and Lady Hooker (who had then left Kew), also stayed at Torquay and came to see him and his family. Later in the month Professor W. G. Adams, who was in the neighbourhood, paid a hasty visit to his fellow Cornishman, when they both enjoyed talking over old times.

This summer the Devonshire Association met at St. Mary Church, an important parish adjoining Torquay. Pengelly, who had long been the Honorary Acting Treasurer, and in other ways intimately associated with the work of the Society, now felt that the time had come when he must relinquish his more active share in connection with it. The prosperity of the

Association bore witness to the soundness of his financial management, for, both in his public and private affairs, he made it a rule never to allow expenditure to exceed income.

. In September he attended the meeting of the British Association at Birmingham, where he read a paper before the Anthropological Section, entitled "A Scrobicularia Bed containing Human Bones at Newton Abbot, Devonshire."

Leaving Birmingham he proceeded to Falmouth to deliver a lecture, whilst his wife and daughters were paying visits, and on Mrs. Pengelly joining him at home wrote thus to his daughter Lydia :—

"*Lamorna, Torquay.*— . . . Your nice chatty letter arrived this morning with the account of your doings and seeings in the Lake district. . . . The Great Chief has duly and safely arrived, and as a matter of course I am dethroned. You will be glad to learn that I bear it beautifully, and am proud to have reason to believe that I am a conspicuous example of humility and resignation. Now don't strike me all of a *Heap* by reminding me of *Uriah*, and thereby play the *Dickens* with me. . . . The upshot of my efforts in the matter of the Natural History Society's lectures, is that I shall have to give three certainly— four most probably. One of the results of inviting other men to lecture, is that other men ask me to lecture. Mr. Statham has just asked me to lecture at and for his Parish Guild, and I have consented. . . ."

In November Pengelly went to London that he might be present at the annual dinner of the Royal Society, and attend a meeting of the Anthropological Institute, of which he was now a member.

In March, 1887, his valued friend Canon Brownlow * gave two very interesting lectures at the Torquay Museum, on "Serfdom," a question to which he had devoted much attention. His volume on "Slavery and Serfdom in Europe," published in 1892, is dedicated to Pengelly.

During the same session Pengelly gave a Lecture at the Museum, entitled "An old Man and Woman," which was a graphic account of some pre-historic human remains found near Newton. The discourse was successful in a marked degree in arousing attention, and was attended by many old friends from a distance.

Pengelly entertained the strongest regard for Professor Tyndall, whom he esteemed second only to Faraday as a lecturer.

* Now Roman Catholic Bishop of Clifton.

Pengelly to Dr. Brushfield.

"Lamorna, Torquay, June 26, 1887.

"I beg to say, in reply to your interesting letter of 25th, that it is my intention to attend the Plympton Meeting. . . . I shall go alone, as my wife and daughters are going to Switzerland, if all be well. I have declined an invitation to a private house at Plympton, and shall put up at the 'George Hotel' there, if I can be taken in. I shall probably return home on Thursday morning. I propose going to London to-morrow to assist at the 'Tyndall dinner' on Wednesday, the 29th, and to return home on the 30th, when I hope to write the Local Secretary at Plympton about the Hotel. I hope it can be managed for us to be together."

Most unfortunately Pengelly took a severe cold at the Plympton meeting. His family, who had just returned from Switzerland, were greatly concerned at the state of his health, and feared that he would not be able to attend the British Association that year. By the end of August, however, he was sufficiently recovered to be present at Manchester. The meeting was an unusually large one, and he was so warmly welcomed by his colleagues, that he many times expressed the pleasure he felt that he had not spared himself the exertion of coming. He was repaid by meeting some friends whom, alas! he was destined to look upon no more, amongst them being Dr. Asa Gray, who died the following January, and Professor John Couch Adams, the astronomer.

Pengelly read a paper on "Recent Researches in Bench Cavern, Brixham, Devon," before Section "C," and again another day before the Anthropological Section, which was presided over this year by Professor Sayce, of Oxford. It was at this meeting that he made the acquaintance of Dr. Moorhouse, Bishop of Manchester, as well as that of the Roman Catholic Bishop of Salford, now Cardinal Vaughan. Dr. Moorhouse and Pengelly were much amused at their non-success in hearing one another the geologist having spent part of Sunday in fruitless efforts to find the cathedral, which he only reached after the conclusion of the bishop's sermon, whilst the latter was unable to find the room where Pengelly was reading his Paper on Monday morning.

The next letter gives evidence of his unremitting labour as Honorary Secretary of the Torquay Natural History Society.

Pengelly to his daughter Lydia.

" *Lamorna, Torquay, October* 6, 1887.— . . . Your very acceptable letter of the 4th inst. duly arrived yesterday. The reopening of the College Hall must have been an interesting occasion. I have now completed cataloguing the books from Mr. Lee's Library* (and the boy has fair copyized my work), but there is still a host of pamphlets bound up in, I think, seventeen vols., and I am now at work on them. Each volume contains on an average twenty pamphlets, I opine, so the cataloguing work still before me is by no means slight. Ah! well! 'twill all rub out when it's dry. You remember, no doubt, that our friend Mr. Ellis informed the Shelley world, through the *Athenæum*, that there was in Mr. Lewin Bowring's possession a manuscript copy of Shelley's poem, 'The Mask of Anarchy'—in other words, the 'Peterloo Massacre at Manchester'—and that the copy differed in sundry places from the printed copy of the said poem. Mr. Lewin Bowring called on me at the Museum on Monday last, and told me that he parted with the MS. to a member of the Shelley Society, and that the Society had printed a fac-simile 'of what had been his MS.,' with an 'Introduction' by H. Buxton Forman. Moreover, he said that six copies had been sent to him, and as he only needed one, he had brought one for the Natural History Society, and one for me if I would accept it. Of course I was 'only too happy,' and, to tell the truth, felt it to be a pretty compliment. You and Hettie may now quarrel as to which of you shall read it first when you and the book are under the same roof. Your mother has finished the translation of the Paper on the Belgian Cavern, and I began to fair copy it last night. . . ."

* Left to the Library of the Torquay Nat. Hist. Soc.

CHAPTER XIX.

1888 TO 1894.

DR. BRUSHFIELD, Dr. Samuel Smiles and his wife, and Professor and Mrs. MaxMüller were at Torquay in the spring. The Professor went over the Museum there with Pengelly, also paying him a very pleasant visit at his own house. He was glad of the opportunity of renewing his acquaintance with Mrs. MaxMüller, who had been one of his favourite pupils in former days.

About the same time the celebrated pianist, Charles Halle, accompanied by Madame Norman Neruda, gave one of their concerts at Torquay, staying there over the Sunday, when Pengelly and some of his family met them. Pengelly much enjoyed making the acquaintance of these accomplished interpreters of the works of the great composers. He had always taken great pleasure in the society of musicians, and loved music. After attending the splendid performance of the "Elijah" at the close of the Birmingham meeting of the British Association, he exclaimed that he would rather have missed the reading of any paper during the meeting, than failed to hear the Oratorio.

Mrs. Pengelly to her Sister.

" *Lamorna, Torquay, March,* 1888.— . . . Dr. Brushfield was here again lately. William was very glad to see him and talk over various literary matters; he gave us a very good lecture on 'Obsolete Punishments' at the Museum. Mr. Stebbing has given us a most entertaining lecture on the 'Shrimp.' He and Mrs. Stebbing seemed to enjoy meeting their old friends again very much. We lunched with them at Mr. Audus Clark's during their visit, and they came to us to meet Sir Jacob and Miss Behrens, the Watsons, Miss Hughes, who is now here from St. Asaph, and one or two others.

"On Wednesday afternoon we went to the Behrens', to meet Dr. Samuel Smiles [*] and his wife. They are both delightful, so easy, that we became friends at once. They are coming to us to-morrow. We find they know the family of William's old friend Robert Chambers very intimately. . . ."

During the Easter Vacation of 1888, Professor McKenny Hughes, of Cambridge, stayed a week or two at Torquay, accompanied by several members of his Class, who were all eager to see some of the geological features of the district under Pengelly's guidance. Amongst other expeditions he took them to the Brixham and Kent's Cavern, and was much pleased to see them at his own house on Sunday afternoons, and also in the evenings after their long "Field Days," when they greatly enjoyed showing their "finds" to the veteran geologist, whose enthusiasm for his favourite science remained as keen as ever. The advice which he had given to a Manchester audience in 1872, he still continued to impress on all young workers.

"Be careful in scientific inquiries that you get a sufficient number of perfectly trustworthy facts, that you interpret them with the aid of a vigorous logic, that on suitable occasions you have courage enough to avow your convictions, and don't be impatient or annoyed if your friends don't receive all your conclusions, or even if they call you hard names."

Though still fairly vigorous, he was beginning to feel the necessity of taking a less active part in scientific matters, than he had been accustomed to do for many years past.

Pengelly to Dr. Brushfield.

"Lamorna, Torquay, July 2, 1888.

"Thank you very much for your nice chatty letter of the 25th ult. I hope to read in due course your paper on Andrew Brice. I am taking things easy this year, having sent nothing to the Devonshire Association, and have no thought of writing anything for the British. . . . I congratulate you on the well-deserved compliment paid you by the Society of Antiquaries. Having been long an antiquarian *student*, may you live to be an antiquarian *study*. . . . I went to Plymouth last Saturday to assist at the opening of the Marine Biological Laboratory, and, as our American cousins say, 'had a good time.' Our host on the occasion was Sir James Clark Lawrence, Prime Warden of the Fishmongers' Company. . . . He came out as one of the brickiest of bricks. He fed us well, and spoke to us in excellent terms and manner. May his shadow never grow less, that is in this latitude."

* Author of "Self Help," "The Life of George Stephenson," etc.

In August Pengelly started with his family for Matlock Bank, with the object of enjoying a thorough change and rest before attending the British Association at Bath in September.   During the meeting he went with Professor Sayce, and some other members, on an excursion to see the remains at Stanton Drew. Unfortunately one or two of the party were missing when the time came for the return drive; this caused so much delay, and the evening became so bitterly cold, that Pengelly, Professor Sayce, Mr. Ussher, and some ladies returned to Bath by train.   The result of this exposure was a very severe chill, which prevented Pengelly from taking any further part in the meeting.

Professor Sayce to Mrs. Pengelly.

"Bath, September 14, 1888.

"I am very sorry that I am not able to come to you this afternoon, as I have followed Mr. Pengelly's example, and am laid up with a severe cold . . . and to-day I am confined to the house.   A British Association cold seems to be worse than any other.   I hope that Mr. Pengelly is recovering by this time."

Pengelly recovered partially from the cold he had taken, and left Bath in time to attend the International Geological Congress in London.   There, though unable to attend all the sittings, he had the pleasure of meeting many foreign geologists of note, including M. Gaudry of Paris, Professor Capellini of Bologna, Baron P. von Richtöfen of Berlin, Professor Stefanescu of Bucharest, and his old friends Professor Otto Torell of Stockholm, Dr. Szabo of Buda-Pesth, and Professor O. C. Marsh from America.

One of the pleasant results of the Congress was an interesting correspondence between himself and Professor Gaudry.   Pengelly often looked back on the meeting with fond regret, as being the last of the many scientific gatherings that he attended with any enjoyment.   His friend Chevalier Dr. Josef Szabo, the eminent geologist and foremost representative of Magyar science, outlived him less than a month, dying on April 10, 1894.

The winter of 1888–9 was one of much suffering to Pengelly, who was troubled with a violent cough.   The rheumatism which had so long affected him also became more painful and acute. Lectures to working men and before the different Parish

Guilds, etc., which it had been such a pleasure to him to deliver, had to be abandoned, and it was only once again that his voice was heard in public.   His final Lecture, entitled " Archæological Discoveries at Hele," was given on April 22, 1889, before the Torquay Natural History Society, for which he had worked so long, so ardently, and so unremittingly, without any other remuneration than the pleasure he found in being of service to those around him.

The Rev. T. R. R. Stebbing was a candidate this year for Fellowship of the Royal Society, and has since been elected.

Pengelly to the Rev. T. R. R. Stebbing.

" Lamorna, Torquay, 8.30 p.m., February 9, 1889.

" I am glad to find your visit to Woodward* was a success ; but then I knew it would be, for, so far as my knowledge of him goes— now of many years' standing—he has never done an unkind thing, nor declined to do a kind one when in his power. . . .

" I always intended that my name should be the last in the list of signatories.

" Please excuse brevity as I am rather busy, but I will write Woodward at once."

As the summer advanced Pengelly enjoyed spending a day with his old friend, Mr. William Vicary, at Exeter ; his health appeared to improve slightly, and his letters show that he still retained much of his old vivacity.

Pengelly to his Wife.

" Lamorna, Torquay, June 10, 1889.

" . . . Yesterday was wet, so Lydia and I stayed at home all day, and had the fires lighted.   To-day is also wettish, but I was able to go to the Museum as usual.   At three I started for the Gladstone Meeting, when I found the Hall very nearly full, but I had a very good seat on the platform.   Gladstone and wife arrived about 3.40.   He spoke for seventy-five minutes, as he only can speak ; he was very eloquent and very consecutive, and very wonderful, and if I didn't know that wives are never proud of their husbands, Mrs. Gladstone must be very proud of him.   Mr. Morton Spark was Chairman, and did his work modestly and well.   Coming out was a serious job, and made me glad that I had no lady with me.   The Hall was densely packed, and the means of exit being so atrocious I was really thankful Lydia had been unable to accompany me. . . ."

* Henry Woodward, LL.D.

Pengelly to his youngest daughter, Hester.

"Lamorna, Torquay, July, 1889.

"Whilst I received your kind interesting letter this morning with great pleasure, I could not but feel that I had not recently written you, and had not earned the pleasure your letter gave me. You know I am always busy when preparing for a Monthly Meeting of the Natural History Society, as was the case this week. Moreover the preparation was more than usually heavy, on account of G. H. White's handsome bequest. The meeting passed off satisfactorily, but my cough was very troublesome after I got to bed that night. . . . Being Sunday I refrained from kicking my best hat all the way down Union Street, by way of expressing my joy on finding that we may look for you this week. But as there is no law against it, I did say ' Hurrah,' and I'll say it again.

"Your Mater and Pater took luncheon at Mrs. Ormerod's the other day, and had a most pleasant time. Amongst the guests were Mrs. and Miss Harley, wife and daughter of my old mathematical British Association friend, Dr. Harley. I am glad that you and Miss Langworthy were so much pleased with your day at Waltham Abbey. All your London visits seem to have been, as we expected, most pleasant. A green lizard was seen again on the Rock-Walk close to the spot where it, or one of its relatives, was seen years ago. You will have heard that these lizards are the descendants of some brought from Jersey more than forty years ago, and placed on Waldon Hill as an experiment, and that ever and anon a representative of them shows itself. Now don't you rush to the conclusion that in this we have an instance of Acclimatization, for it is nothing of the kind. Acclimatization—or, as the word is now often written, Acclimatation—understood scientifically, denotes *that* treatment which (if such a thing be possible) will change the character of organisms to such an extent as to enable them to live where previously they could not live. It is clear that no such change has occurred in, or was required in, the Torquay green lizards.

"Monkeys, left to themselves, would die in England; but if by bringing a pair from Gibraltar to the Biscay shores it were found they throve there, and fifty years after a pair descended from them were brought to Brittany or the Scilly Isles, and they throve there ; and fifty years after that a pair descended from *them* were taken to Torquay and they throve, we should have a case of Acclimatation. Do you follow ?"

At the beginning of August he started with his wife and daughters for a long change at Scarborough, taking the journey by easy stages. The bracing air of the north, however, did him little good, and he made no progress towards recovery. In September he went to Newcastle, hoping to attend the British Association, but was much fatigued by the meeting, and could take but little part in the proceedings. Never again was his well-known figure to be welcomed by his brother scientists. The winter at Torquay was enlivened by the visits of old friends; but he was now only able to take short walks and a few drives, generally to the Museum, and was compelled to lead almost entirely the life of an invalid.

In the spring of 1890, the state of his health compelled him to resign the Honorary Secretaryship of the Torquay Natural History Society, the last scientific office which he had held. Soon after his retirement he was presented, at his residence, with an illuminated address by a few of his old friends, expressing deep regret at his resignation.

The following letter, in which Pengelly congratulates Mr. Isaac Roberts upon his election as a Fellow of the Royal Society, is, I believe, the last he ever wrote :—

Pengelly to Isaac Roberts, F.R.S.

"Lamorna, Torquay, May 5, 1890.

". . . As I see and read various scientific journals, I was acquainted with the general character of your remarkable astronomical discoveries as reported by the Astronomical Society from time to time; when your most valuable and acceptable present of six of your photographs reached me, I was more than delighted. Thank you many thousand times. As I feel that single-handed I cannot thank you enough, I have asked my wife and daughters to assist in the good work, and they have most cordially responded.

"I am delighted to see that the Council of the Royal Society have placed you among the fifteen who are to have the right to affix F.R.S. to their names. (Sir F. Bramwell says the letters stand for 'Fees raised suddenly.') Never were laurels more richly earned than in your case.

"And now, my very dear friend, I must conclude, as my fingers and wrist are getting painfully angry."

Reading still continued to be his greatest pleasure, and, though during the winter his drives had to be abandoned, the long days were cheered for the invalid by visits from his many friends. Amongst those who frequently came to see him were the Rev. E. P. Gregg, Mr. F. S. Ellis, and General Chamberlayne, whose kindness all through his illness was, as he expressed it, "like that of a brother."

In the spring of 1891 Dr. Samuel Smiles was again at Torquay, but as he unfortunately took cold there, he was unable to visit Pengelly, to whom he wrote more than once during his stay.

Dr. Smiles to Pengelly.

"9, Beacon Terrace, Torquay, February 25, 1891.

"I thank you very much for the volumes you have sent me through Miss Pengelly ; and I accept the one inscribed by you to myself with great pleasure.

"Some years ago I occupied myself a good deal, principally for pleasure, in writing out an account of the origin of the various races of men who occupy this country. I went to Friesland, the North Frisian Islands (from which, no doubt, the Anglo-Saxons came), Jutland, the Danish Islands, Sweden, and Norway, as far as Trondhjem.

"The first people of all, however, were the Cave Men, and when I saw that you had been making some extraordinary inquiries as to these pre-historical people, I expressed my desire to my daughter to purchase any treatise you had written on the subject. Now, you have supplied me with as much as I can carry in my head; and I will read your treatises with the greatest pleasure.

"I am sorry that, since I came down here, I have been obliged to keep within doors ; otherwise I would have called and paid my sincere respects to you."

Dr. Smiles to Pengelly.

"9, Beacon Terrace, Torquay, March 20, 1891.

"I return your two volumes, with many thanks. I have read them through, and taken many notes. What labour you must have had in going through all the memoirs on the subject of Kent's Cavern, and unfortunately, you must have martyred yourself in going into that damp hole so often. You are entitled to take rank amongst Dr. Brewster's Martyrs to Science.

"I wish I had been able to see you before I left. But my wife and I have been suffering from very bad colds while here, and we return home on Tuesday morning."

In August, 1891, Pengelly had the pleasure of a short visit from the American geologist, Professor G. F. Wright, of Ohio.

Throughout the year 1892, he continued almost in the same state, though his malady rendered him increasingly infirm. The Meeting of the British Association at Edinburgh interested him greatly, the President being the distinguished geologist, Sir Archibald Geikie, whose address he read with the keenest interest, as well as the reports which his daughters sent him daily of the proceedings at Sections " C " and " H."

An old friend, a daughter of the late Robert Chambers, who came south to see him this year, wrote afterwards to one of his daughters :—

"I am so glad, my dear Hettie, that I had such a pleasant time with you at Torquay, and that I have, and will preserve, a most delightful recollection of my last meeting with the dear gentle philosopher. What an example he was of noble Christian resignation. Laid aside as he was—mentally as strong as ever—only suffering from physical weakness. May his example remain with us."

He was now entirely confined to the house, though able to sit up and be wheeled into another room during the afternoons. The death of his colleague, Mr. Vivian, who had been associated with him in so many scientific undertakings, cast a gloom over the opening of 1893. But the summer was much brightened, as the Devonshire Association met at Torquay, and many of the members visited Pengelly, including Dr. Brushfield (the President), Lady Bowring, the Rev. W. Harpley, Mr. Amery, Mr. Brooking Rowe, Canon Brownlow, and others. It greatly cheered him to see so many of his old friends. In a letter written to Mrs. Pengelly some time afterwards, Lady Bowring says, in reference to this visit :—

"I think much of the years gone by, when my own beloved husband and Mr. Pengelly ever appeared to be so much pleased with each other's companionship. I am so glad I had the pleasure of seeing your invalid last summer, when he kindly received some of the old members of the Devonshire Association for brief interviews. I was gratified to be among the visitors."

Another old friend, whom he had not seen for many years, Mrs. Vaughan, * also paid him a visit this autumn, 1893, accompanied by Dr. and Mrs. Charles Vachell, of Cardiff.

All this time his mind continued as bright as ever. He greatly enjoyed reading the recently published "Letters of Dr. Asa Gray," the American botanist, and on March 6th, 1894, saw for the last time his old friend Prebendary Wolfe. On the day following he felt feverish and stayed in bed, and the progress of the attack was very rapid, lasting only ten days. Through this time of suffering, those who nursed him, never heard him say an unkind thing, or utter an impatient word. On the morning of Friday, the 16th of March, he appeared much weaker, but was able to receive brief visits from his friends General Chamberlayne and the Rev. E. P. Gregg. Both the medical men who saw him that day, Dr. Huxley and Dr. Hamilton Cumming, assured his family, that there was no pain, but considered that the case was one of extreme gravity. Towards evening greater

* Wife of the Dean of Llandaff and sister of Dean Stanley.

difficulty of breathing and entire unconsciousness followed, and the struggle with nature continued only a few hours longer. Just before midnight the end came, and he passed peacefully away in the presence of his wife and both his daughters, leaving behind him the memory of one who was able " to bear good fortune meekly ; to suffer evil with constancy ; and through evil or good to maintain truth always."

On the following Thursday the funeral took place, a service being held at the parish church of St. Mary Magdalene, Upton, which was largely attended by people of every shade of religious thought. The hymns sung were, " Jesu, lover of my soul," his favourite hymn, and that commencing, " Now the labourer's task is o'er," as being in this case especially appropriate. The remains of the geologist were laid to rest in the presence of his two surviving daughters and a large company of mourners, with every token of regard, from the poor as well as the rich.

The respect shown to his memory on all sides gave eloquent testimony to the esteem in which an honourable and upright life, well spent in untiring devotion to study and research, was held.

The news of Pengelly's death was received generally with deep and intense feeling. Letters of sympathy from all parts of this country, from the Continent, America, and even distant Australia, reached his family. Many of them are of far too sacred a character to be published, but all bore witness to the strong affection he inspired, by his nobility of character, his fearless love of truth, mingled with profound reverence for all that is held most sacred.

Clergy and laymen of the Established Church, Presbyterians, Members of the Society of Friends, Leaders of the various Nonconformist Bodies, and Roman Catholics agreed with perfect unanimity in their estimate of his simple though firm faith, strong moral sense, kindliness and unselfish devotion to the welfare of others, and freedom from ambition.

Among scientific men his loss was keenly felt, as will be shown by the following extracts :—

Rev. Professor Bonney, LL.D., F.R.S., to Mrs. Pengelly.

" 23, Denning Road, N.W., March 21, 1894.

" I have seen the sad news in the papers, and must write a few lines to say how deeply I sympathize with you and your family in this sorrow.

"All who had the privilege of knowing your late husband must feel as I do, that his departure leaves a gap which cannot be filled.

"Never have I met with a man who united such strong mental powers, and no less strong sense of what was just, true, and right, to such genuine humour and hearty enjoyment of wit. That was the great charm in his personality. He was so kindly and pleasant a companion, and yet so vigorous, mentally, and strong, morally. When he was obliged to cease from coming to the British Association, we all felt the difference his absence made. There was at once a sense of something missing. He came everywhere like a ray of sunshine. I trust his parting from earth was painless and peaceful, and that he fell asleep. From bodily pain he might have suffered but, I feel sure he would be held up in crossing the dark water by the Saviour in whom he had long put his trust. He has left, as a legacy to all his friends, the memory of a well-spent life, and a good example. Though I doubt not that his life on earth must have been a happy one, yet I hope and trust that now he has entered into a more perfect peace, and an unchanging joy."

Sir Archibald Geikie to Mrs. Pengelly.*

"28, Jermyn St., London, S. W., March 31, 1894.

"On my return to London, after an absence of some weeks, I am much grieved to hear of the great loss which has fallen upon you, and I desire to offer you my sincere sympathy. Mr. Pengelly's death has aroused so wide a feeling of regret, that it must be some slight consolation to you to have proofs of how universally he was respected and esteemed. I can remember him and his bright lectures at the British Association for almost as many years as I have attended the meetings.

"His genial, kindly, and helpful nature, and his invariably bright, cheery, and witty talk, marked him out as a man by himself.

"His death must be a very sad blow to you and the family, and I feel deep sympathy for you, and all the more because I know how entirely he deserved to be loved and honoured."

Professor Rupert Jones, F.R.S., F.G.S., to Mrs. Pengelly.

"March 31, 1894.

"We are all very sorry to know of your great loss, and sympathize with you all. I had been asked to give some information about your dear husband's life and work, since I had known him for so long, and had always appreciated and admired his mental and bodily exertions in the pursuit of knowledge—and so successful a pursuit too,— but I requested a younger geologist to undertake the work. . . .

"Mr. Pengelly will be remembered as a good example of a religious man—earnest, persevering, and exact in scientific research, highly esteemed and appreciated in his own generation, especially by his fellow workers, his work having been carried on in pleasant unison with

---

* Director-General of the Geological Surveys of the United Kingdom.

others, and being too good to die away, as has happened with others, and be forgotten for a while until subsequent discoveries had made it important. . . .

"We shall always remember his cheery way and his genial remarks. . . ."

Dr. Munro, F.R.S.E., to Mrs. Pengelly.

"48, Manor Place, Edinburgh, April 3, 1894.

"It is only a few days ago that a pang of regret and sorrow passed through the heart of the scientific world with the death of your husband. Knowing that during his active lifetime he had a wide circle of scientific friends, and that letters of condolence would be pouring in upon you from far and near, I did not think that my slight personal acquaintance with him entitled me to trouble you with formal expressions of sympathy in your sad bereavement. The receipt of a paper containing such an appreciative notice of our late distinguished anthropologist, affords me now a fitting occasion to do so, and to express to you how highly I esteem and value his works. I am much pleased to have this little biographical souvenir of Mr. Pengelly. . . . I trust, however, it is but the prelude to a more extended biography— one that will be worthy of so conspicuous a leader among the founders of the Science of Anthropology."

Rev. Robert Harley, M.A., F.R.S., F.R.A.S., to Miss Hester Pengelly.

"April 2, 1894.

" I heard of the death of your dear father with sincere regret. He and I were admitted to the Royal Society at the same time, namely, in June, 1863 ; the fifteen that year were :—(1) E. W. Cooke, A.R.A. ; (2) W. Crookes ; (3) J. Fergusson ; (4) F. Field ; (5) Rev. R. Harley ; (6) J. R. Hind ; (7) C. W. Merrifield ; (8) Professor D. Oliver ; (9) F. W. Parry ; (10) W. Pengelly ; (11) H. S. Roscoe ; (12) Rev. G. Salmon (now Provost of T.C.D.) ; (13) S. J. A. Salter ; (14) Rev. A. P. Stanley, Dean of Westminster ; (15) Col. F. M. E. Wilmot. Of these, no fewer than seven, namely, 1, 3, 4, 7, 10, 14 and 15, have now passed away.

" As you are aware, I often met your father at the Meetings of the British Association, and he was my guest on the occasion of his coming to lecture before the Lit. and Phil. Soc. of Leicester, when I was President. A charming guest we found him, as full of humour as of scientific knowledge.

" I had no acquaintance with his special subject, but whenever we met we found that we had many points of contact ; for Mr. Pengelly was not a mere geologist. He did not obtrude his theological opinions, but it was easy to perceive that he was a man of true religious character ; this was shown in his exemplary and upright life. Many will mourn his death, and to you and Mrs. Pengelly and your sister, the loss is irreparable. Yet he had attained 'a good old age,' and you could not be altogether unprepared for the event. His was a long, honoured, and useful life. And now at length—

U

> "He's free,
> Leaving his outgrown shell
> By life's unresting sea."

Sir Joseph Lister to Miss Hester Pengelly.*

"12, Park Crescent, Portland Place.

"In years gone by I had often the privilege of intercourse with your father.

"Looking back to those times I recall vividly the impression of his great intellectual powers, his genial benevolence, and his sparkling humour.

"The importance of his contributions to geology and pre-eminently of his acutely planned and perseveringly conducted cave explorations, is recognized throughout the scientific world.

"I cherish his memory with affectionate admiration."

* President of the Royal Society.   Now Lord Lister.

THE SCIENTIFIC WORK OF

WILLIAM PENGELLY, F.R.S.

By Prof. T. G. Bonney, D.Sc., LL.D., F.R.S.

THE scientific work of Pengelly's long and industrious life, though it admits of sub-division, is connected by a common thread. His duties, his occupations, perhaps also his inclination, prevented him from ranging far afield, and his eminently practical mind prompted him to take up the tasks which lay ready to hand. Born in Cornwall, spending his life in Devon, he devoted himself to studying the geology of south-western Britain, so that his scientific papers, almost without exception, deal with topics which either form part of that subject or arise directly from it. These papers, however, may be separated into three groups—each relating to a particular line of work. One describes the investigation of the Bovey Tracey deposits; another is concerned with the examination of caves; and the third includes a number of miscellaneous geological studies of the south-western district. A further link may be found between the first and the second, for though the work was different in character and lay in separate fields, yet it brings into strong relief that spirit of conscientious investigation, and that patience in the accumulation of facts, which especially characterized Pengelly as a man of science. This it was which most impressed those who came to know him, perhaps because it seemed almost abnormal. One could hardly believe it possible that this witty, light-hearted, almost jovial man, could be identical with the patient and unwearied explorer, who had been toiling hour after hour, day after day, in the dark recesses of a cavern, systematically removing the *débris* layer by layer, sifting the earth, collecting the contents, exactly labelling each specimen, recording every detail, leaving nothing to chance and no loophole for mistake, as he accumulated a mass of facts, which would be imperishable, whatever might be the fate of the inductions framed either by himself or by others.

So, in endeavouring to give, in accordance with the request of his nearest relations, some idea of Pengelly's labours and contributions to geological knowledge, I shall follow the order already indicated, and deal successively with these three topics. I take first the work at Bovey Tracey,* which was also the first to be completed of Pengelly's larger tasks, and was thus the earliest demonstration of his peculiar fitness for that exploratory work with which his name will be ever associated.

Bovey Tracey is a small Devonshire town, just at the foot of Dartmoor and rather near its north-eastern end. It stands on the left bank of the Bovey, about two and a half miles above the spot where this river joins the Teign, at the head of an almost level expanse which extends in a south-easterly direction to the distance of about six miles, with a maximum breadth of about four, not reckoning a narrow prolongation of about a mile and a half towards the south. The aspect of this plain suggests that it is the bed of an ancient lake, an idea which is confirmed by an examination of its deposits. To the west and north-west of this flat basin rises the lofty mass of Dartmoor with its granite tors, on the north "the trappean elevations of Hennock," on the north-east and east are the Haldon Hills, capped by outlying patches of cretaceous rocks, and to the south the rolling uplands which separate the district from the sea. The portion of the plain adjacent to the town goes by the name of Bovey Heathfield. It had been long known that the basin contained a series of deposits very different from the solid rocks of the surrounding hills. First came a few feet of coarse gravel, sand, and clay, beneath which—much thicker and considerably more ancient—were other sands and clays, very distinctly stratified, containing saams of lignite. This material for many years past had been worked†; the most important of the excavations being that

---

* The account is condensed from Pengelly's paper, *Philosophical Transactions,* 1862, part ii. (separately published with a prefatory memoir), and *Transactions of the Devonshire Association,* 1862, p. 29.

† At least a century and a half, according to the historical evidence collected in the prefatory memoir already mentioned.

known as the "Coal pit," situated on the "Heathfield," about a mile from the town and from the western margin of the basin.

This, at the time of Pengelly's investigation, was an open work, nearly 1000 feet long, about 340 feet wide, and 100 feet deep, from which subterranean galleries were carried into the mass, sometimes to a considerable distance, one of them being not much less than 400 yards in length. The clay and the lignite were used in the local potteries, the unpleasant odour of the latter material making it unsuitable for domestic purposes.

The pits had attracted some notice prior to 1860, and the deposits had been more than once mentioned in scientific literature ; but though a pine-cone and a few seeds had been found, very little had been ascertained as to the geological age of the lignitic group. On the whole, however, there was a disposition to regard it as later than the Pliocene period. So matters stood in the year just named, when the late Dr. Falconer brought the subject under the notice of Miss (now Baroness) Burdett-Coutts, as one the investigation of which would be a boon to science. She, "with characteristic liberality," provided the means for Pengelly to undertake the task. He secured the services of Mr. H. Keeping, then living in the Isle of Wight, and known as a most experienced collector of fossils, and the proprietor of the works (John Divett, Esq.) promptly and cordially co-operated in carrying out the investigation.

The object was twofold, viz. to obtain a complete and carefully measured section of the beds which formed the Bovey deposit, and to collect as many fossils as possible, in the hope of placing its geological age beyond all question. In order to accomplish both these, " it was decided to make a fresh section ; in fact, to cut out a series of steps, on a large scale, by which to descend the face of the artificial cliff [of the ' coal pit '] from top to bottom." This would disclose the exact nature, thickness, and order of the successive beds, would afford good opportunities for collecting fossils, and would determine the exact position in which each specimen occurred. By this means it was clearly demonstrated that the upper portion—a mass generally a little more than seven feet in thickness—was very different and quite distinct from the remaining and large part, the beds in which did not lie horizontally, but dipped at an angle of $12\frac{1}{2}°$ to a point 35° west of south (magnetic). The excavation was carried to a depth of full 125 feet, down to the bottom of a seam of lignite four feet thick, the "last bed" of the workmen. This, however, does not form the actual base of the Bovey deposit, but is simply the lowest bed which was quarried in the great excavation, and thus was accessible by the method of working which the explorers had adopted.

Mr. Divett stated that he had once sunk a shaft to a depth of about 13 feet below the bottom of the pit, and had cut two tolerable beds of "coal." Moreover, the topmost bed in the excavation was not the highest in the deposit, as was evident from the direction in which the beds were dipping, so that, altogether, Pengelly estimates the whole thickness as exceeding 210 feet. In order to confirm the succession of beds which had been disclosed by the principal section, two others were made, both of them in the south wall of the excavation, one about 460 feet, the other 680 feet eastward from it. The nature of the ground prevented the explorers from carrying either of these cuttings in a satisfactory manner to much more than half the depth of the main section ; but, so far as they went, they failed to reveal any differences of importance. No remains of animals, whether vertebrate or invertebrate, were discovered, excepting a few fragments of the elytra of beetles ; but a considerable number of plants were obtained. These were sent to Professor Oswald Heer, of Zürich, whose report is associated with Pengelly's paper in the *Philosophical Transactions of the Royal Society.*

The upper part, or "Head," in the section of the Bovey Tracey basin, differs much in character from the main or underlying mass, which it covers unconformably. At the top usually come a few inches of peat, which is succeeded by a fine white sand, and this by a mass of sand with clay, rather irregularly interstratified. At the bottom comes a sandy clay, containing rock fragments, which are usually angular and subangular, and are sometimes rather more than a foot in diameter. These evidently have been derived from the neighbouring hills. On the western side of the basin they are mostly granite, or fragments of the rocks through which it has been extruded. On the eastern side, flint and chert from the cretaceous strata, as might be expected, become more common. This "Head" was generally unfossiliferous, but some leaves were found in one of the clays. Among these Professor Heer recognized the willow—perhaps three species, one being *Salix cinerea,* another probably *S. repens,*—

and the dwarf birch *Betula nana*, which still lingers in the Scottish Highlands, and is so common in more arctic regions. These plants fully confirmed the idea which had been suggested by the rock-fragments just mentioned, viz. that the "Head" had been formed when the climate of Devonshire was much colder than it is at the present day, and ought, therefore, to be referred to some part of the so-called glacial epoch. This discovery at Bovey Tracey is especially interesting, because traces of that epoch are so rare in the south-west of England.

The underlying deposit, which, as already stated, is evidently much the older of the two, yielded a far more ample series of plant-remains, which, however, were not to be obtained from all the beds. The mass consisted, for a thickness of about seventy-two feet in descending, of beds of clay, lignite, and sand; the last, though one layer was thicker than any of the other deposits, being the least common. The remainder of the mass was formed of clay and lignite only, and the whole was free from stones. Thirty-one beds of lignite were cut through in the principal section, varying in thickness from a few inches to rather more than six feet. Thirteen of these yielded distinguishable plant-remains, and these were also obtained from two of the beds of clay. From the collection, which was sent to him, Professor Heer determined fifty species; among these were ferns, conifers, figs, cinnamon trees, an oak and a laurel, with vines, andromedas, a bilberry, a gardenia, a water-lily and sundry leguminous plants—the commonest specimens being a fern, *Pecopteris lignitum*,* and a conifer, *Sequoia Couttsiæ*. Professor Heer, as the result of his examination, referred the lignitic group of Bovey Tracey to the Lower Miocene period.† The flora approximated most nearly, in his opinion, to those of Manosque in Provence, and of Salzhausen in the Wetterau, and it had eleven species in common with the Aquitanien of Switzerland. Of late years, however, the correctness of his inference has been disputed, but with the result of adding to rather than taking from the interest of the deposit, for Mr. J. Starkie Gardner, whose investigations into fossil plants of Tertiary age are so well known, regards the Bovey Tracey flora as contemporaneous with that found at Bournemouth—that is to say, of Middle Bagshot age; but he points out that when Professor Heer wrote,

---

* Referred afterwards by Gardner and Ettingshausen to the genus *Osmunda*.

† Or the upper part of the Oligocene period, according to the more modern nomenclature.

"no Eocene floras of any extent had been described and scarcely any material existed for comparison, except what was of Miocene age . . . it appears to me that in the then state of knowledge regarding these Tertiary floras he could hardly avoid classing the Bovey beds with the Miocene." *

We proceed next to the second section of Pengelly's scientific work, the exploration of ossiferous caves. The Brixham cave was discovered in January, 1858, in extending a quarry on the slope of the hill which rises on the southern shore of Torbay above the small fishing town of the same name. The owner of this quarry had carried the excavation far enough to show that the cave had several branches, and that it contained bones, both on the surface of the stalagmite with which the floor was covered and in the red loam below it. Shortly afterwards, Pengelly visited the place in company with Dr. Falconer; and the latter, on his return to London, addressed a letter to the Geological Society, urging them to undertake the exploration of this new and untouched ossiferous cavern. That Society, however, did not possess any funds which were legally applicable to such a purpose; but its Council brought the matter under the notice of the Royal Society (which was more fortunately situated), and received from it a grant of £100 in aid of the exploration. A second grant to the same amount was afterwards made, £50 was given by Miss Burdett-Coutts, and £5 each by Sir J. Kay Shuttleworth and Mr. R. Arthlington. For the purpose of directing the investigation, a committee of the Geological Society was formed, consisting of Dr. Falconer (as Chairman and Secretary), Mr. J. Prestwich, Mr. Pengelly, Prof. A. Ramsay, Sir C. Lyell, Mr. Godwin-Austen, Mr. G. Busk, Dr. Percy, Prof. R. Owen, Rev. R. Everest, Mr. Beccles, and the President and Secretaries of the Society, while a Torquay sub-committee, composed of Mr. Pengelly, Mr. E. Vivian, Mr. Stewart, Colonel Thoresby, Mr. Sheppard, and Mr. Hogg, was deputed by the London committee to co-operate with them and to superintend the actual investigation of the cave. But as the report on the exploration says, "It is to Mr. Pengelly that the Committee are indebted for the active and constant superintendence of the work and for the record of each day's proceedings. [He] in fact, saw personally to the execution of

* "British Eocene Flora," p. 19, *Memoirs of the Palæontographical Society*, vol. xxiii. (1879).

the whole work, noted all the physical features, and arranged and tabulated all the specimens found in the cave, devoting to the investigation an amount of care and time without which it would have been impossible for the London Committee to have obtained the exact record," which was presented and read to the Royal Society.[*]

Windmill Hill, on the north-western angle of which the cave is situated, rises to a height of 175 feet above the ordnance-datum. The entrance of the cave is about 94 feet above this level, or about 66 feet above the floor of the valley in front of it. The rock is an impure, thin-bedded limestone, belonging to the middle part of the Devonian System ; the district around is generally free from all superficial deposits, except occasionally small depressed patches of sand and gravel, which also sometimes fill narrow fissures in the limestone and extend to considerable depths. A red loam also caps most of the limestone hills. A raised beach on a neighbouring hill, about 30 feet above the sea, is an indication that at a comparatively recent epoch the land was at a distinctly lower level than it is at the present day.

The cave is really a group of enlarged fissures, which cross one another roughly at right angles. The principal entrance faces almost magnetic north, and leads into a long gallery, running southwards, on the eastern side of which (near the entrance) is a narrow nearly parallel corridor, some few yards long. Close to the junction of this another gallery extends eastward for about the same distance, and then, in about a dozen yards farther, the main gallery throws off a larger branch towards the west. On the southern side of the latter come two short fissures, followed by one of considerable size and length, which leads into an irregular shaped chamber, communicating by two apertures with the outer air. The aforesaid branch gallery terminates in a kind of chamber, in which also are two openings, and is crossed by the fissure just named, which is prolonged towards the north, till it joins another one leading back into the western branch, opposite to the second of the small fissures mentioned above. All these, as Pengelly points out, resolve themselves into two sets or systems, which strictly agree with corresponding bearings of the joints in the Devonian rocks of the district.

---

* *Philosophical Transactions*, clxiii. (1875), p. 483. A view of the entrance and a plan of the cave, with sections and other figures, are given in this paper.

The galleries are usually from 6 to 8 feet in greatest width and from 10 to 14 feet in height, and they lie within a space measuring 135 feet from north to south and 100 feet from east to west. The large gallery, leading from the northern entrance, over almost its whole extent, and a part of the great western branch-gallery, were floored with a mass of stalagmite, extending horizontally from wall to wall, the thickness of which varied from about a foot downwards. Beneath this came the detrital accumulations. These, in other parts of the cave, were not covered by stalagmite, and they sometimes filled a fissure up to the level of its roof. They proved on examination to be separable into four beds. The first and second, a breccia of small angular fragments of limestone and an underlying layer of blackish matter, were restricted to the neighbourhood of the northern entrance, and were found to be of minor importance; but the third and fourth extended practically thoughout the cave. Of these two, the former (commonly from two to four feet in thickness) was a reddish-brown tenacious clayey loam, containing many angular fragments of limestone, of all sizes from very small bits to masses even a ton in weight, together with occasional fragments of stalagmite, nodules of brown iron-stone, and (more frequently) pebbles of various rocks. The latter (fourth) bed was a gravel, mainly consisting "of pebbles of different kinds of rock, quartz, greenstone, grit, and limestone—mixed with small fragments of shale common in the Brixham district." The depth of this gravel varied; it was seldom less than six feet, often more, and the bottom frequently was not reached, owing to the contraction of the sides of the fissure.

The floor of the cavern was excavated in successive stages or layers, starting from the entrance, so as to avoid the risk of confounding together the remains which occurred at different levels in the deposit; a risk against which due precaution had not been taken in some previous explorations of caves. Bones were found both in the stalagmite and in the first, third, and fourth beds, and worked flints in the third and fourth beds only; but where the third bed filled the cavern up to the roof, its upper portion contained neither bones nor flints. It yielded, however, in the three principal branches of the cavern, 17 flints and 998 bones. "Two of the former, or about 12 per cent., were nine inches deep in the bed, while the remainder were at lower levels. Of the latter, on the contrary, as many as 372, or 37 per cent., were above the level of the highest flint, and were covered by the overlying stalagmite, in which were found remains of the cave-bear and reindeer. Of the 1621 bones and 36 flints found in the cavern, 7 of the former and 16 of the latter were met with in the fourth or gravel bed."

The cavern was less rich in articles of human workmanship than in the bones of animals. The former were examined and reported upon by Mr. (now Sir) J. Evans. Most of them are flakes, some of which possibly might not be artificial ; but there are three fairly well-made implements of Palæolithic type. It is therefore certain that man either frequented, or at any rate sometimes entered, the Brixham cave while Devonshire was inhabited by various mammals which are now extinct. The following is a summary of the bones and fragments which were identified by the late Mr. G. Busk :—

Mammoth (*Elephas primigenius*)	11	specimens.
Rhinoceros (*R. tichorhinus*)	67	,,
Horse (*Equus caballus*)	30	,,
Urus (*Bos primigenius*)*	28	,,
Red deer (*Cervus elaphus*) ...	12	,,
Reindeer (*C. tarandus*)	72	,,
Roebuck (*Capreolus capreolus*)	13	,,
Cave-lion (*Felis spelæa*)	9	,,
Hyæna (*H. crocuta*)	57	,,
Cave-bear (*Ursus spelæus*) ⎫		
Brown bear (*U. arctos*) ... ⎬ ...	354	,,
Grizzly bear (*U. ferox*) ⎭		
Fox (*Canis vulpes*)	15	,,

Besides these, some bones of birds and small mammals were found, among which were identified the hare (*Lepus timidus*), the rabbit (*L. cuniculus*), the lemming (*Lagomys spelæus*), the water-vole (*Arvicola amphibius*), and the shrew (*Sorex vulgaris*). The bones of the following animals—mammoth, rhinoceros, ox, red deer, reindeer, roe deer and bear, in some instances had been gnawed, almost certainly by hyænas.

Mr. Busk remarks that the remains of the rhinoceros were far more numerous and increased in number in proportion to the distance from the entrance, so that they probably had been dragged into the deeper recesses of the cavern to be devoured by hyænas or by some other carnivora. It appeared also that, in more than one case, the limbs of the horse had been carried in, while the bones were still held together by the soft parts.

* Including probably some bones of *Bos longifrons*.

In the case of the hyænas, teeth preponderated; and like the remains of the lion, a large proportion of the specimens were buried deep in the cave-earth, and became more rare near the surface; the remains of bears were frequent at some depth, but they were also numerous on its surface and in the stalagmite.

The deposits in the cavern evidently indicate the occurrence of changes in its physical history. The gravel must have been brought in by a stream which had flowed over the slates, grits, and shales, on the western side of Brixham, entering by the aperture on that side and passing out by the northern entrance. The bone-earth indicates a change in the hydrographical condition of the district, and it was apparently introduced, not by the western, but by the northern entrance. Prior to this, however, the cave probably was undisturbed for a considerable period, during which a bed of stalagmite was formed, and this afterwards was broken up by the new irruption of water. Professor Prestwich considered it probable that at this epoch the cave was generally dry, but was sometimes flooded by a swollen stream which usually flowed at a level rather below that of the entrance; and that during the dry intervals the cave was frequented by carnivora, while, during the flooding, the relics of their meals were covered up and imbedded in the sediment with which the waters were charged. As the deposit of cave-earth is examined upwards from its lowest part, the remains of elephant, rhinoceros, and lion gradually disappear; those of the hyæna become less common, while those of the bear increase largely in number. At this time the common brown bear seems to have made the cave a place of habitual resort, and as numbers of bones, including those of very young cubs, are found together, and are not gnawed, it may be inferred that the hyæna had by that time ceased to frequent its recesses.

Such, then, was the history of the excavation of Brixham Cave. The results proved that in Devonshire a race of men, in a low stage of civilization, had been contemporaneous with a fauna which has now disappeared from Britain, and, in some cases, is actually extinct.

We proceed next to the most laborious scientific undertaking of Pengelly's life—the exploration of Kent's Cavern or Kent's Hole.* This cave, about a mile due east from Torquay

* The Reports of the Committee appointed for this purpose by the British Association are published in the annual volumes of that Association from 1865 to

Harbour, occurs in a small wooded limestone hill on the western side of a valley, which terminates, about half a mile southward, on the northern shore of Torbay ; this limestone belonging to the middle of the Devonian system. The cavern has two entrances, about fifty-four feet apart, in the face of one and the same low, vertical, natural cliff, running nearly north and south, on the eastern side of the hill. Each of these entrances is about six feet in height, and rather more in width, so as to afford an easy access to the cavern. The base of the northern entrance, which, however, is formed by *débris*, not by live rock, is about 189 feet above mean-tide level, and the base of the southern one is nearly four feet lower.

The existence of Kent's Hole has been known from time immemorial ; but the first exploration, of which any record has been preserved, was made in 1824. This was undertaken by a Mr. Northmore, of Cleve, near Exeter, who visited the cavern with the double object, as he stated, " of discovering organic remains, and of ascertaining the existence of a Temple of Mithras," with the result that, as he was "happy to say," he was "successful in both objects." * He was speedily followed by Mr. (afterwards Sir) W. C. Trevelyan, who is said to have been the first to obtain any results of value to science.† The Rev. J. MacEnery, whose name will be always inseparably associated with the cavern, first entered it in the summer of 1825. It was also his first visit to any such place ; nevertheless, he made an examination in what he conjectured to be a favourable spot, and to his great joy discovered several teeth and bones. For about four years he prosecuted his researches with much energy ; his last visit apparently being on August 14, 1829. During this time he was in communication with Dr. Buckland and other geologists, and he intended to publish a narrative of his investigations, going so far as to arrange for the necessary illustrations ; but his intention was ultimately abandoned, and for some years after his death it was feared that his manuscript had been lost. At last, however, it was recovered, and has been printed entire in the *Transactions*

1880, and are reprinted with prefatory remarks by Pengelly in *Transactions of the Devonshire Association*, vol. xvi. pp. 189-434 ("The Literature of Kent's Cavern," part v.). The account given above is condensed from the latter source.

* Of this gentleman's published researches, an account is given by Pengelly in the *Transactions of the Devonshire Association*, vol. ii. pp. 479-495.

† *Ibid.*, vol. iii. p. 207 ; vol. vi. p. 52 ; vol. x. p. 145.

of the Devonshire Association.[*] For this work also, which obviously must have been one of very considerable and sometimes rather tedious labour, we are indebted to Pengelly. MacEnery clearly proved that the cavern had been inhabited, practically at the same time, by man and by various extinct mammals; but his discovery passed unnoticed, for the recent origin of man was at that time almost universally accepted as an article of belief, and geologists do not always rise superior to the weaknesses of human nature, one of which is a tendency to ignore unwelcome facts.

Some investigations were made in 1840, by Mr. R. A. C. Austen (afterwards Godwin-Austen), and the results were described in a paper on the "Bone Caves of Devonshire," read to the Geological Society of London.[†] Again, in 1846, a committee, consisting of Mr. Pengelly, Mr. Vivian, and Dr. Battersby, was appointed by the Torquay Natural History Society to explore a small portion of the cave. The results of their investigations were communicated to their own society,[‡] and to the Geological Society of London.[§] An account of all these earlier investigations—the literature, in fact, of Kent's Cavern anterior to 1865—has been given by Pengelly, with his usual patient care, in the pages of the *Transactions of the Devonshire Association.*[‖]

These investigations, though perhaps none of them were conducted with that strict observance of method which is now regarded as necessary, proved that the flint "implements" and the remains of extinct animals did occur together in the same deposits. Then, "in 1858, the results of the systematic and careful exploration of Brixham Cavern on the opposite shore of Torbay, induced the scientific world to suspect that the alleged discoveries which, from time to time during a quarter of a century, had been reported from Kent's Hole, might, after all, be entitled to a place among the verities of science." From that time various proposals were made for the further investigation of Kent's Hole. Communications passed between Pengelly and Sir C. Lyell, and finally, at the meeting of the British Association at Bath, a Committee was appointed for the systematic exploration

---

[*] Vol. iii. pp. 196–482, where also the history of the manuscript is given.
[†] *Proc. Geol. Soc.*, vol. iii. p. 286.
[‡] Printed in *Transactions of the Devonshire Association*, vol. x. p. 162.
[§] *Quart. Jour. Geol. Soc.*, vol. iii. p. 353.
[‖] "The Literature of Kent's Cavern," parts i.–iv., in vols. ii. iii. iv. and x.

of the cavern, and a sum of £100 was granted for that purpose by the Association. That Committee consisted of Sir C. Lyell, Mr. (now Sir) J. Evans, Mr. (now Sir) J. Lubbock, Professor Phillips, Mr. E. Vivian, and Mr. W. Pengelly (as Secretary and Reporter). To it the following were afterwards added : Mr. G. Busk in 1866, Mr. W. Boyd Dawkins in 1868, Mr. W. A. Sanford in 1869, and Mr. J. E. Lee in 1873. The proprietor of the cave, Sir L. Palk (afterwards Lord Haldon), most kindly placed it in the exclusive custody of the Committee, and afforded them every facility in carrying on the work, which was commenced on March 28, 1865.

The cavern consists of a number of chambers or galleries, to which names had been given by earlier visitors, or were assigned by the Committee for purposes of reference. These chambers may be regarded as forming two divisions, an eastern and a western, with two external entrances, a northern and a southern, each leading into the eastern division. " The northern entrance opens, through a short narrow passage, into a somewhat spacious chamber termed the Vestibule, measuring about 30 feet from north to south and 35 from east to west. From the north-western angle of the Vestibule, a gallery about 32 feet long and ranging from 6 to 14 feet broad, extends north-easterly, and is known as the North-East Gallery. The Vestibule opens on its southern side into what is appropriately termed the Sloping Chamber, about 70 feet in extreme length from east to west, and 34 in greatest breadth." * From the south-east angle of the Sloping Chamber, a passage, about 22 feet long and from 19 to 27 feet broad, called the " Passage of Urns," leads southward into the " Great Chamber " of the eastern division, and a second passage was found at a later stage of the work connecting this with the western division. The Great Chamber leads southward into another, measuring about 40 feet from north to south and 26 from east to west. This was named the Lecture Hall, since a member of the Committee had occasionally delivered addresses in it. From each of those chambers, narrow branches, apparently parallel, lead in a south-easterly direction, and a passage opens southwards from the Lecture Hall, which is about 17 feet wide and 50 feet long.

Though large portions of the deposits in Kent's Hole had been broken up by Mr. MacEnery and other investigators, very

* *Trans. Dev. Assoc.,* vol. xvi. p. 215.

much ground still remained intact. The Committee selected for their first attempt a part of the cavern—the Great Chamber —which not only was in this condition, but also seemed likely to present no very serious difficulties in exploration. The material which had been dug up by their predecessors had not been removed from the cavern, but had been simply thrown on one side; thus it added considerably to the difficulties of the task, and tended to mix remains from more than one level. All this material was now removed and subjected to a careful examination, with the result that several interesting mammalian remains were discovered. That which occupied the floor of the cave was found generally to exhibit the following succession— (1) Blocks of limestone, sometimes large, clearly fallen from the roof; (2) a layer of mould of an almost black colour, ranging from a few inches to upwards of a foot in depth, called the Black Mould. (3) Beneath this came a floor of granular stalagmite, firmly attached to the walls, seldom less, and generally more, than a foot in thickness, no doubt formed by the drip of water from the roof. (4) A red loam, containing a number of lime-stone fragments, ranging in size from bits not larger than sixpence to masses hardly less than those which lay on the surface of the mould; it exhibited no signs of stratification, and contained, as will be described, various remains. Beneath this came (5) a breccia of angular fragments of limestone and pebbles of sandstone, imbedded in a reddish sandy calcareous paste.

These two deposits varied in thickness, and in this respect seemingly stood one to another in an inverse ratio. The excavation in the cave-earth, and sometimes in the underlying breccia, was at first carried to a depth of four feet below the bottom of the granular stalagmite; but in the last year of their work, the Committee, when they had excavated every part of the cavern to the above-named depth, opened a trench in the vestibule to a further depth of five feet, along a total length of 132 feet. By this the limestone floor of the cavern was actually laid bare for a short distance; in the rest it was practically reached, for the workmen came down to a fissure which was too narrow to admit of their working any lower. In this excavation the material everywhere, except for one or two pockets of cave-earth, was the above-named breccia.

The following was the system adopted in the process of excavation. The accessible portion of the Black Mould was

first removed ; then, after the limestone blocks on its surface had
been broken up, by blasting if necessary, the remainder was
taken away for examination. Then the floor of granular
stalagmite was next stripped off, so as to lay bare the cave-
earth, and this was dug out ultimately to a depth of four feet
in a series of prismatic blocks, a yard long and a foot square in
section, layer by layer. "This material, after being carefully
examined *in situ* by candlelight, was taken to the door and
re-examined by daylight, after which it was at once removed
without the cavern. A box was appropriated to each 'yard'
exclusively, and in it were placed all the objects of interest
which the prism or 'yard' yielded. The boxes, each having a
label containing the data necessary for defining the situation of
its contents, were daily sent to the Honorary Secretary of the
Committee (Pengelly), by whom the specimens were at once
cleaned and packed in fresh boxes. The labels were numbered
and packed with the specimens to which they severally belonged, and a record of the day's work was entered in a journal.
The same method was followed in the examination of the Black
Mould, and also of the granular stalagmite," with the exception
that in these cases, for obvious reasons, the material was not
divided into prismatic blocks, or removed layer by layer.

Of a considerable number of objects found in the Black
Mould, some probably, others certainly, indicated the hand of
man. Among the former were sundry well-rounded stones,
some of them pierced by boring molluscs, and thus evidently
brought from the sea beach, others fragments of slate, which
might have been artificially fashioned. Among the latter were
articles in bronze and in bone, a lump of smelted copper, an
amber bead, pottery, spindle whorls, and flint flakes. The
articles in bronze and bone were neither numerous nor remarkable ; the pottery (except one fragment of Samian ware) was
extremely coarse, and in most cases unglazed ; the spindle
whorls and other "holed" stones were partly of local rocks,
Devonian grit, and Triassic sandstone, partly of a coarse
greenish schist and of "Kimeridge coal," neither of which occurs
in situ in the district. The flint flakes were only four in number,
and much bleached. Bones were numerous ; they were generally
discoloured, and had lost a considerable portion of their weight ;
some also appeared to have been exposed to the action of fire.
Among them were relics of pig, deer, sheep, fox, wolf or dog,

with various smaller mammals ; also of birds and of fish. The mould also contained the shells of molluscs, marine as well as terrestrial. Among the former were the oyster, cockle, limpet, whelk, mussel, and other edible species, together with the internal shell of a cuttle-fish, the unrubbed appearance of which suggested that it had not been picked up on the beach, but had been directly taken from the animal.

The granular stalagmite was broken up and carefully searched, but did not prove productive. It yielded, however, charred wood, marine and land shells, and bones of various mammals, including some extinct species.

Of the four distinct levels in which the cave-earth was removed, the uppermost was the poorest, and the third perhaps the richest, in organic remains ; the lowest contained a large amount of comminuted bone, which was very rare in the three levels above it. In many cases it appeared to be associated with fæcal matter. Large portions of the osseous remains, it should be said, occurred as mere splinters, and teeth were extremely numerous.

The work was carried on from chamber to chamber on the same plan, till at last the cave-earth or underlying breccia had been removed to a depth of four feet from all ramifications of the cavern which were of any importance. The results are detailed in the annual reports, of which the following is a very brief summary. During the first year's work (1865),* in the Great Chamber of the eastern division were discovered bones or teeth of "bear, lion, hyæna, fox, horse, ox, several species of deer, rhinoceros, and mammoth. Remains of hyæna were probably the most abundant, after which came those of rhinoceros and horse. The relics of mammoth included molar teeth and tusks of very young individuals." Several implements were found, the majority of flint, but some of chert, besides a piece of a whetstone of grit and a "hammer-stone." Thus the very first year's excavation fully confirmed the statements made by previous explorers that articles of human workmanship and the bones of extinct mammals occurred in the same deposit, in situations where any subsequent disturbance was impossible. In the second year (1866) the excavation of the Great Chamber was completed, together with a gallery leading from it, and

* The date, as a matter of convenience, is that of the presentation of the report, the work having been done in the earlier part of that year and the later part of the preceding one.

much progress made in that of the Passage of Urns. Bones
and implements were found as before, but nothing specially
novel. By the third year (1867) this passage, the Vestibule,
the north-east gallery, and most of the eastern division had
been cleared out, and in the western one the workmen had
made progress with the Lecture Hall.

In the Vestibule a layer of black soil, consisting largely of
charred wood, had occurred over an area of about 100 square
feet, either immediately beneath the granular stalagmite, or
separated from it by a thin layer of ordinary cave earth. It
"was extremely rich in objects, many of them of great interest,
and including bones and teeth of *Rhinoceros tichorhinus*, horse,
Hyæna spelæa, fox, bear and badger ; as well as human tools of
various kinds . . . implements, flakes and cores of flint, bone
tools and burnt bones." The flint specimens were 366 in
number, "though many of them were mere chips, and the
majority of them simply flakes, no inconsiderable number were
more or less perfect lanceolate implements. . . . The bone
tools included an awl about 3·75 inches long, cut at one end to
a sharp point," and a portion of a harpoon. The granular
stalagmite enclosed a human tooth and four others in a portion
of an upper jaw.* This Report states that blocks of an older,
sometimes ossiferous, stalagmite occurred in the cave-earth,
which indicated the existence of a still earlier floor, a fragment
of which afterwards was found *in situ*. Bones and flint tools,
as before, continued to be found during the year, but nothing of
importance was added to the list. In the fourth year (1868)
the exploration of the Lecture Hall was completed, together
with that of an unnamed chamber opening out of it, but no
novelties were discovered. But in the workings of this year
the breccia beneath the cave-earth appears to have been cut
into more frequently than in previous explorations. It was
often so hard that it had to be split up with chisels, to the
injury of the bones which it contained. "These were sometimes so abundant as to form fully fifty per cent. of the entire
accumulation." With a few exceptions they belonged to bears ;
so that the cavern appears to have been, "during the era of the
breccia, almost exclusively a mausoleum, and perhaps a home,
for bears."

* Nothing of the kind was afterwards found either in or beneath the stalagmite.
The discoverers, from the condition of the relic, were disposed to assign it to a date
more recent than that of the palæolithic implements.

The fifth Report (1869) narrates the clearing out of the south-west chamber and the investigation of one of the most important branches (called the Bears' Den) belonging to the western division of the cavern, in a ramification of which—forming a kind of *cul de sac*—was a pool of water about twenty feet long and eight wide, but of no great depth. This was proved, on examination, to communicate with the south-west chamber, and in the gallery thus formed a number of "initials and dates, amounting probably to upwards of a hundred," were discovered, inscribed on a mass of stalagmite, which blocked the opening into that chamber. Among the dates were 1744, 1728, 1702, and 1618. These are remarkable, for they occurred in a locality where the drip is unusually copious, and yet the deposits had not been sufficient to obliterate them.* The lake was drained, and its floor was found to consist of a pulpy mass of stalagmite, beneath which was cave-earth, and under this more stalagmite to a considerable thickness. In the first-named material were a number of objects—odds and ends of various kinds, obviously thrown into the water by visitors. All were comparatively modern, none being mediæval or ancient, "nor any such as might have been cast in as votive offerings." Bones were found in the cave-earth below, among them a fragment of an elephant's jaw, containing a perfect molar tooth. A flint flake was found in the breccia in this gallery, which was pronounced by Mr. John Evans to be undoubtedly the work of man.

In the sixth year (1870), the excavation of a rather long and irregular shaped fissure, called the South Sally-port, which opens out of the Lecture Hall, was completed and another one (the North Sally-port) was investigated. It was discovered that this differed from the ordinary ramifications of the cave by leading to an external opening in the eastern slope of the hall.† Both contained bones and worked flints. Another ramifying passage was also partly explored (Smerdon's Passage). The excavation of this occupied much of the seventh year (1871), and the cave-earth was proved to be richer than usual in organic remains, no less than 2900 teeth having been discovered, besides bones (many of them mere fragments), and pieces of antlers, together with some flint flakes and chips and a lance-shaped bone tool. In these side-branches the excavations were carried to a depth, sometimes

---

* Several interesting remarks about the rate of growth of stalagmite appear in these reports. This, in Kent's Hole, appears to have been rather unusually slow.

† Two other apertures were discovered in these ramifying fissures.

of five feet, and occasionally of six feet. On the completion of this rather tedious and difficult work one or two minor recesses were investigated, and the excavation of the Sloping Passage, which had been abandoned for a time, was resumed.

In the eighth year (1872), a branch of the cavern leading to the Sloping Passage, called by Mr. MacEnery the Wolf's Cave, which had been begun late in the preceding year, was finished, together with a branch leading from it, in which that explorer had found a large number of teeth of small rodents (the Cave of Rodentia), as well as another recess. This, which was one of a group of fissures, approached by a passage from the Sloping Chamber, was called the Charcoal Cave, from a layer of that material above the granular stalagmite. In this charcoal, which seemed to indicate a place where fires had been lighted, were some bits of very coarse pottery, and a number of bones. Several of them, and two teeth, were human, and were probably the remains of the same individual. In the cave-earth bones and occasional worked pieces of flint or chert were found, as usual, and two more flint implements in the underlying breccia, which was again cut into. The explorers also began work upon the Long Arcade, and were rewarded by a discovery of great interest. Mr. MacEnery had recorded the finding of seven teeth (five canines and two incisors), which were referred to the great sabre-toothed tiger (*Machærodus latidens*).* As this genus previously had occurred only in Pliocene deposits, its association with a Pleistocene fauna was most interesting, so that the committee had been watching carefully for its remains in the hope of placing Mr. MacEnery's discovery beyond all question and of determining the exact horizon at which the remains were lying. Hitherto they had been unsuccessful. Though a large mass of material had been removed, not a trace of *Machærodus* had been found. Now at last they were rewarded. On July 29, 1872, after searching for seven years and four months, the workmen came upon a "well-marked incisor," lying "with the left lower jaw of bear, containing one molar, in the first or uppermost foot-level of cave-earth, having over it the granular stalagmite floor 2·5 feet thick." This, it is strange to say, was the only relic of *Machærodus* discovered in the course of this excavation, so that Mr. MacEnery had been singularly fortunate.

* The history of these specimens, as far as known, with a wood-cut and a lithographic plate in illustration, is given by Messrs. Dawkins and Sanford in "Pleistocene Mammalia," pp. 184-192 (*Palæontographical Society*, 1862).

In the following year (1873), the excavation of the Long Arcade was continued, with the usual results, but some farther investigation of the breccia suggested inferences which will be presently noticed. In 1874, the work was completed in this Arcade, and two or three other galleries were investigated, during which some other inscriptions were examined. These were on a boss of stalagmite, the earliest of them being dated in 1615. The remains of animals, extinct and living, continued to be found, together with flakes or more highly finished implements of flint or chert. The Report of 1875 records the continuance of similar work in various passages and branches of the cavern with the usual discoveries; and the same may be said of the following year (1876). The Bear's Den next engaged attention. In this Mr. MacEnery had dug, and had regarded it as a very productive locality. The task of clearing it out occupied upwards of nine months, but the results (as described in the Report of 1877) hardly fulfilled the anticipations which the earlier accounts had excited, though, of course, the usual "finds" were made in it and in an adjacent passage. Many inscriptions were found on a boss of stalagmite, one of which, dated 1571, is the earliest known to occur in the cavern. The next year's Report (1878) completes the exploration of the above-named passage, and describes the investigation of one of the chambers which were connected with it, but there was no new discovery. The Report of 1879 continues the account of the exploration of minor branches of the cavern, without, however, doing more than augmenting the store of bones and teeth of the cave-animals, and obtaining more objects wrought by the hand of man. The greater part of the cavern, had now been emptied, a sum of more than £1800 had been expended by the British Association, and the results of the last two or three years rendered it highly probable that the continuance of the excavation would do nothing more than supply additional evidence in favour of conclusions which were already sufficiently established; so it was decided to bring the work to an end in the course of the coming year. Accordingly, the Report of 1880 (the sixteenth) records the completion of some work which was in progress on the last occasion, and gives an account of a second and deeper excavation in the Long Arcade. This was carried to an additional depth of four feet, as already stated, or of nine feet in all below the floor of granular stalagmite, and was thus made almost exclusively in the well-known breccia. Only eighteen finds rewarded the explorers. Three good "nodule" tools were discovered in the eighth foot-level, and several flint chips in the ninth or lowest. Of the animal remains, fewer in number than the others, two were bears' teeth and one the crown of a rhinoceros' tooth. No animal relic was found beneath the seventh foot-level.

Thus, on June 19, 1880, the exploration of Kent's Hole was brought to an end. It was the most complete and systematic investigation of a cavern which had ever been undertaken, and on a much greater scale than that at Brixham. A task of this kind is peculiarly exacting. It cannot be entrusted to workmen, however steady and honest they may be ; it cannot be left to a committee, whose members will be uncertain and intermittent in their visits : it demands the constant oversight of one man, who so thoroughly understands the subject, as to know both what should be done at a crisis, and when special precautions must be taken in order to place some discovery of exceptional interest beyond the risk of dispute, by recognizing at once the defects in a chain of evidence, which might afford an opportunity to the critic and an excuse to the sceptic. This superintendence was given by Pengelly. He was indeed occasionally aided or relieved by some of the other members of the Committee, resident at Torquay, for no one man could have sustained single-handed such a continuous and protracted task ; but he made himself primarily responsible for the direction of the investigation. All the specimens discovered passed through his hands, were washed and cleaned, labelled and recorded by him. The labour of this must have been very great, and oftentimes not a little tedious. The number of the specimens was really enormous. It is stated in the fifth Report that on Dec. 31, 1868 (when the study of the bones which had been collected was undertaken by Prof. Boyd Dawkins and Mr. A. Sanford), the number of boxes awaiting examination amounted to 3948, "and though it is true that some of the boxes contained no more than a single bone, it is also true that in many cases there were upwards of a hundred in a box. . . When Prof. Dawkins began his examination there must have been in store for him more than 50,000 bones ; and though many were unidentifiable chips merely, every one had to be passed under review." Judging from the figures which are used in the last Report of the Committee, the

number of " finds," that is of the prisms of material, which not
only had been broken up but also had proved productive,
amounted to over 7300.   Pengelly states in one of his papers [*]
that in the fifteen and a quarter years, during which the excavation was in progress, he visited Kent's Hole almost daily,
and spent over the work, including the time occupied by washing and labelling specimens, in arranging materials and writing
reports, on an average five hours daily.   This is a remarkable
instance of self-devotion on the part of a man, who was not in
independent circumstances and had to earn an income by other
work, for it must be remembered that, in accordance with the
rules of the British Association, no part of the funds could be
devoted to the payment of the secretary of the committee.

The following summary indicates the results of the exploration.   In the first place a lower limit was obtained for the age
of the stalagmite, which, as is stated in the following passage,
could not be less than about two thousand years old.

"Above the stalagmite, and principally in the black mould, have
been found a number of relics belonging to different periods, such as
socketed celts, and a socketed knife of bronze, and some small
fragments of roughly smelted copper, about 400 flint flakes, cores, and
chips, a polishing stone, a ring [made of Kimeridge clay], numerous
spindle-whorls, bone instruments terminating in comb-like ends,
pottery, marine shells, numerous mammalian bones of existing species,
and some human bones, on which it has been thought there are traces
indicative of cannibalism.   Some of the pottery is distinctly Roman in
character; but many of the objects belong, no doubt, to pre-Roman
times." [†]

Thus whatever was discovered beneath the stalagmite must
have been sealed up by it for, at the very least, two thousand
years; probably for a much longer time.   In the cave-earth
were found a large number of chips, flakes, and implements,
generally of flint, but sometimes of chert, together with scrapers
and cores of the same, stones which have been used as hammers
or pounders, and a few pins, needles, and harpoons of bone.
Even if it be granted that some of the chips, flakes, cores and
supposed scrapers, be the results of natural fractures—a thing
which is often possible—and that they have been washed into

---

[*] *Transactions of the Devonshire Association*, 1881, p. 637.
[†] J. Evans, "Ancient Stone Implements of Great Britain," chap. xxiii.   The
passage quoted was written in 1871-72, but the main statements in it were not affected
by the subsequent work in Kent's Hole.

the cave after exceptionally heavy rain or by streams which have now disappeared, still, there can be no question that not a few of the more elaborate implements,* and all the instruments of bone are the work of man; and these, it may be added, resemble similar objects found both in river-gravels and in other caves, in England and in Western Europe, associated with a fauna, which is either extinct or is living only in distant parts of the world and under different conditions of climate.

Pengelly also calls attention † to another matter of great interest.

"A glance at the implements from the two deposits shows that they are very dissimilar. Those from the breccia are much more rudely formed, more massive, have less symmetry of outline, and were made by operating, not on *flakes* purposely struck off from nodules of flint or chert, as is the case of those from the cave-earth, but directly on the *nodules* themselves, all of which appear to have been obtained from accumulations of supracretaceous gravel, such as occur about four miles north-westerly from the cavern. There seems to be no doubt, then, that the Breccia men were ruder than those of the cave-earth; and this is borne out by the fact that, whilst the men represented by the less ancient deposit made bone tools and ornaments—harpoons for spearing fish, eyed-needles or bodkins, probably for joining skins together, awls perhaps to facilitate the passage of the slender needle or bodkin through the tough thick hides, pins for fastening the skins they wore, and perforated teeth for necklaces or armlets—nothing of the kind has been found in the breccia. In short, the stone tools, though both sets were unpolished and coeval with extinct mammals, represent two distinct civilizations. It is equally clear that the ruder men were the more ancient, for their tools were lodged in a deposit, which, whenever the two occurred in the same vertical section, was invariably the undermost. In fact the breccia in which each of the implements was found had cave-earth actually lying on it."

As the deposits differed so greatly in character, as they were often separated by stalagmite, and as a breaking up of this and a partial clearing out of the breccia had preceded the deposition of the cave-earth, Pengelly came to the conclusion that the interval between the two must have been very considerable.

The following list ‡ comprises the more important mammals

* Fourteen of these are figured in the work last cited, with six of the bone instruments.
† Ninth Report (1873). *Ibid.* vol. xvi. p. 346.
‡ J. Evans, *ut supra.* The remains found in the black mould above the stalagmite belong to such animals as the dog, sheep, goat, pig, rabbit, **roe-deer,** and short-horn ox (*Bos longifrons*). These do not occur in the cave-earth.

found in the cave-earth of Kent's Hole, omitting those species which cannot be determined with certainty, as well as birds and fishes :—

Felis leo, var. *spelæa*, cave lion ...	Abundant.
Machærodus latidens, sabre-toothed tiger	Very rare.
Hyæna crocuta, var. *spelæa*, cave hyæna	Very abundant.
Canis lupus, wolf	Rare.
Canis vulpes, var. *spelæus*, large fox	Rare.
Gulo luscus, glutton ...	Very rare.
Ursus spelæus, cave bear ...	Abundant.
Ursus ferox, grizzly bear	Abundant.
Ursus arctos, brown bear	Scarce.
Elephas primigenius, mammoth ...	Not very common.
Rhinoceros tichorhinus, woolly rhinoceros	Abundant.
Equus caballus, horse	Very abundant.
Bos primigenius, urus	Scarce.
Bison priscus, bison	Abundant.
Cervus megaceros, Irish elk	Not uncommon.
Cervus elaphus, stag ...	Abundant.
Cervus tarandus, reindeer ...	Abundant.
Lepus timidus, hare	Rare.
Lagomys spelæus, cave pika ...	Very rare.
Arvicola amphibius, water vole ...	Rare.
Arvicola agrestis, field vole	Rare.
Arvicola pratensis, bank vole	Very rare.
Castor fiber, beaver ...	Scarce.

Brixham Cave and Kent's Hole, though far the most important explorations of this nature, were not Pengelly's only researches in caverns. In the month of October, 1862, during some work on the flank of Happaway Hill, an eminence rising to an elevation of 271 feet above the sea, and north-east of the valley in which lies the principal street of Torquay, a cave was discovered at a height of about 196 feet above ordnance-datum. It was a gallery about 46 feet long, by 10 to 15 feet wide, and about 10 feet high, and the examination of it was entrusted to Pengelly. In order to avert any possibility of malpractices he determined not to employ any labourers but to do the work himself, aided only by his son. It did not, however, prove very remunerative. They found a good many rough flint chips, and one which might be regarded as an implement ; some charred wood, a fragment of the skull of a child, and part of a jaw of a man, whose age apparently was between twenty and thirty years, a tooth of a hyæna, two or three bear's molars, and one or two teeth of rhinoceros, with bones of living mammals. Most of the

discoveries indicated a recent fauna, but as there was no stalag-
mite-floor the deposits were not separable. Pengelly thought it
probable that the cavern had been partly filled in the palæolithic
age, but afterwards had been nearly emptied and then refilled
in more recent times.[*]

Pengelly also visited the famous fissure at Cavillon, near
Mentone, in which a human skeleton had been found. When
this discovery was announced, in the spring of 1872, Sir W. Tite
wrote to him expressing a strong desire that he should investigate
the matter, at the same time generously providing the necessary
funds for the journey. Pengelly arrived at Paris on April 30,
and had an interview with the British Ambassador, Lord Lyons,
in order to secure his good offices, in case any obstacle should
be interposed, after which he visited Professor Milne Edwards
at the Jardin des Plantes, and then examined the skeleton, which
by that time had been forwarded to Paris. It had been very
carefully packed, together with a piece of breccia on which it
was lying, when it was discovered. Pengelly then proceeded to
Mentone, and examined the cave itself. This is a fissure or
triangular slit in the cliff, about 80 feet high, 30 feet wide and
45 feet deep, the threshold being at an elevation of about 103
feet above the sea-level. The skeleton was found at a depth of
seven feet below the surface,[†] and about nine feet from the
entrance. Other fissures exist in the neighbourhood, which
already had received attention.

"The floor [of the cave in question] is composed of dark earth, full
of charcoal and fragments of bones, mingled with blocks of stone
which have dropped from the roof. Below it . . . a skeleton was met
with, as well as flint flakes, rude instruments of bone, and a number of
shells perforated for suspension. The skull was covered with a head-
dress of more than 200 perforated sea-shells. It rested in an attitude
of repose, with the legs and arms bent. . . . The teeth and bones of
hyæna, lion, woolly rhinoceros, mammoth, and other pleistocene animals
occurred both in the soil above and below."[‡]

That this and the other fissures were inhabited in the palæolithic age seems beyond doubt, but it is not so certain whether
the skeleton is of that age, or whether it indicates a subsequent
interment in neolithic times. The discoverer, M. Rivière, stoutly

* *Transactions of the Devonshire Association*, 1886, p. 161.
† Other authorities make the depth about seven yards.
‡ Boyd Dawkins, "Cave Hunting," chap. vii.

maintained it to be a relic of palæolithic man, and to this view Pengelly inclined ; * though he observed that the work of excavation, which was still in process at the time of his visit, was not conducted in a properly systematic way. Professor Boyd Dawkins, however, considers this to be, like more than one other instance in France, a neolithic interment in a cave which had been previously inhabited by palæolithic man, since remains of the former occur in the upper floors of these fissures, and his opinion has found favour with the majority of experts, at any rate in this country.†

We pass over several short papers on points which arose out of these investigations, but we must not forget that, in addition to his work as an explorer, Pengelly did much as the historian of caverns, by collecting the accounts of earlier researches, and by critical notices of those which from time to time were published. These essays occupy many pages of the *Transactions of the Devonshire Association*. They appear under various titles ; sometimes the literature of a single cavern is the subject of a special communication ; sometimes a passing notice of a question relating to cave exploration occurs in a paper which deals with several geological topics. Among the former group we may enumerate the papers on the Literature of the caves at Oreston, at Yealhampton, at Anstey Cove, and at Buckfastleigh, and on the caverns and fissures near Chudleigh. But of these communciations none is so lengthy or so important as that which is devoted to the literature of Kent's Cavern. This is divided into five parts which, if collected together, would form a fair-sized octavo volume. In the second of them Mac-Enery's original manuscript is printed in full ; in the fifth the whole series of reports submitted to the British Association is collected. Caverns also receive notice from time to time in another group of critical and historical papers, entitled " Notes on recent notices of the Geology and Palæontology of Devonshire," from which title after a time the word "recent" was dropped. Of this thirteen parts appeared between 1874 and 1886, and they also would form a goodly volume. In these

* "The Cave-man of Mentone." *Trans. Dev. Assoc.*, vol. vi. p. 293.

† It is, however, right to say that, since this paragraph was written, other ossiferous fissures on this part of the Mediterranean coast have been described which, in the opinion of competent judges, have strengthened the evidence in favour of the view held by Pengelly. See " Address to Section 'H,'" by Mr. A. J. Evans, Reports of British Association, 1896.

Pengelly dealt more especially with such accounts of or comments on the work in the Devonshire caves as had appeared from time to time in contemporary literature. Hence the papers are mainly critical, and are largely occupied by the corrections of errors.* These are sometimes of no great importance, being merely those little slips, which an author, not personally familiar with a locality, can hardly avoid, however careful he may be ; slips, which the present writer fears might be detected in these pages by the keen eyes of his friend, were he still alive ; but certain of them were grave errors as to matters of fact, the correction of which was a matter of great importance. Not a few of the more serious of these errors belong to a special category, misstatements by critics to whom the results of researches in caverns and in the older river gravels were especially unwelcome, as demonstrating that the human race must have existed on the globe for a much longer period than six thousand years. Many men of science still living can remember the excitement which was aroused in certain theological circles by the assertion of this unwelcome conclusion, and how self-appointed champions of orthodoxy rushed into print to discuss, with all the confidence of ignorance, subjects which they did not understand and evidence which they could not appreciate, thus injuring the great cause which they deemed themselves to be aiding.

Pengelly's papers—at this interval of time—teach a valuable if a somewhat saddening lesson, by showing the weapons which would-be defenders of truth sometimes venture to employ in its service. The misstatements are occasionally so gross and so palpable, that, assuming them to have been made in good faith, they indicate either an extraordinary amount of stupidity or a singular form of mental perversity. Some of the worst offenders launched their misrepresentations from behind the ægis of a Society (then newly founded) called the Victoria Institute, which had devoted itself to the task of propping up dubious theology by unsound science. This brings it within the swing of Pengelly's hammer, from which it does not escape without damage to reputation ; for on one occasion he convicts it of continuing to give currency to statements the untruth of which had been demonstrated. A painful chapter truly in the

---

* Somewhat similar to these is another series of papers published in the same *Transactions* (1878-1885), entitled " Notes on Slips connected with Devonshire."

history of the " conflict of science," and perchance it may be not the last !

The third section of Pengelly's scientific work yet remains to be noticed—the miscellaneous papers on geology and kindred subjects. These relate almost exclusively to the south-west of England, and not a few to that part of Devonshire which lies within easy reach of Torquay. One might have thought that the work already described, in addition to his duties as a teacher and lecturer, would have left him no leisure for any other investigations ; but it was not so. As a rule, however, these papers are comparatively short, being the fruits of researches which either did not demand a long time, or could be carried on at intervals as circumstances allowed. They are, in fact, "chips from a workshop," which in many cases are only of local interest ; but still, in not a few, such as were well worth preservation. On this account the majority of them were published in the proceedings of local societies, for Pengelly was not a frequent contributor to the *Journal of the Geological Society of London*. But the variety of subjects covered by these papers so well indicates the energy, many-sidedness, and versatility of the man, that we must endeavour to give some slight notice of their general scope.

One group, among which are some of his earliest contributions to science, deals with questions relating to the Devonian system, its stratigraphy, and its relation to the Old Red Sandstone of other parts of Britain, and to certain of its fossils.* Another group deals with the " New Red Sandstone of Devonshire," in connection with which we may mention an important paper on the " Age of the Devonshire Granites." On this point Pengelly came to the following conclusions : that the granites of Dartmoor are not older than the close of the Carboniferous Period, that they had been stripped bare by denudation when the materials of the red conglomerate were being brought together, and that this conglomerate (or breccia) and the associated sandstone were not of higher antiquity than the lower Trias. There is no very direct evidence for or against the last of these conclusions ; but at the present time, several of the most competent judges are in favour of assigning these deposits to the Permian system, and of regarding the Devonshire conglomerates (or breccia) as the equivalents, speaking in

---

* His first formal paper appears to be that on "The Ichthyolites of East Cornwall," *Trans. Roy. Geol. Soc. Corn.*, vol. vii. (1849), p. 106.

general terms, of the Rothliegende of the Continent. As to the general accuracy of the other two conclusions, no reasonable doubt can be entertained. In other papers, Pengelly discusses the probable physical geography of the region which is now Devonshire, during the age of the "New Red," and he records several interesting facts concerning the well-known Triassic conglomerate of Budleigh Salterton, and the way in which the pebbles derived from it travel eastward along the coast ; besides considering the origin of that curious deposit of chalcedonic silica, called *beekite*, so frequently met with on the limestone fragments in the lower New Red Sandstone of Devonshire.

One of the most important of these papers is devoted to the discussion of a very difficult question—the relation between the crystalline schists which occupy the most southern part of Devonshire, and the slaty rocks to the north of them. In this paper, entitled "The Metamorphosis of the Rocks extending from Hope Cove to Start Point, South Devon," Pengelly gives a general description of the geology of the district, and discusses the age of the schists. On this question two views have been entertained : one, that the schists represent a portion of the Devonian rocks, which have undergone very considerable alteration ; the other, that they belong to a much more ancient series, which had assumed a crystalline condition long before the Devonian period, though they were affected by the mechanical disturbances which produced the cleavage in the slates and gritty rocks of that age. One result of this disturbance has been the production of a considerable fault, running across the country from a point a little distance south of Torcross to Hope Cove, which has thrown down the newer against the older series, and has modified the latter by severe pressure. Pengelly shows that beyond question the alteration was anterior to the period of the "New Red," for not only in Bigbury Bay does the outlier, known as Thurlestone Rock, belonging to that period (regarded by him as Trias) rest upon the edges of highly inclined Devonian slates, but also at the Garrets, a cliff in the same neighbourhood, a patch of conglomerate, of like age, is full of pebbles of quartz and of schist. He gives his reasons for thinking it highly probable that, to the south of the Start Point and the Bolt Head, a mass of granite is concealed beneath the waters of the Channel ; and he is of opinion that, by the intrusion of this rock into the Devonian slates, the latter were converted into crystalline

schists. The question, however, at that time, was not even ripe
for discussion ; it required careful study with the microscope,
and a rather unusually wide experience of rock-structures. His
view still finds some advocates ; but, at any rate, the metamorphosis of the schists certainly differs from that usually caused
by intrusive action, while both they and the slaty Palæozoic
rocks to the north have been indubitably affected by mechanical
movements which took place at one and the same date.

A third group of papers deals with the question whether
any signs of ice-action or, in other words, of the Glacial Epoch
can be detected in Devonshire. These papers contain a number
of interesting observations concerning boulders, which, though
they do not prove the former existence of glaciers, certainly
strengthen the evidence of the " Head " at Bovey Tracey, and
make it highly probable that there was a time when the
climate of this part of England was much colder than it is at
present.

A fourth group of papers deals with the "raised beaches,"
which are rather common features on our south-western coasts,
and adds materially to the evidence in favour of a moderate
depression of the land rather after the Glacial Epoch. One of
these papers describes a number of curious "burrows" in the
limestone rock of southern Devon. These—rather clean-cut
holes, generally cylindrical in form, sometimes two or three
inches in depth, and nearly an inch wide—occur at considerable
heights above the sea level. They are found at elevations of
from 95 to 165 feet near Sharkham, at about 200 feet near the
entrance of Kent's Hole and near Brixham, and near Petitor at
about 235 feet. Pengelly was of opinion that they had been
made by a *Pholas* or some other marine boring-mollusc, and
indicated a submergence corresponding in amount with their
present altitude. In this matter, however, the present writer is
unable to agree with his friend, for he believes these holes to
be the work of snails, for reasons generally similar to those of
which he has already given an account.*

Lastly, there are several papers relating to subjects on the
border-land — in which Pengelly worked so ably — between
geology and archæology. These include notices of more than
one "fossil" forest, of which perhaps the most interesting was
in Torquay. This deposit begins in the Tor Abbey valley, at

* *Geol. Mag.*, 1869, p. 483 ; 1870, p. 267 ; 1872, p. 315.

a distance of about three-quarters of a mile from the sea, and a height of about forty feet above it, and extends below low-water mark, probably rather beyond the five-fathom line. It consists of a dark, peaty material, containing the trunks and branches of trees, with the bones of the stag (*Cervus elaphus*), wild-boar (*Sus scrofa*), and Celtic short-horned ox (*Bos longifrons*). Antlers of the first-named were marked with notches, indicative of the work of man. A single tooth, also, of the mammoth, was dredged up, the general appearance of which suggested that it came from the same bed, though this is later in date than the raised beaches.

Other papers record the occurrence of the remains of whales, which had been washed up on the Devonshire coast or dredged up in its immediate neighbourhood. The bones were identified with *Eschrichtius robustus* (or *Balænoptera robusta*), a rorqual not now known on the British coasts. Beside these subjects we find discussions on the insulation of St. Michael's Mount in Cornwall, on stone-cists and cairns, on bronze celts, on old coins, and on folk-lore, provincialisms, and other subjects, distinctly antiquarian. A number of observations on the Torquay rain-fall must not be forgotten ; these are contained in no less than seventeen short papers, all subsequent to 1863. The list printed at the end of this volume will give some idea of Pengelly's industry, and of his varied interests. It is truly a wonderful record, especially when we remember that Pengelly could not be counted among the " men of fortune and of leisure." Such a number of papers, such diverse subjects, and such careful work in all of them ! Here and there, perhaps, some inference ultimately may have to be modified or set aside ; from this fate no student of a progressive science, where the evidence itself is liable to imperfections, can hope to escape, but we venture to affirm that Pengelly will rarely be found wrong in any statement of facts, and it is this characteristic— its careful and scrupulous accuracy—which gives such a high value to his work.[*]

Full of years, much beloved, and with his scientific work widely recognized, he has gone to his rest. It will be long before this work is forgotten, for his name is inseparably linked

---

[*] The manuscript diary of his geological excursions from 1855–1866, which has been placed in my hands by Mrs. Pengelly, is very indicative of the man ; for it shows how careful and exact his observations were, while its pages are here and there enlivened by some amusing little incidents and experiences.

to the history of caves and the annals of primæval man. We, his friends, in our turn must cease from labour and pass within the veil, but till that hour comes, one memory will remain ever quick in our minds. It is that of the genial presence, the kindly spirit and the playful wit, which could brighten every gathering, and give a zest even to the driest subject.

LIST OF PAPERS

By the late Mr. WILLIAM PENGELLY, F.R.S.,

In the " Catalogue of Scientific Papers " of the Royal Society.

(From Vol. IV.)

1. On the ichthyolites of East Cornwall. [1849.] Cornwall, Geol. Soc. Trans. VII., 1847–60, pp. 106–108, 115–120.

2. Remarks on the geology of the south coast of Cornwall. [1852.] Cornwall, Geol. Soc. Trans. VII., 1847–60, pp. 211–215.

3. Observations on the geology of the south-western coast of Devonshire. [1856.] Cornwall, Geol. Soc. Trans. VII., 1847–60, pp. 291–297.

4. On the Beekites found in the red conglomerates of Torbay. [1856.] Cornwall, Geol. Soc. Trans. VII., 1847–60, pp. 309–315; Brit. Assoc. Rep. 1856 (*pt.* 2), pp. 74–75.

5. The geographical and chronological distribution of the Devonian fossils of Devon and Cornwall. Cornwall, Geol. Soc. Trans. VII., 1847–60, pp. 388–417; Geologist, V., 1862, pp. 10–31.

6. On the ossiferous caverns and fissures of Devonshire. Roy. Inst. Proc. III., 1858–62, pp. 149–151.

7. On the Devonian fossils of Devon and Cornwall, with special reference to the Collection presented to the Oxford University Museum, in connexion with the Burdett-Coutts Geological Scholarship. Roy. Inst. Proc. III., 1858–62, pp. 263–268.

8. On the ossiferous fissures at Oreston, near Plymouth. Brit. Assoc. Rep. 1859 (*pt.* 2), pp. 121–123; Geologist, II., 1859, pp. 434–444.

9. On the chronological and geographical distribution of the Devonian fossils of Devon and Cornwall. Brit. Assoc. Rep. 1860 (*pt.* 2), pp. 91–101.

10. The Lignites and Clays of Bovey Tracey, Devonshire. Roy. Soc. Proc. XI., 1860–62, pp. 449–453; Phil. Trans. 1862, pp. 1019–1038.

11. On a new Bone-cave at Brixham. Brit. Assoc. Rep. 1861 (*pt.* 2), pp. 123–124; Geologist, IV., 1861, pp. 456–460.

12. Recent encroachments of the sea on the shores of Torbay. Brit. Assoc. Rep. 1861 (*pt.* 2), p. 124; Geologist, IV., 1861, pp. 447–453.

13. On the relative age of the Petherwin and Barnstaple beds. Brit. Assoc. Rep. 1861 (*pt.* 2), pp. 124–127.

14. On the age of the Granites of Dartmoor. Brit. Assoc. Rep. 1861 (*pt.* 2), pp. 127–129; Cornwall, Geol. Soc. Trans. VII., pp. 414–432; Geologist, VI., 1862, pp. 11–20.

15. Deer's horns in Brixham Cavern. Geologist, IV., 1861, pp. 288–289.

16. On the Devonian age of the world. Geologist, IV., 1861, pp. 332–347.

17. Geological evidences of the deluge of Noah. Geologist, IV., 1861, pp. 355–356.

18. The lunar seas. Geologist, IV., 1861, pp. 490–492.

19. On the correlation of the slates and limestones of Devon and Cornwall, with the old red sandstones of Scotland. Brit. Assoc. Rep. 1862 (*pt.* 2), pp. 85–87; Geologist, V., 1862, pp. 456–459; Cornwall, Geol. Soc. Trans. VII., pp. 441–445.

20. On the supposed uniform height of contemporary "Raised Beaches." Cornwall, Geol. Soc. Trans. VII., 1862, pp. 446–448.

21. The accumulation of cave deposits. [1861.] Geologist, V., 1862, pp. 65–66.

22. Introduction to O. HEER's paper on certain fossil plants from the Hempstead Beds of the Isle of Wight. Geol. Soc. Journ. XVIII., 1862, pp. 369–377.

23. On the age of the Dartmoor granites. Geologist, VI., 1863, pp. 11–20.

(FROM VOL. VIII.)

24. The lignites and clays of Bovey Tracey. [1862.] Devon. Assoc. Trans. I. (*pt.* 1), 1863, pp. 29–39.

25. On the age of the Dartmoor granites. [1862.] Devon. Assoc. Trans. I. (*pt.* 1), 1863, pp. 48–54.

26. On the chronological value of the new red sandstone system of Devonshire. [1863.] Devon. Assoc. Trans. I. (*pt.* 2), 1864, pp. 31–43.

27. The red sandstones, conglomerates and marls of Devonshire. Plymouth Instit. Trans. I. (*pt.* 1864–65), pp. 15–50.

28. Reports (1–9) of the committee for exploring Kent's Cavern, Devonshire. Brit. Assoc. Rep. XXXV., 1865, pp. 16–25; XXXVI., 1866, pp. 1–11; XXXVII., 1867, pp. 24–34; XXXVIII., 1868, pp. 45–58; XXXIX., 1869, pp. 189–208; XL., 1870, pp. 16–29; XLI., 1871, pp. 1–14; XLII., 1872, pp. 28–47; XLIII., 1873, pp. 198–209.

29. The introduction of cavern accumulations. [1864.] Devon. Assoc. Trans. I. (*pt.* 3), 1865, pp. 31–42.

30. The denudation of rocks in Devonshire. [1864.] Devon. Assoc. Trans. I. (*pt.* 3), 1865, pp. 42–59.

31. On changes of the relative level of land and sea in South-eastern Devonshire, in connexion with the antiquity of man. Geol. Mag. II., 1865, pp. 348–350; Brit. Assoc. Rep. XXXIV., 1864 (*Sect.*), p. 63.

32. The Sahara and the North-east Trade Wind. Quarterly Journ. Sci. II., 1865, pp. 565–566.

33. The submerged forests of Torbay. [1865.] Devon. Assoc. Trans. I. (*pt.* 4), 1866, pp. 30–42.

34. On an accumulation of shells with human industrial remains, found on a hill near the river Teign, Devonshire. [1865.] Devon. Assoc. Trans. I. (*pt.* 4), 1866, pp. 50–56; Brit. Assoc. Rep. XXXIV., 1864 (*Sect.*), p. 63.

35. On cetacean remains washed ashore at Babbacombe, South Devon. [1865.] Devon. Assoc. Trans. I. (*pt.* 4), 1866, pp. 86–89.

36. On the correlation of the lignite formation of Bovey Tracey, Devonshire, with the Hempstead beds of the Isle of Wight. [1865.] Devon. Assoc. Trans. I. (*pt.* 4), 1866, pp. 90–94.

37. On certain joints and dikes in the Devonian limestones on the Southern shore of Torbay. [1865.] Geol. Mag. III., 1866, pp. 19–22.

38. Glaciation in Devon and its borders. Geol. Mag. III., 1866, pp. 573–574.

39. On Kent's Cavern, Torquay. Roy. Instit. Proc. IV., 1866, pp. 534–543; London Instit. Journ. III., 1873, pp. 2–8.

40. The triassic outliers of Devonshire. [1866.] Devon. Assoc. Trans. I. (*pt.* 5), 1867, pp. 49–59.

41. On a newly discovered submerged forest in Bigbury Bay, South Devon. [1866.] Devon. Assoc. Trans. I. (*pt.* 5), 1867, pp. 77–79.

42. On the lithodomous perforations above the sea level in the limestone rocks of south-eastern Devonshire. [1866.] Devon. Assoc. Trans. I. (*pt.* 5), 1867, pp. 82–93.

43. Raised beaches. [1866.] Devon. Assoc. Trans. I. (*pt.* 5), 1867, pp. 103–109; Brit. Assoc. Rep. XXXVI., 1866 (*Sect.*), p. 66.

44. Presidential address on the Geology of Devonshire. Devon. Assoc. Trans. II. (*pt.* 1), 1867, pp. 1–37.

45. The raised beaches in Barnstaple Bay, North Devon. Devon. Assoc. Trans. II. (*pt.* 1), 1867, pp. 43–56.

46. The antiquity of man in the south-west of England. Devon. Assoc. Trans. II. (*pt.* 1), 1867, pp. 129–161.

47. On the deposits occupying the valley between the Braddons and Waldon hills, Torquay. Devon. Assoc. Trans. II. (*pt.* 1), 1867, pp. 164–169.

48. The distribution of the Devonian Brachiopoda of Devonshire and Cornwall. Devon. Assoc. Trans. II. (*pt.* 1), 1867, pp. 170–186.

49. Notes on the meteoric shower of November, 1866, with speculations suggested by it. Devon. Assoc. Trans. II. (*pt.* 1), 1867, pp. 247–255.

50. On the flotation of clouds, and the fall of rain. Devon. Assoc. Trans. II. (*pt.* 1), 1867, pp. 263–266.

51. Fish in Devonian rocks. Geol. Mag. IV., 1867, pp. 284–285.

52. On the condition of some of the bones found in Kent's Cavern, near Torquay, Devonshire. Devon. Assoc. Trans. II. (*pt.* 2), 1868, pp. 407–414; Brit. Assoc. Rep. XXXVIII., 1868 (*Sect.*), pp. 76, 77.

53. The submerged forest and the pebble ridge of Barnstaple Bay. Devon. Assoc. Trans. II. (*pt.* 2), 1868, pp. 415–422.

54. The history of the discovery of fossil fish in the Devonian rocks of Devon and Cornwall. Devon. Assoc. Trans. II. (*pt.* 2), 1868, pp. 423–442.

55. The literature of Kent's Cavern. Devon. Assoc. Trans. II., 1868, pp. 469–522; III., 1869, pp. 191–482; IV., 1871, pp. 467–490.

56. The rainfall in Devonshire during 1866 and 1867. Devon. Assoc. Trans. II. (*pt.* 2), 1868, pp. 560–577.

57. On whale remains (Eschrichtius robustus, *grey*) washed ashore at Babbacombe, South Devon. Brit. Assoc. Rep. XXXIX., 1869 (*Sect.*), p. 116.

58. On the insulation of St. Michael's Mount, Cornwall. Roy. Institut. Proc. V., 1869, pp. 128-137; Nature, III., 1871, pp. 206, 207.

59. The rainfall on the St. Mary Church Road, Torquay, during the five years ending December 31st, 1868. Devon. Assoc. Trans. III., 1869, pp. 113–126.

60. On the submerged forest at Blackpool, near Dartmouth, South Devon. Devon. Assoc. Trans. III., 1869, pp. 127-129; Geol. Mag. VII., 1870, pp. 164–167.

61. The rainfall in Devonshire during 1868. Devon. Assoc. Trans. III., 1869, pp. 153-165.

62. On the alleged occurrence of Hippopotamus major and Machairodus latidens in Kent's Cavern, Torquay. Devon. Assoc. Trans. III., 1869, pp. 483-494; Brit. Assoc. Rep. XXXIX., 1869 (*Sect.*), p. 99; Geol. Mag. III., 1871, pp. 42, 43.

63. The modern and ancient beaches of Portland. Brit. Assoc. Rep. XL., 1870 (*Sect.*), p. 84; Devon. Assoc. Trans. IV., 1871, pp. 195-205; Geol. Mag. VIII., 1871, pp. 78–80.

64. Prismatic ice. Sandstone boulder in granite. Nature, I., 1870, p. 627.

65. Rainfall in England. Quarterly Journ. Sci. VII., 1870, pp. 467–477.

66. On rain. Plymouth Instit. Trans. IV. (*pt.* 2), 1870–71, pp. 115–119.

67. The rainfall on the St. Mary Church Road, Torquay, during the six years ending with December 31st, 1869. Devon. Assoc. Trans. IV., 1871, pp. 42–58.

68. The rainfall in Devonshire in 1869, and in the four years ending with December 31st, 1869. Devon. Assoc. Trans. IV., 1871, pp. 59–72.

69. The Ash Hole and Bench bone-caverns at Brixham, South Devon. [1870.] Devon. Assoc. Trans. IV., 1871, pp. 73–80.

70. The literature of the caverns near Yealmpton, South Devon. [1870.] Devon. Assoc. Trans. IV., 1871, pp. 81–105.

71. Notes on vessels made of Bovey lignite and of Kimmeridge coal. Devon. Assoc. Trans. IV., 1871, pp. 105–108.

72. On the rainfall received at the same station by gauges at different heights above the ground. Devon. Assoc. Trans. IV., 1871, pp. 109–132.

73. The supposed influence of the moon on the rainfall. [1870.] Devon. Assoc. Trans. IV., 1871, pp. 257-290; Brit. Assoc. Rep. XLI., 1871 (*Sect.*), p. 55.

74. Notes on the existence of precretaceous sponges. Devon. Assoc. Trans. IV., 1871, pp. 536–539.

75. Further considerations on the influence of the moon on the rainfall. Devon. Assoc. Trans. IV., 1871, pp. 625–640.

76. The rainfall in Devonshire in 1870, and in the five years ending with December 31st, 1870. Devon. Assoc. Trans. IV., 1871, pp. 654–670.

77. The rainfall on the St. Mary Church Road, Torquay, during the seven years ending with December 31st, 1870. Devon. Assoc. Trans. IV., 1871, pp. 671–693.

78. Notes on the Machairodus latidens found by the Rev. J. MacEnery in Kent's Cavern, Torquay. Brit. Assoc. Rep. XLII., 1872 (*Sect.*), pp. 119, 120; Devon. Assoc. Trans. V., 1872, pp. 165–179.

79. The rainfall on the St. Mary Church Road during the eight years ending with December 31st, 1871. Devon. Assoc. Trans. V., 1872, pp. 139–161.

80. Note on an experiment to predict the annual rainfall. Devon. Assoc. Trans. V., 1872, pp. 162–164.

81. The literature of the Oreston Caverns, near Plymouth. Devon. Assoc. Trans. V., 1872, pp. 249–316.

82. The rainfall in Devonshire in 1871, and in the six years ending with December 31st, 1871. Devon. Assoc. Trans. V., 1872, pp. 371–391.

83. The flint and chert implements found in Kent's Cavern, Torquay, Devonshire. Brit. Assoc. Rep. XLIII., 1837, pp. 209–214.

84. The ossiferous caverns and fissures in the neighbourhood of Chudleigh, Devonshire. Devon. Assoc. Trans. VI. (*pt.* 1), 1873, pp. 46–60.

85. The literature of the cavern at Ansty's Cove, near Torquay, Devonshire. Devon. Assoc. Trans. VI. (*pt.* 1), 1873, pp. 61–69.

86. The literature of the caverns at Buckfastleigh, Devonshire. Devon. Assoc. Trans. VI. (*pt.* 1), 1873, pp. 70–72.

87. The rainfall on the St. Mary Church Road, Torquay, during the nine years ending with December 31st, 1872. Devon. Assoc. Trans. VI. (*pt.* 1), 1873, pp. 117–138.

88. The rainfall in Devonshire in 1872, and in seven years ending with December 31st, 1872. Devon. Assoc. Trans. VI. (*pt.* 1), 1873, pp. 139–158.

89. The granite boulder on the shore of Barnstaple Bay, North Devon. Assoc. Trans. VI. (*pt.* 1), 1873, pp. 211–222.

90. The cave-man of Mentone. Devon. Assoc. Trans. VI. (*pt.* 1), 1873, pp. 293–330; London Instit. Jour. III., 1873, pp. 8–14.

91. Report on the structure and contents of Brixham Cave. Phil. Trans. CLXIII., 1873, pp. 483–495.

92. The Kent's Hole Machairodus. Quarterly Jour. Sci. III., 1873, pp. 204–223.

(FROM VOL. X.)

93. The red sandstones and conglomerates of Devonshire. Part 1. Plymouth Instit. Trans., 1861-62, pp. 15–39.

94. The red sandstones, conglomerates, and marls of Devonshire. Part II., Plymouth Instit. Trans., 1862–63, pp. 15–38.

95. The rainfall on the St. Mary Church road, Torquay, during the ten years ending with December 31st, 1873. [1874.] Devon. Assoc. Trans. VI. (1873–74), pp. 425–446.

96. The rainfall in Devonshire in 1873, and in the eight years ending with December 31st, 1873. [1874.] Devon Assoc. Trans. VI. (1873–74), pp. 447–465.

97. Notes on Dr. RIVIERE's discovery of three new human skeletons in the Mentone caverns, in 1873–74. [1874.] Devon. Assoc. Trans. VI. (1873–74), pp. 560–566.

98. Notes on recent notices of the geology and palæontology of Devonshire. [1874–83.] Devon. Assoc. Trans. VI. (1873–74), pp. 646–685; VII., 1875, pp. 279–324; VII., 1876, pp. 148–244; IX., 1877, pp. 409–448; X., 1878, pp. 618–629; XI., 1879, pp. 525–548; XII., 1880, pp. 591–661; XIII., 1881, pp. 359–402; XIV., 1882, pp. 637–694; XV., 1883, pp. 476–486.

99. The cavern discovered in 1858 in Windmill Hill, Brixham, South Devon. [1874.] Devon. Assoc. Trans. VI. (1873–74, pp. 775–856.

100. Reports (10–14) of the committee for exploring Kent's Cavern, Devonshire. Brit. Assoc. Rep., 1874, pp. 1–17; 1875, pp. 1–13; 1876, pp. 1–8; 1877, pp. 1–8; 1878, pp. 124–129.

101. On the flint and chert implements found in Kent's Cavern, near Torquay, Devonshire. Journ. of Sci., IV., 1874, pp. 141–155; Plymouth Instit. Trans. V., 1876, pp. 341–375 [*With additions*].

102. Notes on boulders and scratched stones in South Devon. Devon. Assoc. Trans. VII., 1875, pp. 154–161; IX., 1877, pp. 177–183; XII., 1880, pp. 304–311.

103. Notes on a tooth of Machairodus latidens in the Albert Memorial Museum, Exeter. Devon. Assoc. Trans. IIV., 1875, pp. 247–260.

104. [Reports (1–5)] of the committee on scientific memoranda. Devon. Assoc. Trans. VII., 1876, pp. 434–441; IX., 1877, pp. 72–87; X., 1878, pp. 74–98; XI., 1879, pp. 78–102; XII., 1880, pp. 70–98.

105. [Presidential address to the Geol. Sect. of the Brit. Assoc., Aug. 16th. History of cavern-exploration in Devonshire.] Brit. Assoc. Rep., 1877 (*Sect.*), pp. 54–66; Amer. Journ. Sci. XIV., 1877, pp. 299–308, 387–394; Nature, XVI., 1877, pp. 318–323; Zoologist, I. 1877, pp. 361–379.

106. The relative ages of the raised beaches and submerged forests of Torbay. Brit. Assoc. Rep., 1878, pp. 531, 532.

107. The literature of Kent's Cavern. Part IV., Devon. Assoc. Trans. X., (*pt.* 4), 1878, pp. 141–181.

108. The geology of the north-eastern coast of Paignton. Devon. Assoc. Trans. X., 1878, pp. 196–202.

109. Remains of whales found on the coast of Devonshire. Devon. Assoc. Trans. X. (*pt.* 2), 1878, pp. 630–635.

110. The metamorphosis of the rocks extending from Hope Cove to Start Bay, South Devon. Devon. Assoc. Trans., XI., 1879, pp. 319–342.

111. On the post-miocene deposits of the Bovey Basin, South Devon. Brit. Assoc. Rep., 1882, pp. 532–533 ; Devon. Assoc. Trans. XV., 1883, pp. 368–395.

112. [Presidental address to the Anthropol. Sect. of the Brit. Assoc., Southport, Sep. 20th.   The antiquity of man.]   Brit. Assoc. Rep., 1883, pp. 549–561 ; *Nature*, XXVIII., 1883, pp. 524–529.

113. The literature of Kent's Cavern.   Part V.   Devon. Assoc. Trans. XVI., 1884, pp. 189–434.

114. Kent's Cavern and glacial or pre-glacial man.   Devon. Assoc. Trans. XVI., 1884, pp. 480–488.

115. Notes on notices of the geology and palæontology of Devonshire.   (*Continuation.*)   Devon. Assoc. Trans. XVI., 1884, pp. 775–824 ; XVII., 1885, pp. 425–449 ; XVIII., 1886, pp. 488–509.

116. Happaway Cavern, Torquay.   Brit. Assoc. Rep., 1885, pp. 1219–1220 ; Devon. Assoc. Trans. XVIII., 1886, pp. 161–170.

117. On a scrobicularia bed containing human bones, at Newton Abbot, Devonshire.   Brit. Assoc. Rep., 1886, p. 841 ; *Nature*, XXXIV., 1886, p. 513.

118. The extinct lake of Bovey Tracey.   Abstract of Lecture. [1885.]   Plymouth Instit. Trans. IX., 1887, pp. 188–196.

119. Recent researches in Bench Cavern, Brixham.   Devon. Brit. Assoc. Rep., 1887, pp. 710, 711 ; Geol. Mag. IV., 1887, pp. 514–515.

For biography and works, *see* Devon. Assoc. Trans. XXVI., 1894, pp. 44–49 ; Geol. Mag. I., 1894, pp. 192, 238, 239 ; Geol. Soc. Quart. Journ. LI., 1895, pp. liii–lvii.

H

I

J

K

THE END.

LONDON : PRINTED BY WILLIAM CLOWES AND SONS, LIMITED.
STAMFORD STREET AND CHARING CROSS.

www.ingramcontent.com/pod-product-compliance
Lightning Source LLC
Chambersburg PA
CBHW051213120726
47905CB00004B/1104